MARGARET DICKINSON

Born in Gainsborough, Lincolnshire, Margaret Dickinson moved to the coast at the age of seven and so began her love for the sea and the Lincolnshire landscape.

Her ambition to become a writer began early. Her first novel was published when she was twenty-five. This was followed by ten further titles, including *Plough the Furrow* and *Sow the Seed*, the first two books of her Lincolnshire trilogy. Magaret Dickinson combines a busy working life with her writing career.

Margaret Dickinson

Plough the Furrow

PAN BOOKS

First published 1994 by Pan Books

an imprint of Pan Macmillan, a division of Macmillan Publishers Limited
Pan Macmillan, 20 New Wharf Road, London N1 9RR
Basingstoke and Oxford
Associated companies throughout the world
www.panmacmillan.com

ISBN 978-0-330-51931-1

3 5 7 9 8 6 4 2

A CIP catalogue record for this book is available from
the British Library.

Phototypeset by Intype, London
Printed and bound in the UK by
CPI Mackays, Chatham ME5 8TD

Visit **www.panmacmillan.com** to read more about all our books and to buy
them. You will also find features, author interviews and news of any author
events, and you can sign up for e-newsletters so that you're always first to hear
about our new releases.

For Dennis, Mandy and Zoë

Acknowledgements

'Brumbys' Farm' has been modelled on Lincolnshire County Council's Church Farm Museum, Skegness, and the locale of 'Fleethaven Point' now forms part of the Gibraltar Point National Nature Reserve, managed by the Lincolnshire Trust for Nature Conservation. My sincere thanks to Ruth Walker, Museum Assistant at Church Farm, for her interest and help in providing background information, and also to Carl Hawke, the Gibraltar Point Warden.

I acknowledge use of material regarding the First World War taken from the *Skegness Herald* dated Friday, August 7th, 1914, printed and published by the Proprietor Jas Morrill, MJI, at the Herald Press, 19 Lumley Road, Skegness; and also general information from later editions of the newspaper, then printed and published by C. H. Major & Co Ltd.

My very special thanks to my family and friends for their interest and encouragement, particularly those who helped me so much by reading the novel in the early stages – my sister and her husband, Robena and Fred Hill; Pauline Griggs; Linda and Terry Allaway; and my daughter, Zoë, who helped with the final draft.

M.D.
Skegness, 1994

One

LINCOLNSHIRE, 1910

'*A GIRL*! A chit of a girl is no use to me.'

Esther Everatt stood before the glowering man and ignored his insult. Inside she was quivering, but she wasn't going to let the old man know that. Her firm chin jutted out resolutely. 'Well, mester, it looks like I'm all ya've got. An' from what I've heard, all ya're going to get.'

'Why you cheeky young wench, Ah'll . . .' Sam Brumby raised his hand and stepped forward as if to strike her. The girl did not flinch. Her green eyes stared at him steadfastly. Her feet were planted firmly on the cobbles of his farmyard as if already she intended to put her roots down in this place.

'Aye,' she said softly now, 'ya can hit me if ya like. I'm used to it. One more blow'll mek no difference.'

Sam's arm sliced the empty air inches from her face. 'Be off with you,' he muttered and turned away, but not before she had seen the momentary shame in his eyes. She guessed it was the first time he had ever raised his hand to a woman, but her impertinence had angered him.

'Ah've no use for the likes of you here,' he was saying gruffly as he went back towards the cowshed. 'It's a strong farm lad Ah want – not a lady's maid!'

Her laughter rang out clear and sweet in the misty, early morning air. 'Mr Brumby – do I *look* like a lady's maid?' Her mouth softened when she laughed; even so, it was a mouth that could harden into an unyielding line of determination.

Despite his insistence that he had no interest in her, he glanced back over his shoulder. She was still standing there, hands on hips, watching him. There was a feline stillness about her. Her feet were encased in boots which had known better days long before her ownership of them. Dust from the road she had travelled encrusted the hem of her long, coarse skirt. She was slim, yet there was an aura of physical strength about her. Her hair was a dark tangle of curls with strands plastered damply to her forehead. Her hands and face were tanned by wind and sun.

But it was her eyes that caught and held the attention of anyone who dared to meet that bold, green gaze. They were still staring at Sam, willing him to listen to her, holding him from turning away.

She saw his moment of hesitation, could almost read on his face the question that was forming in his mind. Where had a young girl like her come from at this early hour? She saw Sam Brumby open his mouth, then clamp his jaw shut again. He was afraid to show even the slightest interest in such a cheeky baggage – she thought, inwardly amused – in case it gave her more ideas.

But Esther Everatt did not need anyone to give her ideas – she had plenty of her own. As Sam Brumby turned away and disappeared into the cowshed, she picked up the meagre bundle of her belongings she had dropped to the ground and marched after him. Outwardly, she was displaying a confidence she did not feel inside. She was determined that this old man should not guess how desperately she needed work and a place to live. She wanted to tell him that she would work morning, noon and night for him if only he would let her stay. But grovelling was not part of Esther Everatt's nature, nor, she guessed, would it find favour with this gruff old man. He would see it as weakness and despise her for it.

At this moment she knew far more about Sam Brumby than he did about her. He had never married and had no family to carry on the farm now that his once-strong limbs were painfully misshapen with rheumatism.

'He needs help,' Will Benson, the carrier, had told her. 'But the miserable old devil's too stubborn to admit it. He needs someone young and strong and not afraid of hard work. Someone like you, lass. And it would get you away from *this*!' Will had jerked his head towards the cottage where Esther lived with her aunt and uncle and their large brood of children. She had stared up at Will as he sat on the high seat on the front of his carrier's cart, hope rising within her. Threading the reins backwards and forwards through his fingers, not looking at her, he had murmured, 'I've always known what a rough life you've got, lass, with yar aunt, an' I've often wished I could do summat to help you.' He had lifted his head and smiled. 'Then last week when I went on me usual trip out to Fleethaven Point and saw how old Sam's getting more bent and slow ev'ry time I sees him, well, I thought to mesen, "he needs a young 'un about the place" and, o' course, I thought of you, lass.'

Now she was here, had walked all through the night to get here, and with all her being she wanted Sam Brumby to need her.

As she followed him towards the cowshed, he banged the lower half of the door behind him, right in her face, but she merely dropped her bundle against the wall, waited a moment or two then drew in a deep breath, lifted the latch and stepped inside. She stood quite still breathing in the pungent smell of the warm beasts – oh how she loved it! She reached out and touched the back of the nearest cow, making soothing noises deep in her throat, standing quietly while Sam Brumby worked.

At last he stretched his aching limbs and stood up from where he had been crouching to finish milking the first of the two cows. Esther saw him rub his knuckles, swollen with rheumatism.

''Ere,' he growled, 'since you're so keen, you can 'ave a go with her – Clover.'

Was she mistaken, Esther thought shrewdly, or did she detect a wicked gleam in the old man's eyes? Her mouth twitched, but she said nothing and moved towards the cow tethered in the corner. Clover turned wild eyes towards her. Again came Esther's soft, pacifying murmur. She ran her hand over the cow's rump, down her legs and along her rounded sides. Down and round and under the cow's stomach until tenderly she touched the bursting udder, all the while her voice crooning softly. She sat down upon the three-legged stool, leant her head against the beast's belly and began to draw milk with steady, rhythmic movements.

Esther refused to look up but sensed that Sam was

watching from under his shaggy white eyebrows that shadowed watery hazel eyes. The white stubble on the old man's face scarcely concealed the hollowness of his cheeks and his wispy hair stuck out from underneath his cap. His clothes – a striped, collarless shirt with the sleeves rolled up above his elbows, black waistcoat and thick corduroy trousers with leather leggings from knee to ankle – hung loosely on him, as if, when new, it had been a much stronger, straighter man who had worn them. Sam was now bent with age, his shoulders permanently rounded, his legs bowed. Each step he took seemed painful; the hobnailed boots too heavy for him to lift.

She heard him sniff and wipe the back of his hand across his mouth. 'You can finish milking her before . . .' he added pointedly, 'you go.' Sam was testing her, she knew it. Esther sensed that Clover was a difficult cow.

'Yes, Mr Brumby, right you are,' she replied, pretending meekness.

As he left the cowshed, closing the half-door quietly behind him, Esther allowed herself a wry smile against the soft hide of the animal. For the first time in her young life she had cause to thank the bad-tempered woman who had reared her. Everything she knew – not only household duties, but all aspects of work on the farm – had been learnt under her aunt's cruel tongue and harsh hand.

Thanks to Aunt Hannah, it would take more than a temperamental cow for Sam Brumby to rid himself of Esther Everatt.

*

5

Half an hour later, Esther tapped on the back door of the house. It opened into Sam Brumby's back scullery. At least Esther presumed it to be the scullery though it bore no resemblance to her Aunt Hannah's, always so neat and clean you could see your face in the shining copper pans hanging on the wall. This place was filthy; unwashed pots and pans were piled in the deep sink and bits of mouldy food littered the draining board.

In front of her was the door leading into the main kitchen. This room was no better than the outer one. To her right she noticed another door leading out of the kitchen and down some steps into what she guessed would be the pantry.

Sam Brumby was standing at the cluttered kitchen table hacking at a lump of fat bacon. He glanced up. 'You still here?'

Esther eyed the food hungrily. She hadn't eaten since the previous day and even Sam Brumby's unappetizing fat bacon in his dirty kitchen looked good to her.

''Ere, sit down and eat,' he said grudgingly and almost threw her a wedge of meat and a hunk of coarse, grey bread. 'Then you can be on your way, wench.'

'Thank you, Mr Brumby.' All politeness now, she sat at his table and ate the food he offered. When she had finished she thanked him, stood up and left the house. But she did not leave the farm. If Sam Brumby wanted her gone, he would have to carry her bodily off his land – and even then, there would be nothing to stop her returning.

She had nowhere else to go. Not now. Not since she had bundled her few possessions into a square of cloth, and, tying the corners together, had crept from her pallet bed in the draughty loft and out into the night. Esther had walked away from the only home she had ever known without looking back. Now, as she stood near the wall of the cowshed, watching the back door of the house but ready to dodge out of sight when Sam appeared, she thought briefly of her journey through the previous night, leaving the village on the edge of the Wolds that had been her home for the first sixteen years of her life. She had left without a trace of sorrow. There was no one she would really miss; certainly not her Aunt Hannah nor her seven cousins, from Mary, the eldest – a pudding-faced, sullen girl – right down through boys and girls of varying ages to the youngest girl – a spoilt, whining brat! Taking the lead from their mother, they had alternately ridiculed Esther or used her to do their share of the chores.

Perhaps her Uncle George was the only one whom Esther would remember with affection. A strong ox of a man, he was kindly but slow-witted and no match for his wife's sharp tongue. He was even overawed by his growing children. Esther had watched his efforts to be close to his family meet with derision. Somehow, she thought, there was a streak of cruelty in all of Hannah's children – and they did not inherit it from their father!

When she saw Sam come out of the back door and go towards the barn, Esther collected the milk and carried it back into the house. She stood at the top of the three steps down into the pantry and surveyed the long, cool room with its red brick floor. At one end similar red bricks formed a raised gantry. Round the walls were shelves cluttered with all manner of stone jars, earthenware basins and bowls, enamelled jugs, scales and weights, knives, spoons and ladles – the conglomeration of years of neglect. On the top shelf was a row of glass preserving jars still holding fruit that was grey with age, a thick layer of dust lining the greased paper tops. Cobwebs festooned the shelves, looped between the jars and spiders scuttled away at her approach.

Her glance came to rest – with a final expression of disgust – upon the dairy equipment on the gantry.

'It's a wonder the folks drinking this milk don't die of disease,' Esther muttered aloud and with pursed lips set herself to clean the bowls, milk cans and the barrel-shaped butter churn. By the time Sam returned, she was pouring the milk into a spotless separating bowl, broad and shallow for the cream to rise to the top.

'Thought I told you to go?' he said, standing at the top of the pantry steps.

'Just thought I'd do this for you, Mr Brumby. After all, this is woman's work. I'm sure there's something else waiting that needs a man's brawn.'

He gave an angry snort. 'Cheeky young wench!' he growled and shook his fist at her before turning away. 'Just dun't let me catch you still here next time Ah gets back. That's all!'

Esther straightened up and eased her aching back. With one last glance of satisfaction at the change she had already wrought in the pantry, even though it had taken her nearly the whole day, she went outside again. She saw Sam disappearing into the cowshed. She stood outside the back door of the house and looked about her.

Just how, she asked herself, was she going to get this stubborn old man to admit that he needed help about his farm? Her help!

Straight opposite her across the yard were some stables, the cowshed and between the two, a small barn. The stables were littered with an accumulation of rubbish slung in carelessly; tools, empty sacks, a barrow and harness badly in need of cleaning and polishing. So, thought Esther, there've been no horses in here recently.

On the right hand side of the yard was a row of small, brick buildings – three pigsties and a tool shed. Beyond that was a large barn with a hayloft.

Four geese headed by a gander came waddling towards her, protesting loudly. The gander spread his wings. Flapping and shrieking, he thrust out his neck and came rushing towards her, his webbed feet slapping the cobbles. Esther stood her ground, hands on hips and faced the fearsome bird.

'Ya can stop that racket!'

He stopped, his vicious beak only inches from her. The wings settled back and, fluffing his feathers, he regarded her with tiny bright eyes. Behind him his mates squawked encouragement from a safe distance. With one last strident screech of disapproval, he turned and, gabbling to his wives, he waddled away. Dutifully, the geese fell into step behind him.

Esther glanced across the yard and saw that Sam was looking out over the half-door of the cowshed, presumably to see what was causing all the noise. For a moment he stared at her, then, even from this distance, she heard him sniff and saw him scratch his white stubble thoughtfully. He glanced at the departing gander and then back at Esther before turning away.

Already the sun was setting, throwing shafts of golden April sunlight across the fenland fields that stretched westward, flat as far as the eye could see till they touched the glowing sky. As dusk closed in on the farm, the tiredness swamped her. She hadn't slept for over thirty-six hours and though the work she'd done that day had hardly been strenuous even in her own estimation, every bone and muscle in her body ached to lie down and rest.

But the work was not done yet. From the cowshed she could hear the sounds of evening milking. She leant on the half-door watching Sam, listening to his rasping breath as he worked. She saw him lever himself up from the low milking stool and a grunt of pain escaped his lips.

As he moved towards Clover in the end stall, the animal lashed her tail and kicked out sideways with her back leg, catching Sam a painful blow on the shin. The old man swore volubly and then, suddenly becoming aware of Esther's shadow at the door, turned his anger on her. 'Ah told you to clear off. Ah dun't want you here. Ah dun't need no help.'

He snatched a leather thong from a hook on the wall and strapped it round the cow's back legs. Now Clover was forced to stand still an submit to being milked.

' "Kicker" would be a better name for that 'un, mester,' Esther grinned saucily and, picking up her bundle, she turned away.

She stood uncertainly in the yard for a moment, breathing in the soft air with a hint of the sea in it. The barn, and its hayloft, loomed before her in the gathering dusk and promised warmth and rest. She glanced back over her shoulder. Let him struggle tonight, she thought, but tomorrow – I'll show him! Esther smiled to herself and went towards the barn.

Two

*S*HE became aware of the early morning light filtering through the cocoon of hay she had made for herself. There was a rustling close beside her. Rats! Esther thought. Her drowsiness vanished. Not that she was afraid of them but she didn't want them running over her whilst she slept.

Without warning the sharp tines of a pitchfork were driven into the hay only inches from her throat. She gave a shriek, flung back the hay covering her and scrambled to her feet. A young man stood there, open-mouthed, the fork he held still embedded in the hay. They stared at each other for a moment before both spoke at once.

'What the 'ell . . . ?'

'Can't you be more careful with that thing? You nearly speared my neck!'

'You shouldn't be 'ere,' he retorted defensively, then as his initial shock faded, he grinned and his gaze travelled up and down her lithe body. 'Oh, I don't know, though.'

He let go of the pitchfork and moved towards her. Esther stood her ground, her eyes challenging him. He was standing close now, too close, but she did not move. He was no taller than she was, but stockily built, the width of his shoulders proclaiming their muscular strength. He wore an open-necked shirt, the rolled-up sleeves showing his arms covered with black hairs. A red kerchief was knotted at his throat, but he wore no waistcoat. His trousers were the usual corduroy with a length of twine tied below each knee. His cap perched uneasily on top of his thick, curly black hair and his skin was swarthy. Three days' growth of stubble darkened his face even more, but his brown eyes glinted as their gaze rested on the gentle swell of her bosom. He ran his tongue around his lips and then grinned showing white, even teeth. He put out his hand to touch her throat where the top button of her blouse was undone. 'It'd be a pity to wound such a lovely neck as—'

Her arm came up smartly to smack his hand away before his fingers could touch her skin. 'Keep ya hands to ya'sen – *boy*!' She uttered the final word with scathing derision. His eyes blazed and a flush of anger spread across his dark features.

'I aren't going to let a little tramp talk to me like that . . .' he muttered. His strong hands gripped her shoulders bruising her skin and digging into her flesh. Instantly she brought her arms up to knock his sideways, loosening his grip on her. Then she tugged on his right sleeve at the same time as she kicked his shin with her sturdy boot. He found himself lying on his back in the hay, staring up at her. The fall had knocked the breath from him. He could make no answer as she said, 'Next time I'll let you have it where it really hurts – *boy*!'

With that she climbed down the ladder.

As Esther sluiced the sleep from her eyes under the icy water from the pump, she heard behind her the clatter of hooves on the cobbles of the yard and turned to see Sam bringing two of his three cows through the farm gate and towards the cowshed. She wondered why he didn't milk the cows in the field like her aunt had done, but watching his hobbling, bow-legged gait, she realized it was easier for him to bring the cows to the byre than to be chasing each one around the field to milk it – especially the temperamental Clover.

As he passed her, she thought he hadn't noticed her until he said, 'What sort of time do ya call this? 'Tis half-way through the day. Ah thought the work'd be too much for a slip of a wench.'

Esther opened her mouth to retort, but for once she thought better of it. She wasn't one to make excuses. Let him think what he liked. Instead she said, 'What do ya want me to do, Mester Brumby?'

He was moving away from her now, but over his shoulder he grunted, 'Ah want you to go, that's what Ah *want* you to do!' He paused, one hand on the door of the cowshed, then turning to look at her, added, 'But seein' as how Ah dun't expect you'll tek any notice of me – you can get on with milking this pair.'

He let his hand fall from the door and began to go towards the house. 'When you've done, turn 'em out into North Marsh Field. Ah'll show you when you're ready. Ah'm off up Top End, but Ah'll be back by you're done.'

There was no further sign of the 'boy'. Who was he, Esther wondered, and what had he to do with Brumbys' Farm? She wrinkled her brow thoughtfully. Maybe what Will had told her wasn't true after all. Maybe Sam Brumby had got some help about the farm. If so, her argument about being the only one he could get to stay would lose its effectiveness.

As she leant her head against the warm flank of the beast and began to pull with easy rhythmic movements, she could almost hear her aunt's shrill voice: 'Not like that, girl, you'll 'ave 'er tits as sore as 'ell,' and, obediently, Esther's fingers were gentle on the cow's udders.

Just as she was finishing milking the two cows, a shadow fell across the straw near the pail and Esther twisted her head slightly to look over her shoulder, although her hands never slowed or faltered in their task.

A girl stood there, though Esther could not see her features for the light was behind her, casting her face in shadow, but outlining her rounded form. She stood uncertainly in the doorway, one hand resting on the rough wood of the door jamb.

'Is Mr Brumby about?' she asked, her voice low and husky.

''Fraid not. He's up Top End — wherever that is,' Esther told her, the milk still squirting steadily into the pail.

'It's yon side the Point,' the girl said. 'I must have missed him somehow — I've just come from there.'

Esther stood up and placed the full pail of milk away from the cow's restless hooves and then moved out of the cowshed and into the light so she could get a better look at the newcomer. Long hair — black, now that she could see it properly in the morning light — straight yet sleek and shining. A grey, knitted shawl covered the girl's shoulders and she hugged it about her, folding her arms across her already womanly breast. She was smaller than

Esther but her body was rounded and buxom. Her eyes were dark brown with long black lashes. Her face was childishly plump, yet her high cheekbones and smooth brow hinted at the promise of beauty as she grew and matured.

She seemed to hesitate as if uncertain what to do next.

'Are you working here?' The dark eyes regarded Esther steadily. 'Matthew told me he thought Mr Brumby needed more help about the place, so – I've come up to see him . . .'

Esther felt her heart lurch. Somehow she would have to give this girl the impression that the job was taken. Esther adopted her forthright pose: hands on hips, feet planted apart, a stance that refuted opposition. But deliberately she smiled, as if to take some of the sting out of her words. 'I heard that too. Sorry – it looks like I've beaten you to it!'

The dark-haired girl shrugged. 'Oh, well, never mind then. It was worth a try.' She smiled in return. 'I reckon he'd have frightened me to death, anyway. I hope you get on all right.'

Esther was taken aback by her friendliness. The girl was not in the least resentful that Esther had taken what might have been her job.

'What's your name?' she asked as the girl half-turned to go.

'Beth Hanley. I live at the Point in one of the cottages with me dad.'

'Oh.' Esther shook her head. 'I ain't seen the Point yet . . .' She grinned ruefully. 'I ain't been off the farm since I got here.' She did not add that it had been deliberate; she was afraid that if she set foot outside the gate, Sam Brumby would find some way to keep her out. Now, more than ever, if there were others wanting the job, she had to prove herself indispensable to Sam.

But Beth Hanley was smiling again showing white, even teeth. 'Mester Brumby'll work you hard, there's no doubt about that.'

'Well, well, well, look what we've got here, then. *Two* pretty girls . . .'

They both turned and Esther saw the young man whom she had encountered early that morning in the hayloft coming towards them looking from one to the other, a broad grin on his face.

At once the smile disappeared from Beth Hanley's face. Her glance went from Matthew to Esther and then back again. 'D'you know her, Matthew?' The friendliness was gone from her tone. 'Did you tell *her* about this job too?'

'Naw, course I didn't. *I* don't know who she is or where she's come from. I only met her this morning.' His insolent eyes raked Esther up and down. 'But – I can't say I'm sorry.'

Obviously, Esther thought, he bears me no grudge for kicking his shins, even though the bruise must still be sore. Perhaps he thinks he can tame me. Well, Mester Matthew – if that's what ya name is – ya can think again! A small smile flickered on Esther's mouth as she met his impudent gaze.

Seeing it, Beth's dark eyes flashed, any sign of a tentative friendship gone in an instant. 'Huh, might 'ave known *you'd* have your eye on her afore she's been here five minutes. Can't keep your hands off anything in skirts, can you, Matthew Hilton?'

'What would either of you do here anyway?' he asked of them mockingly. 'The ploughing?'

He came and leant casually against the other door frame close to Esther, his arms folded across his chest.

Esther stood in the doorway between them. Defensively now, she said, 'Aye, an' I can plough a straight furrow, an' all.'

Matthew threw back his head and laughed, the sound echoing around the yard. There was a sarcastic smirk on Beth Hanley's face as she said, 'Get away, you couldn't handle them great horses, so don't . . .'

'Got time to stand all day gossiping, have you?' Sam Brumby's voice made them all jump. Esther turned back into the cowshed and in her haste, turning from the bright morning light back into the darkness of the shed, she tripped over the pail and fell sprawling into the dirt. The milk spread across the cobbles, running rivulets of white amongst the cow muck.

'Get back to your work, you idle creature!' Sam roared at Matthew and punctuated his words with a blow to the side of the lad's head. 'And forget ya wenching!'

Sam took no notice of Beth Hanley, who nevertheless scuttled out of the yard and up the lane towards the Point as if a nest of hornets were in pursuit.

Esther cursed herself roundly for her own stupidity. The appearance of first Matthew and then Beth had

unnerved even Esther's determination to prove herself
useful to Sam Brumby.

And spilling a full pail of his precious milk would do
her no good at all.

Three

*B*Y the time she had dealt with the one remaining bucket of milk and had come out into the yard again, Sam Brumby and Matthew had disappeared. She sighed, unsure what to do. She badly needed to prove herself useful to Sam. She had nowhere else to go. She would not go back. Not ever! But now she had probably ruined her chances of staying here. She knew just how precious every drop of milk was to a small farmer who had only three cows; and one of those was not being milked just now because it was due to calve at any time.

Esther was standing uncertainly in the middle of the yard when she heard a scuffling from one of the sties and went to investigate. Esther liked pigs. She loved their pink, hairy coats, their snuffling and grunting, and their noisy troughing made her want to giggle. As she looked in over the first door, a half-grown young gilt squealed and rushed excitedly towards her. She expected Esther to be the bringer of food.

Esther laughed. 'You look hungry. I'll go and see what I can find.'

She turned away from the sty and looked back towards the house. There were two buckets of pig swill standing outside the back door. She fetched them and the young pig scurried around her ankles, knocking against her in its eagerness to get at the food Esther carried.

'Let me get to the trough to tip it in, then,' she laughed.

The next sty was empty, but in the end one she found a large Curly Coat sow pacing up and down. She was heavily in-pig and displayed no interest in the other bucket of swill Esther tipped into the trough. The animal was obviously agitated and frothing at the mouth. From time to time the sow picked up a mouthful of straw and carried it about the sty, each time finally dropping it in one particular corner.

Esther moved towards her carefully. 'Now then, old girl,' she soothed. This pig reminded her of one of her uncle's, a restless animal that had turned vicious at the birth and had tried to eat its own young, succeeding in killing all but two of the litter before her uncle had found them. Esther looked around her for something in which she could put the newborn piglets to keep them safe from their mother. There was nothing in the sty, but in the barn she found a battered old tea-chest. She dragged it into the sty and placed it in one corner, pushing some of the straw into the bottom as bedding.

Esther stayed in the corner near the door watching the sow from a safe distance whilst she waited. She had no idea where Sam Brumby had gone. Perhaps she should try to tell him, but she was rather afraid that if she left this pig alone for very long, by the time she returned there could well be a half-chewed piglet or two.

The youngsters slipped out quite easily one by one. The sow tried to rouse herself each time, but her eyes were wild and her mouth frothing. Esther knew she was not trying to suckle her young. This animal was dangerous, just like her uncle's sow. She would kill her litter, given half a chance.

Esther went to one of the other sheds. The door squeaked rustily as she opened it and the fusty smell of neglect met her nostrils. Tools and implements had been thrown in higgledy-piggledy to lie dusty and forgotten. She stood a moment to let her eyes become accustomed to the dim interior and then she spotted what she wanted and pulled it from the heap of implements, disturbing a cloud of dust. She carried the garden hoe back to the pigsty and each time a piglet was born, Esther crept forward, keeping well away from the suffering mother, and as gently as she could pulled the wriggling creature away until she could pick it up. She wiped it as clean as she could with straw, over its face to clear the mouth, and slipped it into the tea-chest in the opposite corner. Then she stood up again and moved quietly back near the door to wait for the next arrival.

A shadow appeared across the doorway. '*Now* what are you up to, wench?' came Sam's exasperated tone.

'Yar pig's farrowing, mester, and it looks to me as if she might try to eat her young 'uns.'

Sam snorted. 'That's nothing new with that sow. Lost half the litter last time, Ah did.'

'Well, not this time,' Esther vowed, more to herself than to Sam.

'What? What d'you say?'

'I'll stay with her, Mr Brumby.'

Sam sniffed again and turned away. 'Well, Ah can't stand here all day playing nursemaid to a pig. You do what you like.'

22

Esther smiled to herself at his oblique reference once more to her sex, but at least this time he had not told her to go.

Esther did not go into the house at midday. Her stomach was rumbling with hunger, but she dare not leave the sow for a moment.

'Ah've brought you a mug o' tea.' She turned to see Matthew grinning at her over the half-door of the sty. He jerked his head back towards the house. 'Mester said you was playing midwife to Curly.'

'Ooh, ta,' Esther said appreciatively, taking the tea. Matthew leant his forearms on the lower half of the door and rested his chin on his arms, watching the sow. 'Awk'ard old devil, she is. You want to be careful – she'll 'ave yar leg off soon as look at ya.'

Esther grinned and held up the hoe. 'That's why I'm armed – and why I'm standing near the door. But I reckon she's a mite busy to be chasing me just now.' They watched together as another piglet thrust its way into the world.

'Here – hold this a minute, will ya?' She moved forward and plucked the tiny animal away, wiped it and popped it into the tea-chest. Then she returned to her place by the door and took the mug back from Matthew, sipping the hot, sweet tea gratefully.

'Well, I'd best be getting back to me hedging and ditching, else I'll have the mester after me again.'

'Thanks for the tea,' Esther said.

'Ya're welcome.' Giving her a saucy wink, Matthew went off whistling.

As the sixth piglet was born – and she could see that the sow was not done even then – Esther heard a familiar shrill whistle and moments later the wheels of the local carrier's cart rattled into the yard.

'Is she here, then?' Will Benson was demanding to know of Sam.

'Who?' Then, understanding, Sam added accusingly, 'Oh, so it's *you* Ah've to thank for landing me with a chit of a girl, is it? Ah can't get rid of the cheeky little baggage!'

Esther heard the carrier's laugh. 'That's our Esther right enough. She's a rare lass. You've met your match there, Sam Brumby. She'll take no notice of your moods and your tempers.'

'What's she to do wi' you then, Will Benson? And what right have you to inflict such as her on me? Ah didn't ask you to bring her. She ain't staying, Ah can tell you that!' It was a long speech for the taciturn Sam, but Will only laughed again.

'*I* didn't bring her, but I admit I told her about you needing a young 'un about the place. I were going to offer to bring her over at least to see you, but when I called at her aunt's – ' he gave a snort of contempt. 'Lord strike me, how I detest that woman – Esther had already left. Set off to walk through the night, her aunt said, so as to arrive by first light.'

''Ow far she come, then?'

'Oh, must be thirteen odd mile, I reckon.'

24

Peeping out of the door, but minding to keep well hidden from the two men, Esther saw the farmer staring up at the carrier and then – a rare thing – Sam Brumby smiled. It twitched the corner of his mouth, unwilling at first, hesitating as if not knowing quite how to form itself after years of neglect, then spreading across his mouth, wrinkling his eyes. From deep within came a chuckle. 'The young . . .' he murmured more to himself than to Will. 'And Ah accused her of being weak because she looked tired this morning. Well, Ah never did!'

The carrier's mouth dropped open. Sam Brumby was actually laughing! It would be a talking point on the carrier's rounds for weeks to come.

Esther saw Sam shake his head wonderingly. He took off the cap he always wore and scratched his balding pate, then pulled his cap on again. 'Well, Ah never!' he muttered again. Esther knew she had, for the moment, earned Sam's grudging respect. And that, she guessed, was not an easy thing to do.

'Ah'll tell you summat else, Will. She got the better of me gander last night. Now, I ain't ever seen old Wellington beat afore – not by anyone.'

'Didn't I tell you, Sam, didn't I tell you she's a rare lass?' the carrier said delightedly.

Will Benson was a dapper little man, dressed more smartly than the farmer. He wore trousers and a striped jacket and matching waistcoat, and the toes of his sturdy boots shone. He sported a ginger moustache which drooped at the corners hiding to some extent the shape of his mouth. Some days he wore a cap and on hot summer days a kind of boater-shaped hat. Esther knew him well for he lived in the same village where she lived – or rather had lived, she reminded herself. She smiled as she saw Will take off his cap. He had a good head of hair for a man of his age, she thought, seeing it smooth and glinting ginger in the sunlight. She liked Will. He had always treated her kindly and even on occasions boldly outfaced her aunt on her behalf. There weren't many who dared to do that, Esther thought ruefully, yet Will Benson always seemed to get away with it.

He was speaking again now. 'She's a good lass, Sam, I can tell you. Treated rough, she's been, by that shrew of an aunt of hers. Mind you, she's raised Esther alongside her own bairns, you can't deny, but only out of a sense of – of *duty*. She never showed the poor lass any affection.' He shook his head and added bitterly, 'She could show it to her own, though. She made the difference between them very obvious, I can tell you.'

Sam said nothing whilst the carrier chattered on. 'She's a hard worker,' and he added a little ruefully, 'she's had to be, with Hannah for her aunt! The lass deserves better. She ought to be given a chance.' Esther felt a blush of embarrassment creep up her face. She had never before heard herself so praised.

'What happened to her folks, then?'

'Her mother, Hannah's younger sister, died giving birth to her,' Will replied briefly.

'What about her father?'

'How should *I* know?' As if to cut off any more of Sam's questions, Will climbed down from his seat. 'I can't sit here chatting all day. I've me rounds to do. I'll just have a word with the lass an' I'll be on me way. Where is she?'

From the pigsty, Esther saw Sam jerk his head in her direction. Even from this distance, Esther heard Sam's dismissive sniff. 'Wasting her time wi' me sow.'

As the conversation between the two men ceased, Esther hung over the half-door of the pigsty. ''Morning, Mr Benson,' she called.

'Eh, there you are, Esther lass.' He gave a wave in greeting and came towards her. 'You settling in all right, then?'

'Ah ain't said she's staying yet,' Sam Brumby raised his voice before Esther could reply.

She grinned at Will. 'He'll find he's a job on 'is hands to get rid of me though, won't he, Mr Benson?'

The carrier laughed, whilst Sam Brumby growled, 'There's nowt Ah want today, Will Benson. You can be on your way.' And with that parting shot, Sam hobbled off.

'Well, lass,' Will said softly. 'Are you all right?'

Esther pulled a wry face. 'I ain't managed to make him see he needs me yet, but I'm working on it.' She grinned suddenly. 'I'm banking on Curly here to help.'

Will Benson poked his head into the sty and a doubtful expression flitted across his face. Esther leant closer and lowered her voice. 'She usually turns nasty with her litter and kills 'em. I'm trying to save 'em.'

Will's expression cleared and he smiled. 'Oh, so that's it – I wondered what Sam meant. Well, lass, it might work. Dun't let that grumpy old beggar get the better of you. Good luck and tek care of yasen. I'll be calling again on Thursday as usual. Tuesdays and Thursdays I come out to the Point.'

'I'll be here,' Esther told him with far more confidence in her tone than she felt.

He turned away, raised his hand in farewell, and went back to his cart.

There were ten strong, healthy piglets by the time the sow had done. The eleventh, a poor, thin little reckling, did not live. Esther bit her lip. She knew the piglets ought to be suckling now. They needed nourishment, particularly that first fluid from the mother's teats, and they needed the warmth of their mother's body, but Esther wasn't sure even yet that the sow's proper maternal feelings had replaced the wild pain.

When the cleansings came away, Esther allowed the sow to eat these. Perhaps that would assuage her unnatural desire, Esther thought. She'd seen it done before and it had worked then. As she watched, the animal seemed to relax. The sow's eyes seemed calmer and she struggled to her feet and went to the trough. Esther smiled. The signs were good.

When the mother returned to the corner and lay down again near the tea-chest, Esther picked one piglet out and placed it to the sow's teats. With inborn sense, the tiny creature nuzzled at the teat to make the fluid come and then began to suck greedily. The sow's eyes closed in contentment and she lay still and quiet whilst Esther placed all the piglets one by one to feed. They'd be all right now. Once the mother had suckled her young, it was unlikely she'd turn on them.

Esther slipped out of the sty and latched the door taking one last look at the now placid scene.

Suddenly, she felt weary. She sank down on to a square of hay and leant back against the rough brick wall and closed her eyes. Already the sun was slanting deep shadows across the yard. She'd been most of the day with the sow without realizing how the time was passing, so intent had she been on saving the piglets. She had not eaten all day.

'All dead, are they?'

Her eyes snapped open to see Sam standing over her.

'Take a look,' she invited and watched as he moved to the door of the sty and looked in. He glanced back at her and then swiftly away again, back to the sow and her litter.

'One of her tits is a windy one,' Esther told him. 'But with only ten young, she's plenty to feed 'em all. One didn't live, but not – ' she added pointedly – 'because she ate it!'

Sam stood looking at the litter as if weighing the piglets she had saved for him against the milk she had lost. He made no comment but as he turned towards the house, over his shoulder he said gruffly, 'Like a bite o' summat, would you?'

Esther grinned as she levered up her tired limbs to follow him. It was the closest a man like Sam Brumby would ever come to a 'thank you'.

Four

ESTHER spent another night in the hayloft, but the following morning, she made sure she was up very early. She had already brought the two milking cows to the byre by the time Sam appeared in the yard.

"Morning, Mester Brumby,' she called cheerfully. His only reply was a sniff and a deepening of his permanent scowl. But at least this morning he hadn't told her to 'clear off'. Instead he seemed to be leaving her to do the milking, for she saw neither Sam Brumby nor Matthew the rest of the morning.

After finishing the dairy work, she attacked the dust and grime of years in the kitchen. She found a long-handled broom and swept the ceiling and then she washed down the walls. As the dirt came off she found the plastered walls were painted a deep red.

Next she scrubbed the wooden table and one by one she cleaned the pans from the hooks on the wall. Then she washed the piles of plates, cups and saucers from the two shelves at one side of the kitchen. There were four huge hooks in the ceiling for hams, but only a storm lantern was hanging from one of them. Perhaps the half-grown gilt was being fattened for killing?

A torn lace curtain was the only covering on the kitchen window and Esther took it down carefully, spluttering as the dust tickled her nose and throat. She would wash and mend that later.

If I'm still here, she thought ruefully.

It was dinner time before she had finished this one room and there was still the huge black range to tackle. She surveyed the clean kitchen with satisfaction. The back scullery and the range would have to wait. Now she would try to find something to make Sam Brumby a midday meal.

She went out of the house and turned to the right. Adjoining the main house was a low building constructed in the same brick and roof tiles. The first door she opened was the wash-house. She sniffed the damp, mouldy air.

'Sam hasn't done much washing in 'ere lately,' she murmured, wrinkling her nose. I'll attend to that later, she promised herself, leaving the door open to let in the fresh air. Beyond the wash-house, on the corner, was the privy. Esther turned again to the right, round the corner of the building and stepped on to grass. To her left was a pond with a beautiful weeping willow tree straggling its graceful fronds in the water. Five green-headed ducks, wriggling their tails, waddled round the edge then flopped into the water. Hens wandered freely about the yard and the grass, scratching and pecking. At the far side of the pond the gander and his geese paraded up and down. The gander held his head proudly and pretended not to notice Esther.

She moved on beyond the end of the house and round to the front. She found herself in what must once have been a well-tended front garden and orchard, but now the weeds were trying to strangle the few surviving flowers. Fruit trees grew up out of the long, unkempt grass but to one side she found a small vegetable patch which showed signs of recent digging. She fetched a fork from one of the small sheds and dug up a spring cabbage and a few leeks. She even found a turnip that had been left in the ground.

Back in the kitchen she washed and sliced the vegetables and put them together with some of the cooked bacon into a clean cooking pot on the fire in the range. Soon the aroma of a kind of stew filled the kitchen. It was a warm, inviting smell which Esther guessed – and rather hoped – had not welcomed Sam Brumby for some years.

Esther was bending over the fire ladling stew into three bowls when Sam entered the house with Matthew behind him. Wordlessly, she placed one bowl on the table in front of the chair where Sam had sat the previous day. She placed another for Matthew and sat down before the third herself.

'By gum, this is good – a good cook as well as pretty!' Matthew grinned.

Esther hacked off a piece of bread for herself making no outward response to his compliment, though she felt a glow of pleasure.

Sam Brumby concentrated on his bowl; he neither spoke nor looked at either of the other two. Esther rose and poured each of them a mug of tea.

As they finished the meal, Matthew stood up. 'I've to go to Mester Willoughby's after dinner today. Shall you be wanting me tomorrow, Mester Brumby?'

Esther saw Sam glance quickly at her and then look away again. He sniffed. 'Aye,' was all he said.

Matthew grinned at Esther, picked up his cap and, whistling jauntily, left the house. Esther cleared away the dishes and carried them into the back scullery. She drew hot water from the tap in the range. As she poured it into the sink in the scullery, she felt Sam Brumby's presence in the doorway behind her and smelt the sweet-sour smell of tobacco smoke as he methodically packed his clay pipe and lit it.

'There's a room – ' he spoke in short bursts between each puff as he drew deeply on his pipe to get it fully alight – 'above 'ere.' He prodded his pipe stem towards the ceiling of the kitchen. 'You can get to it by a ladder in yon corner. It'll – be warmer – than the hayloft.'

He turned away without waiting for her to speak and went out of the back door.

Esther leant on her knuckles in the bowl of hot water and closed her eyes. Two tears of thankfulness plopped into the washing-up water.

The room above the kitchen was no more than an attic boxroom. When Esther climbed the narrow ladder from the corner of the kitchen and poked her head through the trap door, she was met by the musty smell of rotting apples. To one side, spread on newspaper, were apples from the previous autumn; maybe even the one before that, she thought, by the look of some of them. Several were aged to a brown pulp and covered with a thick blanket of dust.

The small, oblong room with a sloping ceiling was

33

littered with bits of broken furniture, a trunk of old clothes and the general clutter of a family who had lived in the same house for generations. In one of the corners, tied up with binding, was a rolled mattress.

Esther surveyed the chaos grimly but by nightfall when she lay down on the mattress, the room was clean and sweet-smelling.

The following morning, as soon as she and Sam had breakfasted and the latter was away out on the farm, Esther went into the back scullery. She sighed as she stood surveying the scene of neglect. It was the same in the wash-house. A mangle stood in the far corner festooned with cobwebs, and tubs and dolly pegs and washboards had been pushed into an untidy heap. On a shelf above stood four irons, a line of cobwebs linking one to another. In the corner opposite the door was the large brick copper with its wooden lid covering the deep bowl. There was evidence that Sam – or someone – had washed a shirt and a sheet which were hanging on a piece of rope strung between two hooks across the room. But in the copper lay a mound of mouldering, dirty clothes.

'Well, Mester Brumby, there's enough work to keep me here a while yet,' she murmured aloud and bent down to rake out the dead cinders from under the copper. Suddenly she felt a smart smack on her rump which was sticking immodestly in the air as she bent double to her task.

'Ouch!' she cried and, coming up suddenly, banged her head on the fire door of the copper. She turned and saw Matthew standing over her, grinning.

34

'Oh, it's you again, is it, *boy*? I might've known!' And she turned back to her chore.

'Aw, come on, Esther, 'ow about a little kiss for a feller in a morning?'

'I got better things to do wi' me time,' she snapped and raked vigorously at the ashes, sending up clouds of grey dust so that she coughed and spluttered as it prickled her throat and stung her eyes. She was forced to draw back and stand up.

Matthew only laughed. 'Serves you right for being so unfriendly.' But he pulled out a spotted kerchief from his pocket and wiped the tears from her eyes. 'Don't cry, sweet Esther,' he said mockingly. At his words she slapped his ministering hand away.

'Cry? Me? You'll never see me cry, Matthew Hilton, I'll promise you that!' They gazed into each other's eyes, hers intense with anger, his fascinated by her loveliness.

'You've got beautiful eyes, Esther. Green, they are. I ain't never seen such lovely eyes . . .' Now the playful, teasing tone was gone from his voice and with surprisingly gentle fingers, he touched her cheek. For once Esther was startled into silence.

The moment was broken by a clatter in the yard. Swiftly Matthew turned away and shot out of the door. 'God, he's back,' he muttered as he went, and Esther was left staring after him with smut on her face and grime on her hands.

An hour later she had a fire glowing white hot under the copper and was staggering to and from the water-butt at the end of the house with heavy buckets to fill it. Each time she climbed on to a stool and tippled the cold water into the huge bowl. Satisfied at last that she had enough, she covered it with the wooden lid and, leaving the water to heat up, she came out into the yard. She glanced at the sun and reckoned it must be nearly midday. The rumblings in her own stomach told her so. There was no sign of Sam Brumby or of Matthew but she prepared a simple meal of bacon and bread and left it set on the table. Then wiping her hands down her skirt, she took a deep breath and opened the door leading from the kitchen into the house beyond.

It led into an ordinary living room with an armchair set on either side of the fireplace and peg rugs on the floor. A table covered with a green plush cloth stood in the centre with four straight-backed dining chairs set around it. In the middle of the table stood a blue and white pot holding an aspidistra, long since dead, its withered leaves rotting and filling the room with a pungent mustiness. The window was covered by yellowing lace curtains which were falling into holes and two huge blue velvet curtains, lined with dust, hung from a wooden pole across the top. The wallpaper had once had a pretty green pattern but now it was faded and dirty. Around the room were several pictures – a large one depicting Jesus in the Temple, with smaller landscape paintings around it. On the far wall at the side of the window was a photograph, brown and faded, of a stern-looking woman, her black dress buttoned to the neck, her dark hair parted in the centre and drawn back severely behind her head.

In the corner, diagonally opposite where Esther had

entered, was another door leading further into the house. She moved slowly past the table, letting her fingers feel the soft fabric of the tablecloth, but it was sticky with dust. She opened the door and stepped into a small hall-way. To her left was the front door which she knew would lead out into the garden and orchard and to her right the stairs climbed steeply to the floor above. Opposite was another door leading to what she presumed on entering to be the 'best parlour'.

The huge fireplace was ornate and bordered by a brass fender, sadly dull. Dusty velvet festooned the mantel-piece and to one side stood an embroidered fire-screen. In one corner was an organ and in front of the fireplace were chairs, a work-box and a footstool. A tall grandfather clock stood in one corner, its hands set permanently at ten to two. On a round table in front of the window lay a huge family Bible and as Esther glanced round the room it seemed that every surface was cluttered with orna-ments and pictures.

She was quite impressed by the size of the farmhouse; to have a living room *and* a best parlour was richness indeed. And yet, Esther felt a sadness sweep over her. It was obvious that this house had once been inhabited by a loving family. Poor Sam, she thought, these neglected rooms echoed his loneliness.

For some reason she could not quite explain, she found herself tiptoeing up the stairs and quietly lifting the latch of a door to her left at the top of the stairs. It was Sam Brumby's bedroom. Her heart pounded in her chest with nervousness. It was one thing to arrive at the farm and worm her way into a job and a place in a dusty attic;

it was quite another to prowl about Sam Brumby's home and go into his bedroom to search for his personal washing. Even Esther, for all her boldness, felt this might be going just a little too far.

The room was surprisingly tidy, though dusty. Sam's Sunday best suit stood on a hanger in the corner, and two faded photographs in silver frames stood on the chest of drawers. Esther bent closer. One was of a man and woman; the woman seated, stiff and straight-backed, her face stern and serious. It was the same face that stared out of the larger picture hanging in the living room. The man, his hand on the back of her chair, had the likeness of Sam about him. Yet it was not Sam. In the other photograph was a solemn little boy, his arm protectively round a smaller girl with a sweet face surrounded by a mass of dark curls.

Esther straightened up and went to the bed. The covers were pulled straight, though the patchwork quilt needed washing. She pulled back the top coverlet and saw that there were no sheets on the bed, only a rough blanket that smelled a little sour. There was no pillowcase on the rough ticking of the pillow either. Her fingers hesitated over a heavy oak chest standing at the foot of the bed. She had no wish to pry into Sam's belongings, but if she were to care for him properly she needed to find fresh bedlinen. Taking a deep breath, she lifted the lid. Inside were sheets and pillow-cases, yellow with age, but neatly folded. She pulled out two of each and bundled them under her arm. The lid dropped with a dull thud and as she was going out of the room she noticed a shirt on the floor behind the door. She scooped that up too. At that moment she heard the back door bang and she scuttled down the stairs without stopping to look at the other upstairs rooms.

Sam was in the kitchen. 'Now what are ya up to, wench?' His words followed her as she rushed past him out to the wash-house.

'Weshing, mester,' she called back over her shoulder. 'Just a bit o' weshing.'

When the sheets, pillow-cases and shirt were bubbling in the copper, Esther went into the barn to search for a length of line to string between two trees in the garden at the front of the house. A good blow in the fresh air was what all these clothes and the linen needed. She glanced down at the coarse skirt and dirty pinafore she was wearing. She wished she could wash her own clothes, but she had nothing to change into and with that cheeky Matthew about, she dare not risk it.

She was possing the clothes in the rinsing tub when he appeared again, startling her as she caught sight of him standing silently in the doorway. She dropped the posser suddenly and cold water splashed her face.

'Oh – ya made me jump!' she said with annoyance. 'What ya doing here? Shouldn't ya be at work?' Sweat plastered strands of hair to her forehead. Her cheeks were red with exertion.

'I've come back to see you.' Matthew grinned and took a step nearer.

She raised her hands, palms outward, as if to fend him off. 'No, there'll be trouble – I dun't want to lose this job. I've come a long way and there's nowhere for me

to go back to, so – so don't spoil it for me, please?'
she pleaded.

Teasing, he said, 'It'll cost you, seeing as 'ow you've
taken it from under Beth's nose,' and without giving her
a chance to argue, he walked away across the yard, a new
arrogance in his stride. He turned once, shouted, 'I'll see
you later,' gave her a saucy wink and a wave and then he
was gone.

Esther felt herself hot all over and knew it was not the
steaming water and the activity of wash-day that had
caused it.

Five

*H*E was waiting in the yard when she finally finished in the wash-house that evening.

'What are you doin' here? You haven't finished milking, have ya?'

'Haven't started,' he replied boldly, and stood before her to bar her way back into the house.

Esther gasped at his audacity and her green eyes glittered. 'You'll have Mester Brumby after you. It should've been done hours ago!'

'I can handle Sam Brumby.'

Esther was at once sceptical. 'Now you're bragging, Master Matthew.'

'Well now,' he said softly, his eyes roaming over her face. 'At least you've stopped calling me "boy".'

She could feel his breath warm upon her cheek as he added, 'I thought mebbe we could take a little walk. I could show you around, like. I could show you where it's safe to walk on the beach – and where it's dangerous.'

'And how do I know you're not the biggest danger out there?'

Matthew threw back his head and laughed. 'You don't,' he said. 'You really don't know.'

Esther made no attempt to rebuff him further. She felt like taking a walk and she was curious to find out more about this place. Since the morning she had arrived at

Fleethaven Point she had not left Brumbys' Farm. But now Sam was some distance away in the field which lay adjacent to the neighbouring farmer's – Top End, he called it. He would not return until after dark. She could spare half an hour . . .

She fell into step beside Matthew. Whistling through his teeth, he swaggered jauntily across the lane and led her beneath the trees growing on the dunes. They climbed to the highest point and paused to catch their breath whilst Esther looked about her, soaking up the feel of the land. Already, she felt an affinity with this place. She shaded her eyes against the red glow of the evening sun and let her gaze travel round, trying to gauge the extent of Sam's holding.

Brumbys' Farm lay with its front windows facing the flat land that stretched westward. About a mile inland were the tall chimneys of a large house surrounded by trees.

'What's that place?' she asked Matthew. He came and stood close behind her placing his hands lightly on her shoulders and putting his cheek against her hair.

Following the line of her pointing finger he said, 'That's the Grange where Squire Marshall lives. He owns most of the land around here.'

'And over there – those buildings?' Esther was pointing to the north-west now.

'That's Tom Willoughby's place – Rookery Farm. Lives there with his wife and her sister. He's a grand chap – you'll like him.'

To the south-west she could see another farm but it

42

was further away – a good two miles at least. 'That's Souters' Farm,' Matthew told her.

Directly below where they were standing was the lane running alongside the dunes leading from the town of Lynthorpe to Fleethaven Point.

'Come on,' Matthew said, grabbing her hand and pulling her down the other side of the dunes. 'I'll show you the sea.'

Esther found herself following him across squelchy marshland, jumping the creeks, wading through green spiky grass and skirting stagnant pools until they came to a lower line of sand dunes. Close by them a skylark rose into the air, hovered above its territory and then glided gently down trilling its song, plunging at the last moment towards the ground.

'These dunes are just forming,' Matthew was telling her as they climbed them. 'A few years back the sea used to come right up here. There you are . . .' As they reached the top, he waved his arm, triumphantly encompassing the view before them as if it were all his own handiwork. 'There's the sea.'

The breeze was cool, but Esther lifted her face and sniffed the salt air and listened to the gentle lap-lap of the waves.

They walked along the shore until they came to the place where the sea curved in to form the mouth of the Wash. Matthew led her along the dunes which ended in a promontory of land sticking out into the water. 'We call this the Spit,' he told her. 'The tide's high at the moment so the water comes right in on either side.'

Esther found herself clutching his arm, afraid of

slipping off the sandy bank and into the swirling water.

'It's what they call an intertidal marsh,' Matthew told her loftily, airing his knowledge. 'When the tide's out, all this – ' he waved his arm – 'is thick mud.'

Matthew let go of her hand and bent down at the water's edge, cupped his hands together and sluiced the cold sea water over his face and head. His black curly hair shone. He shook his head, the droplets of salt water flying everywhere. Then he grinned at her and bent to pick up a flat shell.

'Watch,' he said and then holding the shell between his thumb and forefinger, he skimmed it across the water, the shell bouncing three or four times before it sank into the waves.

'Here,' he said, bending to pick up another. 'You try.' He took her hand in his own, shaping her fingers around the shell. 'Now lean down slightly to one side and flick your wrist so that the flat side of the shell hits the water.'

Esther tried to do as he told her, but the shell merely plopped into the sea and disappeared.

'Look, I'll show you again. Like this . . .'

He made her practise until she could get the shell to skim the surface of the water a couple of times before sinking.

'There you are,' he said jubilantly, 'now you can play ducks and drakes as good as the rest of us. Come on, now I'll show you the Point where I live.'

They walked back along the Spit and retraced their steps across the marsh coming out into the lane once more, but nearer the Point than Brumbys' Farm. This line of dunes – formed many years before and now with trees and bushes well established – curved and formed a solid bank over which the road had been forced to rise.

'We call this the Hump.' Matthew grinned. 'Poor old Will Benson always has a job getting his cart up here. Some days in winter, if it's slithery, he dun't make it and the women from the Point have to traipse across here to meet him when he blows his whistle.'

They stood together on the top of the bank and Esther let her gaze take in the view in front of her. Matthew pointed to a building only a few yards to the left below the rise of ground on which they were standing.

'That's the pub – the Seagull. That's where us fellers all get drunk on a Saturday night.'

'I can imagine!' Esther said drily, but Matthew merely grinned again and swung his pointing finger round slightly.

'And that's where I live, in them cottages.' A stretch of grass in front of the row of cottages sloped gently down towards the river bank. 'The Harrises live in the far end one with all their brood – seven kids there were at the last count,' Matthew went on.

Her mouth tightened. Same number as her aunt's large family. If Mrs Harris was anything like her Aunt Hannah, then Esther had no wish to meet her.

'I live in the next one,' Matthew continued. 'Then Beth Hanley lives next door to that with her dad. He's the coastguard and has a look-out station built on the East Dunes. Last cottage this end nearest to us is empty at the moment.'

Esther's glance travelled around until her gaze rested upon the twisting river to their right.

45

'Whatever's that?' she asked. A boat – a large, black hulk – was set up out of the water close to the river bank on poles and wooden sleepers.

'What's what? Oh, that boat, you mean? That's where Robert Eland lives.'

'Lives? Somebody actually lives in a boat? But it's sort of half on the land and half in the river!'

Matthew laughed then wrinkled his forehead. 'I suppose I've never thought about it before. I've lived here all me life and Robert's parents lived in it before him, so,' he shrugged his shoulders, 'I never thought about it bein' odd.'

'What does he do?'

'Who, Robert Eland?'

Esther nodded.

'He's the lifeboat coxswain. The lifeboat's moored about a mile up the road nearer to the town. All the men that live round are in the crew – Mester Harris, Percy Holmes from the pub, and then two or three from the town. Me too, I'm a launcher at the moment, but one day I'll be in the crew.'

'Is there much need for a lifeboat here?'

He looked at her incredulously. 'Don't you know nothing about the sea?'

Esther shook her head. 'I've come from inland.'

'Ah, that explains it, then. This Point is right on the edge of the Wash and the North Sea and you get a lot of boats coming into the Wash to the ports, an' there's lots of sandbanks and tricky currents, and . . .' He shrugged, finding it difficult to explain to someone what he had known from childhood.

'Is that all they do then? Just man the lifeboat?'

'Course not!' Matthew said scornfully. 'They work on the land – for Squire Marshall, mostly. I told you, he owns nearly all the land hereabouts. And Robert Eland, he helps Dan Hanley with coastguard duties, an' all.'

Esther listened, learning more about the people who lived so close to the sea that it was part of their lives just as much as the land. Sea and land, their life was ordered by the two. To a country girl the sea was a mystery, yet it held a fearsome fascination.

'I'll have to be going,' Matthew said, as the dusk deepened around them, 'else I'll have old Sam after me.'

Before she could stop him, he had planted a kiss on her cheek and had dodged out of the range of her hand, raised at once to deal him a stinging slap. As he broke into a run down the slope of the Hump and back along the lane towards Brumbys' Farm, she could hear him chuckling.

Her swift anger at his audacity softened and she found herself smiling. He was just a cheeky lad with an eye for a pretty girl, she told herself sternly, but the feel of his lips on her cheek still tingled and the thought that he found her pretty warmed her.

She took a last look around from her vantage point, then stretched her arms above her head and breathed deeply in the soft air. What a beautiful, *beautiful* place! Such a feeling of space and freedom. Such stillness and silence – and peace!

Such a peace as she had never known before in her young life.

She gave a final sigh of contentment and let her arms

47

fall to her sides. She ran lightly down the slope towards the farm.

Home to Brumbys' Farm.

Esther had arrived on the last day in April and by the end of May she sensed that Sam was watching for the bloom to appear on his crop of grass. For a small farmer, a good hay harvest together with the corn harvest and root crops which came later meant feed for his stock through the winter.

On the day hay-making began, Esther followed Sam out to the meadow. The morning was bright and clear. Later they would swelter under a hot sun in a clear blue sky.

In one hand Sam carried his scythe and in a holder attached to the back of his leather belt was a honer for sharpening the long, curving blade.

'You bring the forks and rakes out to the field, wench.'

Esther was amazed at the number of workers who arrived. Men, women and even children, from the neighbouring farms and from the cottages at the Point, came to help Sam Brumby bring in his hay. Then in turn Sam, Esther and Matthew would go to work on the other farms. Esther worked alongside the women and children from dawn to dusk and beyond, shaking and spreading the cut grass out to dry during the day and then just before dusk raking it into long rows down the field so as to collect less dampness through the night.

Esther watched Sam at work as he scythed the long grass with easy rhythmic sweeps, moving steadily down the field. The grass seed flew everywhere; it buried itself in Esther's hair and even blocked her nose and made her throat dry and husky.

The next day they spread the cut grass out and collected it again at dusk, until the whole field was cut. Then, after the grass had lain in the field for a few days to dry, it was collected into haycocks.

When all Sam's meadows had been cut into neat rows of haycocks, which were then left to dry in the wind for a while, the time came for loading the hay on to the wagon to be taken to the farmyard. Matthew stood on top of the growing load on the wagon, spreading the grass evenly and expertly as it was thrown up to him on the ends of their long pitchforks by three men below. Under the hot sun Matthew had stripped to the waist, the black hairs on his chest and back glistening with the sweat of his hard work. But he still found time and energy to flirt with the women – young or old, it didn't seem to matter to Matthew Hilton.

Esther, matching his teasing tone, shaded her eyes as she looked up at him. 'Fancy ya'sen up there, don't ya?'

'I'd rather *you* fancied me, lovely Esther.' He grinned down at her, but she noticed that he never paused in the rhythmic swinging of his hay fork, deftly catching the hay as it was swung up to him. For the first time since she had met him, Esther found herself admiring his skill.

Esther herself blossomed under the workload that harvest time imposed and now she felt Sam had really accepted her.

From now on this was her home, this was her land.

When the other helpers left the farm in the evening, Esther went into Sam's kitchen to bake and cook for the next day. Her cheeks were flushed with the heat from the range, her hair straggling in wet wisps around her forehead. Swaying with weariness, late at night she climbed the ladder to her little room.

But the morning found her the first out to bring in the cows and have the milking done before the visiting workers arrived. Mid-morning she would leave the fields and hurry back to the farmhouse to bring out baskets laden with freshly baked meat pies and fruit pasties to the workers in the fields.

All this she did without Sam's instruction, maybe even without his approval.

'Eh, we ain't been fed like this on Brumbys' Farm afore,' one of the workers told her, biting into a juicy fruit pasty. 'This is a rare treat an' no mistake!'

Not a word of praise to her ever passed Sam's lips, but there began a subtle change in his attitude towards her. One morning she overheard him talking to the carrier again.

'She's a way with her, Will,' Sam was saying in one of his rare talkative moods to the man who was perhaps the nearest the reclusive, taciturn farmer had to a friend. 'She laughs and jokes with all the visiting workers, and yet when she wants 'em to do summat, well . . .' Sam paused, lifting his cap and running the back of his hand across the red, sweating mark the band of his cap left on his forehead. 'Well, I don't rightly know 'ow she does it, but she gets t'work out on 'em, and no mistake.'

Will grinned. 'Bit of her aunt in there somewhere, I'll warrant, but Esther wouldn't thank me for saying so. But she's a nicer way wi' her than that old shrew.'

Sam Brumby sniffed and settled his cap back on his head. Squinting up at Will he said slyly, 'Mebbe she teks more after her dad, then?'

'Aye, mebbe so, mebbe so.'

And Will's grin broadened.

Six

SAM Brumby's hay was gathered and stacked in the farmyard. Now it was time for Sam, Esther and Matthew to go to the other farms and offer their help in return, but at least this time Esther did not have to provide the food for the workers. This was the task of the womenfolk on the farms where they went to work.

At Tom Willoughby's farm, Esther was surprised to see Beth coming out to the field carrying baskets laden with food.

'What's she doin' here?' Esther demanded of Ma Harris.

Ma Harris lived in the end cottage at Fleethaven Point. She had a horde of children, but there, to Esther's relief, all resemblance to her Aunt Hannah ended. Ma Harris was shorter than Esther and her plump little body reminded Esther of a cottage loaf on legs. Her grey hair was drawn back into a bun and covered by a white frilled bonnet which she always wore. Esther wondered if she even took it off to go to bed. Ma Harris was a motherly woman, with a ready laugh, a kindly word, and although she often delivered a stinging slap if one of her brood misbehaved, it was a swift chastisement made with rough affection and soon forgotten by both child and mother.

'Who, lass?' Ma asked in response to Esther's question.
'Beth Hanley.'

Ma Harris looked across the field. 'She's got a job as dairymaid for the Willoughbys. Posh, ain't she, in her white apron and cap? Gone up in the world, 'as our Beth,' Ma Harris laughed, opening her mouth to reveal almost toothless gums. She turned back to Esther. 'You ought to wear a bonnet, lass, in this sun.'

Esther grinned at the older woman. 'To protect my milky white skin, you mean, Mrs Harris?'

Ma Harris's laugh cackled out across the field at Esther's sarcasm against herself. Of all the women and young girls in the field, only Esther wore no protection of any kind on her head against the heat of the day. Pride would not let her admit that she did not possess a bonnet. Ma Harris, however, was a wise woman and good-hearted and, within her means, as generous as it was possible to be. The following day, she brought one of her old bonnets and made Esther stand meekly whilst she tied it on the girl's head. ''Twill keep all that grass seed out o' your lovely hair, lass. By, I ain't seen prettier hair than yours. Auburn streaks, it's got, when the sun shines on it.'

Esther thanked her both for the bonnet and the unaccustomed compliment. Working the rest of the day at Ma Harris's side, listening to her prattle and smiling as the woman marshalled her children whilst never pausing in her own work, Esther basked in the warmth of her motherly friendliness.

*

The hay harvest was in and there would be a few weeks' respite before a similar process would begin again with the corn harvest.

Her litter of piglets, as Esther thought of them, had been weaned at eight weeks old and sent to market. One morning after feeding Curly and the young gilt, she went in search of Sam.

'Mester?'

His answer was a sniff.

'I reckon Curly is ready for the boar.'

'Eh?' He looked up, startled. ''Ow does a wench like you know about such things?'

Esther laughed. ''Tis nature, ain't it?'

Sam sniffed again, dropped his hedge knife and walked back with her to the sty to take a look for himself.

Esther giggled as she walked along beside him, and added, 'The chap who used to bring the boar to me aunt's always used to ask, "Is the sow ready, is she flushed – just like a strawberry – at the back?" '

Sam stopped and looked at her. Then a slow smile spread across his shrunken mouth and a chuckle from somewhere deep within forced its way out. 'Eh, lass,' he shook his head. 'You'll be the death o' me.'

Esther grinned back at him.

Sam reached the sty, opened the door and went inside, whilst Esther watched from the doorway. He stood behind the pig and leant his hands on her haunches. The sow blinked but did not move away. 'Aye, lass, I reckon you're right.' Sam stood a moment looking down at the huge sow with her wiry, curling coat. 'Well, old girl,' he said as if to the pig, but at his next words Esther knew he intended her to hear. 'I reckon this wench here has saved your bacon. If ya'd killed yar litter again this year, you were fer me knife come autumn.'

Sam looked directly up at Esther and laughed wheezily again. 'Go up to Tom Willoughby's and ask him to bring his boar as soon as he can. Tell him she's as flushed as a strawberry. He'll like that, will Tom.'

Tom Willoughby did like it. He leant back and roared with laughter, his great belly wobbling, the grey whiskers of his long sideburns quivering, his fat cheeks growing redder by the second. He was a huge man, tall and broad and obviously jovial. 'So it's true what I've heard about you, lass?'

'That depends on what ya've heard, mester.' She stood before him, smiling at his infectious laughter.

He drew a large red and white spotted kerchief from his pocket and mopped his brow. 'Will Benson told us that Sam had got a rare lass working for him now. A rare lass, 'ee said. I reckon 'ee's right.'

Esther's smile broadened but she made no comment. She expected that every farm for miles around on Will's route would know she had come to live and work at Brumbys' Farm.

'Aye, lass, tell Sam I'll be over with the boar tomorrow.'

Soon the corn harvest was upon them. The work for Sam was not quite as hard for he did not do the cutting but allowed Tom Willoughby to send his new reaper.

'Newfangled thing,' Esther heard Sam mutter as he

watched the sails of the reaper crossing the field pulled by three heavy horses. "Spect me corn'll be ruined.'

Sam still worked in the field, tying the sheaves and stooking, all the time keeping a truculent eye upon the machine swallowing up his harvest and spewing it out behind. The stooks stood in the fields for a few weeks to dry in the wind that always seemed to blow across this flat land and when the time came for them to be moved, the wagon was loaded so high at times that Esther held her breath thinking a wheel would crack and it would surely tipple over. But when Sam walked behind the last load to leave the field carrying the last sheaf and placed it on top of the final stack, he knew he had never had a better harvest.

The cry went up amongst the workers, 'Harvest home, harvest home.' Then the gleaners were allowed into the fields and one of the first was Ma Harris, wearing a bag apron over her long skirt in readiness. With her tribe to feed, Ma Harris was thankful that the old traditions still survived. She could usually collect enough corn from all the nearby farms for her family's needs through the winter.

When harvest was finally over, Esther noticed that Sam's walking was more painful, that his back was a little more bent and the joints of his fingers were gnarled with rheumatism. He was tired, yet not too tired to give thanks for a good harvest.

One Sunday morning in September, Sam Brumby bade Esther put on her best frock and be ready in the yard in half an hour.

Esther blinked and looked down at the coarse, well-worn skirt in dismay and then back at Sam. Didn't he realize these were all the clothes she had? Didn't he know that when she washed them each week and hung them on the clothes horse so close to the warm range over night that they almost scorched, it was because they had to be dry for the following morning? Esther wrinkled her forehead and smiled at her own foolishness. Of course he didn't know, for she was careful to strip off and take her bath in the tin bath in front of the kitchen range and wash her clothes long after Sam had climbed the stairs.

'I ain't no more clothes, mester,' she said flatly.

'Huh,' was Sam's only comment, but his glance at her, up and down, spoke volumes.

'You'll have to do as you are then, wench. I'll be waiting in the yard – half an hour,' was all Sam would say. Self-consciously and wondering what this was all about, Esther strip-washed in the back scullery, intrigued to hear the boards above her head creaking as Sam moved about upstairs. In her own small attic boxroom, Esther brushed her hair and shook out her only shawl and put it about her shoulders. Then she climbed down the ladder and opened the back door. She stopped. Her mouth fell open with surprise and then widened into a grin.

Sam Brumby was a resplendent figure in a black suit, a gold watch-chain looped across his waistcoat. He had shaved and his thin white hair was plastered down under a black trilby hat. He was standing stiffly by the gate staring down the long lane leading towards the town, looking as if he hardly dared to move in his starched white collar. Her handiwork, Esther thought, with a stab of pride. It took a moment for her to control her laughter, but knowing that at any moment Sam might turn and see her, Esther cleared her throat and strode purposefully across the yard, her boots scrunching on the cinders.

Sam pulled out the gold Hunter watch from his pocket and looked at it, then giving a sniff he set off along the road towards the town. Esther fell into step beside him, but where exactly they were going, she had no idea for not a word passed between them.

They had walked about a mile when behind them came the rattle of the wheels of a pony and trap. Stepping on to the grass verge to let it pass, Esther looked up to see Matthew grinning down at her. Beth, in her Sunday best bonnet and shawl, was sitting beside him.

As they drew level, Matthew slowed the trap. 'Want a lift, Mester Brumby? 'Tis a long way to the church.'

Sam's frown deepened. 'Thank 'ee – no. Ah can still walk two miles, young feller!'

Above Sam's head, Matthew winked at Esther. ''Spect you'd like to ride in style, Esther?'

Esther grinned back at him but, mindful of Sam's feelings, she answered pertly, 'Thank you kindly, sir, but I'll walk with Mester Brumby.'

As Matthew flicked the reins and urged the pony forward, Beth looked back over her shoulder at Esther, a smug expression on her face. With an obvious gesture, she tucked her hand possessively through Matthew's arm.

When they reached the outskirts of the town, Esther looked about her. She had come this way the day she had arrived, but in the early morning light the houses had been only shadowy shapes. Now, in the sunshine of a

September morning, there was a brightness about the neat houses and well-kept gardens.

'By, them's posh places, mester,' Esther broke the silence. Twisting and turning as she walked she pointed excitedly to right and left. 'Look at that 'un – it's a mansion!'

Esther noticed a brass plate fixed to the gatepost. Laboriously she spelt out the name. 'Doctor Blair.'

Sam neither answered nor turned his head. Esther heard his sniff that indicated disapproval. Evidently Sam Brumby had no time for the town-dwellers.

They walked through the town centre, down the main street with little shops huddled together and living quarters above, and on almost out of the town to a small church. Sam walked up the flagged path, gravestones standing sentinel on either side, to the low porch. Esther followed.

Beth was sitting in a pew half-way down the left hand side of the church, her dark head bowed, her eyes closed piously in prayer. On her left against the wall sat Matthew, but on her right was a thickset man with dark hair. His mouth was completely hidden by a full beard so it was impossible to see if he ever smiled. It was unlikely that he did, for there was no laughter in his eyes beneath heavy, dark eyebrows. The visible part of his face was weather-beaten and lined, giving his forehead the impression of a permanent frown. Esther had seen this man before – he had been one of the visiting harvest workers – but she had never learnt his name.

As if feeling her gaze upon him, the man turned his head slightly and looked straight into Esther's eyes.

59

The frown seemed to deepen.

Wordlessly, Sam motioned Esther to precede him into a pew on the opposite side of the aisle to where Matthew, Beth and the stranger were sitting. Beth seemed not to have noticed their arrival, or was deliberately ignoring them.

The service began and Esther watched and listened. The altar steps overflowed with the offerings from the congregation of fruit and vegetables, flowers and even one or two small wheat-sheaves and corn dollies. The atmosphere was warm and friendly as if the air of thanksgiving pervaded the congregation. She knelt beside Sam and watched covertly as he turned the pages of his prayer book. Esther was no great reader, yet she had learned enough to be able to find the same page in the book as Sam had, and then she proceeded to make a pretence at following the service, moving her lips and miming the prayers, deliberately inaudible.

Esther could not remember having been in a church before. Her Aunt Hannah had been a staunch Methodist and Chapel was the only form of worship with which Esther was familiar.

The service came to an end and Esther stood behind Sam whilst the gentry from the front pews walked down the aisle and out of the church. There was a portly gentleman with whiskery grey sideburns and red-veined cheeks that spoke of too much indulgence of the port. He nodded and smiled to each side as he strutted down the aisle. Esther watched as the men touched their foreheads in a deferential salute, whilst the women smiled self-consciously and nodded. One or two even bobbed at the knee. In contrast to the gentleman's jolly manner, the woman who walked at his side with her hand in the crook of his arm was a thin, miserable-looking creature. True, she acknowledged the greetings of the congregation with a quick, darting look and the briefest of nods, and then her eyes were downcast to the floor as if she almost feared to meet anyone's gaze directly. She looked nervous and ill-at-ease, though why Esther could not imagine, for it seemed her husband was held in high esteem.

Behind them came Tom Willoughby with two ladies whose skirts rustled and swished. One was very large, tall and stately. She sailed along, her breadth filling the width of the aisle. Her face was bloated and the folds of fat beneath her chin wobbled as she moved. The woman with her was thin, with steel-rimmed spectacles perched on her hooked nose. A receding chin and protruding upper teeth accentuated her thinness.

As he drew level with the pew where Sam Brumby and Esther were still standing waiting to leave, Tom Willoughby greeted them. 'How do, Sam? And you, lass?'

Sam nodded briefly and Esther smiled up at the huge figure of Tom Willoughby, causing the two women with him to look her up and down. Their heads bobbed together as they whispered to one another and then they stared at her again. Boldly, Esther returned their scrutiny. As she passed close to Esther, the thin woman pointedly picked up her skirt and pulled it towards herself as if to avoid the merest contact with Esther, even though Sam stood between them.

Sam, Esther noticed, spoke to no one and acknowledged only very few people – the portly gentleman and his wife, Tom Willoughby and the vicar as they left the church – and then only with a sharp nod, a swift pecking movement. All the rest of the congregation Sam deliberately ignored, even those from the Point who were, after all, his nearest neighbours.

As Esther followed Sam from the church the vicar was standing outside the porch shaking hands and exchanging pleasantries with each member of his congregation.

'Ah, Mr Brumby.' He clasped Sam's hand warmly. 'It's good to see you, good to see you.'

'Parson,' Sam murmured.

'And is this the young lady I've been hearing so much about who's come to help you on the farm? Glad to meet you, my dear, glad to meet you.'

Esther smiled broadly at the vicar, her tanned face creasing with smiles, her green eyes twinkling. 'Thank you, sir.'

'Now, come again, my dear, come again. Mr Brumby, you bring this young lady to church again.'

Sam was half-way down the path and made no indication of having heard the vicar. Behind her Esther heard a muffled snort of indignation and a whispered comment between the large woman and her skinny companion. 'Young lady, indeed!' whispered one.

'Fancy,' came the twittering reply. 'Who would have thought it of Sam Brumby?'

Esther whirled around, a stinging reply on her lips, but the retort died as behind the two gossiping women she saw Beth Hanley, her hand on the bearded man's arm.

Esther's gaze met Beth's and she saw the triumph written in the girl's eyes. Esther turned away, sickened by the implications of the two women and Beth's glorying in their insults of her. Still in front of the vicar, Esther turned back to him and said politely, but loud enough for those about her to hear distinctly, 'I'll certainly come back to your church, when your congregation show a little more Christian charity. Good morning.' Ignoring the appalled gasps behind her, she marched down the path after Sam.

It soon became apparent to Esther that Sam Brumby was no regular churchgoer and he had what some might think was a peculiar attitude towards the Being he always referred to as 'The Almighty'. He did not believe in the prayer of supplication; he could never bring himself to pray for things to be given to him. On the contrary his sole purpose in his rare attendances at church was to give thanks. At harvest – good or bad – he would attend the Harvest Service. At Christmas he would celebrate with the Church the birthday of the Son of the Almighty, and at Easter he would give thanks for Christ's sacrifice. But never, ever, would he ask for anything for himself. His lips hardly moved during prayer except to say such words as, 'Thanks be to God'.

Esther was not to attend church again until Midnight Mass on Christmas Eve, but her first visit was not soon forgotten. The very next day when she saw Matthew, she demanded, 'Who was the man sitting on the other side of your girl?'

'Beth's not my girl,' came his swift reply.

'She seems to think so.'

'Well, she ain't,' he muttered and then he grinned. 'You jealous?'

Esther tossed her curls. 'I can do better for mesen than the likes of you, Matthew Hilton.'

'Oh, Miss High an' Mighty, chance'd be a fine thing . . .'

'I asked you who that feller was.'

'Well, you've no chance there, I can tell you. He's eyes for no one but Beth, even though he's years older.'

Esther blinked at Matthew. 'Really? But who *is* he? I thought he were her father.'

'No – Beth's dad never sets foot in a church – not as long as I've known him, an' that's all me life. No – the feller you mean is Robert Eland.'

'Oh, yes,' she said, remembering suddenly what Matthew had told her previously, 'he lives in that boat stuck up on the river bank, dun't he?'

Matthew nodded. 'He's a seaman at heart and dun't really want to live on the land.' He grinned. 'I reckon he tries to get as near to living at sea as he can.'

'Who was the portly gent and the thin woman with him?'

'That's Squire Marshall. He lives at the Grange.'

Esther nodded. She hadn't been required to help out at harvest on the squire's farm. He would employ enough of his own workers, she supposed.

There was silence between them, then Matthew asked, 'Dun't you want to know who everyone else was in church? How about the two women who . . . ?'

'I dun't wish to know who *they* were, thank you very much!' Esther replied.

'The fat one's Martha Willoughby and the thin one's her sister, Flo.'

Rather than display any interest in them, she refused to listen to Matthew any more, picked up two heavy buckets of milk and disappeared into the pantry.

There were others too who would not forget Esther's first visit to the church and two in particular who had no wish to see her there again.

Three days after that first Sunday, a pony and trap bowled along the lane from Rookery Farm, turning sharp right at the junction with the lane running alongside the sand dunes and came to a stop outside Brumbys' Farm. Hearing the rattle of wheels and the horse's hooves, Sam came out from the barn and Esther peeped out of Curly's pigsty, which she was cleaning out.

The two ladies from the church were climbing gingerly down from their trap and coming towards Sam, marching side by side as if confronting the enemy.

'Sam Brumby – Flo and I would like a word with you, if you please,' began Martha Willoughby, taking the lead.

Esther watched the scowl on Sam's face deepen but he said nothing.

'It's about that young girl you have – er – living with you,' put in Miss Flo, but she took care to stand slightly behind her more formidable sister.

'You see, Sam,' continued Mrs Willoughby, 'Flo and I – we don't consider it seemly for a young girl – and one of doubtful character and morals – to be living out here *alone* with you. I mean – did you know what she said to Tom about – about . . .' The woman wafted her hand before her face as if it ill became her to speak of such an indelicate matter. '. . . the boar?'

Flo nodded in dutiful agreement. 'It's all over the town, Sam, just think.'

Esther had heard enough. She came out of the sty and slammed the door behind her. Two pairs of startled eyes turned towards her as she crossed the yard, her green gaze spitting fire, her determined chin thrust forward, the pitchfork she still held in her hands pointing aggressively towards them like a fixed bayonet. Miss Flo gave a terrified shriek and clung to her sister.

Sam put up his hand warningly, as if to fend her off. 'Easy, wench,' he murmured. 'They're naught but a couple of busybodies . . .'

'I'll not be called such names, mester. Not by them nor anyone else. I may be poor, an' I may look like a tramp, but I *ain't* one, an' no one has the right to . . .' Esther jabbed the fork towards them, and Miss Flo began to wail and even the bolder Mrs Willoughby took hold of her sister and stepped backwards. Esther thrust the pitchfork towards them again, so that the two women jerked away. Mrs Willoughby stumbled and fell heavily, dragging her sister down with her.

'I *work* for Mr Brumby on the farm and nothing else. You hear me, missus, *nothing* else.'

She emphasized her statement by prodding the fork ever nearer to the two quivering women on the ground. For a long moment she glared down at them and then, as if satisfied, she lifted the fork away and stood back a pace. The two women, seizing their chance, scrambled up, clinging to each other. Tripping over their long skirts, they scuttled towards the trap. As they went, Esther's anger was turned to laughter. Planted neatly on Martha Willoughby's fat bottom was the perfect brown circle of a cow-pat.

Esther heard Sam's wheezing and she looked sideways at him. He was bending slightly forward, his hands resting on his knees, his head tilted up to watch the two women and laughing until the tears came into his eyes.

'Aye, wench,' he spluttered, 'you'll be the death o' me!'

Seven

'*YOU* coming to the Supper tonight, Esther?' Matthew was grinning at her over the half-door of the cowshed.

Without pausing in her milking, her voice muffled against the beast's stomach, Esther asked, 'Supper? What Supper?'

'Harvest Supper, of course. Ain't Sam told you about it?'

'No.'

'It's at the Grange. Squire holds a Harvest Supper for all the folks around here. Anyone can go – an' they do. It's a grand night. Aw, do come, Esther. Come with me, if you're frit to go on your own.'

She finished milking Clover and stood up, giving the cow a last gentle pat on her rump. 'Good girl, there now, there's a good girl. We'll have to stop milking you soon, shan't we? Ya'll be calving in a few weeks.'

The cow swished her tail but her kicking feet stayed still at Esther's pacifying tone.

Now Esther faced Matthew. 'I ain't frit to go nowhere on me own, Matthew Hilton.'

'Aw, don't take the huff, Esther. I only meant – well – I meant I'd like you to come with me. There's still a lot of people round here you don't know an' . . .'

'Aye, and some as I'd rather not know an' all, judging

68

by them two old biddies in church last week,' she countered.

Matthew grinned. 'I 'eard about 'em coming here. But you sent 'em packing by all accounts.'

Esther smiled at the memory and found Matthew staring at her.

'My, but you're bonny when you smile,' he said softly and his eyes darkened with desire as he stepped towards her.

'Oh, go on with you.' She pushed him away from her, laughing as she added, 'I'll think about the Harvest Supper. Now go away, I've work to do.'

Grinning, Matthew went.

'Mester,' she ventured to Sam at tea time. 'What's this Harvest Supper Matthew's been on about? Do you go?'

Sam sniffed. 'I s'pose I'll have to. I don't reckon much to it, but I don't like to snub the squire. Why d'you ask? You going?'

She shrugged and looked down at her rough work-worn skirt and faded blouse. 'I – I dunno.'

Sam sniffed again. There was a long silence between them. He got up from the table and settled himself in his straight-backed Windsor chair by the range. He reached for his clay pipe on the mantelpiece and began to pack it slowly. Without looking at her, he said, haltingly, 'In that room where you sleep . . .'

Esther looked at him.

'. . . there's a trunk of – old clothes. They – they belonged to – to someone – a long time ago. If – if there's

69

owt you can wear, you can have 'em,' he finished in a rush.

Her green eyes were shining. 'Aw, thanks, Mester Brumby, thanks ever so.'

Sam sniffed, settled his aching bones in his chair and puffed at his pipe.

On the night of the Harvest Supper, Sam Brumby was waiting for her in the kitchen when she climbed down the ladder and stood before him in her finery. She had found a cotton print dress, patterned with blue cornflowers. Its skirt was a little too full to be fashionable and the sleeves too narrow. But, ignoring the fusty smell of material which had been packed away in a trunk for years, she had put it on, pinned up her freshly washed hair with some ivory combs she had found in the bottom of the trunk and arranged her curls to fall over her forehead. She felt like a princess.

Sam was staring at her. His eyes misted over as if he were seeing not her but someone else standing before him. Perhaps he was remembering the person to whom this dress had once belonged. For a fleeting moment, Esther felt awkward. Then Sam brushed his hand across his face, sniffed and said gruffly. 'You look bonny, wench. Come on, we'd best be off.'

The autumn evening was soft and balmy under a clear starlit sky and merry laughter filled the night air as they approached Grange Farm. Lanterns had been festooned all around the edges of the barn which the squire left free for the Harvest Supper. Long trestle tables had been placed down the middle with squares of hay for the revellers to sit on. The tables were piled high with food and when Esther arrived with Sam, people were already helping themselves. There were hams and pickled tongues, pork pies and sausages and for dessert, junkets and cream cheese soufflés. Esther's mouth watered.

Matthew appeared suddenly at her side. 'Come on, Esther, let's get stuck in or it'll all be gone.'

She took a plate and, following his example, piled it high with food. She reached across the table to pick up a cooked sausage when her fingers touched someone else's reaching from the opposite side. She looked up to find herself staring into Beth Hanley's resentful eyes.

'You with Matthew?' Beth asked bluntly.

Esther straightened up. 'Well – sort of. Why?'

There was hurt in Beth's dark brown eyes. 'Dun't you know we're walking out together?'

'No – no, I didn't. I'm sorry – if he'd said then . . .'

Beth snorted. 'Oh, him, he likes to think he's fancy free. He'll flirt with anything in skirts. I knows that.'

'An' doesn't it bother you?'

She didn't answer directly, but stared Esther straight in the face and said, 'He'll come back to me and I'll be waiting for him. You mark my words, Esther Everatt, *he'll always come back to me*!'

For some inexplicable reason the vehement certainty in Beth's tone sent a shiver down Esther's back.

The dark-haired girl turned away and was lost in the throng of people. Esther too turned away from the table and drew breath sharply for she found herself staring into the disapproving faces of Mrs Willoughby and her sister.

'Well, really!' was all Flo could muster.

71

'And what, may I ask, are *you* doing here?' demanded Martha Willoughby.

Esther recovered her senses and smiled brightly. 'Good evening, missus,' she addressed Martha Willoughby. 'And, er . . .' she hesitated and then deliberately her gaze searched the left hand of the thin woman, whom she now knew to be Martha Willoughby's sister. Seeing her ringless finger, she added with emphasis, 'And miss.'

Miss Flo gasped. The edge of sarcasm towards her spinster state was not lost on the middle-aged woman.

'Oh, Martha, come away. I won't be seen talking to this – this creature!'

'Quite right, Flo dear. Really, I don't know what the squire is thinking of.'

They picked up their skirts and with one last glance made as if to turn away in a calculated snub. But in that last glance, Flo had looked Esther up and down properly. She gasped and gripped her sister's arm.

'Oh, Martha,' she squeaked. 'Do – do you *see* what she's wearing? Oh, how could he? How could Sam let her wear one of poor, darling Katharine's gowns?' Flo fished in the sleeve of her blouse for a delicate lace handkerchief and held it to her lips, her eyes wide and staring above the frothy white lace. Martha was made of sterner stuff. She merely eyed the old-fashioned gown with distaste.

'It's absolutely . . .' But exactly what, Esther was not to hear for at that moment Tom Willoughby came up behind them and put an arm about the shoulders of the two sisters. 'Now, now, my dears, making friends. That's the way,' and he gave a great bellowing laugh so that his stomach wobbled and his whiskers shook.

'Oh, really, Thomas. Friends, indeed!' The two women turned away in disgust, but before he followed them, Tom gave Esther a broad grin and an exaggerated wink. 'They'll come around, m'dear, don't you worry.'

Esther stared after the three of them as they walked away. She wasn't bothered one way or the other whether they ever 'came around', but she was intrigued by something Flo had said.

Just who was Katharine?

Thoughtfully, Esther took her plate and sat down in a corner of the barn.

'There you are,' Matthew said and sat down beside her. 'This is good, ain't it, Esther?' he said, his mouth stuffed with food.

'Mmm,' she murmured.

'There's dancing later. Old Joe usually brings his fiddle and plays for us.'

'Dancing,' Esther was startled into replying. 'I can't dance!'

'I'll show you,' Matthew said loftily. 'There's nothing to it.'

He was indeed right. There was nothing to it – at least not the way these happy folk danced, for no one cared that they all just hopped and jigged about in time to the music. There seemed to be no organized dance steps of any kind. But, Esther had to admit, they all certainly enjoyed themselves. Even Beth was dancing and laughing and seemed to have forgotten her rancour for the moment.

'Oh, stop, Matthew, do stop. I'm puffed. I can't dance

another step,' Esther gasped. 'Really, I can't. Oooh, I've got a stitch in me side.'

Matthew laughed. He was by now none too steady on his feet, for he had been partaking liberally of the ale set aside at the far end of the barn. He pulled her away from the other dancers and with his arm about her waist, led her out of the barn and away from the light. Behind them the music and laughter continued but around them now was the black stillness of the night. He pulled her round a corner and towards a straw stack looming in the darkness.

'Oh, just let me sit down. Me feet are fair aching.' Esther giggled and fell into the straw. Matthew stumbled and fell on top of her and in a moment they were rolling and shrieking about in the straw. Then suddenly he was on top of her, his mouth finding hers as he kissed her roughly and his hand was tugging at her skirt. Then she felt his hand hot upon her thigh and felt his fingers working frantically upwards, upwards . . .

She struggled. 'Stop it, Matthew. I won't—'

'Aw, come on, Esther. You'd like it. I know you would. You're ripe as a plum . . .'

'No!' she almost shouted, and then she heard an ominous tearing sound near her shoulder as the fragile material of her dress tore.

Her sudden anger giving her extra strength, Esther shoved him off her and tried to scramble up. The straw caught at her skirt and hampered her escape, so that he caught her by the legs and tackled her to the ground once more. Now she was fighting him in earnest, fighting for her purity.

'Not 'til I'm wed,' she panted. 'I *won't*.'

Suddenly he stopped and rolled away from her. 'Huh, you're a prude, Esther Everatt. You'll die an old maid and never know what it was like.'

Finding herself free, she struggled to her feet and moved a little way away from him. Then she turned and with a parting flourish shouted, 'I'd rather that than bring your bastard into the world, Matthew Hilton!'

She turned and fled back to the safety of the throng of dancers. She found herself a drink and sat in a corner. She was hot and dishevelled, but hoped that everyone was too busy enjoying themselves to notice.

She felt at the back of her shoulder. The tear didn't seem too bad. She had been thrilled to find the dress and had so looked forward to this evening, but now, what with the contempt of Mrs Willoughby and Miss Flo, Beth's angry eyes, and now Matthew's drunken attempt on her virtue – her pleasure was spoilt. She sighed heavily. His behaviour had soured what she had thought had been a friendship. She had liked being with him, quite enjoyed his harmless flirting if she were honest. But no more than that, she vowed to herself, not until I'm married.

Beth Hanley was standing over her. 'Matthew tried his tricks on you, then?'

Esther looked up. 'He tried, but he got nowhere,' she said tartly.

Beth seemed to reflect for a moment as if unable to decide whether or not she believed Esther's claim. 'Funny, he's not one to give up.'

Esther looked up and then slowly rose to her feet

to meet Beth's gaze on a level. 'You don't mean you let him . . . ?'

Beth shrugged. 'Why not? 'Tis natural.'

Esther's lips curled, and she saw anger spark in Beth's eyes.

'Think you're too good for the rest of us, do you, Esther? Matthew not good enough for you, eh?'

Esther shook her head. 'That don't come into it, Beth,' she said quietly, but with candour. 'I – I always vowed I'd be a virgin when I married – that's all.'

For a moment a look of uncertainty crossed Beth's face as if she were struggling with her conscience. Then her dark head came up defiantly. 'Well, it's a mite late for me now to have such high-minded principles. I'll leave you to your lonely bed, Esther Everatt, and wish ya well on it.' With that parting shot Beth tossed her long hair back and flounced away.

Esther, determined to have the last word, shouted after her, 'You're welcome to him.'

Beth disappeared out of the barn into the darkness to find Matthew.

Later that night, for the first time in her life, Esther lay awake with a strange feeling of restlessness. Matthew could be right, she thought sadly, maybe she'd never know what it was like to be really loved by someone kind and thoughtful. Perhaps no one decent would want to marry a girl with a name; 'my sister's bastard' as Aunt Hannah had constantly reminded her.

All she had ever wanted, Esther told herself fiercely in the lonely darkness of the little attic room, was a place to belong. That was why she had left her aunt's house and walked through the night. That was why she had forced herself upon the ailing Sam Brumby. He needed her youth and her strength. But Esther was honest enough to acknowledge that her need of Sam and his farm was even greater than the old man's need of her.

She had no place in her scheme of things for rolling in the hay with the likes of Matthew Hilton!

With harvest time over, now came the preparation of the ground for next year's crops. The work would continue as the weather allowed throughout the winter months, though Sam told Esther he liked to aim to get the ploughing done by December.

'Ah dun't always manage it,' he told her ruefully, 'and there's the threshing to pull in an' all.'

'We'll manage it, mester,' Esther told him confidently. 'Me an' Matthew between us.'

Sam grunted doubtfully. 'Reckon you can manage them great horses of Tom Willoughby's, d'ya, wench?'

Esther grinned at him, her green eyes sparkling. 'You just watch me, mester.'

So on the first day that Tom brought his pair of heavy horses to Brumbys' Farm, both he and Sam followed Esther as she led the animals out to the field; stood watching her as deftly she harnessed them to the plough. She marked out a rig and then cut her first furrow, true and straight. Her clear voice rang out across the field, 'Gee-back, gee-back,' as she guided the horses on a right turn at the end of the rig and began her way back down the field towards the two men. As she approached, Esther's concentration never faltered, her hands stayed firmly on the plough, yet she was aware of their critical scrutiny.

Tom's rumbling voice carried to her ears. 'By heck, lass, that furrow's as straight as I could do mesen. What d'you say, Sam?'

Faintly, she heard Sam's now-familiar sniff. 'Aye, it'll do,' was all he said.

From Sam Brumby that was praise enough.

So day after day Esther took turns with Matthew in following the horses borrowed from Tom Willoughby, guiding the plough as it carved furrow after neat furrow until her legs ached and her ankles were sore from all the miles she had walked on the uneven ground. Her hands were chafed raw from holding the plough handles but doggedly she plodded on through the rain and mud of autumn. The days seemed to grow rapidly shorter and the weather turned colder. Seagulls shrieked above her diving down on to the freshly turned furrow in search of food. Mile after mile she trudged and then, cold and wet, she would return to the farmhouse at night, but only when the horses had been brushed and fed with corn and chaff did she allow herself any respite. In front of the glowing fire in the range she would fall asleep in the wooden chair in the corner by the hearth, often too exhausted even to eat.

Life at Brumbys' Farm fell into some sort of routine for the three of them – Sam, Esther and Matthew. Matthew did not work full time for Sam, Esther found. He helped out on all the local farms and so several days could go by without Matthew being there. Then suddenly he would appear again, grinning cheekily, winking at her and, given less than half a chance, slapping her buttocks, although he was quick to dodge out of the way of her stinging right hand returning the slap.

With the ploughing, Matthew was needed at Brumbys' more than usual. On Mondays Esther washed and ironed, on Tuesdays and Wednesdays she helped with the ploughing when Matthew was needed elsewhere, then on Thursdays she baked and cooked enough food to last the week. Fridays and Saturdays she worked outside again, sometimes more ploughing, sometimes with the stock. But on Sundays, she found that Sam was quite happy to do a minimum of work.

'It's the Lord's Day,' he said gruffly one Sunday morning when he found her black-leading the range. Even the animals were given as little attention as possible.

'Give 'em a sharpener on the Lord's Day,' Sam told her. 'One feed a day instead of two on the Sabbath – they'll be all the more ready to come to the trough tomorrow.'

So on a Sunday, Esther found she had time for herself.

Walking down the lane from Brumbys' Farm towards the Point one Sunday afternoon, when the winter sun lay low in the southern sky, streaking the fields with a golden glow, Esther hummed to herself and every so often she gave a little skip of sheer happiness. She came to the stretch of grass between the cottages and the river bank. Four of Ma Harris's children were chasing each other in a noisy game of tag. Esther smiled to herself. Sabbath or not, Ma Harris would never manage to keep that brood quiet.

79

'Is yar mam at home?' she asked a boy with a runny nose.

'Nah, she's away yonder,' he pointed inland with a grubby finger, 'there's a babby bein' born at Souters' Farm.'

'A babby?'

'Aye, the missus is having her fifth babby. Me mam allus goes to 'elp when a babby's getting borned.' He wiped his nose with the back of his hand and sniffed noisily.

Esther nodded, said goodbye, and walked on towards the river bank.

Now she had time to take a look around her, at the sea and the sand and the river that joined the sea. She was fascinated to see the little fishing boats moored along the river bank, and she followed its curve until the bank gave way to the sea. Esther paused in her walk to look at the huge boat where Robert Eland lived. It was lodged half on the bank, and shored up by sleepers and wooden poles dug deep into the bed of the river. At high water, it would seem to be almost afloat and yet the vessel was firmly anchored and would not move from its place. There was a narrow wooden jetty built up from the firm ground running on to the boat. Esther stood looking up at it in wonderment. She had never seen anything like it. It was a strange place for a man to make his home, she thought. She accepted, though, that there were those who felt an affinity with the sea as she did for the land she helped to work.

'What are you doing here?'

The voice came from behind her, interrupting her

reverie. She turned to find Robert Eland standing beside her. 'Oh, I'm sorry, I didn't mean . . .'

'You're Sam Brumby's wench,' he stated bluntly.

Esther bristled. 'If you mean I work on Mester Brumby's farm, the answer's yes. If you mean owt more . . .' Her green eyes glinted. 'Then you're quite wrong.'

The expression in his eyes lightened a little, but he did not smile. His mouth was completely covered by his wiry beard. He was a dour man, who saw little humour in life in general and even less in his own. 'Aye, I heard of your little – er – rumpus – with Missus Willoughby and 'er sister.' He was glowering again. 'Aye, an' that's not all I've heard about you. You took the job my Beth went after.'

'*Your* Beth, but – but I thought she was Matthew's girl.'

The scowl deepened. 'Huh, *him*!' Robert Eland muttered. He seemed about to say more, but then turned away angrily. As he brushed past her and headed for the gangway to his home, Esther thought she heard him mumble, 'Ah, what's the use?'

Esther walked on and came to a place where the river widened and joined the waters of the sea. On her left – to the east – was marshland, the beach and the North Sea to the horizon and beyond. To the west lay mile upon mile of flat farmland as far as she could see.

Esther shaded her eyes and looked out towards the sea. In the far distance she could see the Spit jutting out into the water, further out even than where she was standing.

She retraced her steps past the cottages and the boat and took the path leading across the old marsh until she came to the dunes. Pushing her way through thick clumps of spiky marram grass, she came to the Spit and walked along the narrow ridge of scrubland to the end until she was surrounded on three sides by the sea. At high tide, the point of land could afford boats a haven from the treacherous currents and sudden squalls of the North Sea. At low tide the River Lynn still wound its way through the mudbanks.

All around her was a magnificent bleakness. She turned slowly in a full circle, but every view was the same – flat as far as the eye could see. With the land so low and level, the glorious sky seemed to surround her entirely. There was so much space, it gave her such a sense of freedom.

She threw back her head and breathed in the exhilarating air. She closed her eyes as the sea breeze wrapped itself around her, lifted her skirt and ruffled her curls, like a man flirting with her. The sound of the waves gently lapping at her feet was soothing.

Whatever happened in her life, she thought, the waves would continue to break upon the shore and the tide would ebb and flow. It gave her a feeling of constancy, a sense of security. Behind her was the land that she loved already. Before her was the sea that she would come to know, too. She belonged in this place, she would make this place her own. She bent and picked up a fistful of the sand. She revelled in the feel of it in her hand. Then she flung it high into the sky and laughed aloud as the particles showered around her.

Esther – unwanted and unloved all her young life – had found a place to stay, a place to love. She had found her home.

Eight

*T*O Esther's disappointment, Christmas Day in Sam Brumby's house was little different from any other day. She had cooked and baked for most of Christmas Eve, so that there was a chicken and vegetables to be cooked on the day itself, and a pudding to be warmed. Even her aunt had made more of Christmas than this, Esther thought disconsolately, as she remembered the shouting and laughter of her young cousins, her uncle carving at a huge goose and the dinner table loaded with all manner of food that they never tasted at any other time of the year. It was the first – and probably the only – time she would think kindly of her aunt.

That night Esther's sleep was disturbed by dreams of a family of children, her own children, with a husband sitting at the opposite end of the table. At first the man in her dream was just a shadowy, indistinct figure, but then the features took shape and it was Matthew who sat at the head of her table. She awoke early, sweating and breathing heavily, but she could not understand why.

That winter on Sam Brumby's farm was a harsh one. Snow came although it never seemed to stay long, yet the north-east winds from the sea were bitingly cold and whipped savagely across the flat land. Matthew still came for a day now and then to find Esther working about the farm huddled in a thick cloak, her hands chapped and her lips blue with cold.

'You want some warming, Esther,' Matthew told her saucily. ''Tis cosy in the hayloft.'

She tossed her head and turned the barrel churn angrily until she heard the flip-flop of the cream turning into butter. 'You never give up, do you?'

He moved closer. 'No, Esther, I'll never give up.' And he reached across and planted a rough kiss on her cheek.

'Oh, go on with you.' But the protest was half-hearted now and there was a faint tinge of pink to her cheek that had nothing to do with the cold.

There was no let-up in the wintry weather and at the beginning of January there came such severe frosts that everything seemed to be frozen solid. The trees were white with ice and the ground as hard as stone. There could be no more work on the land until the cold spell eased, so Sam sent Esther to ask if they could borrow the threshing machinery.

'I ain't no threshing gear, Esther lass,' Tom Willoughby told her. 'Sam must have meant you to go to the Grange.'

'Oh, mebbe he did, Mester Willoughby. He didn't say, but because we borrowed the 'osses off you, I just thought . . .'

Tom roared with laughter. 'I ain't that well off. But dun't you worry no more, lass. I'll see the squire's bailiff for you and see what we can do.'

'Thanks, mester.'

*

One Sunday morning Esther was surprised to see Matthew appear at the cowshed door as she was finishing the milking.

'Hello, Esther. My, but you look bonny this morning. Your cheeks is all rosy.'

''Tis the cold,' she said tartly to his compliment.

'Esther, can you get time off this after'? The pools in North Marsh Field are frozen solid now. I thought we could go skating.'

Esther almost dropped the pail of milk she was carrying. 'Me? But I can't skate.'

'Aw, it's easy. Come on, Esther. 'Tis time you had a little fun. I'll find you some skates.'

'Well,' she said doubtfully, 'all right. I'll be ready after dinner.'

'See you later, then.' Matthew went off whistling loudly.

As she went to and fro between the kitchen and the scullery clearing away the pots after dinner, Sam settled himself in the chair by the range for his Sunday afternoon nap.

'Matthew says North Marsh Field is frozen solid. He's tekin' me skating,' Esther told him.

Sam's only reply was a sniff as he pulled his pipe from his pocket, but a short time later, when she had finished the washing-up and was reaching for her shawl from the peg behind the door, Sam said, 'Wench, watch ya'sen with that lad.'

Slowly she put her shawl about her shoulders and stared at Sam. It didn't register for a moment that Sam was warning her about Matthew. It was the first time the old man had shown the least concern for her. Strangely, the knowledge warmed her.

'Aye, I'll mind him, Mester Brumby,' she said gently.

Satisfied, Sam nodded and, stretching his feet out towards the glowing coals in the range, went back to packing his pipe.

When they reached the field it seemed to Esther as if half the townsfolk of Lynthorpe were there. Happy shrieks of laughter filled the sharp air.

Esther clutched Matthew's arm, convulsed with laughter. 'Oh, look – do look at her over there, she went a right cropper – and her petticoats flying!'

Matthew laughed, 'Look at him, then, he can't control his feet, they're sliding in all directions!' They clung together hooting with laughter.

'Oh, Matthew,' Esther said at last, tears running down her cheeks, 'I don't think I want to try this after all. I'll only mek a fool of mesen.'

'It's much more fun watching everybody else do that . . .' His voice trailed away, and she felt his arm stiffen under her touch. She glanced up at his face to see his lips pressed together into a hard line of anger. A frown creased his forehead and she followed the line of his gaze across the frozen surface to a couple skating slowly and sedately around the far side.

It was Beth and Robert Eland. He held Beth's hand with his left, whilst his right arm was around her plump waist to steady her.

As the couple passed close by them, Matthew slipped his arm around Esther's waist. 'Come on, Esther. Let's give it a try.' Without waiting for her to agree he propelled her forward on to the ice.

They staggered around the perimeter of the ice clinging together, laughing helplessly, aware that they were every bit as funny as those they had been laughing at earlier. They were behind Beth and her partner now. Matthew gave Esther a little push that sent her sprawling on to the ice and sliding into the couple. Beth shrieked and clung to Robert Eland but he was even more unsure on his feet than she and he fell on to his back, clutching at Beth so that she fell on top of him. Matthew, the only one left standing, could hardly hide his mirth at the flailing legs of the other three, the tangled bodies and petticoats fluttering.

Matthew was beside them, holding out his hand to Beth to help her to her feet, leaving Esther to scramble to hers as best she could unaided. As for Robert Eland, Matthew paid no attention to him whatsoever.

'Whatever did you make me go an' do a thing like that for, Matthew Hilton? I've never felt such a fool in all me life!' Esther hissed angrily, but Matthew was paying no attention to her either now.

'Come on, Beth,' he was saying, 'let's show 'em how it should be done.' Before Robert or Esther had a chance to make any protest, he put his arm firmly around Beth and skated off with her.

'Well,' Esther gasped indignantly, 'would you look at that?' she demanded of no one in particular.

'Aye, I see it,' said Robert Eland, having now regained his feet. 'I see it all too well.'

Esther saw the look of anger and jealousy in the man's

eyes as together they watched the other two skating quite expertly. Round and round they went, faster and faster, until the other skaters, most of them still unsteady on the ice, began to move out of their way and to smile and nod towards Matthew and Beth in admiration.

'I'm no judge of skating, mester,' Esther said grimly. 'But I'd say them two's done this afore – and together!'

She glanced up at the man at her side and saw such an expression of hatred as he glowered at Matthew that she was quite startled. That look was far more than just pique because Matthew had stolen his skating partner. Then, just as she heard Robert mutter, 'What's the point of stayin' here any longer?' she saw Matthew propel Beth to the side where they were standing and come to a halt in front of them with a flourish and a shower of ice.

They were breathless and laughing. 'There, didn't I say we'd show you how it was done?'

'Showing off, more like,' Esther said cuttingly.

With exaggerated gallantry, Matthew took hold of Beth's hand and offered her back to Robert. 'Here's your partner back safe and sound. Now, Esther, take that mardy look off ya face and let's see if I can give you a twirl. It's one way of getting the ladies to cling on to you, ain't it, Robert?'

Robert had no chance to respond to his saucy remark, before Matthew pushed Esther back on to the ice and away from the other two.

But for Esther the afternoon's fun was spoilt. She seemed to feel Beth's gaze following her wherever she and Matthew went and Beth Hanley's words seemed to ring yet again in her ears.

'He'll always come back to me, Esther Everatt.'

Towards the end of January the threshing tackle arrived at Brumbys' Farm. Soon the yard was hazy with dust and chaff and noisy with another 'newfangled' machine that Sam hated so much.

'I still like flailing mesen,' he muttered to Esther, but she knew he had accepted the squire's help for the work was beginning to get too much for the old man.

As winter dragged on and spring seemed reluctant to arrive, Esther began to notice a change in Sam Brumby. He rose later each morning, coming down to sit before the range whilst she bustled about the kitchen, singing softly to herself.

'Are you all right, mester?' she asked him finally.

His reply was an ill-tempered sniff. ''Tis the cold, wench. Nothing more. I'll be right as ninepence come the spring.' So Esther continued to cope with the farm with only Matthew for help.

As she finished the milking one morning she heard a clatter in the yard and looked out to see a gig drawn by a fine horse which pawed at the ground and tossed its head.

'Whoa, there, whoa.' The man at the reins was Squire Marshall, whom Esther had seen in church.

Rubbing her hands down the side of her skirt, Esther stepped out into the yard. ''Morning, Squire.'

'Good morning, my dear.' Mr Marshall climbed down from the gig and looked about him. 'Sam Brumby – is he – er – about?'

'He's in the house, sir. Would you like me to . . . ?'

Mr Marshall put out his hand, palm outward. 'No, no, my dear girl. Don't trouble. It was – er . . .' He cleared his throat as if in embarrassment. 'I heard Sam Brumby was – er – not well.' Now he looked keenly at Esther. 'Is that right?'

Esther licked her lips. 'Well, he dun't seem quite his usual self, sir. But he says 'tis only the cold; that he'll be all right come the warmer weather.'

'I'll go in and see him.' Without waiting for an invitation, Mr Marshall turned and walked towards the house. Sam would be sitting huddled in front of the range, she knew, with a blanket wrapped around his shoulders. He looked thin and old now, but he refused to see a doctor.

Esther stayed about the yard pretending to be busy, but in truth waiting for Mr Marshall to reappear. She didn't have long to wait. Ten minutes later, the squire came out of the house closing the door quietly behind him. He seemed lost in thought and didn't notice Esther until he was almost up to her. 'Ah, there you are. Er – well now – I don't like the look of Sam at all, not at all. I've tried to persuade him to let the doctor have a look at him but . . .'

He caught sight of Esther's half-smile. 'Ah, I see you've tried already.' He was silent for a moment, then, stroking his chin thoughtfully, he said, 'Well now, what's going to happen to the farm while Sam's ill, mm?'

'I'll manage,' she said curtly, adopting her usual stance when her ability was questioned – feet apart, hands on hips.

'Well, my dear. I hope you can. I'm not a hard man.

I'm not about to turn a tenant out just because he's ill, especially when his family have held this tenancy for generations . . .'

'Tenant? Mr Brumby is a *tenant* of this farm? He – he dun't own it?'

'Oh no, my dear. Didn't you know? I own all the land around here. I have three tenant farmers in all – Willoughby at Rookery Farm, Souter and Sam Brumby. Sam's family have farmed here the longest. So, as I say, I'm not going to turn him out because he hits a bad patch, particularly if you can keep things going till he gets better.'

Esther's head was whirling. Then she remembered Matthew's words when he'd been explaining about the folk who lived at the Point. 'They all work the land round here – they all work for Mester Marshall,' Matthew had said, but she hadn't understood fully what he had meant then. 'He's the squire – he owns all the land hereabouts.'

Now she understood. Sam Brumby was only a tenant farmer. He didn't own the farm, so what would happen if anything happened to Sam, if he should be ill for a long time, or even die? After all, he was an old man, though Esther had no idea just how old he was. What would happen to her, Esther, then?

She squared her shoulders and looked Mr Marshall in the eyes. She had to make amends for her curtness of a few minutes ago. She knew it was important that she should make a good impression upon Mr Marshall, the real owner of the farm.

'Well, sir, I can manage the farm all right.'

His clear gaze was upon her. 'Can you? Can you really?'

'Oh, yes, sir. Matthew – Matthew Hilton – you know he helps out here quite a lot?'

'Yes, yes, I did know.'

'We've managed everything between us. Nothing's been let slip.'

She went on to tell him about what she intended to plant and in which fields, and which she intended to leave fallow. 'I've tried to talk it over with Mester Brumby, but he dun't seem to have the strength to be interested even.'

The squire nodded. 'Well, you seem to know what you're about – your plans seem eminently sensible.' Mr Marshall glanced about him. 'And, I must say, the place looks every bit as good as when Sam *is* around, I'll grant you that.'

Esther smiled at him. 'I'll cope, sir. I'll keep things right.'

'Well, my dear, I admire your spirit. I can see for myself you're a worker.' He nodded at her as if in approval. 'But don't be afraid to come to see me if you have any problems. I'll be only too glad to help.'

'Thank you, Squire. I'll remember that,' she answered him politely, but inwardly she resolved to prove that she could manage things alone – and manage them well.

Even with the spring, Sam made no improvement, in fact, he seemed weaker.

'You ought to call the doctor in, lass,' Will Benson told Esther. 'Ne'er mind what 'ee says, you get the doc in. It'd look bad on you if owt happens to Sam, an' you hadn't done anything.'

'Would you call on your way back through the town at Doctor Blair's house, Mr Benson, and ask him to call as soon as he can?'

'Aye, righto, lass. I don't mind doing that. I don't like to see old Sam so bad. He's shrivelled away to nothing. All skin and bone he is, now.' Will shook his head. 'No, I don't like the look of him at all.'

As the carrier's cart trundled out of the yard, Esther went to find Matthew. 'Will Benson's going to call and ask the doctor to come out to see Sam.'

'Not afore time neither,' Matthew said brusquely. 'He's poorly, you know. But he's such a stubborn old goat!'

They looked at each other, both thinking the same thing. Just what was going to become of the farm — and of them — if anything dreadful were to happen to Sam Brumby?

Nine

*T*HE doctor came to find Esther feeding the pigs. Above the noise of the scuffling and grunting, Esther heard a loud rapping on the sty door and looked up to see a stranger in a tweed suit.

'I'm sorry, sir. They make such a row at feeding time,' Esther said, hurrying outside and closing the door after her.

Fastidiously, the doctor stepped backwards. 'Quite so, quite so.' There was a pause whilst Esther waited. Then he went on, 'You live here with Mr Brumby, I understand?'

'That's right, sir. I've been here nearly a year now.' Esther felt the doctor looking her up and down.

'Well, my dear.' The doctor's voice had a kindly, concerned note now. 'I'm sorry to have to tell you that Mr Brumby is a sick man. I fear he has not many weeks to live. I'm very sorry, but there's nothing I can do to help him.'

Esther stared at the doctor. 'I – I should have called you sooner. I – should . . .'

Doctor Blair laid his hand upon Esther's shoulder. 'It wouldn't have made any difference, my dear. Don't reproach yourself. He's a tired old man who's worked this land all his life. He's worn out – that's the truth of it.

There's nothing I could have done for him, not even if I had come earlier.'

'Is he in any pain?' Esther wanted to know.

The doctor shook his head. 'Not that I can find out. But his breathing's bad – very bad – and will get worse, my dear, before the end.' He met Esther's steady gaze. 'But you let me know, and I'll do what I can to help him.'

Esther nodded and said hoarsely, 'Thank you, sir.'

Doctor Blair gave her shoulder a friendly squeeze. 'Your being here makes his passing a lot easier, my dear. A lot easier than if he were still living on his own. Just remember that.'

'Why?' she asked candidly. 'I seem to be able to do so little.'

'You being here means he can die in his own home, on the land he has always loved. Otherwise . . .' He paused and took a deep breath. 'I would have had to take him away.'

Esther's eyes widened and her lips parted in a gasp. Grim tales of being sent to the workhouse had been hurled at her by her aunt so often as a threat that she understood at once what the doctor meant. She wasn't sure that it was still a reality that unwanted children, the destitute, the old and the sick actually ended up in the workhouse, but the fear itself was enough.

'I'll look after him, mester – I mean, doctor,' she said in a voice that was none too steady.

'Yes, my dear, I believe you will,' he said, with a final pat of encouragement and understanding.

As the doctor turned to leave, she was surprised to feel

a lump in her throat and a prickle of unaccustomed tears. She realized suddenly just how fond she had become of the grumpy old man.

With the news that Sam Brumby was so very ill, and mindful of her promise to care for him until the end, Esther decided to move out of the attic boxroom above the kitchen for it had no direct access to the upper floor of the house. She needed to be nearer Sam.

Stepping into the room on the opposite side of the small landing to Sam's room, Esther found what appeared to have once been a nursery. Pushed into the corner was an assortment of children's toys – a battered rocking horse, a doll's house, a high chair, a doll with a china face and cloth body and in another corner a full-sized baby's cot.

Esther wondered if all these things had belonged to the sweet-faced girl in the faded picture in Sam's bed-room. Perhaps he could not bear to throw anything away; maybe a lot of the old man's memories of happier days were stored away in this room with these toys. Esther could almost see the little girl with her long hair flowing as she rocked to and fro on the wooden horse; could almost hear her childish laughter . . .

Esther shook herself; her worry over Sam was making her fanciful and morbid. She must concentrate on practical matters, she told herself firmly.

Another door led into a long narrow room with a sloping ceiling, beneath which there was just enough room for the iron bedstead to stand. At one end of the room there was a small chest of drawers and a basin and jug stood on a wash-stand. Although the whole place needed scrubbing out and the bedlinen washing, the room was luxurious compared with the attic boxroom. This room had obviously been the nurserymaid's, but Esther chose it in preference to the larger nursery for it seemed warmer. If she left the two intervening doors open, she would still be able to hear if Sam needed help in the night.

Three nights later, when the room was clean, the bedlinen freshly laundered and the dust banged from the mattress with a carpet beater, Esther moved in. For the first time in her life, she was sleeping in a real bedroom and on a proper bed.

Yet, as she lay awake listening to the rasping, laboured sound of Sam's breathing, she wished she was back in the quiet solitude of the cramped boxroom.

Sam Brumby lived to know that another harvest had been gathered but he had not been well enough to take any active part in the work. Just once, when she was returning from the fields, she saw that he had dragged himself to the kitchen window to watch the final wagon load brought home, but this year it was Esther who had to put the last sheaf on top of the stack. As she did so she turned to see Sam watching her from the window and saw him give her a little nod before he turned and went back to his place by the range.

The following morning when Esther came in from the milking, she found Sam seated in his chair. He was leaning forward, his breathing a rasping, tearing sound.

'Why didn't you wait till I could help you down the stairs?' she said hurrying towards him.

He was seized by a spasm of coughing and waved his hand feebly at her. Helplessly she had to stand and watch as the coughing racked his thin frame. He sat hunched in the chair, growing weaker with every passing day.

'Mester . . .' she began again, but he lifted his hand as if to silence her.

'Lass, get Mester Thompson . . .' He could hardly get the words out, and then only in a wheezing whisper.

Esther bent closer. 'Who's Mr Thompson?'

'I – I want to see him.' He lay back in the chair and closed his eyes. The effort of dressing, coming downstairs and speaking even those few words had exhausted him.

Esther bit her lip. She must find this man, but she didn't know who he was. At that moment she heard the familiar whistle heralding the arrival of Will Benson's carrier's cart in the yard and she flew out of the house and towards him, her skirt held high, her curls flying. All formality forgotten in her agitation, she called the carrier the name by which she always thought of him in her own mind.

'Will, Will – oh, thank goodness you've come . . .'

'Steady, lass, steady. What's wrong? Is it Sam?'

She nodded. 'He's much worse, Will. And he's asking for a Mester Thompson. I don't know who he is, do you?'

Will Benson nodded. His face was grim. 'He's the lawyer in town.'

They stared at each other.

'Why should he – want a lawyer?' Esther asked innocently.

99

'Dun't you know, lass?'

Esther could only shake her head for suddenly there was a funny lump in her throat and she could not trust herself to speak.

'I reckon he wants to make a will, lass.'

'A will? But folks like him dun't make wills . . .'

The carter nodded his head. 'They do if they think they haven't long to go, lass.'

Esther groaned. 'Oh no,' she whispered. 'You reckon he – he knows?'

Will nodded. 'Aye, lass, he knows. He knows all right.'

They stood for a moment in silence. Then Will patted her shoulder in a kindly gesture. 'Go and get yar shawl, or whatever, an' I'll take you back into town and drop you off outside his office.'

'Will, couldn't you . . . ?'

Will was shaking his head. 'Nay, lass, Sam's asked you to go, an' you should do as he's bid. I'll go and have a word with him whilst you get ready.'

She would have enjoyed the ride on Will's cart into town if she had not been so worried about Sam and nervous of presenting herself at a lawyer's office.

'What'll I say, Will?'

Will almost smiled despite the cloud that hung over both of them. He had never seen Esther so irresolute. It was totally unlike her.

'Just go into the office and ask to see Mester Thompson. If he's not available then leave a clear message with – well – with whoever is there. Just tell 'em that Sam

Brumby is a very sick man and that he's asked you to fetch a lawyer out to see him. And could he come as quick as possible.'

'Will he take notice of someone like me?' she asked diffidently.

Now Will did smile. 'Esther lass, just go in there and be yourself. They'll tek notice all right!'

A small smile touched Esther's mouth and her confidence returned. Sam was relying on her.

The young clerk looked her up and down as she entered the office. He moved forward from the tall desk where he was working. 'Can I help you, miss?'

Esther repeated what Will had advised her to say. Without argument the young man consulted a large book. 'I'm afraid Mr Thompson won't be able to come out until tomorrow.' He looked up anxiously. 'Do you think that will be – all right?'

Esther stared at him in surprise. The young man had evidently understood the situation only too well. She relaxed a little. 'Yes, yes, I should think so.'

'Very well, miss.' The young man picked up a pen. 'Mr Thompson will come out to the farm at eleven tomorrow morning.'

'Thank you, thank you very much.'

'Good day, miss.'

Esther hurried along the lane, every so often taking little running steps. She seemed to have been away from the farm and from Sam for such a long time. Even though she worked all day about the farm, she checked on Sam every hour or so. This was the longest time she had left him alone, and because he seemed even worse today, she was anxious.

She turned in at the farm gate at last and hurried across the yard. Beth was standing at the back door raising her hand to knock. At the sound of Esther's footsteps on the cinders, she turned and then let her hand fall.

'Oh, there you are. I've bin knocking for ages.'

'Mester Brumby's very ill,' Esther told her shortly and brushed past her to go into the house, but Beth caught hold of her arm. 'Where's Matthew? I've got to see Matthew.'

'How should I know?' Esther muttered. 'I ain't seen him for days. Just when I could use a bit of help, Mester Matthew decides to do one of his disappearing acts!'

'I thought – he was here – with you.' The statement was an accusation.

'Well, he ain't.' Esther twisted her arm impatiently to release Beth's grasp and added, with a touch of the malice that Beth had used towards her on occasion, 'Mebbe he's chasing a bit o' skirt on one of the other farms.'

The girl turned white and swayed slightly. She put out her hand to steady herself against the wall. With her other hand she clutched at her shawl, pulling it closely around her.

Esther gave her a click of exasperation. Beth's possessive behaviour over Matthew irritated her, and besides she had enough on her mind over poor Sam. She went inside and slammed the door behind her – right in Beth's face.

Ten

MR Thompson, the lawyer, arrived promptly at eleven the next morning. He was a thin-faced, balding gentleman in a pin-striped suit. The broad, stiff white collar seemed too big for his thin neck. His eyes were large behind the thick lenses of his steel-rimmed spectacles, which seemed to be forever slipping down his long, thin nose.

He was closeted with Sam in the front parlour for an hour and a half, at the end of which time he came out into the yard to find Esther talking to Will Benson, who had driven in.

'Come here,' he beckoned her with a long bony finger. 'Would you be kind enough to ask Mr Benson to step into the house for a moment.'

Will followed the lawyer into the house, whilst Esther waited outside in the yard, stroking Will's horses and watching the back door. Will was not required for many minutes for he appeared again almost immediately and climbed up on to his cart.

'Good day, lass. I'll see you later in the week.' He turned his cart around and rattled out of the yard.

'Will . . . ?' Esther called, but he did not seem to hear her shout above the noise of the cart's wheels.

A few moments later, the lawyer too came out of the house, unhitched his pony and climbed into his trap. Touching his hat in a very gallant way to the young girl still standing uncertainly in the middle of the yard, he too turned his conveyance around and left the farm.

Esther watched the cart and the trap disappearing down the lane. Then she turned and went slowly back into the house.

That night it took Esther half an hour to help Sam up the steep stairs to his bedroom and the next day he did not even try to get up out of his bed.

A worried frown creasing her forehead, Esther went out into the pale morning to cope with the milking. She felt more weary than she could ever remember feeling in her young life. Hard work, whatever the weather, had never exhausted her as caring for Sam was doing. Each night she slept restlessly, waking every hour or so to listen to his rasping, painful breathing. Several times a night she would drag herself from her warm bed and, bare-footed, pad across the wooden floors to his room. There was little she could do to ease his suffering, except raise him up on his pillows and give him a drink. Some nights when he seemed even worse, she would go down to the kitchen and heat up some broth on the glowing embers of the range. He scarcely managed more than a spoonful or two and it seemed a waste of time, yet she had to try.

He was so cold that each night she heated three bricks in the range oven, wrapped them in thick, woollen rags and placed one either side of him in the bed and one at his feet.

Now, this morning, he was weaker than ever.

She leant her head against Clover's warm stomach and

closed her eyes. The cow, somehow sensing Esther's distress, stood patiently waiting for her udders to be emptied.

'You sleeping on the job?'

She jumped at the sound of Matthew's teasing voice and, lifting her head, saw his shadowy form in the half-light of the cowshed. Bringing her head up sharply, she snapped back an answer. She was in no mood for his horseplay this morning. 'An' if I am, it's no thanks to you. Up half the night with poor old Sam and all the work to do on the farm. Where've you been? Just when I could use a bit of help, you disappear for days on end!'

Matthew moved forward and now, Esther had to admit, there was genuine concern in his tone. 'Is he worse?'

The anger went out of her as swiftly as it had come. Her voice breaking slightly, she told him, 'He's much worse. He – he had the lawyer here yesterday . . .'

'Oh, Lord!'

'. . . and today he dun't seem to have the energy to try and get out of his bed. Would you go for the doctor, Matthew?'

'Of course, I'll go right now.' He made as if to leave and then, turning back briefly, he added, 'And from tonight, I'll stay here with you and give you a hand with him.'

Esther opened her mouth to protest, but Matthew had gone.

The doctor was sorry but there was nothing he could do. 'I'll leave you this,' he added, handing her a bottle of liquid. 'It may just help him to rest a little at night. Are you sure you can manage, my dear? You're looking exhausted. I could remove him to the cottage hospital, but I very much doubt he would survive the journey into the town . . .'

Esther shook her head vehemently. 'No – no. I dun't want that. I'll manage . . .'

Matthew stepped forward to stand beside her. 'We'll manage, doctor. I'll be staying here now to help Esther.'

Esther saw the doctor glance from one to the other, her own doubts mirrored in his face. 'Well now, I don't quite know if that would – well – be quite right. Isn't there someone – some woman – who could come and help out?'

'If you're thinking of the gossips, doctor, dun't worry. Esther's not one to let their wagging tongues bother her,' Matthew said. For a moment, despite the seriousness of their situation, his cheeky grin was back. 'An' as for keepin' me in me place, well, she's a dab hand at that, an' all!'

The doctor glanced back at Esther and she, seeing that he was still not convinced of the rightness of leaving two young people alone in the farmhouse together, gave him a brief nod. 'We'll be all right, thank you, Doctor Blair. 'Tis Sam we've to worry about.'

Doctor Blair sighed heavily. 'I'm sad to say you're right there, my dear.' He turned away and went out to his gig. 'I'll call again in a day or two, but don't hesitate to send for me if you need me.'

As the gig clattered out of the farmyard, Matthew

said, 'Who's paying for all these doctor's visits, Esther? The likes of us dun't have doctors – not unless we're dying.'

Esther faced Matthew and said quietly, 'Sam is dying, Matthew.'

He stared at her for a moment and then dropped his gaze to look at the ground and shuffle his feet. For once, Esther felt a moment's sympathy for the young man's awkwardness, so she added briskly, 'Besides, I'll see the doctor's paid when the harvest money comes in. Now, let's get back to Sam.'

That night Matthew filled four sacks with straw to form a makeshift bed for himself on the floor in the old nursery between Sam's room and the little room where Esther now slept. 'It's no good me sleeping out in the hayloft, or in that little boxroom you had. I'm no use to you out there.'

'What do you mean?' she asked sharply.

'I'll never hear if you need help, or if Sam gets worse.'

'Oh – oh, er, yes.' Esther turned away but not before she had caught Matthew's grin, and realized that he knew exactly what had been in her mind.

Esther lay in her own bed, every nerve tensed. Any moment she expected to hear the latch raised and Matthew creeping into her room.

He's not stayed here to look after Sam, she fretted to herself, he just wants the chance to climb into my bed and he reckons this is a good excuse to worm his way into the house. She lay there in the darkness, listening. Now that her bedroom door was shut against Matthew, she could no longer hear Sam's laboured breathing. Yet this was worse, she told herself. Now she dare not go to sleep!

But for once Esther was wrong. After some time, she heard Matthew's gentle snoring, and only then did she allow herself to close her eyes and rest.

So they fell into some sort of routine. Matthew rarely helped directly with Sam but he took on most of the farm work, leaving Esther to devote nearly all her time to the old man. Once her initial suspicions as to Matthew's motives had been allayed, she found she was pleased to have him there.

She did not feel quite so alone in the face of death.

When the Sunday of Harvest Festival came, Esther walked the two miles alone to give thanks at the little church as Sam had done all his life. She sat alone in Sam's pew, but as she left the church she found herself being questioned on all sides as to how Sam fared.

'If there's owt you want, lass,' Tom Willoughby boomed, deliberately ignoring the pursed lips of his wife and her sister, 'you just let me know.'

'I'll call and see him,' the vicar promised, and though she nodded agreement, Esther was a little doubtful as to how Sam would view such a visit.

At the church gate she found Beth waiting for her. Her annoyance was tempered by the fact that the girl looked ill. Her face was pinched and although the autumn evening was not cold, she was huddled into her thick winter shawl making her girlish body shapeless. Despite the thick clothing, she still appeared to be shivering.

'He's with you, ain't he?' Beth accused Esther.

There was no point in pretending that she did not understand, so Esther merely replied shortly, 'Matthew's staying to help look after Sam.'

She was surprised to see tears in the girl's eyes. 'I don't believe you. You think you've got him, don't you?'

'I keep telling you, I dun't want him – not that way. But I need his help. I can't manage Sam and the farm on me own.'

'I don't believe you,' Beth whispered again.

Esther shrugged and turned away. 'Believe what you like, then.'

'Esther . . .' Beth cried after her. 'Please – I must see him. Please tell him.'

Esther did not look back or even acknowledge that she had heard the girl's desperate plea, but as she walked along the road from the church, she could almost feel Beth's eyes watching her every step of the way.

Back at the farm, she hurried straight up to Sam's room.

'They all asked about you, Sam,' she told him. 'The parson and the squire. They all sent their regards and wish you well.'

Sam lay in his narrow bed with his eyes closed. It was as if, being unable to go to the church himself, he had given up. He refused all food, and would take only sips of water.

'Parson said he'll come and see you,' she added slyly, hoping that such news would spark some sort of reaction.

But Sam's eyes remained shut and his expression did not alter. Sadly, Esther doubted if he had even understood what she was telling him. His face was like a skull, the skin stretched like dry parchment over the bones. All the ruddy good health of a life working in the open air had gone in the last few weeks. He lay there with his eyes closed, every breath a shuddering, rasping sound, his fingers clutching at the quilt covering him.

'Do you feel worse, Sam?' Esther asked gently, bending down towards him.

There was no answer.

The next morning Esther sent Matthew to fetch the doctor again. 'He's much worse now than when Doctor Blair last saw him.'

Matthew just nodded and muttered, 'I'll go right away.'

It was only when Matthew had disappeared around the bend in the road that Esther realized she had not even thought to tell him that Beth wanted to see him.

Only two nights later, Esther was startled out of her sleep by the sound of the latch of her bedroom door being lifted. At once she was fully awake, lying stiffly, holding her breath.

In the early morning light, Matthew's shadowy form came towards her narrow bed. Ducking his head below the slope of the ceiling, he grasped at the counterpane near her shoulder. She gave a little cry and pulled the cover from his grip. 'Dun't you dare, Mester Matthew . . .'

'Oh, you're awake. You'd better come. I – I can't hear Sam breathing.'

'What?' She sat up suddenly, forgetting the nearness of the ceiling and gave her head a nasty crack.

Fearful of what they were to find, the two young people clung together as they crept through the room Matthew now occupied, across the tiny landing and lifted the latch of Sam's bedroom door.

They found him still warm, yet motionless and silent for ever. He must have died quite peacefully for the covers were unruffled and his hands were folded across his chest, just as he had gone to sleep.

With the dawn, Matthew set off to fetch Doctor Blair to come to Sam Brumby for the last time.

'I'll see the undertaker for you, my dear,' the kindly doctor told Esther as he left the farm later that morning. 'Get Matthew to ask Mrs Harris to come and lay him out.'

Esther nodded, not trusting herself to speak for the lump in her throat. She felt suddenly bereft and very much alone again. She had begun to feel secure and had dared to be happy. Sam had given her a home and had shown her a gruff affection.

Now he was gone.

Sadly, she wandered from room to room downstairs, conscious all the time of poor Sam still lying upstairs and that there was nothing more she could do for him. What would happen to all his family possessions now? she thought. Would his things be auctioned off with people prying and poking amongst his treasured memories? She opened the door into the front parlour – a room she had rarely entered and hadn't even liked to clean properly.

She moved around the room touching the furniture, the ornaments and pictures until she came to the family Bible lying on a small round table under the window. Now, with reverent fingers, she opened the book.

Written on the first blank page was a list of the births, deaths and marriages of the Brumby family.

Esther read the entries and learnt that the first Brumby to farm here had been Sam's grandfather, Joseph. One entry stated that he had been granted the tenancy in 1807. The entry of Joseph's death was in different handwriting, as if the next generation had taken over the duty of recording the history of the family. There was one entry that particularly intrigued her.

'William Joseph Brumby married Sarah Willoughby 27th May 1833.' Her finger moved up and down the page working out the relationships. William and Sarah were Sam's parents. So, she thought, perhaps Sam was some relation to Tom Willoughby.

The next entry was Sam's birth – 'Samuel Joseph Brumby born on 24th August 1833.'

Esther allowed herself a wry smile. There was less than nine months between his parents' marriage and his birth. She closed the Bible and turned away, feeling a little guilty for prying into Sam's secrets. But his parents had married and Sam *had* been born in wedlock, even if only just! Not like mine, she thought bitterly.

Esther sighed deeply. No doubt she'd soon have to leave Brumbys' Farm. But where could she go? No one wanted her.

Tears prickled behind her eyes and the lump in her throat seemed to grow bigger.

Eleven

MA Harris came mid-morning. 'Now then, lass,' she said to Esther. ''Tis all over with the poor old man, then. Aye well, he's been poorly for a while, ain't he?'

'Do – do you want any – help?' Esther asked, not without reluctance. Normally she would tackle anything, but the thought of helping to lay out Sam Brumby made her spine shiver.

'Nay, I'll manage. He were no'but skin and bone towards the end. You get on with yar work. I 'spect you've a lot to do with the funeral, an' all. By, lass, but you've kept this place going, I've got to hand it to ya . . .' and still chattering, Ma Harris heaved her stout frame up the narrow stairs. Esther stood at the bottom and watched Mrs Harris turn into Sam's room and close the door.

So it was late afternoon by the time Esther had finished everything about the farm and had washed under the pump in the yard, changed into her Sunday best frock and pinned up her hair.

When she came down the stairs she found Matthew lingering in the kitchen, warming his hands before the glowing fire in the range. The wood fell and sent a shower of sparks up the flue.

'Thought you'd gone home,' she said abruptly.

He turned slowly and grinned cheekily at her. 'Now –

why would I be wanting to do that, Esther?'

'Well, there's no need for you to stay any longer – not now.' Even to her own ears, her tone sounded more brusque than she had intended.

The smile faded from Matthew's mouth and his eyes glinted in the dancing firelight. 'Oh – dismissed, am I? Just like that, eh?'

Esther gave a click of exasperation. 'Oh, don't be so touchy, Matthew. I've been grateful for yar help, ya should know that.'

He turned away from the fire and moved slowly towards her, almost with a touch of menace. 'No, I dun't know. Perhaps you'd better show me just how grateful . . .'

She put out her hands, palms outward, to fend him off. 'Now, dun't you start that, Matthew Hilton.'

He stopped and regarded her insolently, then said, feigning innocence, 'Start what, Esther? Whatever can you be meaning?'

Esther turned quickly away from him, exasperated. 'Oh, really!' she muttered. Reaching her shawl from the peg, she dragged open the door and was through it and gone before he could say – or do – any more.

The easterly wind whipped across the fields as Esther took the path inland towards the Grange. She stopped to pull her shawl more closely about her as the wind caught at her skirt and tossed her curls. A small smile of satisfaction curved her mouth as she looked around her. Autumn had been gentle and the ploughing was going well, despite her time being taken up with caring for the old man. She smiled ruefully to herself. She did indeed owe

Matthew a debt of gratitude, for without him she certainly would not have kept up the farm work so well. Her smile widened. But it wouldn't do to tell him so, she thought. Matthew Hilton was quite full enough already of his own importance!

The smile faded and she sighed heavily. Everything could be very different from now on. What was going to happen to her now that Sam was gone?

At the Grange, the huge front door was opened smoothly by a tall, thin man dressed in a black suit. His mouth curved downward as if he had a bad smell under his nose. He looked down upon Esther and as she made to enter the house, the man deliberately barred her way. 'I don't think you can have business in this establishment, girl.'

Esther squared her shoulders. 'I am here to see Mr Marshall.'

She waited in vain for any kind of apology from the man, whose expression did not alter. 'I see, and have you an appointment?' He enunciated every word with clipped precision — and with an edge of sarcasm as if deriding the country dialect that was always so strong in her tones.

Esther stood her ground, refusing to be intimidated by him. 'Not exactly,' she said calmly, meeting his cold eyes steadfastly. 'I have come to inform the squire of the death of Mr Brumby.'

The manservant had the grace to look ashamed. But when he left her alone in the hall whilst he went in search of his master, some of Esther's confidence deserted her. She waited nervously, standing first on one foot and then on the other, twisting her fingers together agitatedly as her gaze roamed over the lofty hallway and the elegant sweeping staircase above which hung numerous ancestral pictures of serious-looking men and elegant women. In their company, even in her Sunday best dress, Esther felt like a tramp. The butler emerged from a door to the left of the hallway and beckoned her imperatively. Esther crossed the hall, her boots squeaking on the polished floor. She saw the butler's look of disgust, but the man stood aside for her to enter and as the door closed softly behind her, Esther found herself standing in a book-lined room. In the centre of the room stood a huge mahogany desk, inlaid with a red leather top. The smell of rich tobacco smoke hung in the air. It was undoubtedly a man's room. For a moment Esther thought she was alone, then from a leather wing chair near the fire, Mr Marshall rose and turned to greet her.

'Now, my dear, what is it?'

'I thought I ought to come and tell you, sir. Mr Brumby died this morning.'

'Oh dear. Oh dear me. I am sorry.' Mr Marshall sat down again. 'Come and sit down, my dear girl.'

'Thank you, sir.' Esther sat tensely on the edge of the chair set on the opposite side of the fireplace to Mr Marshall.

'You'll let me know when old Sam's funeral is to be, won't you? I shall attend. As I told you, that farm has been in his family for several generations.'

Esther nodded.

'Is everything all right on the farm? Do you need any help until I can get things sorted out?'

Esther bit her lip. She desperately wanted to ask him what was to happen to the farm — what was to happen to her. Huskily, she said, 'I've kept things going, all the time he's been ill . . .'

'I know you have, my dear, you have done remarkably well. I admire the way you've coped.'

Esther opened her mouth, trying to form the right words, but Mr Marshall was standing now and she found herself on her feet and being ushered towards the door.

Mr Marshall gave her shoulder a comforting pat and repeated his offer of help should she need it. Before she had time to say any more she was being shown out of the front door by the butler and the moment was lost.

She walked back along the lane towards Brumbys' Farm, but at the gate she paused and looked up at the shadow of the farmhouse, still and silent in the dusk. Not wanting to go back into the empty house yet, she turned and climbed the bank bordering the lane. Across the marsh, jumping the meandering streams, she climbed the far dunes and came to the beach. She walked out to the very end of the Spit where the sea and the land and the sky all seemed to meet. She sat down on the damp ground, the wind whipping around her. She could taste the salt on her lips. It was lonely and desolate out here, yet she was not afraid. Her eyes scanned the darkening sea and, half turning, her gaze took in the flat land behind her.

She gave a deep sigh of sadness. She felt as if the niche she had deliberately carved for herself in this place had been taken away from her. He had been a strange man, Sam Brumby, yet already she was missing him. She remembered everything that had happened since the morning she had arrived; Sam's initial rejection of her, then gradually his grudging acceptance and finally his need of her. For the first time in her life she had known real happiness living at Brumbys' Farm. She hoped she had repaid Sam by caring for him until the end.

Poor Sam, she thought, poor Sam.

'What happened?' Matthew demanded, as, back in her working clothes, Esther led the cows out of the byre after evening milking. 'Did Squire say what was going to happen to the farm?'

'No,' Esther snapped. Her moments of reverie out on the Spit were gone. There was work to be done, a funeral to organize. She did not pause in her vigorous sweeping of the cowshed. 'Tek them cows back to the field, will ya?'

'Did he say he would come to the funeral?' Matthew persisted, ignoring her command.

'Yes.' She stopped her sweeping and said briskly, 'Talking of the funeral, I'd best get baking.' She banged the door of the cowshed shut and walked towards the house.

'There'll be a few come, I reckon,' Matthew said following her. 'Old Sam Brumby was a funny old boy, but folks respected him. There'll be Mr Marshall an' his bailiff for a start . . .' On his fingers he ticked off the people he thought would attend Sam's funeral. Esther would be responsible for offering refreshment to them all. It was customary for a spread to be put on at the house following the interment, even if it was over two miles back to

118

the farm from the church. 'The vicar will probably come; all the folks who live at the Point, Tom Willoughby, of course, and Will, the carrier.' There was a pause, then Matthew said, 'What's up with you, Esther? You're not listening to a word I'm saying.'

'Everything will be ready,' she said, 'dun't you worry. You just see to them cows.'

'Huh, I was only trying to 'elp,' Matthew muttered and stomped off.

Late that night as she climbed the stairs, her limbs heavy with weariness, she paused outside the closed door of Sam's bedroom, her hand hovering towards the latch. Then she let it fall. Best not go in, she told herself, I shan't sleep if I look at him again. The funeral people would be here tomorrow to put him in a coffin in the front room. It wouldn't be so bad then. But she didn't like to think of him still lying in his bed, cold and silent – and so close. Holding her breath, she scuttled through the neighbouring room where Matthew had slept, not daring to peer into the dark corners. Only when she was in her own small bedroom and leaning against the closed door behind her, did she breathe easily.

She almost wished she had agreed to Matthew staying another night or two.

Whatever's the matter with you, Esther Everatt? she asked herself fiercely. You're not usually so squeamish. But she had not had to deal with death before. It was not so easy to be rational and strong-minded alone in the darkness of the night with Sam's corpse in the nearby room.

For a long time she lay in her bed listening to every sound; the wind whistling around the farmhouse and the old timbers creaking. She was just on the point of falling asleep when the click of the latch on her bedroom door startled her into wakefulness. She lay there breathing hard, her heart pounding, her scalp prickling with fear. Someone stepped into the room, closed the door behind them and began to move towards the bed.

Esther screamed – a loud, shrill noise piercing the blackness. The intruder fell against the end of her bed and she felt strong hands grasping at her legs kicking under the covers. 'Esther, Esther – it's only me.'

She stopped screaming, panting hard. Now she was angry.

'Matthew! How dare you? What—'

'Esther – please. I thought I'd stay another night or two – just till after the funeral. You dun't want to be here on your own, do you?'

'Well . . .' she said, a little mollified. The memory of her apprehension was still fresh in her mind. Still, she did not trust his motives. 'Mebbe not,' she conceded, 'but that dun't mean I want you in me bedroom.'

'Oh, Esther.' His voice was a hoarse whisper and she felt him sliding along the bed towards her.

'That's quite far enough, Matthew Hilton.' She snuggled further under the covers, pulling them up tightly under her chin.

'Esther – stop tormenting me. It's killing me, sleeping – or not sleeping – knowing you're lying just the other side of the wall . . .' His voice deepened with desire. 'Esther – I want you like I've never wanted anyone before. You've got me all twisted up like no other girl ever has ...'

She gave a snort of laughter. 'Aye, only 'cos I'm the first to fend ya off, me lad.'

'No, no, it ain't that, truly it ain't.'

She felt his breath upon her face and then his lips were on her mouth, but gently, pleadingly. 'Esther,' he murmured. 'I love you, Esther.'

She twisted her head away. 'Matthew – I won't. I've told you I won't – not till I'm married.'

'Then I'll marry you, Esther Everatt, if that's what it takes.'

Twelve

A LL the people whom Matthew had listed attended the funeral, plus a few more besides. Esther recognized most of them. There were the two neighbouring farmers – also tenants of Squire Marshall – Tom Willoughby and Mr Souter. All the men from the Point were there and the squire, together with his farm bailiff, and, of course, Will Benson.

All funerals were sad, Esther thought but she felt the pathos of this one. Poor Sam. There were no close relatives, no one to shed a tear into a delicate kerchief for him. Esther and Matthew kept to their places at the rear of the funeral procession, sitting towards the back of the church in the pew Sam had occupied on the few occasions he had attended a service. The flowers from the previous Sunday were withered and dying. No one had cared enough to put fresh ones in their place. The church was cold and musty with the damp.

The vicar said a few words about Sam, about him being a man of the soil, a man close to Nature, whose life had been ordered by the Seasons of God. Much of what he said was way above Esther's head, but he seemed to be speaking about Sam in a kindly and respectful manner, skilfully avoiding any mention of the fact that he had attended church only about three times a year or that he lived the life of a grumpy recluse.

They stood in a little cluster around the grave as the coffin was lowered into the earth, the damp drizzle seeping through their clothes so that as soon as they could without unseemly haste, the mourners moved away from the cold graveyard and back to their conveyances. Esther saw the squire and his bailiff in conversation. They both glanced across at her, then swiftly away again as they saw her watching them. Then Mr Marshall climbed into his carriage.

Esther unhitched the pony and trap Matthew had borrowed for her from Tom Willoughby and climbed up, slapping the reins so that the pony turned homeward. The rest of the mourners followed Esther back through the town and along the coast road towards the farm.

The spread she had prepared did Sam Brumby proud, though she was a little doubtful as to whether he would really have approved of all the fuss. The atmosphere amongst those present was a little strained. There was no common ground between them for easy conversation, though Esther was painfully aware that the squire and his other two tenants gravitated towards each other and sat together talking quietly as they ate. Esther saw Mr Marshall wave his hand at one point as if to encompass the land all around the farm, and she was sure he was discussing the future occupancy of his holdings. Perhaps even the two farmers whose land adjoined Brumbys' Farm were laying claim to it right now.

Only Will, the carrier, seemed at ease. 'He were a good friend to me,' Will said to no one in particular, and he waved his fork towards Esther. 'An' he gave this young 'un a good start. That right, ain't it, lass?'

Esther nodded. 'Yes. I've learned a lot from Mr Brumby,' she said and purposely she glanced towards the squire. But Mr Marshall was deep in conversation with the two farmers and appeared not to have heard.

Replete at last on ham and pork pie, the mourners began to settle themselves to hear the reading of Sam's will. Mr Thompson, the lawyer, began delivering the legal jargon in a respectful monotone. ' "This is the last Will and Testament of me Samuel Brumby of Fleethaven Point in the County of Lincoln, Farmer. I give devise and bequeath all my real (if any) and personal estates and effects whatsoever and wheresoever of which I have power to dispose by Will unto Esther Everatt . . ." '

At the mention of her name Esther gasped audibly and felt the blood drain from her face. For a moment all eyes in the room swivelled to look at her. But the lawyer did not look up or pause in his reading.

' ". . . absolutely and appoint her sole Executrix hereof. I revoke all former Wills by me at any time heretofore made and declare this only to be and contain my last Will and Testament. In witness whereof I have hereunto set my hand this fourth day of October one thousand nine hundred and eleven." ' Here Mr Thompson looked up. 'The will was signed by Mr Brumby and witnessed by myself and –' his glance rested briefly on the carrier – 'Mr William Benson, whom you all know.'

Now Esther felt the lawyer's gaze come to rest upon her, sitting straight-backed in a chair in one corner.

'You, I presume, are Miss Everatt?'

What old Sam Brumby had actually said to Mr Thompson, as the lawyer was to tell her later, had been, 'I want the wench to have it all,' and it had been left to the lawyer to couch his wishes in legal terms.

Esther licked her dry lips and her reply came out in a hesitant whisper. 'Yes – yes, sir.'

'Well, Miss Everatt, I shall be obliged if you will present yourself at my office tomorrow at ten in the morning for the signing of some documents. Of course there are legal procedures to be gone through, but I see no reason why you may not take it that everything that belonged to Sam Brumby –' he paused for effect – 'is now yours.'

Esther could not stop the words from tumbling from her lips. 'Even the tenancy of the farm – I can stay on at the farm?'

The lawyer held up his hand as if to fend off her eagerness. 'That's quite another matter, Miss Everatt. Presumably –' the lawyer glanced towards Mr Marshall for confirmation – '. . . the tenancy would cease with his death.'

Esther too looked towards the squire and saw him nod in agreement. 'That is correct, Mr Thompson. It is written into all my tenancy agreements.'

'Quite so, Mr Marshall.'

There was a general shuffling in the room as the others present began to lose interest in the finer points of what Sam Brumby's will meant. Not one of them had the right to have expected anything from Sam Brumby, and yet there was an air of displeasure that the girl who had arrived out of the mist one morning from God alone knew where, had got it all.

Only on Will Benson's face was there a smile of satisfaction on Esther's behalf.

Esther noticed Matthew staring at her, as if not knowing quite how to accept the news. She was no longer the waif who had arrived from nowhere and with nothing. Now she was in possession of some valuable belongings and, possibly, even the future tenant of Brumbys' Farm. She saw a slight frown of thoughtfulness appear on Matthew Hilton's young face, but then, as if with silent agreement the gathering made to leave. Esther forgot about Matthew.

She followed Mr Marshall out to his carriage and held the reins for him as he climbed up.

'Mr Marshall – sir – about the tenancy of the farm . . .'

Mr Marshall looked down upon the anxious girl, but his expression was hard and cold. 'This is hardly the time or the place to discuss matters of business. If you wish to see me, come to the Grange.' Without a further word he took the reins from Esther's hand and clicked to the horse to move on.

Esther stared after his retreating back, cursing herself for her mistake. Had she ruined her chances through, in Mr Marshall's eyes, a lack of proper respect for Sam Brumby's funeral day?

The following afternoon – after her morning visit to the lawyer's office – found Esther trudging the muddy lane towards the Grange. There was a fine drizzle and by the time she had walked the distance between Brumbys' Farm and the Grange, the cold dampness was seeping through her cape. Her face and hands were wet and her hair straggled in dripping strands down her face and neck.

'Have you an appointment?' the sour-faced butler asked her loftily. Obviously he had forgotten – or would not acknowledge – the discomfort of his last meeting with Esther Everatt.

'No, but Mr Marshall told me to come and see him.'

'I see.' The man looked her up and down, sighed audibly and then said with pained resignation, 'Then you had better come inside. But please, do wipe your – er – boots.'

She stood just inside the doorway whilst the man walked towards the heavy oak door to the study and knocked. He disappeared inside and closed it behind him.

It seemed an age before the man reappeared, time enough for the rain to seep from Esther's boots on to the polished wooden floor and leave tell-tale puddles. Returning, the man sighed again and then said, 'Would you follow me, please?'

Mr Marshall was sitting behind the huge desk. 'Do sit down.' With a vague wave of his hand the squire indicated a hard wooden chair which had been placed on the visitor's side of the desk.

'Now,' he leant on his desk and his sharp eyes bored into Esther's, 'what was it you wanted to see me about?' It was an oblique reference to Esther's impropriety the previous day. Rather than embarrassing the young girl further, it now made the courage flow into her. 'Mr Marshall, sir, I have come to ask you if you will please grant me the tenancy of Brumbys' Farm. After all, Mr Brumby put in his will that he wanted me to have everything of his and—'

'Whoa there, steady, my dear girl!' The squire put up his hands, palms outward, as if to slow down a galloping horse. 'Not so fast.' He sighed and then leant back in his leather chair. 'The tenancy was not Sam Brumby's to pass on. It reverted to me on his death, to be reassigned as I think fit.'

Eagerly, Esther leant forward. 'But, sir, you know I've managed that farm since Mr Brumby was ill, all this last spring and summer, through haymaking and harvest. You've seen for yourself . . .'

The squire spread his hands in mock helplessness. 'I don't deny it, my dear, you've done a good job, a wonderful job, considering you're a woman. But you see, that's the problem, we don't grant tenancies to women. I have checked with my lawyer and there is a specific clause in the agreement drawn up by my great-grandfather that the tenancy must be in the name of a man.'

'Oh,' she said flatly. Then again, 'Oh.' There was silence in the room between them. Then Esther lifted her head defiantly. 'But why, Squire? Why won't you let a woman have your farm? Can't *you* change the – the clause?'

The squire blinked in the face of her boldness. He had never before met a young woman quite like Esther Everatt and for all his breeding and position, he did not know how to deal with her.

'Well, we never have, in all these years, changed any

thing. I really don't think—' He broke off, as what he thought could be a better idea came to his mind. 'Now, my dear,' he leant forward, 'if you were married, then it would be a different matter entirely.'

'Married? Why?'

'Well, we could put the tenancy in your husband's name.'

Her green eyes flashed, her mind working busily. She too leant forward eagerly, her voice becoming slightly breathless. 'You mean – if I were married, you'd grant the tenancy to me – to my husband?'

The squire nodded. 'Yes, I'd be prepared to do that.'

Again there was a silence between them as they stared at each other. The girl's mind was working feverishly, the man's wondering what was going on in hers.

'There's no one else asked you for the tenancy of Brumbys' Farm?'

'Not exactly, though my other two tenants whose lands adjoin Brumbys' have discussed the idea in principle of splitting it between them. There's no outsider come forward – not yet anyway. Though word may not have got around yet that it's become vacant.'

'How long could you give me before you need to decide?'

The squire shrugged. 'Three weeks or so.'

Esther nodded, her eyes glinting. She stood up and held out her hand. After a moment's hesitation, the squire shook it.

'Three weeks, Squire Marshall. Three weeks it is.'

*

129

She was hanging the washing on the line when she suddenly saw Beth standing uncertainly at the corner of the house leading round from the yard into what Esther called the front garden.

'Is Matthew here?'

Esther stared at her for a moment then looked away. The girl's face was white and there were dark shadows beneath her eyes. She stood huddled into her shawl, her shoulders bent, her arms folded across her body as if protecting it.

'Where is he?' Her voice rose shrilly when Esther did not answer her first question. 'I've got to see him.'

Esther shrugged. She avoided looking directly at Beth and concentrated on stretching out the clothes and pegging them to the line. 'I dun't know where he is.'

'Yes, you do,' Beth said with a flash of her usual vitality. 'He's been here all the time with you since old man Brumby took ill. I thought at least once he were dead . . .' The spark that had flickered briefly died and she sank back into lethargy, almost pleading with Esther. 'Please – tell me where he is. I – I've *got* to see him!'

Esther eyed Beth shrewdly now – she looked dreadful. But if what Esther had in mind was going to work, then she didn't want Beth to meet up with Matthew. She jabbed a clothes peg firmly over a sheet on the line. 'Well, I dun't know where he is. He went off early this morning and I ain't seen him since!'

The girl stared at her, the last vestige of any colour draining from her face. Esther looked away from her again and bent to pick up another sheet from the washing basket. When she looked back, Beth had disappeared.

Esther worked through the day's chores, Beth's visit forgotten, for her mind was busy with her own problems, her own plans.

'Cat got yar tongue?' Matthew appeared in the washhouse doorway as she folded and mangled the sheets from Sam's bed.

'Eh?' She looked round at him. 'What? Oh, no. I was thinking, that's all.'

'You think too much, Esther me girl.' He came up behind her, put his arms about her and nuzzled her hair. For once she did not pull away from him and, encouraged by her lack of rebuff, he kissed her neck.

Esther's eyes darkened. He wanted her, she knew. But did he want her enough to marry her? Had his rash statement in her bedroom the night after Sam had died been made only in the heat of his rough desire for her?

His lips were searching for her mouth, his fingers reaching for the fastenings of her blouse.

'No, Matthew, no!'

'I want you, Esther, I'm goin' crazy for you. Let me love you, Esther, please – please . . .'

'I've told you before, Matthew Hilton, no man's goin' to touch me till I'm married!'

He looked deep into her eyes, his own burning with undenied passion for her. 'Then marry me, Esther, marry me?'

For a long moment they gazed into each other's eyes;

his fervent, blazing with a frustrated passion that threatened to spill over and engulf them both. But Esther's eyes were troubled. She liked Matthew – she liked him a lot. And he worked hard. Without his help she could never have coped over the last few months. But was it really enough for marriage? Could she really spend the rest of her life with him, working side by side on the farm? The farm! She felt a shudder run through her. How could she bear to leave Brumbys' Farm now, the only real home she had ever known?

Mistaking her involuntary shiver for excitement, Matthew murmured in her ear, 'Oh, Esther, you're lovely. I want you so. Please say yes!'

'All right then,' she said at last, 'if you're sure . . .'

'Do you mean it?' His eagerness was almost pathetic.

'Yes, course I mean it. I'll marry you, Matthew.'

His eyes were afire, and his arms were about her again, hugging her, longing to love her. 'When?'

She smiled up at him. 'As soon as you like,' she whispered huskily, clamping down hard on any feelings of guilt. It wasn't just to get the tenancy of the farm, she persuaded herself, she really did like him.

She put her arms about him in genuine gratitude and kissed him.

He groaned as he returned her kiss ardently. 'Esther, oh, Esther!'

It wasn't until a lot later that Esther remembered with a little stab of shame that neither of them had spared a thought for Beth.

*

Mid-morning about three weeks later found Esther dressed in her blue cotton dress and Matthew, stiff and awkward in his Sunday best suit, walking down the lane towards the Grange. They walked side by side in silence, companionable yet not touching.

The grim-faced butler opened the door once more and ushered them reluctantly into his master's study.

'Well, well, Miss Everatt, and to what do I owe this pleasure, my dear?' the squire greeted them.

They stood before him.

''Tain't Miss Everatt now, Mr Marshall, 'tis Mrs Hilton. We were married by special licence at half past eight this morning at the church.' Esther's look challenged the squire boldly. 'Mr Marshall, this is my husband.'

Thirteen

THERE was silence in the squire's study, broken only by the steady ticking of the grandfather clock in the corner.

Mr Marshall recovered his senses, stood up and came around the desk holding out his hand to Matthew. 'Well, well, my boy. Congratulations indeed!'

He turned to Esther and held out both hands to her. 'My best wishes for your happiness, my dear. I'm not a man to go back on his promise, dear me no.' He beamed at them both. 'You've got yourself a farm.'

Esther glanced at Matthew but he was staring at the squire, his mouth slightly open.

'This calls for a celebration.' Mr Marshall went to the side of the fireplace and pulled a red silk cord. When the door opened and the butler glided into the room, he ordered a bottle of Madeira and three glasses. 'My wife would join us, I'm sure, but I believe she has taken the carriage into the town.' He smiled again at them both, his glance flitting from one to the other.

'Well, well,' the squire rubbed his hands together. 'This has all worked out very nicely. I had no idea you two were intending to be married. This is splendid, really splendid news.' He looked towards Matthew and added, 'I'll have the tenancy agreement drawn up by my lawyer and let you know when to come and sign it . . .'

Matthew stared dumbly at the squire, who cleared his throat and turned to Esther for reassurance. 'You must come too, seeing as how really it was you . . .' He coughed in embarrassment and stopped, glancing again at Matthew. The door opened and the butler carried in a tray of glasses and the wine. With obvious relief the squire turned to pour out the wine himself, dismissing the manservant, and handing the glasses to Esther and Matthew. Mr Marshall raised his glass, 'Here's to a long life of happiness and success in your new venture.'

Esther felt that one of them should speak, say something, and since Matthew seemed to have lost his wits, she said, 'Thank you, Mester Marshall. We'll do our best to run the farm right, won't we, Matthew?'

Matthew took a gulp of the wine, spluttered slightly and nodded. He opened his mouth to speak but a fit of coughing overcame him as the wine caught the back of his throat.

Not until they were half-way down the lane leading back to Brumbys' Farm did Matthew speak. They had come out of the big house and walked side by side down the drive and out of the gate. Without even looking at him Esther could feel the rigid anger of Matthew's body as he took huge, furious strides, so that she had to take a little running step every so often to keep pace with him.

Well away from the Grange under a clump of trees that overhung the lane, he stopped and turned to face her, gripping her upper arms with his strong hands so that his fingers dug into her flesh. 'What's going on, Esther?'

'We – the squire's giving us the tenancy of the farm, Sam's farm.'

'Oh? And when was all this worked out, eh?'

'I – I asked him after Sam died, after his funeral. You know I did.'

There was a pause and then his blue eyes narrowed. 'But what did he mean when he said he wasn't a man to go back on his promise? What promise?'

Esther hesitated.

Matthew shook her. 'What did he promise you?'

The words came out in a rush. 'He promised me the tenancy of the farm if I was married.'

It seemed he stared at her a long time, just stared and stared not releasing his hurtful grip, not speaking, just holding her gaze with his own hard, wrathful eyes. His breathing became deeper.

'You mean – you married me – just to get the bloody farm?'

Her chin came defiantly higher and she returned his gaze brazenly. 'So? What if I did? If we dun't take the farm on, what's going to happen to us, eh?'

'You – you – scheming *whore*!' He was beside himself with rage, and could think of no worse insult to fling at Esther who had always held off his amorous advances with such puritanical, virginal fervour. He pushed her so violently from him that she lost her balance and fell on to the grass verge at the side of the lane. He seemed taller in his fury as he stood over her. As she lay on the grass, she felt completely at the mercy of his menacing power. 'You used me,' he spat at her. 'You knew I was crazy to have you, and you used that to get me to marry ya, just to get the farm.'

'Matthew – you dun't understand, t'aint like that . . .' She scrambled to her feet to face him, but he made no attempt to touch her now.

'Ain't it?' He seemed calmer for the moment, yet his composure was perhaps even more frightening than his white hot anger. 'You think I'm stupid, dun't you, Esther, some stupid farm *boy* . . .' He emphasized the derisory name she had first used upon him, as if the implied insult still offended him. 'I 'eard you at the funeral, soon as he'd read the will leaving you everythin' – everythin' in that house – an' still you was after more. "What about the farm? Can I stay on the farm?" you said.' He raised his voice in high-pitched mimicry of a woman's tones, mocking and insulting her now. 'An' you chased out after the squire as he was leaving to ask him the same thing. Oh, by heck, but you're grasping, Esther Everatt.'

In his anger he had forgotten that only a few hours previously she had changed her name to his.

Now Esther's temper was rising to match his own, sweeping away any vestige of fear. 'What about you, then?' she demanded, determined that he should accept his part. 'Why did *you* marry *me*? You asked me, remember?'

'You know why. I wanted you that bad, I'd have agreed to anything . . .'

She stepped nearer to him, her green eyes sparking with fire, her lips parted. Huskily, she said, 'An' dun't you still want me, Matthew? I ain't one to break my

137

promises either. I'll be a good wife to you, Matthew Hilton. You'll not have cause to complain.'

He shook his head wonderingly. 'What is it about you, Esther? God, I hate you for what you've done this day, yet I can't stop mesen wanting . . .' His lips were on hers, crushing, bruising, revengeful, but Esther did not flinch or try to pull away as he half-carried, half-dragged her beneath the trees. He put his hands into the bodice of her dress and ripped the thin material the full length from neck to hem. He took her for the first time, there on the roadside, in a mixture of passion and rage, the culmination of months of pent-up frustration and long-ing. Esther lay submissively beneath him with her eyes closed, the only sound she uttered being a gasp as he thrust deep within her and she felt a searing pain shoot through her groin. The damp ground was cold to her naked back and small stones bit into her skin. In a final humiliation, as the breeze rippled through the under-growth, she felt the sting of a nettle on her cheek.

Esther did not see Matthew the rest of that day. Her wedding day, she thought, and here she was milking the cows, feeding the pigs and churning the butter like any other day of the week. Thoughtfully, she rubbed her cheek. It had not been the way she had imagined becom-ing a wife, the way she had pictured giving herself to her husband and certainly not the way she had wanted it to be.

By nightfall, Matthew had still not returned to the farm. A little after ten o'clock, when Esther was about to give up waiting for him and take her candle up the stairs, she heard his footsteps in the yard. He stopped outside the back door and it seemed a long time before he opened it and stepped inside.

She was sitting near the table mending her stocking by the light from the oil lamp. She looked up as he appeared in the kitchen doorway. They stared at each other. Then Matthew shifted his gaze and moved, a little unsteadily, towards Sam's Windsor chair at the side of the range. For a moment he stood looking at it and then, as if making up his mind, he turned around and sat down in it. Slowly he turned his head and looked towards Esther.

'Well, are we having any supper, then?'

Esther laid aside her mending and moved to and fro between the pantry and the kitchen laying out bread and cheese and mashing a pot of tea. She glanced across at Matthew but he made no move to come to the table, so with a small smile of amusement – for it was obviously Matthew's way of assuming his role as master of the house – she cut him a slice of bread and a lump of cheese, poured a cup of tea and took it to him.

He took the plate and the cup and saucer from her and, placing the tea on the hearth, bit into the cheese.

'Suppose I'd better make a start on the ploughing at Top End tomorrow.' He paused, his gaze on the dying embers of the fire. 'That all right with you?'

Taking her cue from him, Esther said, 'Yes, fine. We'd do well to make the best of the mild autumn weather. Can ya borrow the horses?'

Matthew nodded. 'I saw Tom in the Seagull tonight. He'll bring 'em over in the morning.'

There was silence between them again, whilst Matthew ate and Esther merely nibbled at a piece of bread. She was wondering what was going to happen when they went upstairs. She realized that she should have made preparations for their wedding night, for their first night together in the home that was now rightfully and legally theirs.

She cleared her throat nervously. 'Er – I'll go up. You'll see to things down here, then, will ya?'

Matthew did not look round, but merely grunted.

Upstairs, Esther stood in the room where Matthew had slept on a makeshift bed on the floor. Then she moved into the small narrow room leading off it where she had been sleeping in the single bed. She undressed quickly and then, hearing Matthew's footsteps on the stairs, she scuttled on bare feet back into his room and lay down beneath the rough blankets on the straw-filled sacks on the floor.

As he reached the top of the stairs, she heard him open the door into Sam's room, pause and then close it again.

She was holding her breath as he stepped into the room where she lay. He came and stood over her, the candle in his right hand as he looked down at her. For a long moment, in the eerie shadows cast by the flickering light, they stared at each other. Then he blew out the candle. She heard the rattle as he set it down. In one swift movement the blankets were pulled from her and she felt his weight come down on top of her.

The daily demands of the farm forced them to settle quickly into a routine. The following morning Matthew fetched his belongings from the cottage that had been his home at the Point, and Esther scrubbed and cleaned the bedroom that had been Sam's. Now it was Matthew's Sunday best suit that stood on the hanger in the corner, Matthew's boots set ready beneath. There was fresh linen on the bed and on cold winter nights there would be a fire in the grate.

But Esther did not try to remove every trace of the old man to whom she owed so much. She put Sam's family pictures on the mantelpiece and that night, as they undressed for bed, Matthew padded across the floor to look at the faded photographs.

'By heck,' he exclaimed. 'Is that his pa? He's the spitting image of him!'

'I never dare ask him – but I 'spect so. It's not Sam. I reckon that one's Sam as a younger man.'

Esther pointed to the other photograph in a silver frame. Matthew looked closely at it. 'Not a bad looking fellow, was he?' Then he pointed at the pretty young girl with a cloud of curls. 'Who's this?'

'I reckon that's Katharine Brumby, Sam's sister. There's an entry about her birth in the old Bible in the front parlour – and did you notice at the funeral where Sam was buried?'

'No, can't say I took any notice. I dun't like funerals. I wanted to get out o' there as quick as possible.'

'Sam was buried alongside his parents, but on the other side was the grave of Katharine Brumby, his sister. She was only forty when she died. She can't ever have married.'

Matthew leant forward and peered closely at the faded

picture. 'She looks like you,' he murmured. 'That explains it, then.'

'Explains what?'

'Why he took a fancy to you, of course.' He came and stood in front of her. 'You probably reminded him of her or summat. But then——' Suddenly he grabbed her round the waist and lifted her bodily off the floor and tossed her on to the bed, so that the old springs squeaked and protested. 'Who wouldn't fancy you, Esther?'

He could not quell his hunger for her, yet now there was a look of resentment deep in his eyes.

'Wait a minute, Matthew. There's something else I want to show you.'

He was on top of her, his dark eyes so close, his breathing rapid. She could feel his desire.

'Dun't start mekin' excuses, else I'll . . .'

'I'll not break me promise,' she said quietly, 'but there's something I want to show you.'

'What?' he demanded roughly, his tone still suspicious.

'Let me up, then.'

After a moment's hesitation, he rolled off her on to his back. Esther slid off the bed and bent down to pull out a heavy wooden box from under it. As she lifted the lid, Matthew reared up on one elbow and peered over the side of the bed. His jaw fell open. Inside were a great many coins, more money than either Matthew or Esther had ever seen in their lives.

'The old miser!' Matthew grinned, but there was admiration for the old man, not insult, in his tone. His ill-temper was smoothed away by the sight of so much wealth. Wealth that was now Esther's and – by rights – his too. 'Who'd have thought it?'

Esther let the lid fall and pushed it away. Then she climbed back into bed.

Esther kept her part of the strange marital bargain. Never once did she refuse Matthew his demands upon her body, day or night. He took her whenever and wherever he wanted. In the hayloft, in the wash-house as she bent over the dolly tub, out in the fields where anyone might have seen them – almost as if he were trying to punish her, trying to make her refuse him, just once, so that he could turn on her and accuse her afresh. Certainly, he was trying to humiliate her. But Esther remained stoically docile to her husband's demands. Not a word of complaint or protest passed her lips. Matthew had not reckoned on her strength of will. Nothing he could do to her physically would break her resolve. She had got what she wanted – the farm – and she had been willing to pay the price. And the price was to be a dutiful wife to her husband.

For a time there was an uneasy truce between them, but a week after their marriage, that tentative pact was threatened almost before it had begun.

Beth came to the farm.

From the wash-house Esther saw her talking to Matthew and as she stepped out towards them, drying her hands on her apron, they both turned to look at her. Matthew's face was set in an angry glare, whilst tears trembled on Beth's black lashes. As Esther came closer the weeping girl whispered, 'So it's true, ya got yar way at last?' She turned her tearful eyes to look up into Matthew's face. 'She dun't love you, Matthew. She – she's used you. Mester Willoughby, 'ee told his wife that the squire said he never gives the tenancy of his farms to a woman. She had to be married – to get the farm.'

'Beth, I—'

'It's true!' Her voice was becoming shrill. 'I love you, Matthew, I've always loved you and I thought we was . . .'

'Beth, I'm sorry, I—'

The girl shook her head. 'Mebbe it's me that's the fool. I let you . . .' her voice broke and she took a deep, trembling breath. 'But she – she got you by holding out, didn't she? *Didn't she?*' She screamed at him now, pummelling her fists against his chest and then falling helplessly against him, sobbing hysterically.

'Aw, Beth.' His voice was an anguished whisper, and for a moment his arms were around her holding her tightly against him, whilst Esther stood watching them. She heard Beth give a gulp and saw her pull away from Matthew. Beth turned, her head bowed, as if to walk away, but with a final fury that shuddered through her body, she turned on Esther and came close to her, shaking her fist in her face.

'You'll suffer for this, Esther Everatt, you'll—'

'Esther Hilton now, Beth,' Esther corrected her with brutal calmness.

The girl gasped and the colour flooded into her white cheeks. 'You'll suffer for this,' she spat again so that

Esther actually felt Beth's spittle on her face. 'You an' yours will never know happiness!'

It was like a curse being laid upon her.

'If you plough a crooked furrow an' sow a bad seed, you mun reap a bitter harvest.'

Fourteen

'**Y**OU heard the news then, lass?'

    Ma Harris placed her milk can on the floor of Esther's spotless pantry and watched whilst Esther filled it with creamy milk.

    'No, what's that?'

    There was a triumphant note in Ma's voice as she said, 'Beth Hanley's married Robert Eland, all quick-like. Yesterday, it were. What d'ya think to that – an' only four weeks after yours, eh?'

    Esther almost dropped the small churn she was holding. Slowly, she straightened up to meet Ma Harris's keen gaze. Levelly, Esther said, 'I'm very pleased for her, I hope they'll be very happy.' She forced a smile to stretch her mouth. 'Mr Eland has been – fond of her for a long time, I believe.'

    Esther felt Ma's shrewd glance studying her, but skilfully she avoided meeting those perceptive eyes. 'Aye, that's right,' the older woman acknowledged. 'Strange how things work out, ain't it? Young Beth married to a man old enough to be her father . . .' She cackled at her own joke. 'Well, not really, I'm exaggeratin' a bit. He's thirty-summat but she's only nineteen. An' she's gone to live in that monstrosity of a boat thing – I don't reckon it's safe, mesen,' she added musingly. 'An' there we was all thinking . . .'

146

Esther picked up the full can and held it out to Ma Harris, holding out her other hand for the coppers in payment. 'Shall you want any eggs this week, Mrs Harris?'

'Eh, but call me Ma, lass, everyone else round here does.' The toothless gums widened into a smile and Esther found herself unable to resist smiling in return. 'I'll have half a dozen,' Ma said, 'and they'll want a dozen at the pub.' Slyly, she added, 'An' shall I ask Mrs Eland if she wants to place a regular order for milk and eggs?'

Esther, having recovered her composure after Ma's piece of news, raised a quizzical eyebrow and returned Ma Harris's gaze steadily. 'I dun't reckon the new Mrs Eland will want to get her milk and eggs from me – from us.' She shrugged. 'But ya can ask her, if ya like.'

Ma turned and waddled back through Esther's kitchen. 'Eh, but you've worked wonders with this place. It's spotless. I ain't never seen old Sam's place look so clean. He's a lucky young feller, that Matthew Hilton. Fallen right on his feet, 'ee has, what wi' you gettin' the farm, an' all.' Again she shot Esther a knowing glance. Nothing, it appeared, got past Ma Harris's astute understanding. With what sounded like a note of disapproval, she added, 'But I don't expect he realizes it. Same with all the fellers, lass, they don't know a good thing when they've got it!' She chuckled at her own philosophy. 'But they know when they've lost it.'

As Esther closed the back door behind Ma Harris, she was wondering how Matthew would take the news of Beth's marriage to the man he had always disliked.

Would he start to think about what he, Matthew, had lost?

Esther could not bring herself to speak of Beth to her husband, yet the black-haired girl lay like a shadow over any chance of happiness that their marriage might have had. She guessed Matthew must have heard of Beth's marriage, for the same night that Ma Harris had imparted the news to Esther, Matthew ate his meal in silence and left the farmhouse without a word to her. He had still not returned when Esther banked down the range, took her candle and went upstairs to bed.

She awoke with a start.

A loud crash had disturbed her. Her heart pounded. She heard someone moving through the kitchen, as if they were lurching from side to side, colliding with the table, knocking over a chair. She swung her legs over the side of the bed and reached with fingers that trembled to light her candle. Her mouth was dry with fear as she reached the top of the stairs and heard the door from the living room into the small hall smash open, thrown back against the wall. She held the candle high to see who had dared to invade her home.

'Matthew! Whatever—?'

'Hello, Esh-ter, my beeootiful darlin'. Your husband's come home to hish lovely wife . . .' He hiccupped and reeled backwards falling against the front door behind him. He slithered down into an untidy heap on the floor. In the flickering candlelight, she could see the silly grin on his face.

'You're drunk!' she accused, rather unnecessarily.

Matthew giggled. 'I think I musht be.'

She turned and carried the candle back into the bedroom, leaving him in total darkness. She climbed into bed, blew out the light and lay there shaking with anger as she listened to every blundering step he made, pulling himself slowly up the stairs, muttering to himself then giggling foolishly.

'Esh-ter, bring the candle back here, woman. I can't see a thing. I'll fall down and break me – me neck.'

Grimly, Esther lay still and stared with wide eyes into the blackness.

He gained the top of the stairs and fell into the bedroom, the door thumping back against the bed.

He lay on the floor laughing stupidly. 'Ya know, I reckon I've had – hic – a bit too much.'

Esther said nothing.

She heard him pull himself to his feet and sit heavily on the side of the bed. She listened whilst laboriously he took off his boots. Slowly and with careful deliberation, he took off each item of clothing and laid it across the bottom of the bed. She could feel the heaviness of his clothes across her feet. Then he tugged at the bedclothes and scrambled his way beneath them. For a few moments he lay beside her, breathing heavily. Then suddenly, he rolled over towards her, flung one arm across her, brought up his knee and thrust his right leg over her body.

Although the smell of drink on his breath made her feel sick, she lay rigidly still. He tried to pull himself up to lie astride her, but in his befuddled state the effort was too much. He nuzzled his head against her shoulder and then gave a huge sigh, sending waves of ale fumes into her face.

His breathing became regular and soon he was snoring heavily. After a few minutes she gently eased herself out from under his heavy limbs and pushed him on to his back and on to his side of the bed. She turned her back to him and lay as far to the outside edge of the bed as she could. Her fingers gripped the thin mattress and her eyes stared sleeplessly into the darkness.

What have I done? she asked herself. What *have* I done?

The New Year brought its own problems. January was one of the wettest that the old farmers could remember. The ploughed fields became a quagmire and the swollen river spilled over its banks on to the fields that bordered it. The bitter winds whipped across the flat land, howling around the exposed farmhouse in the dark of the long nights. The winter ploughing was a long way from being finished, but there was no way they could get on to the land.

'We ought to have our own 'osses, two at least,' Matthew said to Esther. 'When the weather lets up, Tom Willoughby'll want his 'osses for his own ploughing. I reckon he's further behind than us.'

Esther nodded. 'He's more acreage than us, he'll not want to be lending us his team when the weather does get better, will he?' She was thoughtful for a moment. 'Do you think the squire would lend us a couple of his?'

Matthew shrugged. 'We could ask, I suppose, but Souters' Farm always has first call on Mester Marshall's 'osses. We ought to try to get our own, Esther,' he persisted. 'Could we find the money to buy a couple of carthorses?'

Esther pulled a face. 'We-ell,' she said slowly as if thinking aloud. 'Last year's harvest was good. We've enough and more to see us through for winter feed. Then there's seven pigs almost ready for market, still leaving us a couple for our own use.'

'What about that money you found under Sam's bed after he died?'

Esther looked up sharply and her eyes narrowed. 'I didn't want to use that. I wanted to hang on to that in case we ever hit a bad time and needed it for the rent and – well – just livin'.'

Matthew appeared to consider. 'Yes, I suppose that's sensible.' There was disappointment in his voice.

Esther looked across at him. It was the first time since their marriage that he had shown positive interest in the running of the farm. Oh, he worked hard, she couldn't deny that, but he seemed determined to remain the hired hand, rather than take his rightful place as the tenant farmer of Brumbys' Farm.

It seemed to her as if he was always angry, as if there was a brooding resentment simmering just below the surface ready to flare into anger at the slightest provocation – particularly towards her. His once merry, ready-to-laugh face seemed to have a perpetual frown, where before there had been laughter lines around his brown eyes. Now those same eyes were often resentful and shadowed with bitterness.

The day they had gone to the Grange again to meet

the squire and his lawyer, who turned out to be Mr Thompson, Esther had felt that Matthew had been deliberately awkward. As they had entered the squire's study, Mr Thompson had risen and come towards them, holding out his hand and smiling at Esther. 'My dear Mrs Hilton, what a pleasure it is to see you again. How are you settling down into married life?'

She had glanced at Matthew in time to see him glowering truculently at the lawyer, and when Mr Thompson had placed the Tenancy Agreement before them, Matthew had pushed it roughly away from him, almost shouting, 'I can't read all that complicated stuff. You'd better ask my wife to deal with all this. *She's* the "mester"!'

Patiently, Mr Thompson had read the lengthy legal document, pausing to explain the obscure parts in simpler words, at last saying, 'Despite all the involved legal jargon, Mr Hilton, I can assure you – both – that this is the standard form of Agreement which Mr Marshall has with all his tenants. There are no catches.' He had beamed across the desk at them.

'Quite so,' Mr Marshall had put in. 'Just sign it at the bottom, my boy, and let me shake you by the hand as my new tenant.'

Matthew had made a great play of signing the Agreement with big scrawling letters, as if he could barely write properly, whereas Esther knew he could sign his name quite easily. She had felt that this behaviour was all part of his punishment of her for having trapped him into marrying her so that she could secure the tenancy of the farm.

Now, as they stood in the kitchen discussing the possibility of buying a pair of horses, for the first time he was showing real enthusiasm in planning their future.

A thought struck her. With a calculated subtlety that was normally alien to her candid nature, she said, 'Why don't you have a word with Tom Willoughby? He would probably know how much a pair would cost. He might even know of some for sale?'

Matthew grinned at her, and for a moment he was the old Matthew. 'Eh, but you're a sharp one, Esther Hilton. Why didn't I think of that?' Then, remembering suddenly, his eyes clouded over. 'Aye, you're a sharp one, all right, an' don't I know it.' He turned away abruptly, the tentative signs of a burgeoning co-operation dying instantly.

'I'll see Tom some time,' he said casually over his shoulder and went out to feed the pigs.

Esther sighed and returned to churning the butter, venting her disillusionment by thumping the wooden barrel of the churn over and over vigorously.

With February came the snow.

It fell heavily and almost continuously for three days. A strong wind sprang up off the sea from the north-east, a bitingly cold wind, drifting the snow and cutting off all communication with the town and even with the other farms.

As the snows began, Matthew brought all the cows into the farmyard. As the weather worsened the animals kept to the byre, munching their way through the hay and watching the white world outside with soulful eyes.

On the first Sunday in the month, as they sat either side of the kitchen table eating the roast beef dinner with no word of conversation passing between them, there came a thumping on the back door. They glanced at each other in surprise. Sunday was not usually a day for callers and no one could get down the coast road from the town. Not even Will Benson had been able to get through on his usual calls during the past week.

'What the . . . ?'

'I'll see who it is.' Esther rose and went to open the back door.

One of Ma Harris's children stood there, his thin frame shivering in the cold, the snow resting on his cap and clinging to his coat.

Esther gasped, 'Aw, Ernie lad, come in, do. Ya look like a snowman!' She laughed and pulled the boy into her warm kitchen. 'Look at him, Matthew—'

'I can't stop, missus, me ma sent me to fetch mester . . .'

'Who? Me?' Matthew rose from table and came towards the boy. 'What is it, lad? Summat wrong? Is it a shout?' Mr Harris was a member of the lifeboat crew too and often the Harris children were sent running to the neighbouring houses, to the pub and to the farms to fetch the crew, and the horses from Tom Willoughby's, when there was a launch.

The boy shook his head, scattering the snow over Esther's floor, where it melted and lay in little puddles. 'Naw, mester, 'tis Mrs Eland. Me mam's with her . . .'

'Beth? What's the matter with Beth?' Matthew's voice was sharp with anxiety.

154

'She's come to her time an' me mam says things aren't straightfor'ard. She—'

'What d'you mean – she's come to her time?' Matthew rapped out.

The boy gaped at him, his mouth falling open. 'She's havin' her babby.'

'*Baby!*' Matthew's voice was a strangled whisper. 'Beth – is – having a – baby?'

'Oh, yes, didn't ya know?' The boy's tone was matter-of-fact, but he was glancing nervously now from Matthew's dark face to Esther's, unable to understand the tension in the air.

The colour drained from Esther's face as Matthew swung round towards her. 'Did *you* know about this?' he hissed at her accusingly.

She hesitated a moment too long. 'No, no, I didn't!'

Matthew's hand shot out and his strong fingers gripped her chin, digging painfully into her cheeks. 'You lying bitch, you did know! It's mine, ain't it? It's got to be! Did you know before we was wed?' He shook her roughly, hurting her neck. '*Did* you?'

'No, no,' Esther cried, but she was remembering Beth coming to the farm asking for Matthew at the time when Sam had been so ill, dying in fact. Twice Beth had come, looking pale and wretched, huddled into a shapeless shawl she must have worn to hide her growing belly. Esther remembered now the desperation in Beth's eyes and how she had pleaded with Esther to tell her where she could find Matthew.

Esther should have guessed, but she had shut her mind – deliberately – to the obvious. She hadn't wanted to know. Then again, after Matthew had married Esther, Beth's hysterical outburst had been caused by much more than just her love for him. She had been pregnant – and desperate!

'I – I swear I didn't know, Matthew,' Esther faltered. But her words sounded unconvincing, even to herself.

'I don't believe you,' Matthew said, through gritted teeth.

The boy, who had been watching them open-mouthed with astonishment, seemed suddenly to remember the urgency of his errand. He tugged at Matthew's sleeve. 'Mester – ya've got to fetch the doctor from town. Me mam can't manage the birthing. The babby's wrong road on.'

Matthew seemed to have forgotten young Ernie Harris's presence. Suddenly he flung Esther away from him and turned back to the boy.

'What? What d'ya mean?'

Patiently, seeming suddenly older than his fourteen years, Ernie explained to the uncomprehending man. 'The babby's coming feet first, like calves do sometimes, mester. Y'know.'

Matthew nodded grimly. Esther saw him close his eyes and heard him groan. She knew what he was thinking. She had seen him have to put his arm inside a cow and pull out her calf, with the animal in terrible pain and the man, fearing for the life of the unborn, heaving and sweating and covered in slimy birthing fluid. She could sense his agony. If it was anything like that – half as bad – for Beth . . .

Esther watched as Matthew pushed the lad aside and

lumbered towards the back door, snatching his coat from the peg on the back door as he went. Ernie too, darting a glance at Esther's face, scuttled outside after Matthew.

Slowly, Esther moved to the scullery window. She saw Matthew reach the farm gate and turn towards the town, wading his way through the knee-deep snow, his arms flailing from side to side in an effort to keep his balance as he went.

Out to the east, over the sea, the sky was low and heavy with more snow as Esther stood alone by the window watching her husband trudge determinedly towards the town to fetch the doctor for the woman who was about to give birth to his child.

It was almost twelve hours later, gone midnight, when Esther, still huddled over a dying fire in the range where she had sat for most of the day, just staring into the glowing coals, heard a loud rapping on the back door.

The sudden noise in the silence of the night made her start suddenly and her heart began to pound.

'Matthew . . .' She jumped up and, snatching the lamp from the table, hurried to the door to open it. But it was Ernie Harris standing there again.

'Missus, me mam sent me to fetch ya.'

'Why, what's wrong? Is it Beth? Mrs Eland?'

'Naw, that's all over.' Even in the pale flickering light from the lamp, Esther could see the delight spread across the young boy's face. 'She had a lad, missus. Doctor were there. Yar man fetched him, but . . .' The smile faded now. ''Ee's bin in the pub ever since, an' now . . .' The voice faltered and the boy dropped his gaze as if embarrassed to look into Esther's eyes.

She put out her hand and gripped Ernie's shoulder. 'Tell me, what is it? What's happened?'

The boy looked up again, the words coming out in a rush. 'Yar man's roaring drunk, missus. An' he's standing outside the boat – Eland's boat – shouting and carrying on. There'll be a fight, missus, if ya don't come. Me dad and some of the other men at the Point have tried to pull 'im away, but . . .' the boy shrugged. 'He's fighting mad, missus. Do come.'

Esther turned back into the house and took down her cape from behind the door and pulled on her boots. Taking the lamp, she snecked the door behind her and bending her head against the sleeting wind, she trudged out into the snow.

Luckily, there had been no further heavy snowfalls so she was able to follow the path trodden by the comings and goings earlier in the day. She followed Ernie's wiry form as he leapt and bounded through the snow. Long before they reached the Point, she could hear Matthew's voice.

Then, as Ernie helped her clamber up the slippery Hump, she saw him.

A small group of people from the Point cottages were standing in a huddled semi-circle behind him, holding lanterns high as if to light the drama going on before them.

Matthew was at the foot of the wooden jetty leading up to Robert Eland's boat. At the top of the gangway stood Robert Eland, shaking his fist at Matthew below.

'Come down here, Eland, and fight like a man – if ya call ya'sen a man. That bairn's mine. There's a cuckoo in ya nest, man . . .'

'Go home, you fool, to your own wife and let mine be,' Eland shouted back.

'Beth's mine. Her bairn's mine, an' ya know it, Eland. I'll not have my son live on a rotten boat that might get swept out to sea wi' the next tide.'

Esther drew in a breath to shout his name, but before she could utter a sound, Robert Eland had run down the gangway and from about half-way up had leapt down upon Matthew, falling on top of him and tumbling him to the ground. They rolled in the snow, grappling to get a hold, trading punch for punch. They staggered to their feet, holding on to each other in the effort to rise. Then they swayed back momentarily and came at each other again, fists swinging. Matthew caught Robert Eland high on the side of the head, whilst in the same second Eland's knuckles found Matthew's nose, and blood, black in the fitful light from the lanterns, spattered the snow.

Esther pushed the lantern she carried into Ernie's hands and ran forward. 'Stop it – stop it, Matthew. You have no right. Robert – please . . .'

Matthew swung his arm back to aim a punch at Eland, but caught Esther full in the chest, knocking her into the snow. She lay there winded, but her attempt at intervention galvanized the other men amongst the onlookers to take action. They moved forward as a body, some to take hold of Matthew, others to grasp Eland. The women amongst the group rushed to help Esther.

'Ee, lass, what a to-do.' She heard Ma Harris's warm voice in her ear.

'I'm – fine,' Esther gasped, not quite truthfully, as they helped her upright. 'Just help me – get him away from here – home.'

She looked across at her husband. He was slumped forward, only held up from falling into the snow by the other men. He was sobbing now, a wretched, distraught figure.

'Beth – oh, Beth. I'm sorry. I didn't know. Ya should have told me . . .' He talked to the empty air because, of course, Beth was not out there in the snow to hear his anguish.

Esther moved forward, resolutely pushing away the memory of Beth's stricken face asking to see Matthew, of her distress at hearing of his marriage. Now Esther put her shoulder under her husband's arm and felt his weight sag against her. She swayed a moment and then straightened.

'Thanks, Mester Harris. I've got him now.' Esther braced her shoulders and half-dragged, half-carried her husband up the lane towards their home.

As soon as they were some distance up the lane, Esther said firmly, 'Shut up now, Matthew. What's done is done. Ya mekin' a right fool of ya'sen.'

He lifted his head briefly. 'Ya made the fool o' me, Esther Everatt. I hopes ya satisfied.'

Still, she thought, he thinks of me by my maiden name and not by the one he has given me in marriage. More than anything, this seemed to accentuate the bitterness he felt towards her.

They stumbled their way through the snow, Matthew still rambling about Beth and his son, and venting his anger upon his wife. By the time they reached the back door of the farmhouse, Esther was exhausted. There was a pain in her chest from Matthew's blow and his weight seemed to grow heavier and heavier. Inside, she pushed him thankfully into the chair by the range and sank down on to the rug herself. The coals still glowed with a little welcome warmth. It was several minutes before she could drag herself upright and move towards the kitchen to fetch a rag to wipe away the blood still trickling from his nose. Two dark shadows were swelling beneath his eyes.

She fetched a bowl and spoon. 'There's some broth here still warm.' Her tone was sharp. 'Come on, Matthew. Stir ya'sen. It'll do ya good.'

There was no response. Matthew leant his head back against the wooden chair and closed his eyes.

'Please ya'sen,' Esther muttered impatiently, but nevertheless she fetched a blanket and wrapped it around him.

Then she went upstairs alone to her bed.

Fifteen

WHEN she came down the following morning, the blanket had been tossed aside and Matthew was not in the house.

Esther cleaned out the range and relit the fire. She laid the breakfast table and was about to go out and start the milking, when he came in. He sat down at the table, picked up the spoon laid ready for him and began to eat the porridge which Esther had spooned into a bowl.

'Ya know,' he began between mouthfuls, his eyes cast downward. 'I reckon we could just afford a pair of 'osses. I was talking to Tom Willoughby at the pub last night an' he reckons he knows of a chap who's got a couple of crossbreeds for sale.'

Esther almost gasped in astonishment. Matthew was acting as if yesterday, and more especially last night, had never happened. She looked closely at him. There was no way he could forget last night's escapade though, she thought grimly, with two black eyes and a bruise across the bridge of his nose. Esther shrugged slightly. Oh, well, she thought to herself, if that's the way he wants it, it suits me. Aloud she said, 'They might be a bit pricey for the likes of us, but there's no harm in 'aving a look, Matthew.'

'Right, I'll go an' see Tom later on today.'

A little later he left the house without ever looking directly at Esther or meeting her eyes.

'By heck,' Ma Harris shook her head. 'Ah dun't want many of them type of birthings. Poor lass were fair worn out, and torn – eh dear!' She clicked her tongue against the roof of her mouth and cast her glance skyward in an expression of regret and shook her head again. ''Ee were a big lad an' wrong road on. She had a bad time, did poor Beth.'

Quietly, Esther said, 'She had a son, then?'

She felt Ma Harris's perceptive gaze upon her, watching her. 'Aye, a fine lad. She's calling him Daniel after her father. The babby's none the worse, just Beth. She'll get over it. She's young enough to have plenty more bairns.' Ma Harris cackled. 'She'll have to go some to catch me up, though, won't she? Me eldest, Ernie, he's nigh on fifteen and the little 'un, Alice, she's just turned three – seven in all livin'.'

Esther smiled and nodded as if in congratulation.

'Ya'll be next, if Ah'm not mistaken,' Ma said. 'How far on a' ya?'

Esther stared at her. 'How – how did you know?'

'Lass – 'tis written in your face.'

'But I scarcely know mesen – I mean – I can't be sure yet . . .'

Ma nodded sagely towards Esther's stomach. 'Ya've one in there, me lass. Ah can tell.'

'Don't – don't say anything, will ya?'

Ma's knowing eyes narrowed. 'Not told him yet?' she murmured.

163

Esther shrugged evasively. 'Well, I didn't want to until I was sure.'

'Aye, all right, lass. I'll say nowt.' A look of concern crossed the older woman's face. 'But are you all right, lass? Ya took a nasty knock last night. Ya've no pains, a' ya?'

Esther shook her head and managed a thin smile. 'No, Ma, I'm fine. Really. I'm tough as owd boots!'

Ma Harris nodded, satisfied.

As swiftly as it had come the snow melted and a wintry sun and a sharp breeze seemed to do their best to dry out the land. Nevertheless the ploughing was still way behind until the day that Matthew came home triumphantly leading a pair of heavy horses.

'They're getting on a bit. Fourteen they are, but there's four or five good years left in 'em yet. The chap said he'd got some young 'uns broken in, but he didn't want to split this pair up. Been together years, they have.'

The horses stood patiently in the yard, submitting themselves to Esther's scrutiny. Their chestnut coats shone and the flaxen socks gleamed. 'They're lovely,' Esther said, smiling and patting their necks. 'Have they got names?'

'This one with the little white mark just below his forelock is Prince and t'other's Punch,' Matthew told her. 'Ya know what, Esther? I can't hardly believe it mesen. The chap as sold 'em to me said Tom 'ad told him all about us. About you and Sam Brumby, and us getting wed . . .' His eyes flickered away a moment, but the excitement of the moment was too great to allow even his bitterness to spoil it. 'An' he said he liked to hear of youngsters working hard and having a go and he wished us well and said we could have a month or two to pay for the 'osses. I give him half as a payment now and . . .'

'I don't like owing anyone money, Matthew,' Esther said firmly, adopting her determined pose; hands on hips, feet planted apart. She saw Matthew look at her, saw his glance falter and flicker away.

'But—'

'Ya'll take the young pigs to market this week and tek the man his money as soon as you get it.'

Matthew's face darkened. 'Dun't mek a fool out o' me, woman.'

Esther's own eyes sparked with anger. 'No need for me to do that, Matthew Hilton, ya make a good job of that ya'sen.' They glowered at each other.

'I'll not be in debt to anyone, Matthew. An' it'll not make a fool of you as long as *you* go and pay the man. But,' she lowered her voice and there was a threat in her words, 'if you don't do it – I will!' She turned on her heel and marched back into the wash-house. Within five seconds the clothes were taking a vicious pounding in the dolly tub.

She heard Matthew leading the horses into the stable. Esther tried to calculate in her head. Would they have enough feed to last through a long, hard winter with two great horses now as well as the cows and other livestock?

In their bed that night, for the first time since before the birth of Beth's child, Matthew took Esther roughly and

165

swiftly, with a bitter fury, as if he bore her a deep resentment and yet he still wanted her. He could not quell his desire for her, yet he despised himself for succumbing to his physical need and for being rendered defenceless by her nearness. His young, virile body could not deny itself the pleasure which she, whilst taking no pleasure herself, never denied him.

Esther was deliberately keeping her part of the marriage bargain.

During the weeks that followed, Matthew worked long hours at the ploughing. He stayed away from the Seagull and the Point – and Beth.

Some days Esther took her turn behind the plough. She came to love the great plodding horses with their gentle eyes and shaggy manes and tails. They were strong with broad, muscular backs and massive hindquarters that pulled the plough through the hard ground as easily as drawing a knife through butter. They were a team and they seemed to know without being told what they had to do. They would turn at the end of a furrow, never faltering, plodding steadily around the rig she had marked out, seeming to slow imperceptibly whilst Esther lifted the plough, ran it along the top edge and then let it down again. Up and down the long straight furrow they plodded, one horse walking in the hollow of the furrow, the other on the unturned turf. Up and down, up and down, whilst above their wise old heads, seagulls screeched greedily and swooped down behind the plough on to the newly turned earth to search for morsels.

One morning Esther caught sight of Will Benson's

cart coming down the lane and heard the blast on his whistle to herald his approach. She halted the horses near the edge of the field that bordered the lane. As the carrier's cart slowed to a stop she could see Will's grinning face. He was wearing a greatcoat over his suit, for it was bitterly cold riding on the front of his cart.

'Eeh, Esther lass,' he said climbing down from his seat high up above the rump of his horses. 'It's good to see ya again. My, it seems ages since I was out this way. What wi' all that snow.' He looked her up and down, and then searched her face more closely, holding her gaze with his own steady eyes. 'How've ya been, lass? How's married life?'

Esther smiled determinedly, 'Fine, Will. Look . . .' She took hold of his arm and turned him to look into the field. 'Matthew bought a pair of horses. Aren't they fine, Will?'

'By, lass, they are an' all.' He looked at her again. 'But should you be doing the ploughing, lass? Ya husband should—'

'Oh, he does his share, Will, and I likes to tek me turn. I ain't no slacker.'

Will's laugh rang out. 'No one could ever accuse you of that, lass. No one.'

'If ya going to the Point first on yar calls, I'm nearly done in this field. I'll come back to the farm and ya can have a bite of dinner with us, Will.'

'Ah'd like that, lass.'

So it became a regular thing that Will had his dinner with Esther and Matthew on the days he came to the Point on his rounds. Soon he was taking their produce to the town markets and selling it for them, bringing the money he made for them on his next visit.

'Why dun't you come into the town on the cart, Esther?' he would ask her. 'Ah could always bring you back if it's too far . . .'

'It ain't that – I ain't keen on the town.' She grinned. 'Tell you the truth, Will, I'd be lost.'

Will smiled indulgently. 'All right, lass. But you'd enjoy a trip now and then. Get that husband of yours to take you.'

'Mebbe, Will,' she hedged, 'mebbe – some time.'

When the ploughing was done and the seed safely sown at last, Matthew suddenly said, 'We should go to church again, Esther. We'll go tomorrow.'

She nodded. 'I'd been thinking the same, it's what Sam would have done after such a bad winter. He'd have wanted to give thanks that we'd got the crops sown, even if we are a bit late.'

Matthew looked at her a little strangely then smiled and nodded. 'That's right, Esther, just what I'd thought.'

He went outside whistling. Esther watched him go, a thoughtful look on her face. She had readily agreed to his suggestion, though she was surprised that the idea had come from him.

The following morning Esther came downstairs in time to set off for church to find Matthew waiting for her in the living room. Her mouth fell open.

'Matthew, what on earth . . . ? That's a brand new suit. Where did ya get that?'

'I went into town yesterday afternoon an' bought it.'

His face clouded ominously. 'Can't a man buy himself a new suit without being answerable to——?'

'Don't fly off the handle,' Esther snapped back. She glanced down at the old dress which had belonged to the long-dead Katharine Brumby. It was already getting very tight around her expanding waistline. Her head came a little higher and her chin jutted out. 'If ya can afford a new suit, Matthew Hilton, then I reckon yar wife deserves a new frock, don't you?'

'Suit ya'sen.' He turned back to the mirror, trying to smooth down his unruly curling black hair but without success. He had shaved, but his dark colouring still gave his jawline a blue tinge however sharp his cut-throat razor.

'I've got to admit it, Matthew,' Esther said, 'ya look very smart.'

He turned to look at her again and suddenly he grinned and she glimpsed the old Matthew; the Matthew who had pursued her, who had tried to tumble her in the hay.

'Ya dun't look so bad ya'sen.' His eyes roamed over her, taking in her long, glossy hair which she had piled high on her head and fastened with the pearl combs; then down her slender neck and lingered on the generous curves of her bosom. He moved towards her, his eyes glinting wickedly.

'Matthew . . .' Esther held out the thing she was carrying in her hands to steer him away from the direction his thoughts were obviously taking. 'I thought you might like to – to have this. Remember? It was Sam's. He always wore it to church.' She held out Sam Brumby's gold Hunter watch. 'Would ya like it?'

'Like it?' Matthew's eyes shone. 'Aw, Esther, it's a fine watch . . .' He slipped it into the pocket of his new waistcoat and looped the chain across his chest and stood there proudly, puffed out like a pouter pigeon.

Esther smiled at him. 'It looks grand, Matthew. Real grand. Well, shall we go?'

The smile faded a little from his mouth and for a moment she thought he looked uncertain.

'Esther,' he began, 'let's not go to church, let's . . .'

Remembering the look of desire which had flared in his eyes a few moments ago, Esther tapped his arm sharply, yet with an air of playfulness, and retorted, 'Oh no you don't, Mester Hilton. You wanted to go to church, so we're going!'

'Esther, mebbe . . .'

'Matthew, do come on, or we'll be late.'

She saw him hesitate, give a shrug of resignation and then he offered her his crooked arm and murmured, 'Very well, but just remember – it was you insisted we go.'

They walked the two miles to the church, Esther's arm through Matthew's. She was wondering if now was the right time to tell him her news, but decided to leave it until they returned home. She was loath to spoil this moment, for she had no idea how he would take the fact that she, too, was to bear him a child.

In the church porch they met the Willoughbys and Miss Jenkins. Tom Willoughby greeted them jovially, asking how their horses had settled down and were they pleased with them? Had they got all their ploughing and sowing done? It was the general talk of the neighbouring farmers greeting each other. A determined smile stretched upon her mouth, Esther glanced at Martha Willoughby and her sister, Flo Jenkins. Their heads were bent close together, whispering.

She caught the odd snatch of their conversation. 'Sam's watch . . . new clothes . . .' And then something she could not understand. 'Fancy him daring to come today of all days.'

Esther's fixed smile faded and her chin came up a little higher. Loudly she said, 'Come, Matthew, we'd best take our place in Sam's pew. I know he'd 'ave liked us to take his seat.'

With satisfaction, she heard the gasps from the two women and a 'tut-tut' as she stepped through the church door, walked up the aisle and took her place in the pew Sam had occupied. Matthew followed her in and sat beside her.

Just before the service began there was a slight commotion in the porch and the sound of a young baby crying. At her side, Esther felt Matthew stiffen. She turned her head to see the colour suffusing his neck and creeping slowly up his face. He stared fixedly straight ahead at the altar. Esther looked behind and saw Robert Eland and then Beth carrying her child wrapped in shawls into the church and taking a seat near the font. Tight-lipped, Esther too turned back and fixed her gaze upon the altar. Morning service began, but Esther was hardly aware of it. Mechanically, she rose and opened her lips to the hymns, mouthing the words. She knelt and whispered the prayers, yet all the time she was uncomfortably aware of the three other people at the rear of the church.

At the end of the service the beaming vicar announced that Robert and Beth Eland had brought their baby son to be christened and that all the congregation would be very welcome to stay if they so wished.

Esther made to stand up to leave, but Matthew gripped her arm and pulled her back down on to the seat. 'We're staying,' he hissed. ''Tis the reason we came.'

Esther gasped. 'Ya knew? Ya . . .'

Heads were turning towards the angry whispers between husband and wife.

'Hush,' someone demanded.

The vicar cleared his throat and raised his voice above the whispering and the shuffling and began the opening words of the service of baptism.

Seething with fury, Esther sat where she was. Not because she was afraid to walk out, far from it, but she was not going to be forced into causing a scene in front of the squire and his family, and the vicar, to say nothing of the Willoughbys. By so doing, she realized, it would be she, Esther, who would be made to look foolish.

When it came to the point in the service where the vicar addressed the parents of the child, Esther felt Matthew make an involuntary movement as if he were about to respond. Now it was her turn to grab his arm and hiss at him, 'Oh no, ya don't. Ya sit where you are.'

He shot her an angry, hate-filled glance, but did as she bid.

Just you wait, Matthew Hilton, she thought savagely, till this is all over.

By the time they were half-way along the lane towards home, Matthew did indeed begin to wish he had never thought of attending his son's baptism uninvited. His wife castigated him, her voice rising shrilly, echoing across the fields until he felt the whole parish must hear her.

'How dare you, Matthew Hilton? Ya knew, didn't ya, that it was his christening today? Didn't ya?' she insisted until he admitted grudgingly that he had overheard the men talking in the pub and had learnt that Beth Eland's son was to be christened that Sunday after morning service.

'I almost changed me mind this morning, when you gave me that watch. But you,' he added, trying as ever to lay the blame on her, 'insisted on us going – if you remember.'

'Whatever possessed you to do such a stupid thing? How could you think you'd be welcome there? Ya've made a fool of all of us.'

He stopped and turned to face her. She stopped too and they stood either side of the narrow lane, the wind whipping loose sand from the dunes around them, the sound of the sea in their ears, and the gulls screeching above as if the wheeling, diving birds were joining in their heated quarrel.

'What d'ya mean?' he argued belligerently. 'Ah've a right to be there. Daniel's my son.'

He uttered the name he had heard the boy given with

pride in his voice and his tone was not lost on Esther. But it served only to fuel her outrage.

'Aye, ya bastard son!' Her country dialect became even more pronounced in her blazing anger. 'Ya've made a fool of ya'sen, and me! An' if that dun't mean nothing, did ya stop to think what Beth must feel to see ya there? And what about Robert Eland – what must that poor feller be feelin'?'

'Beth? Why would Beth mind?' He touched his nose as if remembering Eland's punch. 'And Ah dun't care what *he* thinks! He's leaving me out of the lifeboat crew now on purpose,' he added in an aggrieved tone.

Esther cast her eyes to the scudding clouds above them. 'Are ya so stupid? Can't ya see?' She leant towards him, trying to make him understand. 'Everybody *knows* he's your child, *you've* made sure of that! But you shamed her and she had to marry another to give her bastard a name . . .'

'If that's anybody's fault, it's *yours*, Esther. You knew before you got me to marry you . . .'

'I didn't *get* you to marry me, an' well you know it. You asked me and I said yes, that's all.'

'Only because you held out on me, because you wouldn't . . .'

'Aye, but Beth would and did,' Esther said quietly now. 'And look where it left her. I was always honest with you, Matthew. I always told you I wouldn't bring a bastard into the world, and I meant it.' She paused a moment and then added softly, 'But I'm carrying your child now, Matthew. Your child conceived and born in holy wedlock!'

He stared at her, but his face was expressionless.

'So,' he said slowly. 'Ah'll have sired two calves in a year, eh?' A smile twisted his mouth, but it was a sardonic cynical smile, with no pleasure at her news showing in his eyes. 'Quite the young bull, ain't I?'

Sixteen

*I*T was not the way Esther had imagined giving her
husband the news, but it was done now and over the
days and weeks that followed Matthew made no mention
to Esther about their coming child. He made no enquir-
ies after her health, nor any deference to her condition by
trying to help ease her workload. Not that Esther
expected anything different. She had seen her aunt work
in the fields until a few hours before the birth of a child.
She had been brought up to regard such a condition as
perfectly natural and not an illness or an excuse for
idleness.

Matthew was right about being left out of the lifeboat
crew deliberately by the coxswain, Robert Eland. Pri-
vately, Esther could well understand why and yet
Matthew was a good crew member; whenever the
maroons went up throughout that following summer, she
would see him start forward as if to race down to the
boat-house for the launch. Then angrily he would return
to his work but it would unsettle him. He would be
watching the lane to see the men return, to catch someone to ask what the shout had been, and had it been
successful, and more importantly, had they had a full
crew? But no request ever came for Matthew to join
them again; no sound of Ernie Harris's flying feet across

their yard to pound on the door shouting for 'the mester'.

In the evening following a shout, Matthew would go down to the Seagull to try to join in the chatter and the talk of the rescue. But he was on the fringe now, not welcome amongst the crew members. On such nights he would come reeling home drunk, shouting and singing, only serving to exclude himself further from their number.

At harvest time, their neighbours came to Brumbys' Farm once more to help. Mrs Harris and her brood of children, and workers from Rookery Farm, all came.

This year Robert Eland stayed away.

'He goes out in his little boat cod-fishing more and more now, missus,' Ernie Harris told Esther. 'Mester Eland reckons the land's not for him. His life's the sea, he ses.'

Ernie now helped out frequently at Brumbys' Farm. As Esther's time approached, he would slip in quietly to have the milking done before she came out in the morning. He would arrive again in the evening, often milking the cows out in the field before she came to herd them to the farmyard. Esther smiled to herself. If her own husband had no thought for her welfare, it seemed that the young boy was doing his best to help her.

Ernie was a thin, wiry lad of fifteen now. His brown hair flopped forward over his eyes and he had the habit of flicking his head back and grinning at Esther from under the unruly lock of hair. His face was thin, almost gaunt, but his hazel eyes were bright and he was a quick, ever-cheerful lad. Esther, as her belly swelled, came to rely on Ernie's help more and more. At the end of each week she would pay him for the hours she knew he had worked and then she would add a little for good measure, for the boy never asked for payment, and she was for ever finding jobs that had been done when she knew Matthew could not possibly have done them.

'He's a good lad, our Ernie,' his mother agreed readily when Esther praised Ernie's kindly actions. 'Ah dun't know what Ah'd do wi'out him sometimes. He keeps an eye on the younger ones. Anyway, enough about my brood. How are you feeling, lass? Ya can't have long to go now. Want me to tek a look at ya some time?'

'I'm hoping I can hang on till harvest's safely in.'

Mrs Harris laughed. 'Only if young 'un decides to let ya, lass. They have a will o' their own. They'll come when they'm ready and there's nowt ya can do about it.'

'It's been so wet this year – it's going to be a difficult one. Some of the fields are flooded.' Esther wrinkled her forehead worriedly. 'I'm sure we're going to lose some of the crops.'

'Aye, Ah've seen it happen here afore. Some years back Sam had to take his oats over to one of Tom Willoughby's fields – one of them way over yonder' – the older woman waved her hand westward – 'to spread it all out to dry afore we could stack it.' She glanced again at Esther and said as if warning Esther not to be too hopeful, 'Late we was, that year, gettin' it all in.'

Esther's child decided to wait, however, and when the last sheaf was stacked after a very difficult harvest, Esther heaved a great sigh of relief.

Now nothing could spoil the birth of her child.

*

It was another two weeks, well beyond the time that Mrs Harris had predicted, before Esther felt the tell-tale pain low down in her groin. She carried on milking Clover, murmuring soothingly to the cow as she always did. The pain subsided and died, and Esther pulled steadily on the beast's udders, never slowing, never losing her easy rhythm. She stood up slowly and eased her back. Then she covered the two pails of milk with the wooden lids and picked them up.

She had begun to walk across the yard towards the house, when a second pain struck suddenly and with such intensity that she gasped aloud and doubled over, the bottom rims of the pails catching on the floor and tippling forwards. She gave a cry and tried to pull them upright, but the lids toppled forwards and the milk gushed out on to the yard.

'Oh, no!' Esther cried aloud. The pain was receding now, leaving her vexed and angry with herself for spilling the milk. Half the contents of each bucket was lost and, pursing her mouth, she picked up the two pails and went quickly into the house. If they were to keep up the supply to their regular customers, her own household would have to go short for a day or so. She stroked her swollen belly and glanced down at it.

'But there'll be enough of my milk for you, little one,' she murmured. Already her breasts were tender with ready ripeness for the birth of her child. 'I'll see you never go short – not of anything – if I can help it,' she promised softly.

She left the milk in the dairy. She would have to ask Mrs Harris if one of her girls, maybe Enid, would come and do the dairy work for a few days. And of course Mrs Harris herself would attend her at the birth. She went out again into the yard. The September day, which already had the hint of autumn gentleness about it, was warm and sultry.

'Huh,' Esther said aloud. 'Never anyone here when ya wants 'em.' The yard was silent save for the occasional stamping of a hoof from the cowshed. Esther gave a click of exasperation at herself. She had quite forgotten that she had not yet turned the cows back out into the field after the morning milking. As she opened the byre door, she was forced to lean against the wall as another pain, beginning low down, gripped her in its vice-like severity. As the wave passed she loosed the cows from the cowshed and drove them across the yard and into the lane where they idled along the verges, tearing at the grass and beginning the whole process of milk production once more.

Again Esther looked about her and chewed at her bottom lip with uncertainty. She did not want to have to go to the Point herself. Ma Harris's cottage was over-looked by the Elands' boat and the last person Esther wanted to meet at this moment was Beth Eland.

She was still hesitating, debating whether to go into the house and upstairs and prepare the bed for herself, trusting to luck that Matthew would come home before . . .

Another pain clenched her abdomen, more strongly than ever and she could not prevent a low grunt escaping her startled lips. The pain was so swift and intense, like nothing she had ever before experienced. She found herself doubling over and squatting down on to the verge panting until the pain began to ebb away. Sweat trickled down between her breasts and for a moment she closed her eyes as the heat of the day danced and swam before her eyes.

In the distance she heard a shrill whistle and the faint rattle of cart wheels coming closer and blissfully closer. Esther licked her dry lips and made as if to pull herself upright, but another pain was already beginning, swelling and pulsating, so that she gasped again and toppled forwards on to her knees.

Will Benson's cart appeared round the bend in the lane and drew to a halt. She heard, rather than saw, for her eyes were still squeezed tightly shut against the pain, Will scrambling down from his seat and running with uneven footsteps towards her.

'Aw, lass, what is it? Is it the bairn? Ya shouldn't be out here on yar own. Where's that husband of yours? Where's Matthew?'

Esther almost laughed – if the pain had not been so bad, she would have done – at the flurry of anxious questions.

'Stay there, lass. I'll go on to the Point right away and fetch Ma Harris. Now, don't you move, lass.'

She wasn't planning on going anywhere, she would have said, but she just nodded and bent over her throbbing belly, hugging it with her arms. Will hobbled back to his cart and pulled himself up, catching the reins and flicking them to urge his horses forward. The cart trundled past with Will's anxious eyes upon her as he went by. The pain had subsided a little now and she was able to look up and give him a weak smile. Heartened, he slapped the reins again and drove on.

By the time Ma Harris was puffing up the lane towards the farm, Esther had managed, between the pains, to get back to the house. She paid a visit to the privy next to the wash-house and was at the back door about to go in, when she heard Mrs Harris's voice.

'Here I am, lass, and not afore time, by the look on ya.'

Esther thought she had never been so pleased to see Ma Harris's toothless grin as she was at that moment. She could feel the sweat glistening on her face now, and her hands and legs seemed to be shaking. She felt Ma Harris's firm, comforting grasp upon her arm and thankfully she leant against the older woman.

'There, there, now, ya'll be fine. Just do as Ah tell you, and everything'll be fine.'

It was. The most difficult part, Esther thought afterwards, had been heaving herself up the stairs, with Ma Harris lending a helping hand from behind.

Once she was lying on the bed, propped against pillows, with the older woman taking complete charge and issuing orders, all of which Esther did her best to obey, the birth was surprisingly quick and easy.

'Ya doing wonderful. Child-bearing hips ya've got, me lass. By, but you'm lucky. Push, lass, now a deep breath and push. There – good lass – that's the head.' Esther heard a little whimper and Ma Harris's raucous laugh. 'Aye, that's it, young 'un, let us know ya coming. Now, Esther lass, wait a bit – wait a bit – now push, lass, push.'

Esther gave a little cry as her belly emptied and her child thrust its way into the world.

'Eh, Esther lass, it's a lovely little girl.' Ma Harris's capable hands wrapped the baby in a shawl. 'No need to slap this one,' she laughed above the now squalling infant. 'She means showing ya she's a good pair o' lungs.'

As she laid the baby in Esther's arms, she asked, 'What ya going to call her, lass?'

Two bright spots of colour burned in Esther's cheeks from her efforts, and sweat still shone on her face. There were dark shadows of exhaustion under her eyes, but she was smiling. 'I don't know, Ma, we – we haven't talked about it.'

She heard Ma Harris give a soft sigh, but it was more the sound of understanding than of disapproval. 'Men are never very good at making up their minds. Ya'll end up deciding, lass, Ah can tell ya. So ya might as well think about it now. Just while I gets you sorted out. Now, we've got to get this afterbirth. Can you give a cough?'

Esther looked up in surprise. 'What?'

'Cough, lass. Just cough.'

Obediently, Esther coughed and felt the afterbirth slither from her. 'Aye, that's it. All nicely away. Good, good.'

Esther began to giggle helplessly, the emotion manifesting itself in a gentle hysteria. 'I – I feel like Curly the pig,' she spluttered.

Ma opened her mouth and laughed too. 'Aye, lass, but I hope you're not going to present me with as many as her.'

The two women shook with mirth, their happy laughter mingling with the wondrous sound of the newborn baby's wails.

Some time later, when Mrs Harris had washed her and the baby, and both were lying in clean linen, the infant in the crook of Esther's arm, they heard the back door slam and Matthew's voice. 'Esther. Esther! Where are you, woman? Where's me dinner?'

Ma Harris lifted the latch on the bedroom door and went out on to the top of the stairs. 'Matthew,' she called down. 'Ya'd best come up here.'

Esther heard her husband come to the bottom of the stairs. 'What? Oh, it's you,' she heard him say, then she heard his heavy footsteps mounting the stairs, almost reluctantly, it sounded to her. Ma Harris popped her head round the door.

'Ah'll be away now, lass, but Ah'll be back later. An' dun't you fret, our Ernie'll see to the milking and the dairy work.'

Her head disappeared and Esther heard her say to Matthew, 'In ya go, lad, Ah'll let her tell ya 'ersen.'

Slowly the bedroom door was pushed wider open and Matthew stepped into the room. Esther looked up at him and smiled. His face was expressionless as his glance passed over her and to the small bundle, now quietly asleep, in Esther's arms.

'You have a daughter, Matthew.'

She saw his mouth twist into a wry smile. 'Huh, is that all ya can give me? A girl! What use is a girl?'

Esther gazed at him, conflicting emotions struggling

on her face. But she said nothing. His reaction to her news had, for once, left her quite stunned and bereft of any answer.

He sniffed and passed the back of his hand across his mouth. 'Well, 'tis a good job someone's given me a son, ain't it? What good is a girl to any man?'

He turned and went out of the bedroom.

Esther laid her cheek against the soft ginger-coloured down of her baby girl's head. Her eyes glistened with unshed tears at his unkindness. Yet suddenly his brusque words reminded her of Sam Brumby on the day of her arrival here, and a smile trembled on her mouth at the memory.

She rubbed her cheek gently against the baby's head. 'That's what I'll call you, my little one. I'll name you after old Sam's sister, Katharine. Though perhaps,' she added reflectively, 'Kate would suit you better. Yes, that's it. Kate Hilton.'

The baby stirred, wriggled a tiny finger in the air, and slept on.

Seventeen

TOWARDS the end of November, a sudden storm blew up. Lightning split the sky and thunder crashed directly overhead. High winds gusted the sea into a fury and the farmers rushed out to tie down their stacks before the wind tore them apart and scattered them. Doors and windows rattled and the cows moved towards the gateway leading from their field into the farmyard as if pleading for shelter.

'Let 'em in the yard, Matthew,' Esther said, 'an' leave the cowshed door open. Poor things. They don't like the wind. Neither do I, come to that,' she added, shuddering. It was the only weather she really didn't like. She hated the way the wind clattered the roof tiles and shook the doors and windows. It sounded a live, vengeful, relentless being that wrought damage and disaster.

'Sneck the door and come away in to the fire,' she begged Matthew at dinner time as the wind howled around the lonely farmhouse. 'Ya can't do much out there in this lot until milking time. The bairn won't stop crying. I reckon the wind is bothering her, too.'

Matthew slapped his hands together and blew on them to warm them, before sitting down on the wooden chair near the range to pull off his boots. He glanced towards the wicker cradle in the corner of the kitchen and then grinned up at Esther. 'Her wind, or the gales, d'ya mean?'

Esther laughed. 'Fool!' she chafed him, but secretly she was pleased. It was the first time he'd made any sort of comment about the baby or taken any notice of her. Ever since her birth, Matthew had ignored her existence, even though the child had played her part in trying to arouse some sort of response from him by crying half the night. Resolutely he always turned over in their bed, pulled the covers over his ears and left the child to Esther.

'I mean that racket outside. It's enough to upset anyone.' Esther shuddered. 'I pity anyone who's got to be out in this lot when it gets dark.'

They had eaten their midday meal and Esther was scuttling backwards and forwards between the kitchen and the draughty scullery with the pots, whilst the wind battered at the back door and blew in underneath it, when they heard a loud knocking.

Esther turned wide eyes on Matthew. 'What . . . ? Who . . . ?'

'How should I know, woman? Go an' answer it.'

The wind snatched the door out of Esther's hand as she unsnecked it, and almost lifted their visitor bodily and blew him into the house.

'Ernie!' Esther exclaimed. 'Whatever's the matter?'

'Where's the mester?' the boy panted, his eyes dark with anxiety.

Esther pointed into the kitchen and then followed Ernie as he went through.

'Hello, Ernie. What's up?' Matthew asked.

'Me dad sent me to ask ya . . .' He paused, shifting uneasily from one foot to the other.

'Yes,' Matthew prompted. 'What?'

'Well, he knows – well, he feels awk'ard asking you like . . .'

'Get on with it, Ernie.'

The words came out in a jumbled rush. 'It's Mester Eland. His fishing boat's about two miles offshore with a distress signal hoisted . . .'

Matthew was on his feet in a moment.

'He's out cod-fishing. Two fellers on the front saw his sails whipped away by the wind. Nobody knows what to do, 'im being coxswain, like. Me – me dad wants to launch the lifeboat. It'll be hard work rowing in these seas, he ses, and – well – he needs you to – to make up the number.'

Matthew and the boy stared at each other whilst Esther gasped aloud. 'No, oh no, not in this lot!'

'Shut up, Esther, and go and get the 'osses ready. We'll need them, and ours are nearer than going all the way to Willoughby's. Ernie, run and tell yar dad and the others to get up to the station and I'll come with me 'osses.'

Ernie's eyes glowed. 'Me dad says I can come on the boat if you agrees?'

Matthew regarded the young lad steadily for a moment. 'You sure?'

Ernie nodded, unable to speak with excitement.

'Right, then.'

Esther opened the back door and bent her head to the wind. 'Fancy being fool enough to go fishin' in this weather,' she muttered to herself. To be fair, she realized, the gales had blown up suddenly and unexpectedly. At milking time that morning, which would have been roughly when Robert Eland had set sail in his boat, the weather had been deceptively calm.

Punch and Prince were reluctant to leave the warmth of their stable. They flattened their ears and bent their heads as Esther pulled on their harness and then coaxed them outside. They tossed their heads and clattered their hooves on the cobbles and tried to pull backwards into the stable again.

'Stand. *Stand!*' she bellowed, but the wind whipped the words from her mouth and hurled them away. Matthew appeared in the yard dressed in warm clothes. He came close to her, his mouth against her ear, so that she could hear him above the gale. 'Ya'll have to give me a leg up.'

She bent down and cupped her hands and as he put his knee in them, she hoisted him on to the back of the nearest horse. Taking the reins of both horses in his hands, he urged them out of the yard and turned to the left up the lane towards the boat-house set in the dunes nearer the town.

Esther shivered and went back into the house to be met by the wails of her baby girl. She picked her up and opened the front of her blouse for the child to suckle, crooning soothingly. For once, however, Esther's thoughts were not on her hungry child, but on her husband.

As dusk fell the wind seemed to get even stronger, raging around the lonely farmhouse as if it would pluck it from the ground. Esther laid the now sleeping child in her cradle in the corner of the kitchen and pulled on her coat and boots. She checked the fire in the range and then went out into the wild night and across the yard to the byre. The cows were huddled together wild-eyed and restless, disturbed by the storm. With a calmness she did not feel inside herself, Esther crooned softly to each of the beasts in turn, dreading the moment when she would come to Clover who, in the end stall, was already lowing and stamping her feet. But strangely, when Esther came at last to the stall, and ran her hands caressingly over Clover's rump and uttered guttural noises deep in her throat, the animal seemed to quieten at once. The wind still rampaged and rattled the door and the rafters, yet inside the cowshed it seemed safe and warm. Docilely, Clover stood to be milked and as Esther rose and moved the milk away, the cow turned sorrowful eyes upon her.

'I know, old girl, I don't like this storm either, but ya'll be all right snug and warm in here for the night. I aren't going to turn you out into the field.'

Esther chuckled as the cow, seeming to understand, turned back to pluck some hay from the stall and chewed on it placidly.

Back in the kitchen where her baby slept soundly now, Esther threw more wood on the range fire and warmed her chilled body. She had quietened her child and soothed the restless animals. Now that there was nothing to busy herself with, it was Esther who felt unsettled and worried. There had been no word of how the rescue was going. Every nerve in her body seemed to be twitching so that she could not keep still. She paced the small space that was the hearth, walking across to the cradle and back again to the fire, hugging her shawl around her for comfort as much as for warmth.

Why didn't someone come and tell her what was happening?

She paced the floor again. It was no good. Afraid as she was of the storm, it was far worse waiting here alone and not knowing what was going on. She glanced across at the cradle and bit her lip with indecision. There was no way she could take the child down to the shore on such a wild night, nor could she leave her here alone in the house.

The waiting was dreadful. In the darkness with the storm still raging round the farmhouse, Esther's imagination ran riot. What if they were all drowned – Robert Eland and the men who had tried to rescue him? What a devastating effect it would have on this small community. Only widows and fatherless children would be left, and poor Ma Harris, she would lose both husband and son.

'I know,' she said aloud at the thought of Ma Harris, 'she'll look after her.'

If she wrapped the baby warmly, Esther told herself, and carried the wicker cradle to the cottages at the Point, Ma Harris would keep an eye on Kate, just for an hour or so whilst Esther went down to the beach.

'I can't bear this dreadful not knowing what's happening any longer,' she muttered.

Once her decision had been made, within minutes Esther was pulling the door to behind her. Hugging the cradle close to her, she struggled against the wind along the lane towards the Point and Ma Harris's cottage.

The door was opened reluctantly by a thin-faced girl of about fourteen or so. It was 'our Enid' as Ma always called her. Esther smiled, 'Is yar ma in?'

The girl shook her head. 'Naw, she's gone to the beach to see if she can see me dad . . .'

'Aren't they back yet?'

Another shake of the head.

'Oh.' For a moment Esther was uncertain.

'What did ya want?' the girl ventured.

'I – I just wanted to go to the beach mesen, and I wondered if Ma – if ya mother – would keep an eye on the bairn for me.'

The girl's white face broke into a smile. 'Ah'll look after her, missus.' She opened the door wider inviting Esther to step inside. 'The young 'uns are all in bed, so they'll not disturb her and . . .' She led the way into the living kitchen and pointed to another cradle set on a chair in the corner by the range, 'Ah'm already looking after young Danny.'

Esther stopped abruptly in the doorway and drew breath sharply. She had never stopped to think that she might encounter Matthew's other child.

'Come in, missus,' the girl was saying, her eyes on Esther's face. 'It'll be all right, honest it will.'

Esther managed a weak smile, torn by conflicting emotions. She could hardly retreat without looking foolish, and she couldn't bear to return home to continue that awful, lonely waiting.

She sighed and came to a decision. Living so close, she could not hope to avoid meeting the Eland family for ever, she supposed. Pressing her lips together she stepped determinedly into the room and placed her cradle on a chair in the opposite corner of the room. She stood a moment looking towards the other cradle.

'Want to have a look, missus?' Was there a note of slyness in the young girl's voice? Did she know the full story? Esther sighed inwardly. She supposed so, and thought ruefully, who around here didn't know?

Esther nodded and stepped closer as Enid drew back the blanket from the baby.

'He's a grand lad. Black hair, 'ee's got, and the darkest brown eyes you ever saw in a bairn. He'll break a few hearts when he's grown.'

Esther said nothing as she looked down upon the child and saw for herself that there was no mistaking who his father was. Matthew could never have denied his paternity of this boy even if he had wanted to, nor could anyone else. She felt a moment's pity for Robert Eland who seemed to be the only really innocent person in all of this.

She turned away abruptly. 'I won't be long, but I – I just have to go and see . . .'

The girl nodded understandingly.

Leaning into the howling wind, Esther dragged herself up the last dune. As she ran down the other side and on to the beach, she gasped in surprise. There was a large crowd gathered on the sands, several holding lanterns so that the lights shivered and shook in the wind, but showed a welcoming light for the lifeboat to come home.

Esther threaded her way amongst the crowd, glancing

into the dark faces for someone she knew. Before them huge waves crashed on to the sand and rushed up the beach. People were standing near the water's edge, but from time to time were driven back when the waves raced towards them.

'Esther, lass, over here.' In a brief lull in the noise of the wind, she heard Ma's voice calling to her. Esther looked about her and then felt a grip on her arm and turned to see Ma's face, for once not beaming, but serious and anxious.

'Is there any news?' Esther put her mouth close to Ma's ear. 'What's happening?'

Ma lifted her shoulders and shook her head. 'We dun't know nothing. Hours they've been gone now.'

It was then that Esther saw Beth standing a little apart from the rest of the crowd; a silent, motionless figure, hugging her shawl around her and gazing steadfastly out across the black, heaving waters.

Who, Esther wondered, filled Beth's mind? Whose safety twisted at her heart? Her husband's – or Matthew Hilton's?

'A light! There's a light – I saw it,' someone in the crowd shouted. Suddenly there was a buzz of excitement and everyone moved forwards, craning to see.

'There! There it is, did you see it? Only a flash, but it was there.'

'Aye, I saw it. Come on, lads, they'll want a hand.'

Men moved forward out of the crowd, splashing into the thundering waves, reaching with willing hands to help the boat – whatever boat it was – coming ashore. Then Esther saw the lifeboat, riding the crest of a wave, being borne almost on to the beach and coming to rest finally in the shallows. Urgent hands grasped the boat and held it steady, reached in to help the crew climb out. Strong shoulders were offered to the cold, exhausted men of the lifeboat. The onlookers surged nearer, holding their lanterns aloft to give more light.

At that moment Esther saw Matthew.

He was half-carrying, half-dragging Robert Eland ashore, his arms grasping him strongly about the waist. Robert Eland's arms were draped about Matthew's neck and his head lolled forward in a semi-conscious state. Esther did not need to be told that a few more hours out in his boat would have been the death of Robert Eland.

She saw Beth waiting, still standing in the same place on the sands. Beth had not moved even a step forward. In the eerie, flickering light from the lanterns, Esther could see Beth's gaze fixed upon Matthew as he brought her husband back to her from the sea.

As Matthew drew near to Beth, even from here Esther could feel the intensity of their gaze upon each other. She saw Beth reach out with fingers that shook towards the two men. But to whom she was reaching in that tentative, thankful gesture, no one could have said, for her gaze never left Matthew's face. When he gently gave over her husband into her arms, and watched as she took the man's full weight upon herself, it was Matthew's face Beth reached up and touched. Matthew grasped her hand and held it to his cheek for a timeless moment before the crowd surged forward to help, and they were forced to draw apart.

'Here, lass, let us help ya.'

'Is he alive?'

'Matthew — you're a hero. Ya mun be exhausted ya'sen, lad.'

'Here, drink this, Matthew, 'tis rum. 'Twill warm ya.'

'The doctor, get the doctor for Robert Eland.'

Unobserved, Esther slipped away from the back of the crowd, the dark beach enfolding her as she hurried away to collect her child from Ma Harris's and be home before Matthew.

She would never, she vowed, tell him that she had even been on the beach. She could never tell him what she had seen pass between Beth and him that night.

For a while Matthew basked in the glory of being a hero. The local paper recounted the courageous rescue and stated quite categorically that Matthew Hilton, and the rest of the lifeboat crew, had saved Robert Eland's life. It was Matthew, the paper reported, who had plunged into the icy waters and battled his way through mountainous seas to Robert Eland's little boat when they found it drifting helplessly towards a sandbank. Robert Eland, weak with exhaustion and only semi-conscious, could not rouse himself to climb into the lifeboat as it had come alongside in such treacherous, swelling seas. Had it not been for the bravery of Matthew Hilton, the small fishing boat would have been grounded on the sandbank and probably would have capsized, plunging the fisherman to his death. The journalist who wrote the report was unstinting in his praise, though of course he knew nothing of the strange connection between the two men which, had he but known, made the gallant rescue even more praiseworthy.

From that night, Matthew was welcomed back into the lifeboat as a permanent member of the crew. He was fiercely proud of the place he had earned in the lifeboat and even though there was still guarded wariness between Robert Eland and Matthew, whenever there was a shout the two men seemed able to leave their differences ashore. Esther found this difficult to understand and yet she could not help but feel a grudging admiration for men who could hate each other and yet still work as a team to help someone else in distress.

From the time that Matthew had undoubtedly saved his life, Robert, magnanimous in his own quiet way, came back to help out with the harvest on Brumbys' Farm. Matthew still went down to the Seagull at the Point from time to time but he caused no more drunken scenes and whilst they never could be friendly towards each other, there seemed to be an uneasy truce between the two men.

Esther did not know – nor did she enquire – whether or not Matthew ever saw Beth and his son, Daniel. Esther had her own growing child now and always she had the farm.

Through the months that followed, they settled into a routine. Matthew, despite his bitterness against her which sometimes surfaced, nevertheless worked very hard on the farm – and his physical need of her never diminished. Even though now words of love never passed his lips, he still wanted her as much as he had ever done. As for Esther, although she had never pretended to love

Matthew, she had believed that they could find some sort of happiness together. But resentment had changed Matthew and now Esther knew herself to be locked in a loveless marriage.

Nevertheless, she reminded herself resolutely, she had what she had always told herself she wanted most – a place of her own and a family. Now she had someone to cherish and to love – her baby daughter.

If Matthew took little interest in his daughter, there was someone else besides Esther who made up for his deficiency.

From the moment he saw Esther's child, Will Benson was besotted by the little girl. Whenever his cart drew into their yard, it became a ritual for him to climb down and go in search of Kate. Finding her, he would pick her up and, as she grew, offer his pockets for her to delve into with her tiny hands and searching fingers. She would giggle and pull out sweets and pretty ribbons and trinkets one after the other.

'You spoil her, Will,' Esther would admonish, but she would smile as she said it. It was difficult not to spoil the bright-eyed child, though she was not always as cherubic as she appeared to Will. Sometimes there were childish tantrums if she did not get her own way, and it was left to Esther to administer the sharp smack of correction. At such times, Matthew would frown and turn away, irritated by Kate's naughtiness.

'She only does it when you're around,' Esther would say. 'She does it to get your attention. If only you would take a little notice of your own daughter sometimes . . .'

Matthew would be gone, slamming the door behind

him. With Will Benson, however, Kate had no need to provoke his attention – it was hers without asking. For him, Kate was all smiles and dimples and angelic behaviour. He fussed over Kate like a hen with one chick and when she began to walk it was as if he would like to cocoon her against all hurt.

'Should you be letting her play in the yard, Esther?' he asked one bright, breezy washing day, when Esther let the child play whilst she moved between the wash-house and the clothes line in the front garden. 'Won't she get dirty?' A worried frown creased his forehead.

Esther laughed as she slapped the wet clothes on to the mangle and turned the handle rapidly, the suds flowing back into the dolly tub. Then the garments fell into the cold rinsing water in a tub on the other side of the mangle. 'A little dirt won't hurt her. Let her play,' and added softly as she remembered her own harsh childhood, 'children need to play.'

'But what about the pond? What if she fell in?'

'Oh, I'll mind she doesn't get near that,' Esther promised him. 'I'll have it fenced off by she's really walking.'

The subject of their conversation turned solemn eyes from one to the other as they spoke and Esther smiled as Will squatted down and pulled a tiny doll from his jacket pocket. At once Kate scrambled to her feet and tottered towards him, her chubby hands outstretched. A smile of satisfaction spread across his face.

Esther shook her head. 'I dun't know, Will Benson, you've a way with the women even yet,' she teased him, as he swung Kate up into his arms and walked round to the front of the house with Esther as she carried a basket of wet clothes to hang on the line.

'Eh, lass, I ain't been round the front here lately. You've done wonders with this garden.'

The trees had been pruned and promised apples and pears and plums in a few weeks, and the grass beneath had been neatly cut. At the far end, an oblong had been dug to make a kitchen garden and already Will could see potatoes, cabbages and carrots growing.

So the year of 1913 and the first half of 1914 passed peacefully enough for the small community of Fleethaven Point and Brumbys' Farm prospered under Esther's hard work and common sense.

It was a time of calm before the storms that were to follow; storms that were to tear asunder the fabric of their lives.

Eighteen

AFTER morning service on that first Sunday in August 1914, Esther was gratified that not only did the vicar now greet them warmly, but the squire took the trouble to stop and shake Matthew's hand and ask how they both were and was everything going well on the farm. 'Old Sam would have been very pleased, very pleased,' he boomed. 'Almost three years now, isn't it? It doesn't seem it. How time flies.' He smiled benignly down at Kate's upturned face and tickled her under the chin. 'What a sweet child.'

Kate dimpled at him and pulled in her chin playfully, already artful in the ways of attracting and receiving attention. The squire looked up and winked at Matthew. 'And plenty of time to add to the brood, eh Hilton?'

He glanced back with pride at his own two sons escorting their mother from the church. 'Nothing like family life, Hilton. Nothing in the world to beat it. My eldest boy is going up to Oxford in October. We've just heard he's got a place.'

Matthew nodded as if he fully understood and murmured, 'That is good news, sir,' and hoped it was the right thing to say. There was no mistaking the pride in the squire's voice that must suggest a great achievement on the part of his son.

'What's he mean, "going up to Oxford"? It's a place,

ain't it?' Esther whispered as the squire passed out of earshot.

Matthew shrugged his broad shoulders.

'I'll ask Will,' Esther murmured, 'he'll know.'

She was smugly satisfied to see that the Willoughbys, walking down the aisle only a few paces behind the squire and his family, could not have failed to overhear the conversation, but as usual Martha Willoughby and her sister swept past them, holding their skirts with delicacy and all but sticking their noses in the air.

Walking home, Matthew said, 'It's a Bank Holiday tomorrow, Esther. I'll tek ya on the pier.'

She looked at him, their eyes on a level for Matthew was no taller than she was. 'The pier? What's the pier? I ain't never seen one. Where is it?'

He stopped in surprise and turned to face her in the lane. 'Dun't ya know what a pier is? Why, we've a fine one off the main beach,' he said, jerking his head backwards towards the town. He looked at her closely. 'You pulling my leg, Esther? You must have seen it.'

She shook her head. 'No, honest.' She gave his arm a little shake. 'Tell me, Matthew.'

They walked on slowly. 'Well,' Matthew began hesitantly. He was not adept at describing things. 'It's a long wood and iron thing built out into the sea. Ya can walk down it, an' at the end is a saloon where they have music concerts on a Sunday afternoon. I 'spect there'll be one tomorrow too. I thought you might like to go.'

'I've heard of concerts, Matthew, but I've never been to one. I'd love to go, I really would.'

202

'Well, we'll go, Esther,' Matthew said generously. 'We'll go tomorrow.'

'Have you been before?'

The moment the question was asked, Esther realized her mistake, for his eyes clouded over and his brow creased in the familiar frown. 'Yeah, a few years back,' he muttered shortly.

He must have taken Beth, Esther thought, and now I've reminded him of her. She sighed inwardly. It was not the first time during the three years of their marriage that she had unthinkingly said something that had reminded him of Beth, or his son, Daniel. It was impossible to go through life trying to avoid saying or doing anything that would remind him of them. So in the end, Esther had given up worrying. How could any of them ever forget when they all lived so close to each other? They just had to live with it.

Esther had thought that Matthew would forget his promise to take her on the pier, but the following morning he said, 'Well, aren't you ready? You're not going into town dressed in yar pinny, are ya?'

'What?'

He was already dressed in his Sunday best suit, the gold watch-chain looped proudly across his chest. With a great play at being a gentleman, he pulled the watch from his pocket and let it rest in the palm of his hand. He looked at it, then lifted it to his ear to listen to its tick. 'Get a move on, Esther, if Ah'm taking you to the pier, else it'll be dark by we gets there.'

Esther's eyes glowed with excitement as she hurried

upstairs to put on her best dress and bonnet and to dress Kate.

So on Bank Holiday Monday, the third day of August 1914, a hot summer day, with just a light, friendly breeze blowing in from the sea, they walked towards the town along the lane that was now so familiar to Esther. Kate walked a good distance on her sturdy legs, but when she cried that she was tired, it was Esther who humped her on to her hip and carried her.

When they reached the outskirts of the town, Matthew turned up one of the avenues leading to the dunes, through a pathway bordered by prickly sea-buck-thorn and on to the beach itself.

Esther gasped at the sight before her. In the distance she could see the pier, a long arm extending right out into the water, with a building at the end. She could see tiny ant-like figures moving along the pier. Then on the sands there were roundabouts and swings and stalls sell-ing whelks and mussels.

A smile curved her lips and she gripped Matthew's arm. He laughed at her excitement; she was just like a child on a Sunday treat. Wasn't that just what she was? A child who had never known anything but cuffs and knocks and hard, grinding work, with never a moment given over to sinful pleasure, as her aunt would have called this outing. But Esther wasn't giving a thought to her aunt today. Today was for fun.

'What is it, Matthew? What are all these people doing on the beach? Won't the tide come in and wash away their stalls and such?'

'The sea dun't come up this high, not in summer.

204

Mebbe in winter or spring when the real high tides come and the winds whip 'em up too. But these folks is all gone by the winter. These are summer folk.'

'Look at all these people – where are they all from? From the town?'

Matthew laughed again. 'Naw, they're the holiday-makers and the day trippers. They come on the trains.'

Esther shuddered. 'Ah dun't like trains.'

'Why, have you been on one, then?'

'Not me!' she cried. 'But the railway ran through the village where I lived before. Great noisy thing – an' dangerous too. Killed a sheep once.' That, to Esther, was sacrilege.

'Ah've never bin on a train,' Matthew mused. 'Ah'd like to tek a ride on one some day.'

'Well, dun't ask me to come with ya,' she said resolutely, and Matthew laughed at her again. She did not take offence but laughed with him. They wandered around the stalls, watching the folk. Women dressed in their Sunday best and carrying parasols, their long skirts sweeping the sand; the men sweating in their dark suits and starched white collars and bowler hats. A little boy, dressed in a sailor suit, skipped past them bowling a hoop. A small girl in a frock with such stiff petticoats that she hardly dared to move, walked sedately by her mama. Esther watched the child enviously, imagining her Kate in such a pretty dress. But the subject of Esther's daydreams lay heavily in her arms now, asleep against her shoulder, oblivious to all the shouting and laughter of the holiday-makers.

'Look,' Matthew pointed out to sea. 'See the paddle

steamer just leaving the landing-stage at the end of the pier. It takes trips out to sea. D'ya want to go?'

Esther shook her head. 'I'll keep me feet on dry land, Matthew, if it's all the same to you.'

Matthew shrugged. 'I dun't mind. I gets all the sailing I want on the lifeboat.'

They walked on in silence for a time, watching the crowds thronging the beach and the pier. Merry laughter filled the air and the shouts of children at play mingled with the sounds of the sea.

'Come on, let's go on the pier then,' Matthew said and, taking hold of her hand, he led her up to the entrance, through the barrier and out on to the pier, laughing as Esther caught at her bonnet which was in danger of being whipped from her head. 'The wind seems stronger out here,' she gasped.

They walked on and soon the waves were breaking beneath them. Esther looked down between the gaps in the planking to see the water swirling below. She clung tightly to Matthew's arm. 'Oooh, I feel as if I might fall in.'

'Dun't be daft, woman, how could ya fall through them little cracks?'

Esther grinned at her own foolishness. 'I know, but – but it *feels* as if I could.'

She shifted the sleeping Kate to a more comfortable position and the child stirred and whimpered. She rubbed her eyes, gave a huge yawn and then smiled prettily at her mother. She wound her chubby arms round Esther's neck and pressed her pale pink cheek to her mother's.

'Mamma,' she murmured.

Esther patted the child's back. 'There's my clever girl.'

At her side she felt Matthew stop suddenly and having moved on a pace herself, she stopped and turned to look back at him. He was staring at the child incredulously. 'She's talking. She – said a proper word.'

'Well, I should hope so!' Esther pretended indignation. 'She's almost two.'

Matthew moved closer. Kate turned her face towards him and smiled, her cheeks dimpling, her green eyes laughing and her red baby curls dancing in the breeze. She unwound her arms from her mother's neck and, with a child's artfulness, held them out to her father. 'Dadda, Dadda.'

Matthew's gasp was audible. 'She – she called me Dadda,' he exclaimed unnecessarily.

Esther almost giggled but then as she watched the softening expression on Matthew's face, her mirth turned to a deep pleasure. Matthew reached out to take the child from her. He held her carefully, almost like a china doll, his large hands encompassing her waist. He lifted her up to look at her properly. The child gurgled and laughed and repeated the word that had won her such attention. 'Dadda, Dadda.'

Matthew grinned suddenly and settled his daughter in the crook of his arm. 'Ah'll carry her for a bit, if you like. She must be heavy for you after a time.'

'She is,' Esther admitted and eased her aching shoulders thankfully.

They could hear the music from the saloon now, music such as Esther had never heard before. Inside, they sat down to listen to the sweet melodies from violins and then a man with a strong, vibrant voice began to sing. She couldn't make out the words, but she enjoyed watching him waving his arms and closing his eyes and tossing his head. He knows what he's singing about, she thought, even if I don't. Then at the end everyone stood whilst the orchestra played 'God Save the King' and even some members of the audience were singing now, Esther noticed. Then it was over and they all went out once again on to the pier. It was cooler now than when they had gone in, and the breeze was even stronger so that Esther had to hold on to her bonnet and bend her head against the wind.

'We'd best get back, Esther. Looks as if it could turn to rain.'

Esther smiled up at him. 'It'd be worth a soaking. I don't know when I enjoyed mesen so much.'

Playfully Matthew doffed his hat towards her and made a little bow. 'We aim to please, ma'am.' Then, still carrying Kate in one arm, he put the other around Esther's waist and held her close to him as they hurried along the pier and towards home.

Esther was to look back on that day with a sense of regret. There had been, on that bright August Bank Holiday, the tentative hope that things could be better between herself and Matthew; that with a little time, they could become a family.

But the happenings in the weeks that followed were to smash any chance they might have had of a lasting happiness.

Nineteen

WHEN Will Benson's cart rattled into the yard on the following Friday morning, Esther called out from the back door, drying her hands on a towel as she went to meet him, 'Whatever are you doin' coming on a Friday? You was only here yesterday.'

Instead of answering her question, he asked her another. 'You heard the news?'

'News? What news?' Esther was shocked by the solemn expression on his face. She couldn't remember ever seeing Will Benson without a smile beneath his moustache and a twinkle in his eyes. 'Will – is summat wrong?'

He climbed down slowly, a folded newspaper in his hand, and came towards her. Fleetingly she thought, something must be very wrong. He hasn't even looked around for Kate, or asked about her.

'We're at war, Esther lass.'

'War? What d'ya mean, war?'

Will unfolded the newspaper he was carrying. 'It's in the paper.' He glanced up at her. 'Dun't you get the local paper that comes out on a Friday?'

Esther shook her head. 'No, I dun't bother with it, though I reckon Matthew sees it at the pub on a week-end. He's sometimes mentioned bits of news – like a lifeboat rescue he was involved in, that sort of thing.' A

209

smile flickered briefly on her mouth, but died when there was no answering response from Will.

He spread the paper out and began to read slowly but unfalteringly. ' "War declared. Note rejected by Germany. The following statement was issued from the Foreign Office at twelve fifteen this morning: 'Owing to the summary rejection by the German Government of the request made by His Majesty's Government for assurances that neutrality of Belgium will be respected, His Majesty's Ambassador at Berlin has received his passports and His Majesty's Government have declared to the German Government that a state of war exists between Great Britain and Germany as from eleven p.m. on August the Fourth.' " '

Esther gasped. 'But – but the fourth – that was Tuesday.'

Will nodded.

'But on Monday, we – we were on the pier with – with all the holiday-makers. We – we had a lovely day . . .'

Will nodded again. 'Ah know, lass, and so did a lot more all over the country, never thinking that the very next day we'd all be at war. Oh there's been talk and rumour for a bit now, but Ah dun't think anyone – well, not the likes of us, anyway – took it serious. But the town . . .' He jerked his head in the direction of Lynthorpe, through which he had just passed. 'It's fair buzzing with rumour and gossip. They reckon there's boats patrolling along the coast. They say Lynthorpe Territorials left by the eight o'clock train this morning and that boy scouts over thirteen are being required for running despatches and such.'

'What will it mean? It – it won't make any difference to us, will it? Not here at the Point?'

'Ah dun't know what it'll mean, lass.' He shook his head sadly. 'It might all be over very quickly, but – ' he sighed heavily – 'on the other hand . . .'

'What?' Esther prompted, her tone sharp with anxiety.

He looked at her with sorrowful eyes and added gravely, 'It could change all our lives.'

They were still standing together, poring over the newspaper and the snippets of news about the war, when Matthew came into the yard a hedge knife in his hand. He had been working in the fields, trimming hedges. His forehead glistened with sweat and there were dark wet stains on his shirt under his arms.

'Ah've just heard. Is it true, Will?' There was an air of excitement about him.

Will nodded and held out the newspaper towards him. Matthew took it eagerly and scoured the page. 'It says there's a rumour there's been a naval engagement off Flamborough Head.' He looked up at Will. 'That's up north from here, ain't it, on the Humber?'

Will nodded. 'Aye, just north of the mouth of the Humber.'

Esther glanced in the direction of the sea, as if she suddenly expected to see soldiers appearing over the sand dunes and advancing in steady lines across the land – her land. She shook herself and said firmly, as if by doing so she could refute the possibility, 'Oh, come in and have a cup of tea, Will. It'll not affect the likes of us.'

Just as she turned away she saw the two men exchange a knowing look. The older man sombre and afraid, the younger with an air of anticipation and exhilaration.

It seemed to Esther that the days that followed were filled with nothing but the talk of the war. Even young Ernie Harris, his eyes bright with excitement, came with news for Matthew.

'The squire's leading a recruiting rally tonight in the town. Shall ya tell the mester for me?'

Esther swung round to stare at him, her eyes dark with anger. 'Ah'll do no such thing, an' you're not to think of going, Ernie Harris!'

He grinned at her cheekily, a newborn confidence in his manner. 'Just try and stop me!'

'You're not old enough, Ernie. Ya can't—' But the boy had turned and was running out of the yard, giving a little hop and jump every so often, capering almost, as he ran home.

Esther shook her head. 'Madness,' she murmured. 'Sheer madness.'.

When Esther found out that her husband planned to attend the recruiting rally in the town on the first of September, she asked Ma Harris if Enid would come to the farm and look after Kate so she could attend too.

'Aye, she can come, lass,' Mrs Harris said, but added doubtfully, 'Yar man'll not like it. Men dun't like women interfering in such things.'

Esther snorted. 'Then he'll have to lump it. If he thinks he's got any grand notion of volunteering, he's got another think coming.'

Instead of laughing, as Esther might have expected,

Ma Harris merely shook her head and sighed. 'Dun't mek a fool of him, lass, ya'll regret it.'

Esther stared at her. 'Ya not letting Ernie go, are ya?'

Ma shrugged. 'Can't stop the young 'uns, lass. Nor the old 'uns, come to that.'

Tuesday evening was clear and fine when Esther watched Matthew walk out of the yard dressed in his best suit, his watch-chain looped across his chest, and set off purposefully in the direction of the town. She saw Ernie Harris running down the road from the Point, saw him draw level with Matthew and fall into step beside him. She watched them until they turned a bend in the lane and were lost from her sight. At that moment, Enid arrived to sit with Kate, and Esther put on her coat and hat. Pulling the back door to behind her, she set off across the yard. As she drew level with the barn she heard footsteps in the lane and, not wishing to be seen, she hid behind the corner of the building, peeping out to see who it was. She almost gasped aloud. A group of men from the Point, all dressed in their Sunday best, were walking towards the town. She spotted Robert Eland with the landlord of the pub. There was Mr Harris and Beth's father, Dan Hanley, too.

Esther clicked her tongue with exasperation. Now she would have to wait until they were well up the lane before she could set out. When they too had taken the curve in the road, she left her hiding place and followed them at what she hoped was a safe distance.

'Esther – Esther, lass. Wait for me!'

She turned to see Ma Harris hurrying towards her as

fast as her little round body would allow. 'You going to the meeting, lass?'

Esther nodded grimly. 'I don't want Matthew to see me though.'

'Huh, I don't want my old man to see me either,' Ma Harris replied with feeling, but tonight there was no toothless grin, no attempt at humour.

On a green stretch of grass on the sea front, a huge crowd had gathered. At one end on a raised dais were a table and several chairs where some of the local dignitaries had gathered. When Esther arrived and joined the throng, weaving her way through the crowd in order to hear better, Squire Marshall was on his feet addressing the meeting, shaking his fist in the air.

'We are fighting for our very existence, for freedom and democracy. In Belgium ordinary men are being shot and their women violated . . .' A horrified gasp rippled amongst the crowd. 'And when they have overrun Europe they will turn upon us, upon Britain. We must unite for God, for our King and for our country . . .'

Cheers broke out all around Esther, as the squire thumped the air with his raised fist. Then he turned and gestured towards a middle-aged man in army uniform, with several medals on his chest. He was introducing him to the crowd. 'We are privileged to have Major Langley with us this evening. He is a recruiting officer for Lincolnshire. Major Langley, I invite you to address the gathering.' The squire almost bowed towards his honoured guest as he rose and stepped forward.

The major's booming voice rang out over their heads, echoing in the dusk of the evening. He entreated all the local men between nineteen and thirty-five to enlist. 'You all stand and sing the National Anthem or Rule Britannia, but now we ask you to prove your patriotism by your sense of duty.' His voice suddenly softened, and yet it still carried out into the night air. 'I pay tribute to the great self-sacrifice of the women of our country during the past few weeks. Bravely, they have waved goodbye to their loved ones who have given themselves – their very lives – in the service of their King and country.'

His voice rose. 'No young woman should allow herself to be seen with a man between the ages of nineteen and thirty-five unless he wears the King's uniform.' A few in the crowd applauded and he leaned towards them. 'For any man who does not wear the uniform will make a rotten lover . . .' the crowd cheered – 'and a very much worse husband.' The cheers grew louder.

Oh, he's clever, thought Esther, he's very clever. First he fosters a sense of outrage by his stories of the violation of women and children in Belgium, then he appeals to a man's pride and sense of honour and as a final weapon he states blatantly that only a man in uniform is worthy of a woman's love and pride. He's making it a matter of a man's virility.

Major Langley was speaking again, issuing a veiled threat. 'If the young men of our country do not answer the call, the same fate will befall our women and children as those in Belgium. I know our fine young men cannot – will not – let that happen!'

Loud cheering and applause broke out and there was a

surge towards the platform as from all sides young men moved forward to volunteer.

To a great roar from the crowd, the squire's elder son, Rodney Marshall, was the first to step up on to the platform and be greeted by a vigorous handshake from the major. The squire beamed and surveyed the crowd, holding out his arm to show off his boy, as if it were the proudest moment in his life.

Others were following, climbing up on to the platform to be greeted by Major Langley.

Esther grabbed Ma Harris's arm. 'Oh no,' she breathed. 'There's Ernie! We've got to stop him.'

Ma Harris, though her eyes were fixed upon her son, remained motionless.

'Come on, Ma. We've got to—'

Ma was shaking her head. 'No, lass,' she said quietly, so softly that Esther had to bend her head closer to hear what she said above the excited hubbub. 'No, let him be. He'll not thank me for interfering. Neither would his dad.'

'Ma, you *can't* let him go. He's not old enough anyway.'

Ma shook her head ruefully. 'That'll not stop him – nor them taking him.'

'Then I'll tell them,' and Esther made as if to push her way through the crowd towards the platform.

''Ere, who you shoving?' The man in front of her turned round to see who was trying to elbow their way through. 'Wait ya turn . . .' When he saw it was a woman, he grinned and his tone changed. 'Hello there, darling,' he leered. 'Want to do ya bit for King and country, eh?'

'Let me through,' Esther said, outraged. 'One of the volunteers on the platform is under age and I mean to stop him.'

'Oho, I can't let you do that, me darling. If the lad wants to go, then—'

'Get out of my way,' Esther spat and pushed the man in the chest with the flat of her hand.

'Esther, don't—' Ma Harris tried to intervene, but no one was listening to her.

At once anger replaced the man's teasing tone and he grasped Esther roughly by the arms. 'Oh no, you don't . . .'

Esther cried out, more in frustration than in pain. She struggled and kicked the man's shins. He gave a yell of pain and those close by now turned round to watch the scuffle.

'Not a German, is he?' some wag shouted, 'having a go already?'

'Let me go!' Esther yelled again.

Suddenly there was Matthew standing before her. The fight went out of her instantly as she looked into his face. His eyes were dark with fury.

'Leave her alone!' Matthew said in a low, controlled voice that held more menace than if he had roared.

'What's it to do with you?' asked the stranger, still holding Esther.

'She,' Matthew said with deliberation, 'is my wife.'

The man let go of Esther as if she had burned him. 'Aw, mate, I'm sorry, I didn't know. I'm sorry . . .' He turned and shouldered his way through the crowd, escaping before the vengeful husband could retaliate.

Matthew was not concerned about the man. He was glaring at Esther, who was rubbing her forearms where the man had gripped her. 'What the hell are you doing here?'

She returned his glare with equal rancour. 'Making sure you don't do anything stupid, like volunteering.'

Colour suffused his face and his eyes bulged. 'Christ, you've got a bloody cheek, woman! You'd do anything – anything to make me look small, wouldn't ya? I've a good mind to go up there this minute and—'

'That's right, mate, you tell 'er. Don't you hide behind a woman's skirts,' a voice from those nearby joined in their quarrel. Neither Matthew nor Esther took any notice.

She put out her hands and took hold of his shoulders. 'Please, Matthew, don't do anything foolish, anything rash. You're needed here, on the farm. You have a family now . . .'

Matthew's mouth twisted sardonically. 'Aye, the farm! Always the farm, isn't it, Esther?'

He brought his arm up and knocked her hands away, twisting out of her grasp at the same time. Then he turned and blundered away through the throng. In a moment he was lost from her view.

'Oh, Esther,' mourned Ma Harris. 'Ya've done it now, lass. He'll join up just to spite ya.'

Twenty

MATTHEW did not join up, but he did not arrive home until the early hours of the following morning, staggering up the stairs to tumble into bed beside her and fall into a state of drunken unconsciousness rather than of sleep.

Talk of the war dominated everyone's conversation and seemed to rule their lives, even though it was happening hundreds of miles away in another country between peoples whom Esther had only heard of in her days at the village school. Foreign places became part of everyday speech, and when lists of casualties began to appear in the local newspaper, suddenly it was very real and very close.

Ernie Harris came to say goodbye, looking somehow bigger, more filled out already. All at once, he was a young man going off to war.

'Oh, Ernie!' In a sudden surge of emotion, Esther put her arms about him and hugged him to her. 'Do you really have to go?'

The boy wriggled with embarrassment at her unexpected display of sentiment. 'I want to go, missus. I'm a soldier now.' His thin face beamed at her as she stood back to look at him. She shook her head sadly and murmured again, 'Oh, Ernie, I – we shall all miss you.'

'I'll be back, missus, when we've taught these Germans a thing or two. Besides, everyone says it'll be over before Christmas.'

As she followed him to the gate, it seemed as if everyone who lived at the Point had turned out to wave Ernie off to war. They shouted after him as he walked proudly down the lane, a slight figure growing smaller and smaller. At the curve in the road, he turned and gave a final wave. Then he was gone. The gathering dispersed, leaving the lonely figure of Ma Harris standing in the road staring at the place where her eldest son had disappeared from view.

Esther went over to her. She put her arm about the older woman's plump shoulders. 'Come and have a cup o' tea with me, Ma.'

It took some considerable urging to make Ma move, but at last she allowed Esther to lead her into the farmhouse.

On the Sunday following Ernie's departure, Esther insisted that they should attend church. As they might have expected, the service revolved round the war. The hymns the rector had chosen were full of patriotic fervour and self-sacrifice, and the prayers appealed for God's help on the side of righteousness and the fight for freedom from oppressors. Stubbornly, Esther refused to mouth the words she could not believe in. However, when the prayers took on a more personal note, and the vicar prayed for all those from this parish who had volunteered, Esther was glad to join in. Fervently she added her own prayers, closing her eyes and pressing her hands together.

As she stood up at the end of the service and looked about the church, she was saddened to see, already, so many empty spaces. The squire and his lady now had only their younger son in attendance, and yet it was their absent elder son who was the main topic of interest. As Squire Marshall passed down the aisle he was stopped at every pew to be grasped by the hand and congratulated.

'A fine boy, Squire.'

'You must be so proud.'

'Good luck to your boy, sir.'

A few pews in front of where Esther, Matthew and Kate were sitting, and on the opposite side, the Willoughbys waited their turn to greet the squire.

'My best wishes to your boy, sir,' Tom Willoughby's voice boomed around the church. 'He does our little community proud and no mistake.'

The squire shook the man's outstretched hand. 'Thank you, Willoughby, thank you.' He nodded towards Martha Willoughby and her sister, Flo Jenkins.

Martha's shrill voice echoed down the church. 'There's some here as might take a lesson from your boy, Squire.' Her glanced swivelled towards Esther and flickered to envelop Matthew. The gathering still in the church had all fallen silent to listen to the exchange. It was as if the congregation was holding its breath.

'And you, ma'am,' Martha was addressing Mrs Marshall. 'What a fine example you have set all women. So brave, so patriotic, ma'am.'

Flo was leaning forward over her sister's shoulder. 'There's some – far be it from me to name names – but there's some who'd keep their men at home, making out they can't be spared from the work on the land.'

Martha nodded vigorous agreement. 'Aye, and the men are all too willing to stay at home. Slackers, they are, ma'am, and worse!'

Flo pursed her already thin lips to a slit. 'Cowards, Squire, that's what *we'd* call them. Cowards!'

A gasp rippled through the listeners and shocked whispering broke out. Beside her Esther heard the hiss of Matthew's breath and felt it on her cheek.

It sent a shudder of premonition down her spine.

She turned to look at him and saw that colour had suffused his face and that his dark eyes were fixed upon the Willoughby family.

'Take no notice, Matthew. It's all right for her to talk. She's no sons to send and she knows Tom Willoughby's too old to be expected to volunteer. *She* can talk – she's safe.'

Through clenched teeth, Matthew muttered, 'Shut up, Esther. What do you know about it, anyway?'

Irritated and angered by what she saw as a misplaced patriotic fanaticism, Esther swept Kate into her arms and stepped out of the pew. She hurried from the church before the squire and his party had reached them. No doubt that would give the congregation further cause to speculate about her and her family. It was an unheard-of discourtesy for anyone to precede the squire and his family from the church. Even the vicar, as she swept past him, gaped at her open-mouthed and did not gather his wits in time to speak to her before she was down the cinder path and out of the gate.

Esther walked home alone, alternately carrying Kate and getting the child to walk a short distance.

The smell of roasting beef greeted her from the range oven as she stepped into the house. Esther sighed. She doubted her husband would return until very late, and more than likely he would be in no state to eat a Sunday dinner.

At ten thirty that night, Esther was about to turn down the lamp and go up to bed when she heard singing in the yard. She hurried to the back door and opened it. In the bright moonlight, Matthew was standing in the middle of the yard, holding on to the pump for support and waving a bottle in one hand.

' "Rule Britannia, Britannia rules the waves, Britons never, never, never, never . . ." ' He sagged against the pump. 'Hello, Esh-ter. Come and kiss your soldier husband.' He slithered down to sit on the ground propped against the pump.

Esther moved forward slowly. '*What* did you say?'

' "Britons never, never, never . . ." ' he began again.

'No, no, not that. After that.'

His head wobbled from side to side. 'I – I forget.' He took another swig at the bottle as if he wanted to obliterate the remotest chance of remembering.

She took the bottle from him and flung it across the yard with all her strength. It smashed against the hen house and the frightened birds set up such a squawking that it sounded as if a fox had got in amongst them.

223

She bent over him – as always when she was angry, hands on hips, feet spread apart. 'Matthew Hilton, have you gone and volunteered?'

Suddenly he seemed painfully sober. 'I – I think I must have done, Esther.' Slowly from his pocket he pulled a piece of crumpled paper. Awkwardly, he dragged himself to his feet, but Esther made no move to help him. Instead she took hold of his arm roughly and pushed him towards the house. 'Then you'd better go back and un-volunteer.' Inside she steered him into the kitchen. 'Just you sit down there, me lad, and let's have it. Just what have you done in your drunken state?'

Matthew fell back into the wooden chair and passed a hand, which shook slightly, across his forehead. Beads of sweat glistened on his face. 'Oh, Esther, I don't know what I've done.'

'*Have* you volunteered?'

Matthew raised apologetic eyes to look at her. Slowly he nodded.

'Whatever made you do such a stupid thing? You can't go. What about the farm? I can't manage the farm on my own.'

Matthew's smile was without humour. It was a smile of sadness. Soberly now, he said softly, 'You don't need me, Esther. You never did.'

'Of course I need you, Matthew. Don't be so stupid. If you can't think about me and the farm, what about your daughter? What about Kate?'

'Kate?' He spoke her name almost as if he didn't remember who she was. 'Oh, Kate. Well, she dun't need me either. You're mother *and* father to her. We both know that.'

'Matthew, will you stop being so – so deliberately stupid,' she screamed at him.

As her tone grew shriller, his by contrast grew softer and more patient – more resigned to what he had done. 'Stupid? Yes, I'm stupid. At least I was.'

He sat staring into the glowing embers of a dying fire. Esther, stunned by his manner, was quiet now.

'I knew you only married me to get the tenancy of this farm, Esther,' Matthew was saying quietly. 'At least I didn't give much thought to it afore we was wed . . .' The ironic smile twisted his mouth again. He had sobered swiftly, yet he was more talkative, more expansive and confiding than she had ever known him. She sank down on to the rug watching him as he talked, his face half in shadow illuminated only by the red glow from the fire.

'I – ain't been quite fair to you, Esther. I know that now. I blamed *you* for tricking me into marrying you, when really I – I should have married Beth.'

There, it was said now, Esther thought, but she remained silent, sitting on the rug, hugging her knees up to her chest and staring into the glowing coals.

'I wasn't being fair to you, Esther,' he repeated. 'You were right when you said it was me who asked you to marry me. I did – 'cos I was mad to have you. I wanted you as I never wanted anyone before – not even Beth – in that way.' He leaned forward and touched her cheek with unexpectedly gentle fingers. 'Oh, Esther, I still want you – that way.'

She bent her head and for a moment pressed his hand closer to her cheek, but she could not speak.

'But I – I never stopped to really think things out,' he went on. 'Beth was always there, had always been there for me, and – ' he sighed and moved restlessly – 'and daft-like, I suppose I thought she always would be somehow. I never realized, y'see, that Beth was the only one who really loved me.' His voice broke as he added hoarsely, 'I'm sorry, Esther. I've not done right by you – or Beth. Mebbe, just mebbe, I've chance now to prove I'm not all bad.'

She moved then, knelt in front of him and put her arms around him and leant her head against his chest. 'Oh, Matthew, you're not bad, not wicked at all.' She hugged him tight. 'Don't go, Matthew.'

He buried his face in her hair and for once held her close in an embrace that was affectionate rather than lustful. 'Oh, Esther, I've no choice – now. It's too late.' His voice broke on a hoarse whisper. 'Too late.'

They clung together in a timeless moment, closer, now that they were to part, than they had ever been.

The following morning when Esther opened the back door to go out to do the milking she saw that a swirling fog was rolling in from the sea, enveloping the farm, cutting it off from the outside world. How she wished that they could stay like that, cut off from everything outside the farm gate, a little island of their own, safe from the war and the cruel tongues of neighbours that had driven Matthew to prove himself not a coward.

As she finished milking and was carrying the pails

across the yard, Matthew came out of the back door, dressed in his Sunday best suit. Sombrely he met her gaze. Slowly he drew the Hunter watch from his pocket and unhooked the gold chain from his waistcoat. He held it out to her. 'Here, Esther – ' he cleared his throat – 'you'd best keep it till – till I come back.'

Carefully, she set the pails down and took the watch from him. 'Of course, Matthew, I'll keep it safe for you – till you come home again.'

They stared at each other wordlessly.

She saw Matthew swallow, saw him pull in a deep, shuddering breath.

'I'd best be off then.' He tried to smile, but it did not reach his eyes. 'I – I don't want 'em to think I've changed me mind.'

'Have you seen Kate?'

He nodded. 'Aye.' He glanced away and said gruffly, 'Look after her – and ya'sen.'

'Do you want me to come into town with you?' she asked softly.

He shook his head. 'No – no, thanks.'

'You'll write, won't you?'

He shifted his feet. 'I'm not much for writing, Esther. But I'll try to let you know where I am and, well, if I'm all right – if ya want.'

'Of course I want.' She was about to add 'don't be stupid', but for once she bit back the sharp retort in time.

There was an awkwardness between them as if neither knew what to say and yet didn't want the final moment to come.

He bent and picked up the pails of milk. 'I'll carry these in for you.'

Surprised, she merely nodded. She followed him into the house but stood in the scullery whilst he took the milk through to the pantry. She leant against the wall at the side of the window, her hands still cradling the watch. He came back and stood before her.

'I'll be off, then.'

She nodded. 'Take care of yourself, Matthew.'

He nodded and stepped out over the threshold. Esther stood by the window near the back door watching Matthew walk across the yard and out of the gate. She could just see his shape through the swirling mist as he pulled the gate to behind him and turned towards the town. Then she saw him hesitate and stop. Slowly he turned around and took a few steps in the opposite direction towards the Point.

Beth, she thought, he's going to say goodbye to Beth – and to his son.

She saw him falter and stop again. He stood in the lane, a lonely figure, gazing towards the Point, straining to see the Elands' boat home through the mist.

Esther closed her eyes and laid her forehead against the cool glass.

'Oh, Matthew, Matthew,' she whispered.

When she opened her eyes and looked again, he had disappeared from view.

Twenty-one

LETTERS had always been rare amongst the small community at the Point. The arrival of one used to cause anything from delighted surprise to worried consternation, and everyone knew about its coming within minutes, sometimes even before the real recipient.

Now, letters, cards – news of any sort – were eagerly awaited and pounced upon. The first card, delivered by Will Benson on his rounds, came from Ernie Harris telling his parents he was still in training and had not yet heard of being posted abroad.

A month after Matthew had left, a postcard arrived from him addressed to his wife. As Will handed it to her, Esther read the words Matthew had written so laboriously. 'I am well. I hope you are too. Matthew.' As an obvious afterthought, he added at the bottom, 'And the child'.

Esther sighed and a wry smile twitched her lips. Which child was he really thinking about, she wondered. Kate? Or his son who lived in the boat on the river bank?

She pulled the back door wider. 'Come on in, Will, ya dinner's on the table.'

'Eh, ya're a grand lass and no mistake.'

'You've always been good to me, Will. An' I never forget those that's done me good turns.'

Will grinned amiably, and said shrewdly, 'Aye, an' I reckon you dun't forget those that's done you a bad turn either, eh, lass?'

Esther laughed aloud, her bright eyes glinting. 'How well you know me, Will Benson.'

'Aye,' Will murmured more to himself than to her. 'I reckon I do at that.'

Esther handed Matthew's postcard back to Will for him to read. He smiled. 'Not much of a letter writer, is he?'

'No, but at least he's actually written to me.'

They exchanged a glance of understanding. Will nodded but said nothing more, deliberately concentrating on the meat and potato pie she had placed before him. As always, after the first few mouthfuls, Will made a pretence of looking around the room as if he had just remembered. As usual, he said with careful casualness, 'Where's the little one, then?'

It had become a ritual between them. Esther replied, 'Sleeping upstairs, but I'll fetch her down before you go.'

Satisfied, Will nodded. 'I've got a present for her.'

'Oh, Will, really! You spoil the child. You really shouldn't bring her something every week.'

Will grinned. 'Well, if I can't spoil me – ' he cleared his throat and finished – 'me favourite little girl, then I dun't know who can.'

Gently, Esther said, 'Didn't you ever have any children, Will?'

There was a long silence whilst Will kept his eyes downcast, concentrating on his plate as he mopped up the last vestige of gravy with a piece of bread, savouring every morsel. Esther thought perhaps she had trespassed too far on his privacy, that he was going to ignore her question, but at last he raised his head slowly and looked directly into her eyes.

Choosing his words carefully, he said, 'It never happened with me and the wife, and then not very many years after we was wed she – well – she didn't like that side of things. Y'know . . .' Their eyes held together in a steady gaze. 'But she were a good wife in every other way, *every* other way. And I – never wanted to see her hurt. I still don't.'

Slowly Esther inclined her head. 'Yes,' she whispered. 'I can understand that. You're a good man, Will Benson.'

Colour suffused his cheeks and his voice was a little husky with emotion. 'Mebbe I ain't always been.'

Esther stood up, not wanting to embarrass him any further. She grinned. 'Not many of us are perfect all the time, Will. I reckon we're all allowed a little slip now and again.'

Will laughed, blowing away the moments of awkwardness between them.

'I'll go and fetch Kate down to see you.'

Minutes later as she sat her sleepy daughter on Will's knee and watched as he pulled a toy from his pocket, his head bent towards the child, Esther knew for certain what had lain hidden in the recesses of her mind, and her heart, for years. If only Will would say the words she longed to hear. But from their conversation a few moments before, it looked as if she would have to wait a long time – maybe for ever.

There were a number of familiar faces missing at the Harvest Supper that year. All the young men had gone to war, and the last of the harvesting had been left to the old men, the women and children. Esther found herself meeting new people from more distant farms whom the squire had prevailed upon to help, and she in turn had to go some considerable way to help out in turn.

'By, but we're late getting it all in this year. How's things with you?' Tom Willoughby asked her.

'Not too bad, Tom, thanks. We got it all in just before Matthew volunteered.' Her mouth was grim at the memory of that night, nor could she forget the part Tom's wife and sister-in-law had played. Esther was fair-minded enough, however, to know it was none of Tom's doing.

'Come up to my place in the morning, Esther, lass,' Tom was saying, 'and hitch a lift with my workers. We're off to Browns' Farm tomorrow and it's five miles or more. You can't be carrying your little girl that far.'

Esther smiled her thanks and the morning saw her and Kate perched on the front of the wagon beside Tom Willoughby under the malevolent glare of his wife as the cart trundled out of the yard of Rookery Farm. Tom Willoughby never seemed to worry what his wife and sister-in-law said or did. He was far too intelligent, Esther thought, to be ignorant of their mischief-making, but no doubt long ago he had decided that the best way to treat it was to ignore it. Well, thought Esther, if he can then so can I, though inwardly she had to admit that she still felt resentment towards the two women for having goaded Matthew into volunteering.

Esther found that her horses were much in demand too, and she received payment from some of the farmers for their use of Punch and Prince.

'You'm lucky you've still got yar 'osses,' Mr Souter told her. 'They took the team I reckon to borrow from the squire in the first month of the war.'

'What d'ya mean, Mr Souter? Who took them?'

'This government official came – from the War Office, or whatever they call 'em. Commandeered them for service, he said.'

Esther gasped. 'Can they do that?'

'Huh, can they just!' Mr Souter said grimly.

'Well, ya're welcome to borrow mine, Mester Souter.'

'Thank 'ee, Mrs Hilton. I might at that – while ya've still got 'em!'

So it was not quite such a shock for Esther the day a thin-faced, hunch-backed little man with steel-rimmed spectacles and clutching a sheaf of papers under his arm knocked on the back door of Brumbys' Farm.

'I am sorry to inform you that you are required to give up your two farm horses, Mrs Hilton.'

'I ain't no 'osses,' Esther said boldly, but at that moment, Punch decided to kick his stable door.

The man's eyes narrowed and he smiled thinly. 'Really, Mrs Hilton,' he said. 'Well, I am informed—'

'Oh, yes, and who informed you, might I ask?' Esther said belligerently and added beneath her breath, 'as if I didn't know.'

233

The man cleared his throat nervously. 'There is another little matter, Mrs Hilton.'

'Oh, yes.' Her tone was uninviting.

'Yes – it's about your grassland. Meadows.'

'What about it?'

'We need you to plough up some of your grassland for—'

'I ain't ploughing me grassland up and that's final!' Esther's eyes sparkled with defiance and she stood, hands on hips, facing him.

'Well – er – Mrs Hilton – the Government . . .'

'If the Gov'ment want to plough me land up, the Gov'ment can come and do it! And . . .' she added menacingly, 'I'd like to see 'em do it without 'osses.'

'But, Mrs Hilton—'

She flung her hand out to encompass the cows munching happily in the field to the left of the farmyard. 'Where are you goin' to get milk from if the cows ain't no grass to feed on? You tell me that!'

'Er – well, I don't rightly . . .'

'Exactly! I've never heard anything so daft in all me life. An' if I lose me hay harvest, I can't feed my livestock through the winter. If you tek me 'osses, I can't bring either me hay in nor me corn harvest.'

'Well, I do take your point about the grassland, but the horses, I really must insist—'

'And I must insist,' Esther said, her tone heavy with sarcasm, 'that you leave me farm. This is private property.'

'Madam.' The man's tone became lofty. 'There is a war on.'

'Dun't I know it. Where do ya think me husband is? Out in France more than likely, when he should be here helping with the ploughing and the threshing.' She took a step towards him and the little man backed away.

'Well – er – I'll see what I can do. I'll – er – bid you good-day, Mrs Hilton.'

'Good-day, mester.'

Through narrowed eyes, she watched him go.

Early the next morning, as the dawn stretched fingers of light across the sea, Esther led Punch and Prince across the marshland towards the East Dunes. Finding a sheltered hollow, she tethered them to a sturdy elder bush and left them, returning at night to lead them back to the farm to feed and again in the early morning leading them back again into the dunes. So, during the second week when the official came back with two men to lead her horses away, Esther was able to say, quite truthfully, 'They ain't here. They've gone.'

'You mean someone's taken them away?'

'That's right,' she said, deliberately misinterpreting his meaning.

'Well, really,' muttered the little man. 'I really do wish my colleagues would keep me informed of what they're doing. Good day, Mrs Hilton. I apologize for having wasted your time.'

Not until the little man and his helpers were safely out of earshot did Esther laugh aloud. It had been worth all the loss of sleep with her early morning and late night treks to the dunes to keep her horses!

*

Life for Esther had never been easy nor did she expect it to be, but caring for her child, running the farm and helping others in return for their help was beginning to take its toll even upon her strength and determination.

'You're losing weight, lass,' Will told her, and not for the first time, 'and you look tired.'

Esther tried to smile but found that her brave act didn't fool Will Benson anyway. 'I am, Will. I'm very tired,' she admitted to him as she would not have done to anyone else. 'But,' she added stoically, 'what else is there to do? I made me own bed, an' now I'll have to lie in it.'

'Aye, I know, lass, I know. But ya didn't reckon on lying in it on ya own.'

At that moment, Kate came toddling towards Will on her chubby legs, her arms outstretched to him asking to be picked up. Fondly, Esther watched them together, the greying wisps of Will's hair, which still glinted red in the sunlight, close to the bright red-gold curls of the child as she wrapped her arms about his neck.

'You'll never guess, Esther, who came on the cart with me this morning.' Will rocked Kate back and forth in his arms. She chortled and played with his watch chain.

Esther wrinkled her forehead. 'No one I know, was it?'

Will nodded. 'Young Ernie Harris.'

Esther's eyes lit up. 'Ernie! Oh, that is good news. Is he home from the war? Home for good? He's not hurt, is he?'

Will laughed. 'Whoa there, steady, lass.' His face sobered. 'No, he's got a bit of leave because he's to be sent out to France very soon.'

'Sent to France?' Esther's voice dropped to a bewil-

236

dered whisper. 'They can't send him out there. He's not old enough!'

Will shook his head. 'He'll have to go, Esther. He signed up.'

Esther stared at him in disbelief.

Later that day, Ernie arrived at the farm to see Esther. When she opened the back door to his knock she scarcely recognized the young man in army uniform. He seemed to have grown taller and certainly he had filled out. But his face still beamed at her with the familiar grin of Ernie Harris.

"Evening, missus. I couldn't go again without seeing you.'

'Oh, Ernie, how fine you look in your uniform. And how well, too.' She laughed. 'The food can't be as bad as they make out, eh?'

She held open the door as an invitation for him to step inside. He pulled his cap from his head and manoeuvred his pack through the doorway and into the kitchen.

'Are you leaving already? I thought you only came this morning.'

'I did – but I've got to catch the train back tonight.'

'Train! Have you been on a train, Ernie?'

Ernie nodded. 'All the troops are moved about by train.'

So, Esther thought irrationally, Matthew would be getting his longed-for ride on a train. I hope he thinks it's worth it.

Ernie looked bulky and awkward standing in full kit in the cramped space of her kitchen. 'Lynthorpe is a bit of a difficult place to get to by train and be sure to be back in time,' he was explaining. 'I mustn't be late reporting back to camp or I get put on a charge.'

'A charge?'

'Yeah, they're very strict. You have to stick to all the rules and reg'lations. It's a good life, though. I dun't regret going, missus. I'm seeing a bit more of life and I've met some great fellers.'

Esther nodded, her gaze travelling up and down the figure before her.

His eyes were bright with excitement. 'I'm really off to France.'

'You – you want to go?'

'Oh, yes, missus, I do.'

'I – I don't suppose you've seen anything of Matthew?'

Ernie shook his head. 'I did ask about him. We're in the same regiment – the Fifth Battalion the Lincolnshire Regiment – but in different companies. I reckon Mester Hilton's in the same company as Master Rodney, the squire's son. If I ever bump into him, missus, I'll tell him I've seen ya.' There was no mistaking the pride in Ernie's voice as he talked about his regiment.

'Will he – will they be going to France too?'

Ernie wrinkled his forehead. 'I suppose so. I don't know if we all go together or what, but I'll keep a look out for him, missus,' he promised finally.

There was a moment of awkwardness between them before Ernie said, 'I'd best be off. Goodbye. I hopes everything goes well on the farm for you. I've told our Enid to come and help you when she can. I hope that was all right, missus?'

Esther nodded. 'Thank you, Ernie. I'd be glad to have

her.' It would be a little bit of Ernie Harris close to her, she thought.

Esther had been surprised by her feelings after Ernie had gone. She missed him about the farm, missed the help he had given so willingly, and was lost without his cheerful good nature to lighten the days. Especially the days when Matthew had sunk into one of his dark, silent moods.

With an unaccustomed lump in her throat, Esther said, 'Goodbye and – and good luck. Take care of yourself.'

He put on his cap, placing it carefully at the right angle, pride in every movement. 'I will, missus. I'll be seeing you again.'

With a cheerful wave, he was gone. Across the yard and out of the gate, where he turned to wave again and then set off up the lane towards the town.

It was to be the last they saw of Ernie Harris.

Twenty-two

CHRISTMAS that year – the time by which they had all believed the war would be over – came and went. It lacked the usual festive feeling. The adults had to force themselves to make merry for the sake of the children, but a cloud hung over everyone.

A small package came for Esther who, never having received anything like that before, fingered it nervously before opening it. Inside was a Christmas card from Matthew. There were also two copies of a photograph of him in uniform. On the back he had written, 'Some of the lads had their pictures took, so I did too.'

From the photograph, Matthew's solemn face stared up at her. He looked very grand in his uniform. It looked grey on the photograph, but she knew from having seen Ernie that it would be khaki, buttoned up to the neck. He stood stiffly, with his feet set slightly apart, his legs encased to the knees in a sort of bandage – there must be a name for them but Esther didn't know what it was. On his feet were sturdy boots. Well, she thought, Matthew's used to wearing them, but he looks thinner in the face. His eyes, staring straight into the camera, held a scarcely concealed fear. He had been plunged into a strange and violent world, and he must now be seeing sights and experiencing tragedies he had never before imagined even in his worst nightmares. Already he looked a very different man from the one who had left Fleethaven

Point only a few months ago. He looked as if he had aged ten years in as many weeks.

The photographs were identical and Esther wondered why he had sent two. Perhaps it had been a standard fee for so many and, not having had anyone else to send one to, he had sent them both to her.

The thought struck her suddenly, flashing unbidden into her mind. Perhaps he wanted Beth to have one, but did not like to send it to her direct because of Robert Eland.

Esther sniffed. Well, he's had that! she thought with a trace of belligerence and tucked the spare photograph into a drawer, slamming it shut with an air of finality. She carried the photograph of Matthew upstairs. Taking the old picture of Sam Brumby's parents out of its silver frame, she found that the new one of Matthew fitted perfectly in its place. Downstairs again, she stood it on the mantelpiece in the kitchen. Alongside it she placed the pretty Christmas card. It was the first card she could ever remember having received.

She picked Kate up and pointed to the photograph. 'Look, Kate, that's your daddy.'

The child pointed. 'Dadda,' she said obediently. 'Where Dadda?'

'He's away, darling,' Esther murmured. 'Maybe for a long time.' As the child wriggled to be set down to run outside to play, Esther was left staring at the photograph of her husband.

Three months later on a blustery Friday in March, the news made headlines in the local paper which Will

Benson now brought out to the Point each week. Alongside a notice of yet another mass meeting for recruitment with the clarion call to 'Come and Join His Majesty's Forces' were the words:

BRITISH CASUALTIES
Local squire's son and estate worker killed on the same day.

The sad news has reached our town of a tragic loss to our community. Corporal Rodney Marshall, of the Fifth Battalion, the Lincolnshire Regiment, son of Mr and Mrs Marshall of Fleethaven Grange, has laid down his life for his country. Corporal Marshall was one of the first from this district to enlist when Major Langley gave his stirring address at a meeting in the town at the beginning of September last, only a month after hostilities had broken out.

Corporal Marshall was born at the Grange and had attended a boarding school in Lincoln where, only this year, he gained a place at Oxford, which, but for the outbreak of war and his immediate courageous enlistment, he would have taken up last October. A fine young man who undoubtedly had a brilliant career ahead of him, has made the greatest sacrifice of all. Our deepest sympathy is extended to his parents and brother, but we share in their pride at the great sacrifice he has made.

Killed also on the same day and from the same Regiment as Corporal Marshall was Private Ernest Harris, a worker on Squire Marshall's estate.

'Oh, Will.' Esther looked up from the newspaper she held in her hands, having laboured over the printed words, needing to read for herself before she could believe it true. 'Oh, Will, I must go to Ma. Does she know?'

He nodded sadly. 'It were me that told her, lass. Eeeh, but I thought they'd have been told – that they'd have had one of them awful telegrams.' He took off his cap, ran his hand through his greying hair. 'But they hadn't. Oh Esther, lass, they didn't know till I showed 'em the paper.' His eyes were troubled, almost tearful. 'I never thought.'

Esther put her arms around Will and for a moment they clung together. 'Don't, Will, don't. It ain't your fault. It's the – the authorities. They should have told them.'

She felt him shake his head against her and his words were muffled against her shoulder. 'Aye, but there's that many, Esther. That many.'

He pulled away from her gently and patted her shoulder, a little embarrassed at his emotional display.

'What do you mean?' Esther whispered, her eyes wide.

'The main newspapers give lists of casualties every day. I 'eard as how lots of families learn of the death of their relatives that way. Then a telegram arrives a few days later. It ain't really anyone's fault, they're just snowed under with the number that they've to deal with.'

Esther gasped. 'You mean, there's that many getting killed every day?'

Will nodded but could not bring himself to meet her eyes.

Esther sighed. 'Poor Ernie and poor young Rodney Marshall, too,' she added as a dutiful afterthought. She glanced at the clock on the mantelpiece behind which there were now three postcards from her husband. They came about every five or six weeks, always with just the same brief message and whilst Esther had toiled painstakingly over her letters in reply, asking questions, telling him news from home, he had never once answered any of her direct comments.

I wonder, Esther thought to herself, if Matthew is still alive or whether somewhere, sitting on someone's desk, is a telegram waiting to be sent to me?

Ma Harris accepted the news of her son's death in the stoic manner with which she met all life's tragedies.

'I knew when he went, lass,' she told Esther sadly, 'that I might never set eyes on him again. I love all my bairns, lass, all seven of 'em – an' even the two babes in the churchyard that died before they scarcely drew breath . . .'

Esther hadn't known before of that particular heart-break in Ma Harris's life. But now was not the time to be asking.

'But Ernie was me eldest. The man of the family – after his dad. I'll miss him.'

'We all will, Ma, truly we all will.'

There was a memorial service held in the church for the squire's son, Rodney, and where the newspaper had given only two lines to Ernie Harris's death, Mr Marshall, even amidst his own grief, was more generous. He gave explicit instructions to the vicar that the service should give equal recognition to both young men and he sent his own carriage to take Mr and Mrs Harris and all their family to the church.

For the first time in her life, Esther warmed to a member of the gentry, whom she had always believed cared little or nothing for her and her kind. Squire Marshall, his wife and one remaining son sat in their family pew, the empty place beside them a poignant reminder.

Mrs Marshall's sobs could be heard throughout the service. She left the church clinging to her husband's arm, her face, covered by a black veil, buried against his shoulder. By contrast, Ma Harris, though there was deep sadness in her eyes, seemed to be the mainstay of her family, shushing the weeping little girls, Enid amongst them. Taking her husband's arm, she walked down the aisle and out of the church with dignified pride. Her indomitable spirit was battered but certainly not broken.

Now that a soldier's death had touched Esther in the loss of her young friend, her anxiety for Matthew's safety grew. Although cards still arrived from him, they were spasmodic and Matthew never thought to write the date on his cards, so Esther had no way of knowing how long they had taken to reach her. She had no idea where he was, except that he was definitely in France now. Every day she feared the arrival of a telegram, became more afraid for him if the time between his postcards seemed too long. Every week she had to compel herself to read the growing list of casualties in the local paper.

So 1915 passed and soon the war was a whole year old and there was another Christmas to face – this time knowing that Ernie would never come home.

Although her anxiety for Matthew's safety was never far from her thoughts, the farm took up all Esther's strength and time. Another harvest was safely over but there was the ploughing and the threshing through the winter. Without Tom Willoughby's help, Esther doubted she could have coped. He sent men and machinery to help her whenever he could, so that all her ploughing was done to time in readiness for the spring sowing. The squire rarely visited now, but it was understandable, Esther thought. If the gossips were to be believed, it seemed his wife had taken to her sick-bed since the loss of their son and the poor squire had virtually lost his wife too.

Esther was always tired and had no time for anything now except her work and caring for Kate. Yet there was after all a strange security in the changing seasons and the demands of the farm which must be met no matter how she felt. She could not just give up. The war had robbed her of her young friend, Ernie, and had enticed her husband away; she would not allow it to take away her home and her livelihood too. She must keep everything going until Matthew came back . . .

Enid Harris, and now one of the younger boys, Luke, coming up to thirteen, helped her. Willing though the girl was, Enid was not Ernie and certainly she could not do the work Matthew had done. Esther suggested that Enid should take over the dairy work and looking after Kate. The child adored the older girl and began to run after her towards the Point as Enid went home.

The first time it happened, Esther rushed out of the stable where she had been putting the harness on Punch and Prince, and called after them. 'Come back, Katie, you're not to go with Enid just now. She's going home.'

The child pouted and shook her curls, which glinted in the sunlight. 'I want to go an' play.'

'No, stay here.'

'It's all right, missus. She can come and play with our young 'uns. Me ma won't mind.'

Esther bit her lip. She had no objection whatsoever to her daughter playing with Ma's children, but she knew that Danny Eland often played with the Harris brood.

Esther sighed deep within herself. How could she hope to keep Kate and Danny apart for ever when they lived only a few hundred yards from each other and in such a small, self-sufficient community? She bit her lip and wondered what Beth too felt about the matter.

'All right then, but only half an hour, mind.'

'I'll bring her back for her tea, missus,' Enid promised and held out her hand to the child who trustingly put her own small hand into it.

Esther watched them go, then turned away and went back to lead the two horses out into the early spring sunshine. She groomed them, brushing away the last shreds of the winter coats they were shedding until they gleamed.

'My, you pair have got fat through the winter,' she said and was rewarded by Punch tossing his head and butting her gently. She laid her head against the horse's neck, drawing comfort from its warmth. 'I don't know what I'd do without you two now Matthew's gone,' she murmured. Silently, she acknowledged that her husband had indeed done her a favour when he had bought the pair. She drew back and patted their necks in turn.

'But, me lads, it's work for you tomorrow.' Tom

Willoughby had promised to lend Esther his seed drill and another of his horses for sowing the fields at Top End.

She screwed her mouth up thoughtfully. 'I hope he remembers I need at least another feller to help me. That's one thing I can't manage on me own,' she told the two horses as she led them out of the farm gate and along the lane into the first grass field.

It was as she was closing the gate to the meadow and about to turn back towards the farm gate that she saw a distant figure striding purposefully along the lane towards the Point. She stared, straining her eyes to see if she could recognize him. She saw that the man was carrying a pack on his back and that he was in uniform.

'Matthew?' she whispered and involuntarily took a step towards the approaching figure.

It was not Matthew. As the figure came nearer she saw that the man was a stranger to her. He was taller than her husband and his fair hair fell forward in a gentle flick over his forehead. His skin was a smooth light brown, but his face was thin, his cheeks hollowed. As he walked along he seemed to be deep in thought, for he was frowning slightly. As he drew level with her, he looked up and saw her standing there. A smile crinkled his face and lit up his blue eyes.

'Good afternoon, ma'am.' His voice was deep and soft, with a well-spoken gentleness in it. 'I wonder if you can help me?'

Esther ran her tongue over her lips and smoothed her palms down her skirt. She felt suddenly hot and dirty — and ridiculously shy.

'I – I'll try.' Her mouth was dry and her voice came out in a croak.

His face sobered as he said quietly, 'I'm looking for Mrs Harris. I understand the family live at the end of this road?'

Esther nodded. 'The – the end cottage at the Point itself. There's a row of four.'

He smiled again, but there was a sadness that did not leave his eyes this time. 'I've – er – come to see her about Ernie?'

There was a moment's silence between them as they stared at each other. 'Did – did you know him, then?' she asked.

The man nodded. 'I was with him . . .'

Esther drew breath sharply. 'Not – you mean – when he – he was killed?'

The man nodded. 'Yes. I've – er – brought her a letter from him. At least – I wrote down what he asked me to tell her. I've not been able to get here before now, and I particularly wanted to bring it to her myself. I didn't want to just send it. Perhaps I can reassure her' – there was pain in his eyes as he remembered – 'that he didn't suffer – not too much.' His glance flickered away and Esther wondered if he were being quite truthful. But his good intentions could not be doubted.

There was a lump in Esther's throat as she said, 'It's kind of you to come and see Ma . . . I mean, Ernie's mother.'

He shrugged. 'It's no more than we do for each other all the time – out there.' There was a trace of bitterness in the final two words.

Esther did not argue, although she could not imagine Matthew sitting beside a dying boy, listening to his last message home, and then travelling to a remote part of the country to deliver that message in person to his mother.

Esther continued to gaze at the stranger and he returned her trance-like stare. He seemed to be searching for something to say, anything to say, that would keep him here, talking to her.

At last he said reluctantly, 'Well, I suppose I'd better be getting on. Maybe I'll see you when I come back?'

Esther nodded. She was conscious of her ruffled hair, her face shiny with sweat and the smell of horses still on her hands and clothes.

'Thank you for your directions.' He smiled again and began to walk away, glancing back once to give her a cheery wave, to which her hand fluttered nervously in response.

Close by her, just beyond the gate, Punch stamped his feet, lifted his head and whinnied loudly. Esther jumped, startled from her reverie by the sudden noise. She moved slowly down the lane towards her own farm gate, watching the striding figure as he reached the Hump and climbed to the top of the bank. She saw him pause, turn and look back once more towards her. Then he disappeared down the other side and was gone.

Esther hurried into the back scullery and sluiced cold water over her face. She ran lightly up the stairs and brushed frantically at her tangled curls until her hair gleamed. She bit her lip as she glanced down at her working clothes. Pulling open the top drawer of the chest she took out a clean white blouse and a starched pinafore.

He'll be there now, she thought, meeting Ma Harris and being asked into her kitchen. She'll sit him down and bustle about making tea and bringing out scones and cakes, wanting to hear his news, wanting to talk of Ernie and yet putting off the moment, postponing the renewal of the pain the visitor's news must bring.

She'll be sitting down too now, Esther imagined as she went downstairs and stood in the scullery looking out into the back yard, and beyond, into the lane. Ma would sit down at the scrubbed table and face the stranger across it and listen to what he had to tell her about Ernie.

How long would they talk? How long would it take for him to impart his message? And how long afterwards would he stay?

Esther rubbed her palms down her clean apron, turned away from the window and went back into her kitchen, but a moment later she was back at the window. She went outside and stood in the centre of the yard, biting the edge of her thumb uncertainly. She didn't want to intrude, yet she wanted to go down to Ma's cottage.

She wanted to meet the stranger again.

'What on earth's the matter with you?' she said aloud. 'You're a married woman!'

Still her feet would not take her back indoors to start getting Kate's tea ready – which was what she should have been doing. A strange fluttering somewhere under her ribs would not let her dismiss the smile of the stranger quite so easily.

Then she realized she had a ready-made excuse to go to

251

Ma's cottage. Kate was not home. She was still down at the Point with Enid. Eagerly Esther almost ran towards the gate and out into the lane. She must fetch Kate, she told herself, trying to justify her action. It's way past her tea-time.

There were no children playing outside the cottages; no sign of Danny Eland or – thank goodness – of his parents.

Outside Ma Harris's cottage Esther hesitated, feeling diffident about being here. She clicked her tongue against her teeth, impatient with herself. She was still trying to decide what she ought to do, when she heard a tapping at the window and she turned to see Kate's beaming face pressed against the pane, jam smeared around her mouth. The door opened and Enid beckoned her in. 'Kate's all right, missus. I'm sorry I didn't bring her back, but this feller's come to see me ma . . .' Her eyes were shining, and her voice dropped to a whisper. 'Ooh, he's a lovely feller, missus, real handsome. Come in an' meet him. He knew our Ernie.'

Shyness swept through Esther – an unaccustomed feeling for her. 'Well, I don't want to intrude, I just came to fetch Kate home . . .'

'She's had her tea.'

'Yes, but . . .'

'Oh, do come in, missus, please,' Enid urged her, and Esther needed no more persuasion.

Twenty-three

AS she had imagined, they were sitting around the kitchen table, the stranger in the place of honour in Mr Harris's Windsor chair at the head, whilst Ma sat at the opposite end. Mr Harris had come in from work and in deference to his honoured guest had sat down at one side of the table. The children stood together, wide-eyed and curiously silent, just staring at the visitor.

As Esther came in, the man glanced towards her and rose politely. Their eyes met and the wonderful smile spread across his face.

'Hello – we meet again,' he said in his rich, deep voice.

Esther smiled self-consciously. She felt Ma Harris looking from one to the other in puzzlement, but Esther's own gaze was fixed upon the stranger's face.

'You know Esther – Mrs Hilton?' she asked him.

Did she imagine it or did the faintest trace of disappointment flicker across his face?

'Not exactly,' he was saying evenly. 'We met in the lane and – er – Mrs Hilton directed me to your house.'

Esther found her voice. 'I'm sorry – I didn't mean to butt in. I came looking for Kate.'

'Nay, lass, you ain't butting in. How could ya? Sit down a minute and have a cup of tea.'

'Well . . .' she murmured, but the stranger, still standing whilst she remained so, was already pulling out a chair near him and inviting her to join them around the table. 'If you're sure.'

For a few moments there was an embarrassed silence, covered by Ma busily rattling cups and saucers and filling the teapot.

'Are – are you on leave?' Esther asked him, remembering that he had said in the lane that he had not been able to come to see Ernie's mother before now. In a few more weeks it would be a year since they had heard the news of Ernie's death and it seemed strange that it should have taken quite so long for him to make his visit. His reply soon answered her question.

The smile twisted a little wryly. 'Sort of. A few days after Ernie was hit, I was injured and eventually sent back home to hospital.'

Before she could stop herself, her gaze roamed over his body. A lean, lithe body, now he was divested of the uniform's shapeless greatcoat.

As if reading her thoughts, he said, 'Don't say it – I don't look injured.'

She looked up to meet those brilliant blue eyes watching her with amusement. She drew breath sharply and laughed, 'How did you know what I was thinking?'

'It was written on your face.'

Ma pushed a cup of tea in front of her and Esther gave a little start. She had forgotten that there was anyone else in the room. The kitchen was crowded with people – Mr Harris and Ma, six of their children and her Kate, yet for a few moments she had felt herself completely alone with the stranger.

254

'Mr Godfrey—' Ma began, but was interrupted by the soldier saying, 'Please – call me Jonathan.'

Ma rewarded him with her toothless smile and nodded. 'Jonathan,' she corrected herself, 'is going to stay with us a few days, Esther, at least he's going to stay at the pub . . .' Ma grinned. 'Ah dun't reckon he fancies sleeping with all my brood!' The family all laughed together and two of the younger boys started a rough-and-tumble on the hearth-rug which earned them a quick cuff from their mother. Suddenly the kitchen was full of noise, for although the soldier had come on a sombre errand, he had somehow lifted their spirits and helped to ease their loss.

They could not bear to let him go – not just yet – and so had prevailed upon his good nature to stay a while in their midst.

Carefully – though her heart was beating in a most peculiar manner – Esther said, 'That's nice. Where – where are you from?'

'Lincoln. You know it?'

Esther shook her head.

He was smiling at her again. 'Well, I've never been to Lynthorpe before, and to be honest–' the laughter lines around his eyes crinkled – 'I'd never even heard of Fleethaven Point until I met Ernie.' His voice dropped a little as he added, 'He made it sound like the most wonderful place on earth.'

'It is!' Esther replied without thinking.

The stranger, who was by the minute becoming less of a stranger, threw back his head and laughed. '*Now* I know who you are. You're the missus from Brumbys' Farm, aren't you?'

Esther felt the colour rising in her neck and flooding up her cheeks. 'Is that what Ernie called me – *the missus from Brumbys' Farm*?'

'He talked a lot about you.' The blue eyes were teasing her gently and yet she knew by his tone that Ernie's tales of her had been flattering. Very softly, he added, 'I had to come and see – ' he paused as if deliberately – 'for myself.' Louder he added, 'Everything – the sea, the marshes, the farms . . .'

'We'll show ya, mester, we'll show ya.' The two boys were either side of him, both talking at once. 'We'll tek ya crabbin' and shrimpin' . . .'

'That would be nice,' he answered the boys, placing an arm across each of their shoulders, but his gaze never left Esther's face. 'I'm looking forward to seeing the sea.'

Esther liked the way the newcomer spoke, his voice was deep yet gentle and to her his words seemed well pronounced.

'Esther had never seen the sea before she came to live here,' Ma was telling him, 'had you, lass? Now ya can't keep her away from it. Always up at the Point she is, staring out across the water.'

Esther coloured with embarrassment and could think of nothing to say. She pushed back her chair with a scrape on the stone floor. 'I'd best be goin'. It's way past Kate's bedtime.'

As she rose, the soldier got up too.

'Goodbye, Mr Godfrey,' she said, a little breathlessly, wanting to add 'I hope we meet again' but not daring to in front of the Harris family. Then the thought struck her – Esther Hilton not *daring* to do something because of what someone else might think? It was unheard of. What had come over her?

But the stranger had no such inhibitions. There was a twinkle in his eyes as he held her hand in his and said, 'I hope I see you again whilst I'm here, Mrs Hilton.'

As she walked home, Kate skipping along at her side and hanging on to her hand, Esther could not stop the tiny thrill of pleasure from flooding through her at the thought that Jonathan Godfrey would be staying for a few days at least.

She would see him again.

Esther thought about him several times during the following morning.

About mid afternoon she saw his tall figure coming along the lane, the two youngest Harris children hopping alongside him. They were carrying home-made shrimping nets. The soldier was bending his head slightly to one side to listen to their chatter whilst a small smile played on his mouth. Watching them, Esther moved towards the gate. He looked up and saw her and raised his hand in greeting. His smile broadened, crinkling the laughter lines around his eyes. It was impossible not to return his smile.

'Georgie and Alice are taking me shrimping.' His blue eyes danced with merriment. 'We wondered if your little girl – Kate, isn't it? – would like to come along.'

'I'm sure she would. Please come in a moment.' She opened the farm gate and they followed her into the farmhouse. 'Would you like a drink of milk, Georgie – Alice?'

'Yes please, missus,' they chorused.

Esther turned to Jonathan Godfrey. 'Please – sit down. Can I offer you anything – a glass of home-made wine perhaps?'

'Thank you – as long as I'm still sober enough to wield a shrimping net!'

The children giggled and the sound of their laughter brought Kate downstairs from her room.

'You comin' shrimpin' with me an' our Alice an' Mr Godfrey?' Georgie asked her, a rim of milk on his upper lip.

There was pleasure on Kate's face, but then it faded. 'I – I ain't got a shrimpin' net.'

The Harris children exchanged glances. 'Ya can borrow ours,' Georgie offered generously. 'We can take it in turns.'

Kate brightened again and as Jonathan stood up, she slipped her hand trustingly into his. 'Can Danny come too?' her piping voice asked and she smiled winningly at the tall man, her red curls dancing.

Jonathan glanced at Esther. 'Danny? Who is Danny?'

Before Esther could answer, Kate spoke for herself. 'He's my friend. He lives at the Point – in the big boat.'

'You know, mester. He was playing cricket with us this morning.'

Above the children's heads, Jonathan exchanged a glance of wry amusement with Esther. Laughing, she said, 'It sounds as if you're in great demand.'

'He's bin teaching me an' Danny to bowl overarm,

ain't ya, mester?' Georgie turned back to Esther, awed admiration in his tone. 'He's played cricket afore the war with a proper team in Lincoln.'

'Fancy!' said Esther, dutifully echoing the young boy's respect.

Kate was tugging at his hand. 'Well – can Danny come too?'

'Of course he can.' Jonathan looked again at Esther. 'I'll take good care of them,' he promised her.

As she watched them go, Esther felt disappointed that she had not been asked to join them. Just for once, she thought forlornly, she would have liked to have left her work and responsibilities for an hour or so and joined in the childish games on the seashore.

Suddenly, she felt very much older than her twenty-two years.

He brought Kate back to Brumbys' Farm at tea time, carrying her in his arms, her head lolling sleepily against his shoulder. Esther met them half-way across the yard and as she took the child from him, she saw him wince.

'You shouldn't have carried her. She could have walked.'

He smiled wryly. 'Poor little mite's tired out.' He drew the back of his hand across his eyes and yawned. 'Oh, I'm sorry, but that sea air's strong.'

'They've worn you out, that's what it is,' she teased him, and was surprised at how easy it was to talk naturally to him, as if she'd known him weeks or months instead of just two days.

'You could be right there,' he smiled ruefully. 'Perhaps I'm not as fit yet as I thought I was.'

'What – happened? I mean – where were you hurt?'

'My shoulder.' He gestured to his left one. 'A piece of shrapnel was lodged in it. I was shipped back to this country to have it removed. They think they've got it all out, but the wound seems to be taking a long while to heal properly.'

'I'm sorry.'

His smile broadened as he said candidly, 'I'm not. It gives me an excuse to stay here a little longer.'

Esther was surprised to feel a strange excitement just below her ribs.

'Well – I suppose I'd better let you put the little one to bed.' There was no mistaking the reluctance in his voice. 'Maybe I'll see you tomorrow?'

Esther nodded.

It was as she emerged from one of the pig sties early the following morning that she caught sight of him passing the farm gate, walking towards the town. Involuntarily, she made a move towards him, to shout after him, but she checked herself. Jonathan Godfrey was leaving and he had not even bothered to call to say goodbye. As one of the growing pigs from a recent litter pushed past her legs and scampered about the yard, grunting and snuffling in its excitement at being free, Esther gave a click of annoyance. Seizing a broom, she chased the pig back into its sty.

Fool! she chastised herself, getting dreamy about a handsome face and smiling eyes.

'I'm off to play with Danny, Mam,' Kate came skipping across the yard, her pinafore on inside out.

'Oh no you're not,' Esther began and then seeing the child's disappointment, she forced a smile. She picked her up and swung her round and round till Kate giggled. Then setting her down on the yard again, Esther added, 'At least, not until you've collected the eggs for me. You're getting a big girl now, Katie, you'll soon be four and I need you to help with little jobs you can do.'

'Then can I go and play with Danny?'

Exasperated, Esther sighed, but relented. 'Yes, then you can go.' As the little girl skipped away to fetch a basket, Esther shouted after her, 'And don't break any, Katie.'

'No, Mam, I won't.'

But when Katie had left the farm, running on her sturdy little legs towards the Point, Esther's thoughts turned once again to Jonathan Godfrey. Her irritation stayed with her all day. She was angry with herself for having read more into his glances, his smiles, his words. How could he just go off like that, without a word? He was just another flirt – like Matthew, she told herself crossly.

Then she sighed. Only the stranger had been so very good-looking and so kind. How many other men she knew would have spent the whole afternoon shrimping with four small children? Certainly not Matthew! He had hardly ever taken any notice of his own daughter, let alone anyone else's.

Despite her vexation, she still found herself glancing

261

up the lane, half-hoping she would see Jonathan Godfrey walking along it, back towards the Point.

But the lane was deserted – not even Will was due for a visit today.

When Kate returned at dinner-time, Esther questioned her eagerly. 'Has Mr Godfrey gone?'

The child wrinkled her smooth brow. 'Dunno. Nobody said.'

'But – he's not there now?' Esther persisted.

Kate shook her curls. 'He was nice, wasn't he, Mam?'

'Yes, Kate,' Esther murmured, more to herself than in answer to the child. 'He was nice.'

Twenty-four

AS Esther spooned stewed apple into a bowl and placed it before Kate, there came a knock at the back door.

Mother and child exchanged a glance.

'Mebbe it's Danny.' Kate picked up her spoon and as Esther moved to answer the door, the child added, 'Tell him I'll come when I've had me dinner.'

But it was not Danny.

Esther found herself gazing into a pair of blue eyes, the laughter lines crinkling around them. Then her glance went to something he was holding out to her.

'I made this for Kate. Is she here?'

Esther nodded. 'I – thought . . .' she began, then, gathering her reeling senses, pulled the door wider open to invite him in.

Esther saw her daughter's eyes light up and she gave a little squeal of delight. 'A shrimpin' net! Is it for me?'

Jonathan nodded. Kate jumped down from her place at the table and took the net from him. 'Ooh, it's lovely. I must show Danny—'

She was gone, rushing out of the back door, her feet flying across the yard.

'Kate! Kate, what do you say to Mr Godfrey?'

But Jonathan only laughed. 'Let her go. Her delight is thanks enough.'

'Mebbe so – ' Esther pursed her lips – 'but she shouldn't forget her manners.'

His smile disarmed her chagrin at her impulsive daughter, and in an instant dispelled the feeling of disappointment that had lingered all the morning.

He had not gone away. He had not left without so much as a goodbye, as she had believed. They were standing in the kitchen, just looking at each other.

Esther was searching for something to say but could think of nothing. She smoothed the palms of her hands, suddenly moist, down her white apron.

'Well, I'd better be off,' he said. 'Robert Eland is taking me out in his boat, fishing.' But still he made no move to go.

There was silence between them as they stared at each other.

'Well, er . . .' he said at last. 'Maybe I'll see you later?'

Esther nodded. 'Don't fall in the sea,' she teased him.

Esther went about her work during the afternoon in a daze. Ever before her mind's eye was a smiling face with brilliant blue eyes. By dusk, when Kate was in bed and Esther began the evening milking, she had given up hope of seeing him again that day.

'Hello,' came the soft, bass voice, and Esther looked around Clover's rump to see a dark shadow framed in the early evening sunlight leaning over the half-door. She felt a sudden flutter beneath her ribs, and her fingers stopped their gentle pulling on the cow's teats and involuntarily she tightened her hold.

Clover, unused to such ungentle treatment particularly from Esther, lashed her tail and kicked out sideways with her hind leg. The cow's hoof struck Esther's knee and the swishing tail cuffed her cheek. Surprised, she toppled backwards on to the cobbles of the cowshed.

In an instant he was bending over her, dropping to one knee in the slurry, his blue eyes clouded with anxiety.

'Are you hurt?' He put his arm under her shoulders and bent as if to put the other under her knees to pick her up, but, more startled than hurt, Esther struggled to rise.

'No – no, really. I'm fine.' She gave a nervous laugh as she gained her feet, disturbingly aware that he was still supporting her, standing very close and holding her arm.

Clover had turned her head and was looking at Esther with soulful eyes. Esther reached out and patted the cow's back. 'It's all right, old girl, it was my fault,' she crooned gently. Embarrassed, she looked up into Jonathan Godfrey's face and explained, 'She – she's temperamental and needs a lot of coaxing . . .' Feeling an unaccustomed foolishness, she let her voice trail away.

Gently, he said, 'It was my fault entirely, I startled you – and her.' Tentatively, he put out his hand and stroked Clover's hide. The cow moved under his touch, but it was a movement of pleasure rather than of restless irritation.

Esther laughed in surprise. 'She likes you. You must have a special touch.' Immediately the words were spoken, she flushed with embarrassment, and more so when she realized he had still not let go of her arm.

She pulled away and bent to pick up from underneath the cow the pail of milk, which, miraculously, was still upright.

'Here, let me,' he offered and without giving her chance to refuse, gently but firmly, he took the pail from her hands. 'Where do you want it?'

'In the house, please,' she said a little breathlessly. 'In the pantry.'

'Right you are, Ma'am,' he teased, then added more seriously as he noticed her limping slightly as she left the cowshed, 'Did she hurt you?'

'Not much – but she caught me right on my knee.'

He pulled a face as if he shared her pain. 'Ouch!' he murmured with feeling.

Esther laughed wryly. 'Too true! But it'll soon go. It's not the first kick I've had by a long way, an' I don't expect it'll be the last, either.'

Whilst he set the milk carefully in the pantry, she lifted the kettle from the hob and mashed a pot of tea.

He came back and stood before the range, spreading out his hands towards the warmth of the fire, for the early spring evening had grown chill. He gazed into the flames and there was a far-away look in his eyes.

Esther came to stand beside him, holding a cup of tea. She looked up at him, watching his profile in the flickering light, the straight nose and smooth, firm chin, the well-shaped mouth that smiled so readily. But now there was no smile upon his lips. Whatever his thoughts were, they were grave. Slowly he turned to look at her and for what seemed an age they just stood there looking deep into each other's eyes.

At last Esther stammered, 'Er – would you like a cup of tea?'

He started visibly as if she had woken him from a

daydream. Perhaps she had, but in the next instant he was taking the cup from her and as their fingers touched, she felt a tingle run through her.

Alarmed that the touch of a stranger could arouse such a feeling in her, Esther stepped backwards and put the distance of the hearth rug between them. As if realizing what her action meant, there was a fleeting look of disappointment upon his face that this time she did not imagine. He smiled sadly and, taking a mouthful of tea, looked around him. His eyes rested upon the silver-framed photograph and the several postcards stacked behind it.

He nodded towards it. 'Your husband?'

'Yes – yes. That's Matthew. He's – he's a soldier, like you. I think he's somewhere in France. He sends me a postcard every six weeks or so, just to let me know – he's – he's all right. He doesn't write much.'

'We're not allowed to say much at all,' Jonathan Godfrey defended Matthew. 'You're lucky to hear anything, believe me.'

'What's it like out there?' Immediately she had spoken the words aloud she wished them unsaid, for the haunted look of anguish that came into his eyes filled her with guilt.

'I'm sorry,' she said at once. 'I shouldn't have asked. You want to try to forget for a time, while you're home.'

He shook his head sorrowfully. 'There's no way of forgetting. Not ever.' His voice was a hoarse whisper and once again he just stood gazing down into the fire.

He was not seeing the fire in the range in Esther's kitchen. He was seeing flashes of gunfire and mangled flesh, hearing the thud, thud, thud of the guns and the screams of his comrades.

'Oh, you try to push it out of your thoughts,' he said slowly, 'but then it all comes flooding back when you least expect it – or want it. At night, just when you're falling asleep. Or in quiet moments like this. Moments that should be peaceful and – ' he raised his head and looked directly into her eyes – 'savoured.' There was a long pause then he added, flatly, 'But back it all comes to torment you.'

Now she moved back closer to him. 'I'm sorry,' she whispered again.

'It's – all right. It's natural that you think you want to know. But you don't, believe me you really don't.'

Esther returned his gaze steadily. 'I'm not afraid of the truth, however bad it is.'

'No – no, I don't believe you are.' His eyes roamed wonderingly over her face, her hair and then came back to look once more into her eyes. Those steadfast green eyes that returned his gaze so directly. He leaned forward, lifting his hand to touch her cheek with gentle fingers.

For one breathless moment, she thought he was going to kiss her, but as his fingertips brushed her cheek, he jumped physically as if he had been stung and stepped back abruptly. In the fading light of the evening, the firelight glinted on his hair and highlighted his cheekbones, his fine nose and firm jawline. His eyes were shadowed, but she could hear his rapid breathing.

Brusquely he said, 'I shouldn't be here – I must go.'

He turned, went out into the scullery and wrenched open the back door.

Esther followed him, the words bursting from her lips before she could contain them, 'How long are ya staying?'

He stood very still, his hand on the latch, but he did not turn round. Muffled, the words came to her in staccato jerks. 'I don't know – but I must leave. Tomorrow – I'll have to go – tomorrow.'

She felt the disappointment flood through her. 'But I thought you were going to stay longer – a few days, you said.' The words were out of her mouth before she thought to stop them. They were like a reproach. 'Why must you go so soon?'

'I must. Goodbye, Mrs Hilton.' He dropped his hand from the door and the action was like a gesture of despair. He took a step forward, but still he did not look back. He walked away from her and though she stood watching him through the dusk all the way to the gate and into the lane, not once did he turn or wave.

By the set of his shoulders, it was as if he were afraid to look back at her.

Esther lay awake for most of the night haunted by the feel of the feather-light touch of his fingers on her cheek and then his sudden brusqueness.

She could not bear to think of his leaving in the morning, knowing that she would never see him again. She groaned aloud and buried her head in the softness of her pillow. What was she thinking of? What was the matter with her? She was a married woman with a child.

She had only just met him and yet when she closed her eyes, she could see his face so vividly; his smile, the kind blue eyes, and yet his jawline was firm and his handsome face showed strength and honesty . . .

The following morning seemed to drag and Esther found herself watching the lane leading from the Point to the town. The lane he must walk down when he left. She snapped at Kate every time the child tried to catch her attention. She raced through the milking, even shouting at Clover and slapping her rump sharply when the cow moved restlessly, to be repaid by the cow kicking over the pail of milk and wasting it all.

Common sense would have told her she was being foolish and very unfair to Kate – and the animals.

But common sense seemed to have deserted her.

By lunch time when Enid arrived, Esther was so irritable that she decided that the only thing to do was to go up to her favourite spot at the end of the Spit to see if the place where the land and the sea and the sky became one would soothe and calm her – and maybe bring her to her senses.

Beyond the lane she climbed over the bank and crossed the marshland towards the East Dunes heading for the beach.

He'll have gone by now, she told herself firmly. She must have missed seeing him pass by her farm gate. Yes, she reminded herself sharply, her farm gate. That was all that mattered. Her farm, her land.

She reached the Spit and walked the length of it, breathing in the sea air deeply. She bent and picked up a handful of earth, clutching it in her hand, holding it close to her body in that space beneath her ribs where she had felt, and still felt, that peculiar fluttering of nervousness when she saw Jonathan Godfrey – or even thought of him.

'This land is mine,' she said aloud to the sea and the sky as if daring them to refute her words. She threw back her head and closed her eyes and swayed with the soft breeze, wrapping the place around her like a cloak or, more to the point, a suit of armour. Nothing and no one mattered to her more than this land.

His face was still before her; she could not blot out the memory of his smile . . .

'Mrs Hilton – Esther.'

The deep voice spoke so softly behind her that for a moment she thought she had imagined it carried on the wind, brought to her ears by her thoughts.

'Esther?' There was uncertainty in his tone now when she did not respond, did not move.

She opened her eyes and slowly turned to face him, tilting her head to look up at him. The wave of hair flopped forward over his forehead on which now there was an anxious furrow. Involuntarily, her fingers fluttered to smooth away his worry, but she fought off the desire, clenching her hands together and squeezing the earth she already held.

'I – thought you were leaving. Have you come to say goodbye?'

He shook his head slowly, as if he didn't quite believe it himself. 'No. No, I'm not going yet.'

For a timeless moment they stood and stared at each other whilst the tiny waves lapped at their feet and the seagulls wheeled and dived and screeched above them.

Slowly she dropped the handful of earth she was holding and brushed the dirt from her fingers.

'I saw you from my bedroom window in the pub, crossing the marsh, coming this way,' he was saying. 'I was all ready to go – to leave, then I saw you walking out here all alone. And I couldn't go,' he ended simply.

He held out his hand to steady her as side by side they walked back along the narrow strip of land.

After a moment's hesitation, for something told her that she was about to take a step from which there would be no turning back, she put her hand into his.

Twenty-five

*T*HEY met every day. At some point in every day, they were together. Sometimes for a few snatched moments, sometimes for an hour. And for the rest of the time, he filled her mind.

'When must you go?' she would ask, fearful of the answer yet needing to know. 'How long can you stay?'

'A few more days,' he would answer gently, 'then I should go.'

The few days stretched into a week and then two and soon she ceased to ask 'how long?'. She could make him stay, she told herself, she would make him stay. He had no need to go back to France. He'd been wounded, hadn't he? He'd done his bit in anybody's book!

They walked the seashore, side by side, not quite touching, and yet the closeness between them was like a physical embrace. They walked the dunes and they found a sheltered hollow that became their special place to sit and talk.

'Where is it you come from?' she asked him. 'Lincoln, did you say? It's a city, isn't it? I've never been to a city.' There was a wistful note in her voice.

'Should you like to go?' Jonathan asked softly.

She leant against his shoulder and looked up at him coyly. 'Maybe – with you. Tell me about it?'

'Well,' he began, idly tracing lines in the sand,

drawing a rough sketch-map to illustrate his words. 'There's a cathedral high on the hillside – built by the Romans, would you believe? It dominates the city. Wherever you are, you can see it standing proudly overlooking us all. Then the houses and streets sort of radiate out from it. There's a steep hill climb with old houses built close together on either side – buildings so old you'd wonder sometimes how they still stand.'

Esther watched his face as he talked. Watched the memories of his home flitting across his face. Memories in which she had no place. She loved the sound of his deep voice. There was little trace in his speech of the Lincolnshire dialect that was so prevalent in the countryside, and so strong in hers.

'Quaint little shops,' he was saying, 'and old bookshops – dusty and musty, but fascinating – all huddling together on the hillside. Near the cathedral there's a castle with dungeons. It's old too, though I can't remember when that was built.' He grinned at her ruefully. 'I expect I was told at school, but somehow in your own home town you take things for granted. They're there. You expect them always to be there, so you don't bother.'

Esther nodded eagerly. 'It's like the sea here. It fascinates me. I love to stand on the Spit and watch it come swirling in around me, but the folks who've lived here all their lives never come to look at it. They just know it's there.'

Jonathan nodded. 'All the same, I bet if you took them away from it – inland – they'd soon miss it.'

'Do you miss the city?'

He looked up from his sand drawing and gazed out

across the wide expanse of beach, across the water as far, if he could have seen it, as the foreign shoreline. 'Not while I'm here, no. But when I was over there – oh, yes, I missed my home town – my home country.'

Esther's gaze followed his own as she murmured, 'I suppose they all do.'

By saying 'they' and not 'you' it was as if she was separating him from the men still over there, trying to make him believe he need not go back.

He was so totally unlike Matthew – like no man Esther had ever known. He held her hand and raised it to his lips, kissing each work-roughened finger with such tenderness that tears sprang to her eyes. He made no demands upon her. He never tried to touch her intimately, to fondle her breast or unbutton her blouse. He didn't even kiss her mouth. He didn't lunge at her in a frantic, boyish manner. He was courteous and caring and undemanding. But there was a look in his eyes when she met his intense gaze. Such a look as she had never seen before in any man's eyes. There was desire – oh, yes, she knew that look – but with Jonathan there was more, so much more.

Esther was bemused and spellbound by him.

If they had not met during the day, as darkness fell Jonathan would slip away from the Seagull and come quietly into the yard of Brumbys' Farm.

'Look,' he told her, holding out his hand to her as they stood in the shadows of the barn. On the flat of his palm lay a door key. 'The landlord said I should have a key in case I wanted to go into the town and see a bit of night life.'

They smiled at each other. Now he could come and go freely from the Seagull, with no awkward questions asked.

Esther moved close to stand looking up into his face. She wanted so badly to put her arms about him, to lean her head against his chest, to feel his arms holding her tightly. The desire was so strong it was almost a physical pain. She steeled herself deliberately not to touch him.

'Oh, Esther, Esther,' he whispered hoarsely and touched her cheek with tender fingertips. 'Every morning I get up and I say firmly to myself, "Today, I must leave." ' He smiled ruefully, 'Yet by nightfall, I'm still here.' He shook his head in disbelief at his own actions. 'I would never have believed that a woman could make me shirk what I know is my duty. But you're . . . ' He hesitated, searching for the right word. 'You're something very special. Do you know that?'

She reached up and pressed his hand against her face, holding his gaze with her own intense eyes. Slowly his head came down, as if he were fighting the impulse and yet losing the battle. Their lips touched, a gentle, feather-light brush. She heard him make a low sound in his throat. His lips moved against hers, his eyes closed and his arms came about her drawing her into his embrace. She put her own arms about his neck and pulled him even closer to her.

He lifted his head and loosened his embrace. He shook his head. 'We shouldn't. We mustn't . . .'

His green eyes blazed. 'Why? I love you, Jonathan, and you love me, don't you?' The words – never before spoken to anyone by her – came so easily and so naturally

276

to her lips that she never paused to wonder, to savour the sound of them and to revel in the meaning behind them.

He gasped at her directness, then smiled, won over by her honesty.

'Don't you?' She was insisting on an answer from him. When he didn't give one, she too released her hold on him and stood back, away from him. Quietly, she said, 'Say ya don't love me, and I'll turn around and go. And ya can walk away from here – and never think of me again.' She saw the pain in his eyes. She stepped closer again. 'Say it – say ya *don't* love me . . .' She was daring him to deny her. In a whisper, she added, 'If ya can.'

He groaned, reached out for her and enfolded her in his arms. 'You know I can't. I didn't know it was possible to fall in love so quickly, so easily and – so completely.'

Triumphant, she laughed softly against his ear, standing on tiptoe to nibble his lobe with gentle teeth until he buried his head against her neck. 'Why did I come here? Why did I ever have to meet you?' he murmured.

'Do you wish you hadn't? Do you wish we'd never met?'

He lifted his head and cupped her face between hands that were gentle. 'Oh, no. Never that! Maybe it would have been better if we hadn't. But whatever happens, I shall never say I wish I hadn't known you.'

He began to help her about the farm. She taught him how to milk the cows, how to harness and drive the horses into the fields.

'I've told Mrs Harris that I'm staying on to help out a bit with the spring sowing,' he told Esther. 'I'm still on sick leave from the army . . .' His voice trailed away and he avoided meeting the enquiry in her eyes.

Esther had to bite her lip to stop the question being spoken aloud. How long? How long have we got left?

'It'll look better if we're working together, if . . .'

'Jonathan, I don't care what it looks like.' She spoke sharply, trying to hide her fear of his leaving. At least she was determined to make the most of every minute. 'I don't care what people think – or say.'

He shook his head sadly at her. 'Oh, Esther, but I do. I care for your sake. I wouldn't harm you for the world and when I think what people must be thinking, must be saying, about us – about you . . .'

'Let 'em!' Esther faced him squarely, her chin jutting forward. 'It isn't anyone else's business. I'm not liked around here, except mebbe by the Harrises.' She shrugged her shoulders. 'So what's it matter?'

'It matters to me.'

'Well, it shouldn't. Besides,' she added and was unable to stop the note of sarcasm creeping into her voice, 'there's nothing to know really, is there? For all your fine words, ya don't show me ya love me!'

She turned away from him and with an abrupt 'walk on' to the horses, she moved away down the field leaving him staring after her. When she turned at the far end of the field, he had disappeared.

'Will you stop that silly crying, Kate,' Esther shouted.

The child's weeping was quelled but she continued to hiccup uncontrollably. 'Stop that noise, or I'll give ya something to cry about.'

'I (hic) can't. Danny Eland pulled my hair ribbon off and wouldn't give it back.'

Esther stiffened. Danny Eland! Her impatience at her daughter died. She was being so unfair to take her own irritability out on her child.

Where was Jonathan? Why had he gone off like that the previous afternoon and not come back? All the morning they had been together mucking out the stables and polishing the harness and then leading the horses out to the field.

'You'll have to show me what you want me to do to help with the sowing,' he had grinned, and then she had made that stupid remark and off he'd gone. Why did she always have to open her mouth and let it say what it liked? she groaned inwardly.

All the evening she had watched for him. She had moved restlessly about the yard, going out to the field to do the milking instead of bringing the cows into the shed so that she could watch the lane. Any minute she expected to see his tall, slightly stooping frame appearing at her gate.

As darkness had fallen she had hustled Kate to bed and then she had stood most of the evening by the scullery window near the back door overlooking the yard and the lane.

He did not come.

Didn't he love her any more? Had she driven him away so easily by her bluntness? Was he disgusted because she had hinted she wanted more from him – that she wanted him physically? She had not realized just how naïve and inexperienced in matters of love she was, even though she was a married woman and a mother. She didn't know what was expected of her, how a man like Jonathan expected her to behave.

And there was no one she could ask. There was no one she could confide in. Not even Ma Harris and certainly not Will Benson – not this time.

Now, this morning, when Jonathan had still not appeared, she was venting her frustration on her innocent daughter.

'There, there, Katie, Mamma didn't mean it.'

She sighed, picked up her daughter and carried her outside the back door and round to the front of the house to sit on the grass in the sunshine. Taking the child on to her knee, her arms about her, her cheek resting against Kate's hair, Esther gave her mind over to the problem of Danny Eland.

She should have guessed it would happen. He was only behaving just like the brother to Kate that he was. She prayed that they should never find out about their relationship to each other.

'Boys are like that, Katie,' she explained, stroking the little girl's glowing curls, remembering her own boy cousins pulling their sisters' hair and her own if they had half a chance. 'You'll have to learn to stick up for yourself, darling.' As I had to do, she thought. For a moment the life she had led in her childhood came flooding back – the taunts of the other children about her bastardy, her aunt's harsh tongue and rougher hand. Only for her gentle-natured Uncle George had Esther any kindly memories.

'When you go to school there'll be lots of boys like

Danny Eland. You'll have to learn to put up with being teased.'

Kate looked up at her mother. She had stopped crying now, though salty lines still streaked her face. 'I don't think I want to go to school, Mamma.'

Esther smiled down at her. 'You'll like it when you get there. You'll learn all sorts of things – how to read and do sums and . . .'

'But I don't want to be teased – I don't like being teased.'

'No,' Esther murmured. 'No one does, but if you greet their taunts with a smile and a cheeky answer back, they'll soon give up. You see, they're only trying to upset you, to make you cry. If you don't cry but laugh at them instead, they'll give up.'

Kate seemed thoughtful, solemnly analysing her mother's advice in a peculiarly old-fashioned way for one so young.

'When do I start school? Danny says he's going next year.'

Esther sighed. Danny, Danny, Danny – always Danny Eland. 'About the same time, I think, though you're a bit younger than him. I'll have to see the teacher.'

'But Danny and me – we'll go to the same school? We'll be together?'

'Yes,' Esther was obliged to tell her. 'You'll be going to the same school as Danny Eland.'

Kate scrambled up from her mother's knee and ran across the grass towards the yard and the gate into the lane.

'Kate. Kate, where are you going?'

The child shouted back over her shoulder as she skipped across the cinders, 'To tell Danny I'm going to school with him.'

'Well, really!' Esther said, half-exasperated, half-relieved that childish quarrels could so soon be forgotten. Yet Kate's association with Danny Eland brought Esther no comfort, no peace of mind whatsoever.

It was late afternoon before she saw Jonathan.

She had walked across the marshland beyond the road opposite her farm and up the rise of the far dunes. From here she would be able to see the houses at the Point and the Seagull. She could see the children playing round Ma Harris's cottage, Kate amongst them and undoubtedly Danny Eland too. She could see Robert Eland on board his boat home spreading his nets, examining them for holes that would let the fish slip through.

She thought briefly of Beth. It was strange how they never seemed to run into each other. She could remember having seen her only once or twice since Danny's christening, then only in the distance and Danny was four now. Certainly they had never met and spoken even though they lived only a few hundred yards from each other.

Then she saw Jonathan.

He was standing at the end of the Spit – her own special place. A lonely, motionless figure just staring out to sea.

As she watched him, the familiar fluttering began just below her ribs and she felt as if, even though she was out in the open, there was suddenly not enough air to breathe.

Then she was running, running. Bounding over the tufts of grass, jumping the sandy hollows, splashing through the rivulets winding across the marshy ground.

A little way from him she slowed, panting hard, watching him. Now she moved slowly towards him.

'Jonathan.' She breathed his name like a prayer. A prayer for forgiveness, for understanding.

He did not move.

His name caught in her throat on a sob. 'Jonathan!'

She saw him jump physically and turn swiftly. She caught a fleeting glimpse of the sadness that was in his face before his joy at seeing her there filled his eyes with love.

He held out his arms to her and she ran into them. In that moment both of them were oblivious of the fact that they could be seen plainly from the cottages even though they were quite a distance away – and even more easily seen by Robert Eland on his boat if he cared to shade his eyes against the dazzling water and look in their direction.

Jonathan was kissing her mouth, her eyes, holding her fiercely in his arms.

'I thought you'd gone,' she gasped. 'Gone away and left me. Forgive me . . .'

Between urgent kisses, he murmured, 'We shouldn't – we'll be seen . . . Come – let's go in the dunes.'

They ran along the narrow bank, clutching at each other, laughing with nervousness, with mutual joy. They gained the dunes and came to their special place, a natural hollow, sheltered from the sea breeze and safe from prying eyes, hidden even from the coastguard's look-out.

They sat down in the sand and she snuggled against him. He wrapped his arms around her and laid his cheek against her hair.

'I couldn't sleep last night,' he said. 'I stood at the window of my room in the Seagull, looking out towards your home.'

She giggled nervously. 'I stood at me scullery window half the night watching the lane. I didn't sleep a wink.'

He stroked her hair.

She rested her head on his chest. 'We won't quarrel ever again, will we, Jonathan?' she murmured sleepily, for the sun was high and here in the hollow it was sheltered and warm. They lay back in the sand.

After the sleepless night tormenting herself that he no longer loved her, Esther just wanted to stay here safe and warm and happy for ever.

When they awoke the fickle sunshine had disappeared and a cold mist had crept in from the sea and surrounded them as they slept.

'Jonathan – oh, whatever time must it be? There's the milkin' to do. And Kate will be looking for me!' Esther scrambled to her feet and rushed headlong towards the twisting track which led back across the marsh and the dunes to the lane.

The mist swallowed her.

'Esther – Esther, wait.' He was instantly fully awake. 'You're going the wrong way. Esther!'

She could hear his voice but she could not see him.

The mist swirled about her obliterating her sense of direction completely. 'Jonathan,' she shouted, 'I can't see you. Where are you?'

Suddenly Esther knew real fear. She had never been lost like this. She heard his voice just once more. 'Now just stand still, Esther, and keep talking to me and I'll come to you.'

There was silence.

'Jonathan,' she shouted. 'Jonathan! *Jonathan!*'

There was no answering shout.

Twenty-six

ESTHER called his name until she was hoarse. She stumbled over thick tufts of grass, fell into sandy hollows, until she was almost weeping with fear. Her heart was pounding and her breathing painful. She ran first one way and then stopped, unsure, turned and ran another way. Prickly sea-buckthorn loomed out of the mist and scratched at her hands and forearms. She thought she had found the footpath which led back across the marshland to the lane and began to follow it, still calling his name all the time. She shivered in the dampness of the mist and yet she was sweating with fear.

She trod in a rabbit burrow and twisted her ankle, giving a cry of anguish as she fell to the ground. She pulled herself up again and plunged on blindly. The path she was following gave way to a stretch of sand and she knew she was on the beach. She turned around and began to go in the opposite direction which she now knew must lead her back to safety. Then she stopped. What about Jonathan? She could see nothing but the grey, clinging mist all around her.

Suppose Jonathan, who didn't know the beach and the ways of the sea at all, were to wander in the mist out towards the sea? What if he was caught by the incoming tide as it swirled inward, forming creeks and sand islands? That much at least she had learnt about the sea and the tides since coming to live here. Jonathan knew nothing. He would be cut off, caught by the rushing water . . .

'Jonathan,' she cried, fearing more for him now than for herself.

There was silence all around her, the mist wrapped itself about her like a shroud.

She stood still and listened intently. Was that a seagull crying?

Suddenly it was clearer, though faint. 'Eeestheer!'

'Jonathan, Jonathan – I'm here. Where are you?'

His voice was nearer and now she continued to call his name and steadily he was coming closer and closer, the sound of his voice in answer to her own becoming stronger and louder. 'I'm coming, Esther. Stay where you are and I can come to you.'

The mist cleared a little and his dark shape came towards her. She was so thankful to see him that she flung herself against him, winding her arms about his neck, kissing his face, crying and laughing all at the same time.

'I thought you'd gone towards the sea. I thought you could have drowned.'

Jonathan's arms were about her, tight and protective and thankful. Their mouths were warm against each other, whilst the cold mist enclosed them.

'Oh, darling, my love, my dearest love,' she was murmuring, her endearments echoed by his deep voice. She was shivering as much from fear as with the cold. Jonathan took off his jacket and wrapped it around her, hugging her close to him. He kissed her, soothing away her terror. His lips were gentle, but as she returned his kisses, his mouth became more urgent.

'Esther, oh, Esther,' he whispered and they sank down together into the sand.

In their relief at finding each other safe, having for a few brief moments believed each other in danger, their longing overwhelmed them and they were lost. They yielded to the hunger that had been between them almost since their first meeting – an inexplicable craving that had shocked and engulfed them both.

And now their bodies came together in a flood of ecstasy. It was as if they were the only two people in the world. Swept away on a tide of emotion, there was no Matthew, no Kate – even no farm. It was as if for the whole of her life, Esther had been waiting for this moment, for this man. Her need of him was a physical pain. Her body ached for his. Nothing and no one else mattered . . .

'I never knew it could be like that,' she said, lying back on the sand.

Jonathan kissed her forehead, her eyelids and then her mouth, his lips gentle and caressing. 'Oh, my dear love, neither did I.'

She opened her eyes to find his blue eyes, full of concern, searching hers. She could feel his breath upon her face as he whispered, 'You're not – sorry?'

Her own eyes widened. 'Sorry? How could I be?' She reached up to trace the line of his jaw with her fingertips. 'I love you,' she said simply and no other explanation was needed.

His arms tightened around her and his lips kissed her neck, moving down, down to her breast and she felt the flutter of desire begin again. They made love again, slowly now, exulting in each other, murmuring endearments until again the waves of passion bore them to the heights of exquisite happiness.

Afterwards they still lay together in the sand. The mist enveloped them, but they were oblivious to the searching damp, reluctant even yet to leave. Holding her, Jonathan said, 'Esther, what about your – husband?'

Esther, her cheek against his chest, said, 'Matthew doesn't love me. He never did.'

'What?' There was astonishment, and disbelief, in the one word.

'I think,' she said slowly, 'it's time I told you the truth about my marriage.' She shivered suddenly, as if for the first time becoming aware of the cold and, noticing, he wrapped his jacket around her and held her close, warming her with his body.

'I suppose,' she mused as much to herself as to him, 'we should not have married. I—' She stopped as realization came creeping unbidden into her conscious mind. 'I didn't know what love was.' She heard the surprise in her own voice and paused, as understanding at last flooded through her. 'But now I do,' she added. There was a sadness too mingled with her present happiness. A sadness for Matthew – and even for Beth. She sighed deeply and began to tell Jonathan from the beginning.

'I was born a bastard,' she began bluntly, and felt his arms tighten about her. 'My mother died at my birth, refusing to name my father.

'My mother's sister – my Aunt Hannah – brought me up. She didn't love me, though I have to admit she taught me all I know and her harshness has made me a survivor. But as soon as I was old enough, I left.'

She told him how she had come to this place, walking through the night to arrive out of the early morning mist at Sam Brumby's farm. How she had made herself useful to Sam and how, by the time he died, she believed that the old man at least had had some affection for her in his gruff way.

'From the moment I arrived here, Matthew was – well – after me. I always vowed I'd never give way to any man before marriage.' Bitterness crept into her tone. 'I wasn't going to bring another bastard into the world!'

'Oh, sweetheart,' she heard Jonathan murmur.

'I knew there was something between him and Beth but when the squire refused to give me the tenancy of Brumbys' Farm in my own name just because I'm a woman . . .' At the indignation in her voice, he raised her hand to his lips and held it against them. 'I just never stopped to think. Matthew wanted me, asked me to marry him and I agreed.'

There was silence. 'But – but why, darling, if you didn't love him?'

'I liked him well enough. He was the only one of my own age round here who'd been friendly. But it was the farm. I wanted the farm – a home of my own. Somewhere I could belong, and I had to be married to get the tenancy. It was the only way. The only way.'

'Then he – he must have loved you, Esther. He wouldn't just ask you to marry him for no reason.'

She buried her face against him, aware of a kind of shame only now when she had learnt the difference between real love and mere physical lust. 'He – he only wanted me – physically.'

There was a long pause, then Jonathan said quietly, a little ruefully, 'Well, I can hardly blame him for that, now can I?'

She curled up against him, winding her arms around his waist, pressing her head against his chest. 'I think Beth truly loved him, and at the bottom of him I think he loved her. But you see Matthew's the sort of man . . .' She hesitated for a moment searching for the right words to express a knowledge that she was only just becoming aware of herself. 'He's the sort of man who can't resist a challenge – any sort of challenge. Do you know what I mean?'

'I think so.'

'Poor Matthew. It was the same when he volunteered. It was only because Martha Willoughby and her bitch of a sister made loud remarks in church about cowards and that Major Langley . . .' She paused. 'God – I'll never forgive that man! His speechifying altered all our lives. He whipped up such patriotism in his speech at a rally in the town, well, poor Matthew, he couldn't resist it, could he? If something was out of his reach or denied him, he wanted it all the more. At first I was that challenge, whilst Beth was always willing. When he had married me, he had me whenever he wanted. I never said no. Maybe,' she mused thoughtfully, 'it would have been better if I had said no now and then.'

She let out a long sigh and continued. In the circle of

Jonathan's arms, his cheek against her hair, Esther was quietly remembering just how her marriage had been, seeing it clearly for the first time. For now, in this moment in the dunes, she had learnt the difference.

'Matthew seemed to change. I know he was bitter about the farm and why I'd married him. He knew that it was really me that Mr Marshall gave the tenancy to – not him in his own right but only because he was my husband. It sort of – lessened his manhood. In his own eyes, if no one else's.'

'That's understandable,' Jonathan murmured.

'Before we married, when I held out against him, all he could think of was getting me, even if it meant having to marry me. When at last he'd got me, he began to hanker after Beth again. I think he had some funny idea that Beth would still be his even after he'd married me, would always be his. So when she married Eland and was out of Matthew's reach, it made him want her all the more. Then, of course, she had Matthew's baby.'

She felt Jonathan's whole body stiffen and she raised her head to look up at him as he asked, 'Little Danny is *Matthew's* son?'

'Yes.'

'I – see,' he said slowly, trying to comprehend how it must affect the close-knit community of Fleethaven Point. 'It must be difficult for you – for everyone.'

Esther shivered suddenly. 'I'll have to get back to the farm.'

She got up from the sand and held out her hands to him. 'Let's try and find our way back to the road and this time I'm keeping tight hold of you,' she laughed artfully, 'in more ways than one.'

They stood together for a moment, gazing deeply into each other's eyes, sharing again that special intimacy.

'You'll come to the farm tonight?'

'Esther, I don't think . . .'

She placed her forefinger against his lips to still his objection, and whispered urgently, 'Promise me you'll come?'

He nodded, his breath touching her fingers in a soft sigh. 'But only after dark. I don't want the gossip to start.'

'I don't care . . .' she began, but firmly he said, 'It would hurt you, my dear. You – and Kate. I don't want that.'

They parted just before the bank of grass bordering the lane, he to turn off towards the rear of the Seagull and Esther to cross the road to her farm.

She walked as if in a dream. All round her the familiar scene seemed unreal and yet suddenly so much more vibrantly alive. The pungent smell of the yard met her. She breathed deeply revelling in the air around her.

How wonderful it was to be alive – and to be loved.

A smile curved her mouth, softening its hard, set line to tenderness. She hummed softly beneath her breath, and every so often she gave a little skip of sheer happiness.

The farm seemed quiet and unusually still as if waiting for her return. There was no sign of Kate. She would be at the Point with Enid – or Danny.

As she pushed open the back door, she saw it.

Lying on the floor, delivered whilst she lay in Jonathan's arms, was a postcard from Matthew.

Twenty-seven

*S*HE stood holding the card in her hands, tensing herself against the expected flood of guilt. But it did not come. It was as if the card was from a stranger, or from someone she had known a long time ago – a person from another life.

She moved jerkily into the kitchen, and raised her head slowly to look up at the photograph of Matthew on the mantelpiece. She stared at it, but she could not even summon up memories of the real person; she could not hear his voice in her mind, or feel his touch.

To her, now, Matthew was only a face in a photograph.

It was Jonathan who was real. It was Jonathan's face she saw in her mind every waking moment; how the laughter lines crinkled round his eyes when he smiled. The way his mouth was a little lopsided, but how his blue eyes sparkled when he looked at her. How the flick of blond hair fell continually over his forehead so that she longed to brush it back and to feel his face beneath her fingers. It was his deep voice she heard, not Matthew's. It was Jonathan who loved and held her. It was his touch she craved.

Esther tucked the latest card behind the picture at the back of the others. She would tell no one of its arrival, she thought, but then remembered ruefully, doubtless everyone at the Point would already know of its delivery if the postboy had cycled all the way from town.

'Where's my little girl, then?' Will asked climbing stiffly down from the front of his cart as Esther came running around the corner of the house from the front garden, a wet shirt in one hand, clothes pegs in the other.

'Oh, it's you, Will. I thought . . .'

'Aye, lass, it is.' He eyed her shrewdly. 'Expecting someone else, were ya?'

'Yes – no, no of course not.'

His gaze dropped to the man's shirt she was holding in her hands. His eyebrows rose fractionally. 'Matthew home, is he?'

It was an odd question, and there was a peculiar tone in his voice, as if he already knew the answer. There was more behind his remark than the mere words implied.

Esther looked down at the garment she carried, and then she tried to hide it behind her back. 'Er – no, but I'm just doing a bit of weshing, that's all.' Will was the only person, other than perhaps Ma Harris, whose opinion mattered to her. Suddenly she was angry for allowing herself to feel that way. In her own estimation it was weakness.

She overcame her moment of confusion and glared at him, her chin coming higher, defying him to question her further. She turned away and strode round to the front of the house again, her back rigid against his prying. Will followed her and stood watching whilst boldly she shook out the shirt and pegged it wide on the line.

'There's talk, lass,' he said gently.

Esther whirled around to face him, a sharp retort on her lips. She met Will's steady gaze and read in his eyes not the malicious meddling of the Willoughby women, nor the gossipy tittering of the Harris family, but a genuine concern for her. The anger went out of her. She walked slowly towards him and put her hand on his arm.

'Will,' she whispered, as if sharing a secret, as indeed she was. 'I am happier than I have ever been in me life – than I ever knew it was possible to be. Don't begrudge me a little happiness, Will. Not you – of all people!'

She saw his old eyes water. 'Eh, lass, Ah'd never do that, you should know that. But Ah can see you getting hurt. Real bad.'

She nodded. 'I know – I know it can't last for ever. One day, he'll walk away from me down that lane and maybe I – I'll never see him again. But for the moment . . .' she shook her head almost in disbelief at herself – 'I can't help myself.'

'We've all bin young, lass. An' who am I to judge?' A small smile quivered on Will's mouth, then he was serious again. 'Be careful, Esther lass, dun't get hurt. And don't give them vicious tongues the chance to wag all the more.'

She sighed. 'I think it's too late for that warning.'

They stood together for a moment and then Will repeated his initial question. 'Where's my little Katie?'

In the daytime, Esther met Jonathan on the seashore at his insistence. He was still hoping to protect her from the prying eyes of those at the Point.

'I think they know anyway,' Esther told him.

He sighed. 'I was afraid of that.'

Esther didn't care about the gossips, but she loved Jonathan all the more for his concern for her. Theirs was a love that would not – could not – be denied. Sometimes they walked quietly hand in hand at the water's edge, sometimes they cavorted in the shallows like children, splashing each other, till their clothes were wet and clinging. Their eyes would meet and desire would flash between them and they would fly into each other's arms, the salt water mingling with their kisses. Then they would run towards their own hollow in the dunes, pausing to kiss and running again, eager for the moment their bodies would entwine, their souls meet and they were the only two people in the world.

All through that summer of 1916 he stayed. She tried to keep the war news from him, clinging to the hope that if he was cut off from how things were, he would not be forced to go back by feelings of guilt. But he must have seen the newspapers at the Seagull for some days he would come to work on the farm silent and solemn. She would watch him at work, seeing deep in his eyes that he was reliving the horror.

Nineteen sixteen was a year of killing. Daily, terrible reports appeared in the papers and names that were to become synonymous with tragedy – Ypres, Verdun, the Somme and Passchendaele – were on everyone's lips. The people of the little community of Fleethaven hardly knew where these places were and yet they became as familiar on their tongues as their own home town.

Still Jonathan stayed.

Through haymaking and into the corn harvest, he

worked on Brumbys' Farm and at night they made love in the loft in the barn, warm and snug in a sweet-smelling bed of hay. Late at night they took reluctant leave of each other, lingering in the soft starlight, the sound of the sea music to their love, the salt air its perfume. Esther would creep back into the farmhouse whilst Jonathan sneaked in the back door of the Seagull.

One night as they lay in each other's arms in the aftermath of their passion, Esther said, 'You still haven't told me about yourself. You know all about me. What you don't see for yourself, I've told you.' She ran her fingers across his chest. She revelled in the feel of him – his smooth, slightly bronzed skin, marred only by the bandage wrapped around his shoulder covering the wound he refused to let even her see.

'What kind of house do you live in?' Esther asked him. 'I can't imagine what it's like to live in a big city.'

She felt the laughter rumble in his chest. 'It's in a little side street; what they call a terraced house. You know, all the houses in one long row, like the four cottages where the Harrises live, but a whole street of houses on either side. Three small bedrooms upstairs and two rooms down with a back scullery and a privy across the yard.'

'No garden?'

'No. No grass, no trees, no flowers. Just the back yard where my mother pegs out the washing and brings it in all covered with smuts from the works' chimneys.'

'Do you live with your parents?'

'Yes – and my sister, Peggy.'

'What does ya dad do?'

'He's a schoolmaster. He teaches at a boys' school in

299

the city. And my mother's a dressmaker. The front parlour in our house is always littered with paper patterns and pins.' But he was smiling fondly as he said it. It sounded to Esther a genteel sort of occupation for a woman. She imagined Jonathan's mother would be a real lady with soft, smooth hands spending her days sewing fine garments. Not like Esther – out in all weathers with red and roughened hands.

It was obvious to Esther that Jonathan came from a warm and loving family and she felt envious. How she would love to belong to such a family – to Jonathan's family. She was eager to hear all about them. 'You said you have a sister. Tell me about her. How old is she?'

His eyes clouded as he murmured, 'Almost twenty. Poor Peggy.'

Esther checked the question that sprang to her lips. Why 'poor Peggy'?

'She's going through an awful time,' Jonathan told her. 'She was engaged to a young chap who worked with me. We were friends – that's how Peggy met him. We volunteered together.' He was silent, remembering. Memories in which Esther had no part. 'He – he was killed only a month after we went out there. Poor Peggy,' he murmured again. 'She used to be so jolly, always laughing and teasing. Now she's thin and so unhappy.' He stroked Esther's face with the tips of his fingers. 'I wish you and she could meet. You'd be so good for her. You're so strong . . .'

Esther kissed his cheek gently in a gesture of comfort. 'I would love to meet her, too. And your mother and father – they sound wonderful.'

300

Jonathan drew her into his arms and as she leant her head against his shoulder, he stroked her hair, pulling out the pins and combs so that it tumbled down her back. Then he buried his face in the rich tresses. 'You've such beautiful hair . . .'

Somewhere there was suddenly a loud banging and a shout, 'Missus, missus!'

'What is it?' Esther whispered and scrambled to her feet, pulling the front of her blouse across her exposed breast. 'Where's me skirt? Quick!'

Jonathan too was buckling his trousers and reaching for his shirt.

'No,' she whispered urgently. 'You stay here. I'll – I'll see who it is.'

She almost fell down the ladder from the hayloft and ran out of the barn.

'Enid, what is it?' She hurried across the yard, hastily brushing the tell-tale wisps of hay from her clothing.

Enid turned and, closer now, Esther heard the girl's gasp of surprise. 'Where've you – ?' the girl began and then seemed to think better of it.

'What's the matter?' Esther asked again.

'Me dad sent me for yar 'osses. There's a ship been sunk out at sea. He's got to take the lifeboat out.'

'Right,' Esther said, 'come on, we'll . . .'

As they moved to go towards the stable, they both heard, thinly through the walls of the house, the wailing of Esther's child.

Esther gave a click of exasperation through her teeth, 'There now, your knocking has woken Kate.'

'I'm sorry I'm sure,' Enid said, her tone stiff with

sarcasm. 'But I heard her crying as I got to the door, afore I even knocked.' She tossed her head and glared defiantly at Esther, as if to say 'the fault's not *mine*'.

Ignoring Enid's attitude, Esther snapped, 'You go in to Kate and I'll see to the horses.'

Prince and Punch were reluctant to leave the warmth of their stable. They didn't take kindly to a night shift as well. Punch let out a whinny which echoed through the night air then he kicked his huge hoof against the door as Esther struggled to harness them.

'Whoa there, stand, damn you,' she shouted, so unlike the gentle tones she normally reserved for the animals that the horse only kicked all the more.

'Esther, here, let me.' All at once Jonathan was beside her in the stable, stroking the animal's mane and speaking in soothing tones to them. Silently, he harnessed Punch, whilst Esther dealt with Prince, the more docile of the two. Then they each led one out. At that moment Enid came out of the house carrying a lantern. She held it aloft and in its light Esther could see her glancing from one to the other.

'I'll stay with the bairn whilst you both take the 'osses,' the girl said and added with an unmistakable note of censure, 'She's wet through and been crying for ages. But you go on, *I'll* see to her.'

Esther pursed her lips. Their secret was well and truly out now. Not that she cared, but she was very afraid of the effect it would have on Jonathan. Already he felt guilty for seducing the wife of a soldier at the front, a man who was one of his comrades. And he liked and respected the Harrises. What would he do now?

They led the horses up the lane towards where the boat-house lay amongst the dunes. As if reading her thoughts, Jonathan said quietly, 'She'll tell her mother, won't she?'

'Aye, an' anyone else who'll listen. An' they'll all be only too willin' to listen.'

'Esther – I'm sorry . . .'

'Don't be,' she retorted swiftly. ''Cos I'm not. And don't let it spoil things between us.'

'But your daughter, little Kate, we shouldn't have left her alone.'

Even in the middle of all this, Esther was gratified to notice that he said 'we' and not 'you'. How readily he shared the blame. She loved him all the more for it, if that were possible.

More gently, she said, 'No, no, we won't leave her any more. You'll come into the house . . .'

'No, Esther, I –'

'Oh, I'm not asking you into me bed,' she said swiftly, knowing that Jonathan would flatly refuse to go into the bed Esther had shared with her husband. She smiled in the darkness and there was coyness in her voice. 'There's a nice soft peg rug in front of me hearth.'

'Oh, Esther, you're the giddy limit!' She heard the responding laughter in his voice and knew he could not resist her any more.

When Esther returned home a little while later she opened the back door to the sound of her child still crying.

'Oh no!' she breathed. Had Enid gone home and left

Kate alone again, even though she had promised to stay? Esther ran through the kitchen and up the stairs, Kate's wails growing louder to her ears.

In the gentle glow from the night-light, Esther could see her child sitting up in the narrow bed, tears coursing down her red cheeks, her eyes tightly screwed up, her small hands balled into fists beating the patchwork counterpane. Enid was there, sitting on the bed, trying to take the child in her arms to comfort her. Kate was hysterical.

'I can't do nowt with her, missus. I've tried.'

'It's all right, Enid. It's not your fault.' Esther sighed. No, she thought, it's all mine.

She sat down on the side of the bed and wrapped her arms around the child and rocked her and soothed away her night terrors. Kate was wet and frightened and lost. She had cried out and her mother had not come.

'I haven't even been able to change her bed, missus. She won't let me . . .'

Esther nodded. 'You run along home. Enid . . .' she added as the girl paused at the door and looked back at her. In the dim light they faced each other. 'Enid, thanks for staying.'

Enid nodded but said nothing and as Esther listened to the girl's footsteps going down the stairs, she knew that by the morning, Ma Harris would be regaled with all the sordid details of the night's events.

As she changed Kate's nightgown and bedding, Esther felt the first real stab of guilt despite her brave words to Jonathan. Whilst she had been making love with Jonathan in the hayloft, her little girl had been crying for her.

Anything could have happened, she told herself fiercely. Kate could have been sick, or choking to death – and you wouldn't have known. Or cared. Yes, yes, I would. Of course, I care. I'm not that bad, I'm not wicked.

But, said a nagging little voice inside her, you left a small child alone in the house whilst you . . . Now you've been found out and you'll have to take the consequences.

'I can't give him up,' she whispered, as later she lay sleepless in her own lonely bed, 'I just can't.'

The following morning Ma Harris arrived as usual to collect the milk and eggs from Esther. But her manner was nothing like as usual.

'Well, lass, this is a fine how d'ya do, ain't it?'

Esther faced the older woman's stare boldly. There was no point in feigning misunderstanding. Besides, Esther was never one to tell lies.

'You don't understand . . .'

Ma Harris nodded, her toothless mouth pursed to nothingness. There was no familiar cackle of laughter this morning. 'Oh, yes, I do, lass. I understand only too well. I know you hadn't the perfect marriage with young Matthew. But you made yar bed, lass. Ya shouldn't be lyin' in it with another, now should ya? Specially not when yar man's away fighting the war.'

'I didn't want him to go, you know that,' she replied belligerently. 'In fact I begged him not to go – *if* you remember?'

'I remember all right. I suppose the next thing you're goin' to tell me is that none of this would have happened if he hadn't gone?'

'Well, it wouldn't, would it?'

'Dun't lay the blame at Matthew's door. This ain't his fault.'

'Oh, I suppose you're like everyone else around here,' Esther responded heatedly. 'Blaming me for tricking Matthew into marrying me. Matthew should have married Beth, we all know that now, don't we? But wicked Esther Everatt stole him away from poor, innocent Beth. Poor, innocent Beth indeed! She lifted her skirts for him, didn't she, let him have his way with her and bore his bastard? But of course, it's all *my* fault.'

'I ain't talkin' about all that, lass. That's all over and done with.'

'Over it may be,' Esther retorted, 'but I dun't reckon it'll ever be done with. People's got long memories round here for minding other folks's business.'

'So – what's going to happen when Matthew gets back and he hears about – about this feller? What's going to happen then, eh?' Ma Harris persisted.

Suddenly the fight went out of Esther and she sank down on to the cold stone of the gantry where the milk stood in its churn. 'I haven't had a card from Matthew for months, Ma. I – I dun't reckon he's ever comin' back.'

She raised her eyes to meet Ma's and watched the fleeting expressions on the woman's face as she tried to come to terms with what Esther was now telling her, tried to find it within her to understand Esther, to forgive her even, but failing, as she said, 'Well, it still dun't give you the right to take up with another man. And worse, leave yar bairn alone in the house whilst you're – you're . . .'

For all her bluntness, even Ma Harris could not bring herself to put it into words.

Esther stood up. 'On that score, I happen to agree with you. It won't happen again.'

'Ya mean . . .' For a moment there was a hint of relenting in Ma's expression. 'You mean you're going to end it?'

'No, no, I don't.'

Ma Harris sucked in air through her sunken mouth. 'Esther – you dun't mean you – you'll take him into yar bed? Not Matthew's bed!'

Esther faced her brazenly, then yielded. She didn't care what any of them said about her, but she couldn't bear them to think ill of Jonathan. She shook her head. 'Jonathan would refuse anyway. Whatever you think of me, you shouldn't blame him, he's a gentleman.'

Ma shook her head grimly. 'I dun't blame him. Ya can't blame a man. I blame you.' With that she turned and went out of Esther's pantry and out her house. Esther followed her to the back door. Half-way across the yard, Ma turned and shouted back, 'I'll be sending Enid for the milk and eggs in future, Esther Hilton.'

She was surprised just how the older woman's attitude hurt her. She had thought herself tough and hard and totally resilient to the opinions others had of her. But she had always liked Ma Harris, had valued her friendship and, at times, her help. Now Ma had literally turned her back on her.

Determinedly, Esther shook herself. I'll survive, she told herself. Of course she would – but still, it hurt.

*

307

Esther was sure Jonathan would feel obliged to leave, but still he stayed. Now, however, he came into the farm-house. Some nights they just lay quietly together in each other's arms. Too tired by the day's work to make love, yet wanting to be together, just close to each other.

As the summer grew older, workers from the neighbouring farms began to arrive to help with Esther's corn harvest. She knew they whispered about her and Jonathan, for she saw them in little huddles, nodding towards her. Sometimes a guffaw of laughter would echo across the field. Sometimes she would catch the fleeting disapproval in their eyes, especially amongst the women. There were many more women helpers now on the farms than ever before, for their menfolk were gone. There were a lot of new faces too, but the one familiar face she wanted to see did not come. This year there was no Ma Harris rounding up her brood and setting them to work.

It was obvious that all these workers had heard about Esther Hilton and the soldier. Her chin would go a little higher, and deliberately, she would move towards Jonathan. She would touch his arm and look up into his face then glance towards the whisperers coquettishly, defying their disapproval.

'Esther, you shouldn't . . .' he would murmur, but she would not listen.

'I dun't care,' she would tell him, her eyes flashing rebelliously. 'I'll give 'em something to tittle-tattle about.'

Towards Jonathan, however, the workers' manner was deferential. The men – the few who by reason of age or ill health were left – would gather round him, watching him and quietly helping him. It was like a silent accolade on their part for his suffering, for his bravery. Perhaps it was also a wordless apology for the fact that they were still here, whole and almost untouched by the war.

Doggedly Jonathan kept pace with them and Esther watched with concern as the sweat poured down his face and his shirt clung damply to him. But she knew he would hate her to fuss over him, particularly in front of everyone.

She was returning from the farmhouse to the field with cool drinks for the workers when Kate came running towards her across the stubble. 'Mam, Mam! He's bleedin'. Come quick!'

Esther glanced to where the younger children were playing at the edge of the field. She squinted against the bright sunlight. 'Who? I dun't see—'

'Not them – him!' Kate was pointing, not in the direction of her playmates, but towards the menfolk further down the field.

They had stopped work and were gathered around one of their number lying on the ground.

Jonathan! She couldn't see Jonathan.

'Oh, no!' Esther breathed and began to run.

Twenty-eight

'WHAT is it? What's happened?'

Esther pushed her way through the group. Then she dropped to her knees beside Jonathan. He was sitting on the ground, bending forward, holding his injured shoulder.

'Let me see . . .' she began.

'No! It's just the wound – opened up. Don't fuss, Esther.'

She gasped at his sharpness and sat back on her heels, staring at him.

Immediately, he was contrite. 'I'm sorry,' he murmured softly, and as he raised his head, she saw his face was grey with pain and streaked with sweat.

In her anxiety for him, she had been oblivious to the fact that the gathering were standing silent and watchful, listening for every word that passed between them. Yet even in his pain, Jonathan had not forgotten.

She stood up. Stiffly, she said, 'You'd better come to the farmhouse.' Then she turned to Ben Harris. 'Perhaps two of you would help him?' Then she marched away across the field towards the farm without looking back.

But her eyes were brimming with unshed tears.

When they were alone in her kitchen Esther bathed and dressed the jagged line of the wound which had opened

310

up a little at what had been its deepest point. 'Why didn't ya tell me it was as bad as this? Ya shouldn't be doing *anything*, let alone heavy farm work.'

'I'm not going to be beaten by a little scratch.'

'Please, Jonathan . . .' she began and took his hands in hers. She saw him wince and slowly she turned them over. The edges of his forefingers were covered with blisters.

'What on earth . . . ?' she gasped.

'It's tying the sheaves.' He grinned ruefully. She put her arms around him and he nestled his head against her breast.

Kate's running feet sounded on the yard and Esther moved away from Jonathan as the child appeared in the doorway. Her eyes were wide with alarm. 'Danny ses you was hurt. Are you?'

Jonathan smiled at her and his face softened. 'A little – it's nothing.'

'Nothing, indeed!' Esther muttered.

Kate moved towards him and as he held out his good arm to her, she climbed on to his knee.

'You mustn't do any more work on the farm, you—' Esther began.

'Oh, yes, I will!' His mouth was a firm, determined line. Above the child's head they glared at each other.

'Oh, you're so stubborn. You're just like . . .' Esther bit back the words. She had been going to say 'just like Matthew' but instead she finished lamely, 'You're all the same, you men!'

She was aware of Kate's glance shifting from one to the other. 'If you can't help Mam on the farm, mester,' the child said, beaming up at him with a beatific smile, 'then you can take me shrimpin' tomorrow.'

The look of defeat on Jonathan's face was so comical that Esther turned away and smothered her laughter with her apron. Then she heard his deep chuckle as he ruffled Kate's curls. 'All right, you win. I can't beat the two of you!'

But on the third day, Jonathan was back in the fields doggedly keeping pace with the other workers.

Despite his grief at the loss of his elder son, Squire Marshall was determined that life on his estate should go on as near to normal as possible.

'We shall hold the Harvest Supper as usual,' he told each of his tenants in turn. 'I expect you all to come and bring whatever friends you like.' He paused a moment reflectively and added, haltingly, 'There'll be too many empty places.'

Visiting Brumbys' Farm, he said to Esther, 'And this is the young man I've heard about who's visiting poor Mrs Harris.' He held out his hand to Jonathan and gripped it warmly. 'Did – did you know my boy?'

His voice deep with regret, Jonathan replied, 'Not personally, sir, but by sight, yes.'

'Well, my boy, I trust our good air is returning you to full health. I expect you'll – er – be going back soon, will you?'

Jonathan's normally steady gaze flickered away for a moment. He took a deep breath and then looked back to meet the squire's gaze squarely. 'Yes, sir,' he said softly, but nonetheless firmly, 'I will be going back.'

Esther, hearing the exchange, felt as if the breath had been knocked from her body. Her whole world seemed to crumble and even in the sunlight she shivered. Mechanically, she stretched a smile on to her mouth when the squire wished her good day. She stood staring after him as he mounted his horse and rode out of the farmyard gate.

When he was out of sight, Jonathan put his arm about her and led her into the barn. 'I know what you're thinking – feeling,' he said gently. 'But you've known all along that I must leave eventually. I'm well now – that's obvious to anyone who sees me working in the fields. I shouldn't be here. Every day I'm on borrowed time.'

She looked up into his face. 'But your wound isn't healed properly. You know it isn't.'

'It's – well enough that I ought to be going back. If I don't report back very soon, they'll come looking for me.'

'You could hide here. No one from the army knows where you are, do they?' She flung her arms about him crying, 'Don't go. Stay with me. Please!'

He held her close. 'A little longer, my love, just a little while longer.' More than that he would not promise.

Later she asked, 'You'll come to the Harvest Supper with me?'

'I'll go to the supper – but not with you.'

'Whyever not?'

'Esther, we'd be flaunting our – our affair in front of all your neighbours. We'd only be asking for more trouble. These people care for Matthew. You must go to the squire's supper as the wife of a tenant farmer, the wife of a

313

man who is a soldier at the front doing his duty for his country – as Matthew's wife.' Despite his reasoned argument, his voice wavered a little on the final words, but Esther was too angry to notice.

'Don't be stupid,' she began hotly. 'Matthew only went because he got drunk and volunteered when Martha Willoughby called him a coward.'

'For whatever reason, he's there – in the thick of it. I'll go with the Harrises. That is, if they'll have me.'

For once Esther could not shake his quiet resolve.

Esther dressed with care on the evening of the Harvest Supper. She was as nervous as a girl on her first outing with a young man.

She had to take Kate along, for on this night there was no one who wanted to miss the supper to stay at home with Esther's daughter.

'Will Enid be there? And the others?' Kate chattered incessantly, catching some of Esther's excitement.

'I expect so. Do hold still, child, whilst I tie this ribbon in your hair. Such thick curls you've got, just like mine.'

'Will Danny be there?'

Esther's fingers were stilled a moment. Then she brushed Kate's hair vigorously.

'Ouch, you're pulling.'

'I really don't know,' Esther said, answering her daughter's question but unable to keep the sharpness from her tone. 'But I'll be there tonight to make sure he doesn't pull your hair again.'

'Oh, he doesn't pull my hair any more,' Kate said airily.

'I'm very glad to hear it.'

'No – now he tries to kiss me.'

'What! For heaven's sake, child, you're only four! You shouldn't be kissing little boys . . .' Esther pursed her lips and muttered, 'He's his father's son, all right, and no mistake.'

'What did you say, Mamma?'

'Nothing for you, missy. You stay away from Danny Eland, d'you hear me?'

'He's my friend. I like Danny.' The small mouth quivered and tears trembled, but Esther hardened her heart.

'You'll do as I say, Kate.'

The merriment was in full swing when they arrived at the huge barn at the Grange. At least on the surface it appeared to be, but after a few moments there, Esther could feel that the atmosphere of gaiety was forced. Although everyone was doing their best to put on a show of enjoying themselves, there were so many faces missing now, so many who would never be coming back. Every day the casualty lists grew longer and news of fearsome battles, won and lost, dominated the newspapers.

She scanned the bobbing heads for sight of him and saw him deep in solemn conversation with the squire. She felt Kate's hand tug itself from her hold.

'Kate, you . . .'

The child was gone, darting between the dancers to the stack at the end of the barn where several children were playing, sliding down and tumbling each other. At least, thought Esther wryly, I can't see Danny Eland amongst them. Then forgetting the children, her eyes again sought Jonathan.

Drawn towards him, she threaded her way through the throng, coming to stand a little way off, just watching him. Her gaze roamed over him, drinking in every feature. The flop of golden hair, the smooth skin tanned to a healthy bronze now by all his outdoor work. Reluctantly, she had to admit that he looked the picture of health – not a wounded soldier on sick leave. The realization terrified her.

As if feeling her close by, he lifted his eyes and met her gaze. She saw the fire burn in his eyes, saw the hunger in them as he took in her appearance. He had never seen her in her best dress, for he never accompanied her to church and that was the only time she ever wore it other than for the Harvest Supper. Suddenly, another memory pushed its way unbidden into her mind. She had worn this dress on that last Bank Holiday – when Matthew had taken her on the pier. So long ago, it seemed now. Another world, another life away.

Squire Marshall, following Jonathan's gaze, greeted her. 'My dear Mrs Hilton.' He held out his arm to her as if to draw her closer, to include her in their conversation. 'I'm so glad you've come. Of course you two know each other. I was forgetting – I met you at Brumbys' Farm the other day, didn't I?'

Esther looked sharply at the squire but the remark had been made so innocently and without guile. So, she thought, the gossip hasn't reached the squire's ears, or at least if it has he's choosing to ignore it. She glanced

316

at Jonathan and that special look of a secret shared passed between them.

She held her hands clenched at her sides, willing herself to resist the urge to go up to him, to put her hands against his chest and reach up and touch his lips with her own. Instead she said, 'How is Mrs Marshall, Squire?'

The older man's face seemed to age before her. 'Ah, my dear, she's frail and weak, I fear. She's never recovered from our great loss, you know.'

Esther's green eyes filled with genuine sympathy. 'I am sorry, Squire,' she said softly.

'Thank you, my dear, thank you.' He smiled, making a great effort to play out his self-appointed role as host of the party alone. 'Ah, there's Tom Willoughby. Willoughby, over here a moment.'

Tom Willoughby's huge bulk came towards them.

'Squire,' he greeted his landlord cordially but with due deference. 'Hello, Esther lass. Any news from Matthew, then?'

Esther drew breath sharply and avoided looking at Jonathan. 'No – no, I'm afraid I haven't heard from him – in ages.' She had told no one about the last postcard from Matthew, but even that had been several weeks ago now, so her answer was not exactly a lie. Yet Esther, always truthful, felt it to be. Her heart thudded a little faster, and she was sure her cheeks grew pink.

'I'm sorry to hear that, lass, real sorry,' Tom was saying.

There was a moment's awkward silence between them, then Tom Willoughby and the squire both began to speak at the same moment.

'I wanted—'

'How—?'

'Sorry, sir, after you . . .'

'No, no, Willoughby, it was nothing really, just idle conversation. If you'll excuse me I'll get round to some of the other guests.'

He nodded and smiled at the three of them and as he moved away, Esther said, 'What were you going to say, Tom?'

'I was about to say that I wanted a word with you, Esther. I've a bit of bad news. I don't know if you'll be able to borrow the threshing tackle the squire lends us. It's at my place now, but I'm having the devil's own job wi' the blessed traction engine! The man we usually get when it plays up has volunteered and I don't know of anyone else who knows about engines.'

'Oh, no,' Esther groaned. 'With so many hands short, I was relying on that.'

'Er, perhaps I might be able to help,' Jonathan's deep voice put in quietly. 'What sort is it?'

Tom Willoughby told him. A smile spread across Jonathan's face. 'I'll take a look for you, Mr Willoughby, if you'd like me to?'

'Well, if you think you can do owt, young feller, I'd be chuffed. Er, 'ow do you know about steam engines, then?'

'Made in Lincoln, wasn't it?'

Tom Willoughby nodded.

'That's where I worked before I joined up. I maybe even worked on it, Mr Willoughby.'

'Well, I'll be damned!' exclaimed Tom Willoughby

with such a comical look on his face that both Esther and Jonathan burst out laughing.

It was the only unfeigned laughter heard all evening and then it was heard by many only with disapproval.

Later the following day, Esther went to Rookery Farm to find Jonathan up to his elbows in grease and oil, clambering all over Tom Willoughby's huge traction engine.

She had not seen him all day. Frustrated and feeling neglected, she had guessed that was where he would be. She didn't stop to think of the consequences that parading her friendship with Jonathan before Martha Willoughby and her spiteful sister could bring.

She had to see him.

It was like a craving that would not be assuaged until she was with him. Even then, when he was near, all she wanted was to be in his arms, lying with him, being loved by him . . .

'Have you mended it, then?' she asked, truculence in her tone. His face wore a rapturous expression.

'Oh, hello, Esther, what are you doing here?' Without waiting for her answer, almost as if he were uninterested in it, he had turned away and bent his head once more into the workings of the great machine.

'Good evening, Mrs Hilton.' Martha Willoughby's voice spoke behind her, with an underlining accent on the 'Mrs'. 'And to what do we owe this particular pleasure?'

Esther turned and her chin went a little higher. 'I came to see how Jonathan – Mr Godfrey – was getting on with repairing the engine.'

'Really?' There was a simulated sweetness to Martha's tone. 'I hadn't realized that his – er – services were your particular property.' The sarcasm was evident and Esther was left in no doubt that Martha Willoughby knew exactly what the relationship between Jonathan and herself was.

Esther smiled with false amiability in return. 'I'm sure Mr Godfrey is pleased to be able to help. In fact . . .' She glanced over her shoulder at the two men laughing and talking together, gesturing to the internal workings of the engine, and there was a note of jealousy in her voice. 'He seems to be thoroughly enjoying it.'

Martha nodded, a malicious smile on her mouth, the fold of fat beneath her chin wobbling. 'Yes, he seems to enjoy his life here. Made himself quite at home, so I gather. Nicely hidden away from the war.'

'He came to see Ma – Mrs Harris – to tell her that he had known her Ernie, *if* it's any business of yours, Martha Willoughby, which it ain't. And he was wounded, you can see that for ya'sen.'

Martha smirked. 'Convenient though, ain't it, that he can hide in a little out-of-the-way place like Fleethaven Point where the authorities won't find him in a month o' Sundays?'

'Well, at least he's done 'is bit. I see you hang on to your man well enough. You ain't goaded him into joining up. Though I'm surprised the poor man hasn't – if only to get away from you!'

'Dun't you get high 'n' mighty with me, *Mrs* Hilton. We all know how you come to be where you are. A tramp from the Lord knows where who took old Sam Brumby for the poor old idiot he was . . .' She wagged her finger in Esther's face. 'Getting him to change his will when he was on his deathbed.'

Esther gasped. 'I never did—'

Martha's tirade continued. 'My Thomas's family was related to old Sam's way back. All that should have been ours, by rights, not left to a scheming hussy like you!' Martha was in full flow now, enjoying having Esther at her mercy. 'To say nothing of how you tricked young Matthew into marrying you. Telled him you was pregnant by him, I don't doubt. 'Tis the oldest trick in the book, that one.'

'That's not true,' Esther shrieked, 'and you know damn well it ain't. My Kate was born nearly a year after we was wed.'

Martha cackled. 'Huh, ya dun't have to *be* pregnant to catch 'em. Only tell 'em you are.'

Esther's eyes narrowed. 'Oh,' she said, her tone heavy with sarcasm, 'is that how you caught poor old Tom Willoughby, then?' It was a particularly cruel remark considering that the Willoughbys had no family.

Martha's fat cheeks, already marked with tiny red veins, grew purple. 'Why, you, you—'

At that moment behind them the great steam engine spluttered into noisy life and drowned Martha's abuse.

Esther turned on her heel and marched away from Martha and off their farmland. She returned to Brumbys' Farm. It *was* her farm, and everything in it, no matter what Martha said.

Esther wished now she had never gone up to Rookery Farm, particularly as Jonathan had hardly seemed to notice her. His indifference had hurt her far more than Martha's scathing attack.

So, Esther thought furiously, if he prefers a smelly old engine puthering steam and smoke to me, then he's welcome.

Nevertheless, she found it impossible to sustain her anger for long, for when he came back to the farm, his face was grubby with oil and smuts and his eyes were shining like a little boy's on Christmas morning.

'It was good to get me hand in again, Esther,' he told her as he sluiced away the grime under the pump in the yard. 'Eh, but I've missed it – my work. I hadn't realized just how much until . . .' He spread his hands out before him and looked down at them and laughed. 'Until I got them all mucky with oil and grease again.'

She watched his lean body rippling in the sunlight and longing burned inside her. Again she saw the bandage covering the wound on his shoulder; that jagged, purple scar that was a constant reminder of what he had seen and suffered.

It was a reminder to her too that he was still a soldier and that the war was not yet over. Not for either of them.

That night their love-making was as tender as ever and when they lay together quietly afterwards, she cried against his shoulder, and kissed the scar with tender lips, her tears falling on to it as if to wash it away if she could. But it would always be there. It was as if the scar on his body was like a scar on their happiness. An unceasing reminder that it all must end.

Twenty-nine

*E*STHER watched the rotund figure of a man on a
bicycle riding with solemn concentration along the
lane towards the Point.

The sun glinted on the silver buttons of his black
uniform and her heart gave a lurch of fear as she saw him
dismount and lean his bicycle carefully against the gate.

A policeman! Why was a policeman coming to her
farm?

He walked slowly across the yard towards the back
door of the house. 'Mrs Hilton?' he greeted her.

She nodded and ran her tongue over lips that were
suddenly dry.

'We've – er – reason to believe that there's a soldier
staying hereabouts, Mrs Hilton.' He paused, but she
returned his gaze steadily and remained silent. Her heart
thumped so loudly she was certain he must hear it. She
was praying that Jonathan would not appear out of the
cowshed.

'Well, now . . .'

At that moment there came a clang from the cowshed
and the sound of a man's voice. 'Steady, girl. Steady,
Clover.'

The policeman raised his voice so that it carried across
the yard. 'This 'ere soldier, been in these parts a while
now, so we understand. And – er – whilst he might have

323

been on sick leave at first, if you understand me, well, time's gone on, so to speak, and if he's fit and healthy enough to be working on a farm, then . . .' The man spread his huge hands palms upwards.

Esther caught her breath. Over the man's shoulder she could see Jonathan emerge from the cowshed and walk across the yard towards them. She made an involuntary movement to stop him, to try to prevent the inevitable. But purposely Jonathan avoided noticing her gesture and came to stand quietly beside the policeman. The older man turned slowly to look at him as Jonathan asked, 'Could it be me you're looking for?'

'I really couldn't say, sir.' The policeman was polite with a hint of apology in his tone. 'I have to follow up these – er – reports we get, you know. People get some funny ideas, about deserters and such.' He lifted his huge shoulders in a shrug. 'Ugly name, isn't it, for a man who's probably done more than most for his country and rightly deserves a bit of respite, but – well – you know how it is, sir?'

Jonathan nodded, his mouth set in a grim line. 'I do indeed,' he said quietly. 'You have your duty to do.'

'I'm glad you see it that way, sir.' He paused, his keen eyes searching Jonathan's face. 'So may I take it,' he added quietly, 'that you will be reporting back to your unit in the very near future?'

Jonathan nodded. 'Yes, officer, you may.'

'Perhaps you'd call in at the station when you go for the train?' He paused, glanced towards Esther, and back again to Jonathan. 'Shall we say in a couple of hours?'

324

There was sympathetic understanding in his tone, but nevertheless an underlying firmness.

Esther gave a little cry and her hand fluttered to her mouth to still the sound. She watched, wide-eyed, as Jonathan slowly nodded agreement.

'I'll bid you good day then, sir.' The policeman touched his forefinger to his helmet in a gesture of farewell, nodded to Esther and turned away.

As the man mounted his bicycle and rode off, a little unsteadily, Esther could contain her anger no longer.

'How dare he? How dare he come here . . . ?' She was shaking with fear. Fear that the moment she had dreaded had come. Now Jonathan would leave her.

Jonathan put his arms about her. 'Don't, my darling, it had to come.' He put into words her dread. 'We both knew that one day I would have to go. I'm lucky it was not the military who came looking for me. They would have arrested me on the spot.'

'Why?' she cried. 'You've done nothing wrong? They—'

'Esther, my darling. I should have gone back weeks ago. But I—' His voice broke with emotion and he buried his face in her neck, his words becoming muffled. 'I couldn't tear myself away from you.'

'You mean – you mean you'll be in trouble when you get back?'

Jonathan did not answer her.

She tightened her arms about him, as she realized at last how much he did love her. He loved her just as much as she loved him. She knew what it must have cost this man in terms of pride and principle to have overstayed his term of sick leave and run the risk of being put on a charge.

'Oh, my love, my darling,' she murmured.

At that moment over his shoulder, parked a little way along the lane Esther saw a pony and trap. Sitting in the trap were two women, one tall and stout and the other thin and angular.

Esther stiffened and as Jonathan lifted his head to look at her, she gave a low growl of rage and tore herself from his grasp. She was running across the yard, her skirts held up in one hand and shaking her other fist and yelling at the two women in the trap.

'You bitch! You fat old beezum, Martha Willoughby. And you, Flo Jenkins, you wizened old maid—'

Martha made valiant efforts to turn the trap around in the lane, but Esther was upon them before she could do so. She grasped the side of the trap and shook it, making it rock precariously.

The two women screamed in terror, but Esther's frenzy had driven all sense and reason from her mind. All the fury she had held against these two women for years was unleashed.

If it had not been for Jonathan reaching her at that moment, she would have tipped the trap over on to its side, throwing the two women into the road and undoubtedly causing them physical harm. He took hold of her, pinning her arms to her sides so that she struggled and kicked against him and continued to mouth insults at the two women, but no longer could she hurt them.

Jonathan raised his normally quiet voice above Esther's screeching. 'Go, Mrs Willoughby, just go!'

Martha, red and flustered, scrabbled in the bottom of the trap for the reins and sat up. She cast one anxious look back at Esther and then flicked the reins and the pony moved forward. As the trap moved off down the lane, the two women stared back at Esther, fear in their eyes.

As if to confirm that there was reason for the trepidation on their faces, Esther yelled after them, 'I'm not finished with you two old biddies yet. You'll pay for this day, Martha Willoughby!'

He took her back to the farmhouse and into the kitchen. He made her sit down near the range whilst he poured her a strong cup of tea from the pot on the hob.

Esther was still shaking with rage and now with fear, as the realization overwhelmed her. She moaned and closed her eyes and rolled her head from side to side. 'Don't go. Please, don't go!'

He knelt in front of her and took hold of her hands. 'My darling – I must. But I want you to remember that wherever I am, I shall be loving you still. If we never meet again . . .'

Her cry of anguish broke into his words, but he stroked her hair and held her even closer, comforting her as he might a child. 'If we never meet again,' he repeated bravely, 'our love will last for ever.'

'I love you, I want us to be together. Don't go back. I'm begging you!' Her tears flowed, and she clung to him. 'Don't leave me, I can't bear it.'

He eased himself back from her clinging arms and gently held her tear-streaked face between his hands, forcing her to look at him. He brushed the strands of hair, wet with her tears, from her eyes.

His own sorrow and his heartache for her misery filled his eyes with compassion. 'My own dear love, my only love, you don't mean it . . .'

'I do, I do!' she sobbed wildly.

He shook his head. 'No, you don't, not really,' he insisted with a quiet firmness. 'If I were to stay, I'd be a deserter – a man always running from the authorities. See how easy it is for the local bobby to track me down?'

'They've reported you – I know it! Then they couldn't resist coming to gloat . . .'

'Hush, my love, hush.' He put his arms about her once more. 'I couldn't run for ever. Eventually, I'd be caught and probably sent to prison—'

'You'd be alive!' she cried bitterly.

'What kind of life would that be? A life of shame. You'd come to despise me . . .'

'Never! I just want you here with me – alive. I don't care . . .'

'But I do, Esther,' he said, giving her a very gentle yet nonetheless deliberate shake. 'I'd hate myself. I couldn't live the rest of my life like that – not even with you, my own darling.'

Hysterical now, she pulled away from him and stood up, moving backwards behind the chair, deliberately putting a barrier between them. 'You don't love me. Not as much as I love you – you can't do, or – or you wouldn't go.'

In her passion, she didn't see the hurt in his eyes that her words inflicted. But the pain was in his tone. 'Oh,

Esther, don't say such a thing – not to me. Not to me, my love.'

She stood before him, holding on to the back of the chair, her whole body shaking, racked by heaving sobs. Taking a handkerchief from his pocket, he moved closer. Tenderly he wiped away her tears. Even as he did so, more came to take their place. He could not stem the flow of her misery.

Gently he released her grip on the chair and enfolded her once more in his arms, just holding her close until she was exhausted and her sobs subsided to a forlorn, childish hiccuping. All the while, he murmured soothingly and stroked her hair.

When at last she was calmer, he said again, 'I could not live a life of dishonour, my dear, not even for you.' He tensed waiting for her crying to burst forth again, but she was quieter now, drained of the passion and resigned to his going.

'Esther, you must be strong. We must get through this and then, when it's all over, well, we'll see how things stand.'

It was the only hope he could, or would, give her. She would perhaps never quite understand, never quite accept his reasons, but she realized that despite all her courage, her forthright, strong will, this gentle man was made of even stronger mettle than she.

Jonathan's arms tightened about her and, against her hair, his voice was deep with poignant longing as he whispered, 'Love me one more time, Esther, before I go.'

*

Later, she watched him walk away from her, down the lane and out of her life.

When he reached the bend in the road that would hide him from her view, she gave a cry of agony and began to run after him. Not yet, she told herself, I must see him still. Reaching the bend in the road herself, she stopped and stood watching the figure striding away from her, growing smaller and smaller.

Not once did he turn and wave, not once did he look back. In her heart she knew why. If he looked back now, he would not be able to go.

'Jonathan.' She breathed his name like a prayer. 'Look at me, Jonathan. Turn around, my darling.'

But the figure grew smaller and smaller until, through the blur of her tears, she could no longer see him.

Thirty

*T*HE days following his going were long and lonely.
Ironically, when Jonathan left, it was two years
almost to the day since Matthew had walked away into
the mist down the same road.

'Danny ses that nice man's gone away. Has he, Mam?'
Kate wanted to know.

Esther swallowed the lump that rose in her throat. She
took Kate on to her knee, the child leaning her head
against Esther's shoulder. 'He had to leave suddenly.'

'But he didn't say goodbye to me.' Kate's mouth
quivered.

'He asked me . . .' Esther added, inventing the lie, 'to
give you his love.'

'Is he coming back? I want him to take us fishing
again.'

'I – don't know. Maybe some day.'

'I hope he comes back. I liked him – and so did
Danny.'

'Yes,' Esther murmured. 'So did I, Katie. Oh, so did I.'

Mechanically, Esther went through the motions of living.
The demands of her daughter and the farm were all that
kept her going. There was a numbness in her mind and
an ache in her heart that was an actual physical pain in
her chest. She worked till she dropped, hoping to find

oblivion in exhausted sleep. The nights were the worst, when she lay alone in the darkness and relived the times she had lain in his arms. Even tears would not come to give vent to her misery.

Her grief was too deep for tears.

In the cooling days of autumn she walked the shore close to the water's edge, hearing the ghostly laughter they had shared. She sat in the sandy hollow, the place where they had made love, her arms wrapped around herself, her body aching for his touch. Now, all she felt was a gnawing emptiness below her ribs. Even her favourite place at the end of the Spit failed to bring her solace. It seemed forsaken and lonely, and the wailing seagulls overhead seemed only to echo her own isolation. It seemed as if all feeling had gone, even her love of the land failed her now.

Without Jonathan, her world, the land she had once loved so fiercely and fought so hard to win, had become a desolate and melancholy place.

Now she watched for the postboy, praying that Jonathan would write to her. Was he missing her as much as she missed him?

No word came. As the days passed she found resentment against him growing. He hadn't loved her. He couldn't have done – or else he would have written. He would have found some way to send word to her – to let her know he was safe, to tell her he loved her still.

She heard nothing.

What had happened to him when he reported back to his unit? Maybe he was safe, she tried to tell herself, in prison for his wrongdoing, but safe. But in her heart she knew that even if he faced charges, eventually they would send him back out to the war front.

Why, oh, why, hadn't he written to her? He didn't love her, not really, she tormented herself. Already he had forgotten all about her. Letters and cards came through from the front. Even if he had been sent out to France again, he should still have been able to write to her. Then cold fear would clutch at her heart. He hadn't written because he couldn't – because he'd been killed. And here she was hating him for deserting her so coldly, whilst he was lying dead on some battlefield.

Yet she could not, would not, believe that she would never see him again, that he was gone from her for ever. It was the only shred of hope she had and she clung to it with all the tenacity that was in her nature.

One November night about a month after Jonathan had left, a night so calm and still that the sound of the sea drifted in clearly over the land, Esther came wearily down the stairs from seeing Kate into bed when she heard the strangest noise, faint at first, then growing louder. A cacophony of banging and clattering, like copper pans being beaten, rattling pots and whistles and horns. Nearer it came. She stepped outside her back door and saw lights bobbing in the lane outside the gate to her farmyard. Then, distinctly in the black stillness of the night, she heard the sound of chanting voices:

> 'Her husband's gone to war,
> 'So she becomes a whore.
> 'She leaves her work, she leaves her child

'Her husband's name she has defiled.
'Her sins to the world we'll tell,
'Come out, come out, you Jezebel!'

Esther stepped back inside and slammed and bolted
the door. She leant against it breathing hard. She closed
her eyes and moaned aloud. They were ran-tan-tanning
her! Her heart was pounding in her breast. Then a hot
anger surged through her. She had not stayed outside
long enough to see who was in the group, but now in
comparative safety she looked out of the scullery window
overlooking the yard. In the fitful light of the swinging
lanterns, it was almost impossible to discern the faces,
yet there were two figures which were recognizable by
their shapes. The tall, looming bulk of Martha Willoughby and the stick-like thinness of her sister, Flo
Jenkins, were in the forefront of the mocking group of
ran-tan-tanners. Behind them, the other figures, laughing and chanting their crude verses, remained anony-
mous in the shadows, though she suspected there were
one or two from the Point.

As the noise and shouting continued, echoing all
around her farmhouse, she heard the frightened wail of
her daughter from upstairs. She was about to turn away
from the window to go up to Kate, when, for a brief
instant as the lanterns swayed, she caught sight of a still,
silent figure set apart from the rest, standing on the bank
on the opposite side of the lane. Motionless, with her
hand clutching a black shawl around her head, taking no
part in the proceedings but just standing and watching –
was Beth Eland.

334

For a long moment, Esther stood looking back at the woman, although she knew Beth couldn't actually see her inside the darkness of her home.

Why was she there? Esther wondered. Had she thought up this escapade? Or had the Willoughby woman and her sister dragged Beth along to see her rival's humiliation?

At that moment, Esther heard Kate's sobs closer and turned to see her daughter standing in the doorway.

She went forward now and gently pushed Kate back into the kitchen. Closing the door behind them blotted out some of the noise.

'What is it, Mamma? What's that noise?'

'Just some people had a mite too much to drink, and acting very silly. Tek no notice. Come . . .' she offered, sitting down in the wooden chair and opening her arms to her daughter. 'Come sit on me knee near the fire till they've gone.'

They sat together, their arms about each other, Esther's tightly around her daughter's shaking body, whilst Kate wound her sturdy, childish arms about Esther's neck and leant her head against her shoulder.

'I wish that nice man was still here with us,' she murmured. 'He'd make them stop. He'd make them go away.'

Esther stiffened and held her breath. 'Who – who do ya mean, Katie?'

The noise still went on outside, but the child seemed less afraid now. She wrinkled up her smooth brow as if trying to remember. 'The man who made me a shrimpin' net – I don't remember his name.'

335

Esther said quietly, 'You mean J— Mr Godfrey.' To herself, she added, and he's the reason that mob's outside yawping their heads off. Thank goodness you can't understand what they're calling your mother!

Suddenly the noise ceased. The woman and the child sat up, glanced at each other, then Kate slid to the floor and Esther got up. Hand in hand they tiptoed out to the back door. Making as little noise as possible in the silence that followed the din, Esther slid back the bolts and lifted the latch. They were still there, the lanterns swaying, feet shuffling, but they were quiet. All the banging of pans and whistling and chanting had stopped. In front of them stood the huge, avenging figure of Tom Willoughby.

'. . . Get away to yar homes. Ashamed of ya'sens, y'ought to be. As for you, wife – if you ever, ever, do this sort o' thing again to this lass and her bairn, I'll tek off me belt to ya. Aye,' he wagged his finger in the faces of those grouped behind Martha and Flo. 'Aye, and then you'll have cause to ran-tan-tan me as a wife-beater, won't ya?'

'She's a bad 'un, Tom, is Esther Hilton,' came an unidentifiable man's voice from the back. 'No better than a tramp when she came and—'

Tom knew the speaker. He raised his voice. 'Oh, aye, young Percy Souter. Does yar ma and pa know yet that you'm got a lass in Lynthorpe in the family way, eh?'

There was a ripple of embarrassed laughter amongst the crowd, but no answer from the youth. Tom was not finished yet. 'And what about you, Joe Bridges? Why, I remember when we was lads together . . .'

'Eh, steady on, Tom lad. Fair's fair, no need to rake up a young feller's wild oats, not when he's a respectable married man.'

'Respectable married man!' Tom threw back his head and let his roar of laughter ring out into the night. 'Eh Joe, that's the best yet!'

'All right, Tom, you win. We're off home. Come on, lads, let's get away afore he ses any more. You know a mite too much, Tom Willoughby, a mite too much.'

'That I do,' Tom said, his tone grim now. 'There's not one here amongst you that has the right to cast the first stone at her. Not one!'

It was as if the biblical reference finally shamed them all, for one by one they melted away into the blackness until only Tom was left to take a none-too-gentle hold of his wife and sister-in-law and march them off up the lane back towards Rookery Farm.

The weeks and months dragged on. Christmas was a hollow sham for Esther. She had hoped that she and Kate might still be invited to the Harrises' as they had been on the two previous Christmases since Matthew had gone to war.

'It'll be company for the bairn being with my lot and I expect you could do with the company, lass,' Ma Harris had said that first year in her warm, all-embracing way.

This year, no invitation came.

Since their quarrel Ma Harris had never come near Brumbys' Farm, though she still allowed Enid to help Esther with the dairy work and to look after Kate. Even the younger boys helped about the farm and Enid still took Kate to her home. By what Esther could gather from Kate's chatter, Ma treated the child no differently.

It's just her mother she's no time for now, Esther admitted ruefully.

She had thought that even Ma might relent in her coldness towards her at Christmas, if only for the child's sake, but on Christmas Eve Kate hung her stocking on the kitchen mantelpiece and went alone to her room, whilst Esther sat in front of the range and thought of Jonathan. There was a goose cooking slowly in the oven and holly decorated the living room. There were mince pies and puddings in the pantry and only the two of them to share the festive fare.

How stupid and useless it all seemed, yet she had to try, she was obliged to try, for Kate.

But all she wanted was to go down to the beach, even in the cold of the winter, to their special hollow and try to relive those stolen hours in Jonathan's arms.

Esther was relieved when Christmas was over. In the first few days of the New Year the weather had suddenly turned bitterly cold and, still struggling alone with the ploughing, Esther was in a state of near exhaustion each evening.

'Esther, Esther!'

From the depths of fatigue she was roused by a loud banging on the back door and someone calling her name. She must have fallen asleep on the rug in front of the range, for the fire had gone out and the ashes were cold.

She shivered and pulled herself to her feet, staggering

almost drunkenly with the tiredness that never seemed to leave her now, to open the door.

Robert Eland stood there in the darkness. 'Esther, I'm sorry – but one of Tom Willoughby's stacks is afire and the others are in danger. We need everyone we can get to help put it out. Will you come?'

'Oh – of course,' she hesitated, 'but I must make sure Kate's all right first.'

Robert Eland nodded and hurried away whilst Esther ran lightly upstairs to check on her sleeping daughter. Kate was not given to night terrors any more. Esther stood over the bed looking down upon the angelic face of her child. She bit the edge of her thumb and glanced around the room. The night-light! She dare not leave that burning. She put it out and then drew back the curtains. It was a clear, frosty night and the moonlight flooded the room. Kate would not be frightened now, even if she awoke.

Downstairs Esther checked that the fire in the range was out. Now everything was safe, she reassured herself. Within minutes she was half-running, half-walking up the lane towards the Grange and branching off towards Rookery Farm. The coldness of the night banished all sleep from her eyes. Ahead of her she could see the figures of the other men and women from the Point, all hurrying towards the glow in the sky that all farmers dread to see. As she neared the farm, she could smell the acrid smoke and see sparks showering into the night sky, dancing against the blackness and drifting dangerously towards the other stacks in the yard.

Between the burning stack and the well, they formed

two chains, one to pass the water and one to return the empty containers for refill. They used anything they could lay hands upon. Two boys – Peter and Luke Harris – worked the well bucket, and the women and children made up the human chains, whilst Tom Willoughby and Robert Eland were nearest to the burning stack.

'I don't see Martha and that sister of hers taking their places,' Esther remarked to the woman nearest to her and, turning to glance at her, found herself looking directly into the dark eyes of a familiar face illuminated by the flickering light from the fire.

Esther caught her breath. 'Beth!' The name escaped her lips before she could stop herself.

'Hello, Esther,' Beth said quietly. As she passed a full bucket of water to Esther, their eyes met and held for a moment, until Esther turned away briefly to pass on the bucket. Her gaze was drawn back to the woman at her side standing patiently waiting for the next bucket to reach her.

Esther searched about her mind for something to say. But it was Beth who asked, scarcely above a whisper, 'Have you heard any news from him lately?'

There was no need to ask who she meant.

'No – no, I haven't had a card for months now.' Esther paused, but she felt Beth was waiting for her to say more. 'They can't always write, you know. It dun't mean that anything awful's happened to him. Besides, if it had, I'd have heard from the authorities . . .' She stopped, suddenly aware of the strange circumstance. Here she was standing in a farmyard in the middle of the night whilst the flames of a burning stack leapt and danced and cast eerie shadows and grotesque shapes, trying to comfort Beth of all people! If it hadn't been so heartrending, it would have been comical.

Beth said nothing. Esther watched her, wondering about her. There was a calmness and a quietness about Beth now. She seemed so much older than the girl who had shaken her fist in Esther's face and laid a curse upon her for taking the man she loved. It was as if Beth had grown old in the space of a few short years. The promise of beauty that had been in her young, round face had never flowered. She was much thinner than Esther remembered, the high cheekbones and hollowed cheeks giving her a gaunt look, accentuated by the flickering shadows. Her eyes were dark, unfathomable pools of loneliness.

Was that what the loss of true love did to a person? Esther wondered. Would she, Esther, grow old, too, waiting and longing for Jonathan?

There was nothing else Esther could think of to say so they just carried on working side by side to save what they could of Tom's stack.

By the time dawn was spreading cold fingers of light across the flat land, the fire was out and the helpers were trudging home, smut-faced and weary. Esther turned away, sickened by the sight of the blackened and smouldering hay which the men were still spreading and turning to make sure it would not blow up again into a blaze.

She felt someone grasp her arm and as she began to turn to see who it was, a hand slapped her face hard. Caught off balance by the sudden attack, Esther fell to the ground.

Martha Willoughby stood above her. 'So, you thought you'd have revenge for your ran-tan-tanning by setting light to our stack, did you?'

Esther opened her mouth to protest, but the tirade was not finished. 'Well, let me tell you, Esther Hilton. They all know you now round here for exactly what you are. A scheming hussy who tricked a dying man into leaving her everything that rightly belongs to others; who stole another girl's sweetheart and her baby's father and then – to cap it all – when he went to fight for his country, took another man, a deserter no less, into her bed. You're a trollop, Esther Hilton. A whore and—'

Anger flooded through Esther and she struggled to her feet. She stood facing Martha, her eyes flashing fire, her hands on her hips. But before she could utter a word, Tom's booming voice rang out in the early morning light.

'That's enough, Martha.' He stepped between them, but his face was in shadow so that Esther could not see his expression. When he spoke his voice was so hard and cold that Esther was shocked. 'Ya'd better go home, Esther.'

She stood before him now, swaying slightly. This was too much. Martha's malice she could take, but not Tom's animosity. Never Tom's. The fatigue of the night's work, her own very personal misery and now this threatened to overwhelm her. Esther's shoulders sagged and her arms hung limply at her sides. All her strength drained from her. She looked up at Tom and tears welled in her eyes as she whispered, 'Not you too, Tom. You don't believe I'd fire ya stack? Surely you don't!'

Tom shook his head as if not knowing what to believe. 'Just – go home, Esther. It'd be for the best, lass.'

Martha was quiet now, watchful and triumphant. For a moment it had seemed as if her husband was going to take Esther's side, but he had not. Even though he had not exactly taken his wife's side either, Esther could feel Martha's sense of victory.

She turned away hurt and sick at heart.

One day merged into another, each the same as the last. The work she had once loved, had revelled in, became drudgery.

Where was the reason to go on living now that he was gone?

She wandered the shore, grieving as if Jonathan were already dead, lost to her for ever.

During the time that he had been with her she had attended church infrequently. It was as if she had been afraid of retribution, for her early childhood had been spent beneath the flailing arms and chest-beating, fire and brimstone preacher in the pulpit, who had instilled fear of eternal damnation into the young child, which even the maturity of later years and reasoning found hard to dispel completely.

Now she returned taking Kate with her and hoping to find comfort and understanding. Unashamedly – though only in the silence of her own heart – she prayed for Jonathan's safety.

'If only I could know that somewhere he is alive and safe, then I could find the will to go on living.'

She emerged from the church to shake hands with

343

the vicar and nod to the members of the congregation she knew.

'Ah – er – Mrs Hilton. Good morning. Er – so nice to see you.' The vicar greeted her, but he seemed oddly ill-at-ease, and his handshake was swift and too brief. He seemed to snatch his hand away after the merest contact with hers, and turn away quickly to greet, with an exaggerated enthusiasm, the couple walking behind her.

Esther nodded to two or three people she knew by sight, but there was no courteous raising of hats by the gentlemen or answering smile from the ladies. One or two pointedly turned their heads away, deliberately cutting her. Esther held her head high, her chin jutting forward defiantly as she marched down the pathway and out into the road. It was obvious they had all heard about her and the soldier who had come to the Point, no doubt thanks to Martha Willoughby. So what? What did they know about falling in love and being loved by such a man as Jonathan Godfrey! Never, ever, would she allow anyone – least of all these people she hardly knew – to make her feel ashamed of loving Jonathan.

Esther walked all the way home, her anger making her quicken her pace until Kate begged her to slow down.

'I'm getting a pain in me side, Mam,' she wailed.

'I'm sorry, Katie,' Esther said, immediately contrite.

Kate, soon sunny-natured again, asked, 'Can I go and play at the Point when we get home?'

'Yes, yes, you can,' Esther decided suddenly. 'I'll come and see Ma, too.'

When they reached the stretch of ground between the cottages and the river bank, they saw three of the

344

younger Harris children and Danny playing soldiers, marching up and down with sticks on their shoulders for rifles.

'You can't play, Kate,' shouted Georgie Harris. 'We're going to war. War is men's work.'

Esther looked down at her daughter to see the child's lower lip quivering.

Then Danny was standing in front of them. 'Dun't cry, Katie. Course you can play. You can be a nurse when we gets wounded – like Mester Godfrey.'

Esther felt a lurch in her chest at the mention of his name, but Danny, unaware of the effect his words had upon her, was taking Kate by the hand and leading her into the game.

Esther wandered towards Ma Harris's cottage. She tapped on the door, opened it and was about to step inside when Ma's ample frame appeared in the doorway. Esther gasped aloud as she looked into Ma's set face. Her eyes were cold and her mouth set in a hard line.

'Well?' she asked shortly. 'What do you want?'

Esther shrugged. 'I just came – to – to see you.'

Ma stood her ground, making no move to invite Esther in. 'Well, Ah dun't want to see you,' the older woman said harshly.

'Ma, I . . .'

Ma Harris turned away. 'Please go, Esther. We've nowt to say to one another. Not any more.'

Esther turned and blundered away before anyone might see her tears. She picked up her skirts and ran and ran across the marshland and along the Spit. Running, running until she felt her lungs would burst. At the end of the Spit, close to the water's edge, she picked up a handful of stones and hurled them one by one into the water.

Angry tears blurred her vision.

Why was she being punished for having loved Jonathan? When at last she'd tasted – oh, so briefly – real happiness, it had been cruelly snatched away. Now, even her tender memories were being soured by the condemnation of those around her.

Down the years, in brutal mockery, came the echo of Beth's curse.

'You an' yours will never know happiness.'

Thirty-one

*I*T seemed incredible to all of them that the war had been going on for over two and a half years. Mothers dreaded the passing of the months as their sons who were still at home grew older, nearer and nearer the age when they could volunteer, or be called up. Esther heard – through Enid – that Peter Harris, now fifteen, was already planning to volunteer. Esther shuddered and, despite Ma's present coldness towards her, she prayed that the woman who had once shown her such friendliness would not lose yet another son to the war.

As men were killed and went on being killed in their thousands, the Military Service Act had been passed the previous February and all men between the ages of eighteen and forty-one who did not have special exemption were being conscripted. Wives feared that any day their husbands, who had believed themselves too old, would have to go too. Would Robert Eland and maybe even Mr Harris and Tom Willoughby be next? Esther wondered.

She dragged herself through the weeks and months, through the ploughing, through the spring sowing. Now no one came to offer to lend her their machinery, horses or manpower. Whether it was because they were no longer able to offer the help or because they no longer wished to help Esther Hilton of Brumbys' Farm, she did not know. She managed most of the ploughing with her own pair of horses, but the seed drilling was beyond her strength and she was obliged to go back to the old way of broadcasting the seed from a carrier hung around her neck and shoulders.

'Thank you, Aunt Hannah,' she said to herself, grudgingly admitting that the reason she at least knew how to do the sowing this way was once more due to her aunt. How was it, she mused to herself as she walked up and down the fields, casting the seed from side to side as she went, that she could not bring herself to think of her aunt with any shred of affection? Yet she was forced to acknowledge that all the learning and the know-how she was now drawing on in her lone struggle to survive, she had acquired from her aunt. Even her stubborn resilience – going to bed each night to sleep the sleep of the exhausted and rising still as bone-weary to face another lonely day – had been fostered by her aunt's harshness. Esther had survived a loveless childhood and grown the stronger for it. But having known love, Jonathan's love, and for that matter Ma Harris's friendship, it was harder now to live without affection. She had the farm, Esther told herself sternly when weakness threatened to overwhelm her. She had Kate and always, she had Will. He still came each week, as faithful and uncritical as ever.

Esther never spoke of Jonathan to anyone – was never able to say his name aloud. Not even to Will, for whilst he stood by her, defended her sometimes in the face of the censure of those around, she knew that even he had disapproved of her love for Jonathan.

Her heartache and her loneliness had to remain locked silently within her own heart. The days stretched ahead, unendingly desolate. She would face them – and she would survive – but, oh, how she missed the feel of Jonathan's arms around her!

On a bright summer morning in 1917, Esther woke with a sense of foreboding. It stayed with her through milking. The animals were restless and obstinate, and later, in the dairy, the heat of midday affected the milk and the butter would not come. She churned and churned until the sweat prickled her armpits and ran in rivulets down between her breasts.

'Mrs Hilton, Mrs Hilton.'

'Now what?' she muttered, passing the back of her hand across her damp forehead. Giving the churn one last vicious turn, and then letting the handle swing loose, she stepped out of the pantry, through the kitchen and out of the back door into the sunlight. She screwed up her eyes against the glare and shaded her face with her hand trying to see who the caller was. A dark uniformed shape stood before her, thrusting a white square of paper into her hand.

'It – it's a telegram, missus.' The young man's tone was apologetic.

Esther stood staring at it, not moving, until he thrust it towards her again, anxious to be gone before she read what awful news it must contain.

Jonathan! Oh no! Her lips formed his name, but she made no sound. With trembling fingers she reached out and took the telegram. The young man turned, mounted his bike and pedalled away quickly.

The words blurred before her and she had to blink

and read it several times before the truth penetrated her consciousness.

Beneath the heading 'POST OFFICE TELEGRAMS' and some small printing which she did not trouble to read, the message was handwritten, the wording terse and impersonal:

OHMS. War Office, London. To Hilton, Fleethaven Point, Lincolnshire. Deeply regret to inform you that Sgt M. Hilton, Lincolnshire Regiment, was posted missing 21st May. Secretary War Office.

There was not even the name of the sender to soften the harsh, dispassionate wording.

For a long time Esther looked down at the piece of paper in her hands, reading and re-reading the words until they blurred before her eyes. She walked slowly into the house. In the kitchen she stood, dazed, in front of the mantelpiece. With shaking fingers she reached up and took down the photograph of Matthew in its silver frame. The postcards stacked behind it slithered down and scattered around her, floating down on to the floor like falling petals. She picked each one up and sat down at the table, resting her arms on the plush green tablecloth. She placed his photograph in front of her and then read and re-read every postcard he had sent.

'Oh, Matthew,' she murmured aloud, 'Matthew, I'm so sorry. I never wanted this to happen.'

She stayed a long time in the house on her own, coming to terms with the news. Learning to live with the knowledge that now she was really on her own. Thoughts of Jonathan intruded, but resolutely she pushed them away. Now was not the time to think of him.

At last she sighed and heaved herself up from the table. She replaced the photograph and the postcards on the mantelpiece and then gently touched the face in the picture with her forefinger. 'Poor Matthew,' she murmured.

She went across to the sideboard and opened the drawer. Lying face upwards was the companion photograph to the one in the frame. She took it out and closed the drawer. Picking up the telegram from the table, she left the farmhouse and turned towards the Point.

There was something she had to do.

Esther walked the short distance from her farm to the Point. At this time of day there was no one about outside the cottages or the pub and for this she was thankful. She didn't yet want to face the inevitable questions. She stood on the bank below the towering bulk of the Elands' boat home. She waited uncertainly. There was no one in sight and she did not want to venture up the gangway uninvited and unheralded. She heard a footstep on the wooden planking of the deck and saw Robert Eland appear at the end of the wooden jetty.

With the hand that still held the telegram Esther shaded her eyes against the sun and met Robert Eland's gaze unflinchingly. She saw his glance switch to the piece of paper rattling gently in the breeze, then come back to her face.

Levelly she said, 'Robert – can I speak to Beth, please?' She heard him draw in breath quickly between his teeth and for a moment his eyes seemed to widen.

He nodded briefly, turned away and disappeared, leaving Esther standing on the river bank below.

It seemed an age that Esther waited, and yet it could not have been more than a few moments that she stood in the sunlight, staring at the black bulk of the boat in front of her. Her eyes took in the peeling paint exposing rotting wood. Poor Robert, she thought, he hasn't had time to keep his own home in good repair. Being one of the few able-bodied men left, Robert Eland always helped out on the estate when needed. And he was often needed.

I wonder why no one has called him a coward for not volunteering? she thought and then answered her own question in her mind. It would be difficult for anyone to accuse Robert Eland of cowardice; many times he had risked his life out at sea in the lifeboat rescuing others. The war had brought a greater number of tragedies at sea. She bit down hard upon her lip as she remembered it had been just such a reason that had brought Enid rushing to the farm for the horses; the night the girl had seen Esther emerging from the barn, her clothing in disarray. I mustn't think of him, she told herself, not now!

She waited in the hot sun, breathing in the scent of the countryside, yet unaware of it. Seagulls screeched overhead, bees hummed busily and butterflies fluttered aimlessly. But the bright day seemed only to mock her. How can it be such a beautiful day, how dare it be, when I . . . ? She closed her eyes a moment against the glare and when she opened them again she saw that Beth was standing at the end of the planking.

The two women stared at each other and then Beth

came slowly down to stand in front of Esther.

Neither of them spoke, yet their eyes held each other's. Wordlessly, Esther held out the telegram for Beth to read. The woman, who had borne Matthew's son, reached for it with shaking fingers.

Dragging her gaze away from Esther's she lowered her eyes and read the words. At last she raised her head, eyes closed and a low moan of anguish escaped her lips. 'Oh, no! *No!*'

Gently, Esther eased the piece of paper from Beth's rigid fingers. 'Beth – I know how you feel. I never – understood – not before. Now I do.'

No more explanation was necessary. The two women regarded each other sadly. In that moment of mutual loss, they came the closest they ever would to understanding one another.

Esther had not known love before Jonathan, but if Beth had loved Matthew in the same way, then there was room for compassion.

Esther held out the photograph. 'I thought you might like to have this. Matthew sent me it soon after he – first went.'

Beth took his likeness and stared at it and then held it to her breast. 'Don't you want it?' she whispered.

'There were two,' Esther explained simply. 'I have the other in a frame on the mantelpiece.'

Beth nodded. Her eyes filled with tears that spilled over and ran down her pale cheeks. 'Thank you, Esther. And thank you for coming to tell me.'

Beth turned away and, like an old woman, dragged herself back up the slope of the gangway.

Thirty-two

*T*HE small community was shocked by the news.

The squire rode over in person to visit Esther. 'Of course, my dear,' he said taking her hand and patting it comfortingly, 'it does say "reported missing". There is room for hope, my dear. It must be chaos out there, you know. Maybe he's been wounded and carted off to some field hospital and not able to tell them who he is. Anything like that can happen. You must – we must all – continue to hope that he is alive somewhere. It's not definite – you must cling to that hope.'

Esther tried to smile. 'Thank you, Squire, you're very kind.' She bit her lip. She wanted so much to ask him what was to happen about the tenancy of the farm, but suddenly the picture of his angry face and his censorious words after Sam Brumby's funeral made her bite back her question. Now was not the time!

Life continued much as before through the summer of 1917 – day after day the same. What had she to look forward to now? What had she to hope for? Indeed, with this dreadful war snatching all the young men from their midst, fathers, husbands – and lovers, what hope for the future had anyone?

The day that Esther had dreaded arrived without warning and before she could take the evasive action she had done the last time. The little man with the sheaf of papers under his arm arrived so unexpectedly that she had no chance to move Punch and Prince from the meadow.

'I am quite aware, Mrs Hilton,' he began without preamble, 'that on the occasion of my last visit you were able to deceive me. I don't intend to make trouble for you.' His voice softened. 'I'm not really the hard-hearted villain you take me for – but I have a job to do and I am afraid I really must commandeer your horses.'

'How am I to get the harvests in? There's no fellers and . . .' She stopped and bit her lip. She had been about to tell him that she no longer had the usual help from her neighbours now that they were ostracizing her at the instigation of Martha Willoughby and – yes, she had to admit it – even Ma Harris.

'I really am sorry,' the official was saying again. 'The squire has been allowed to keep three horses on condition that he loans them out to anyone nearby who has real need . . .'

'How do you think just three horses can cope with all the work around here at harvest? The grass and the corn dun't wait, mester.'

The man sighed. 'I do understand . . .'

'No, ya don't. Ya can't!' She turned away before he should see her tears. Before she would let any man – other than Jonathan – see her cry, she turned her back on him. With an angry gesture she waved him away. 'Oh, take 'em, then. Only, don't let me see.'

She sat in the kitchen, her hands lying idly on the table, staring out of the window that faced on to the front garden, determined not to risk catching sight of her beloved horses being led out of the meadow and up the lane towards the town.

Two pairs of small feet pounded across the yard and Kate, followed by Danny Eland, came bursting into the kitchen.

'Mam, Mam, they're taking Punch and Prince. Mam, stop them.' Tears ran down her daughter's face and even the boy seemed to be having difficulty in holding his mouth from quivering. Esther held out her hand and Kate came and stood at the side of her chair. The child leant her head on her mother's breast and the tears flowed. Esther held out her other hand to Danny and he came and stood close beside her, and rested his head against her shoulder.

'It dun't seem fair,' he muttered. 'They're old, yar 'osses, anyway. What use can they be in – in the war?'

'I know,' Esther murmured. 'I can't rightly understand it myself, Danny. But there it is, they've got to go.'

Through the open back door the three of them listened to the distant sound of clopping hooves going up the lane, growing fainter and fainter until they could hear them no more.

So many leavings, Esther thought sadly. How many more beings she loved – human and animal – were to walk away down that lane never to return?

Danny twisted his head and looked up into her face. 'I'm sorry about the mester.'

Esther looked down into the boy's dark brown eyes and for a moment rested her hand on his black curly hair. He was so like Matthew that one day, as he grew older, he would surely have guessed just who his sire was, if Matthew had still been around. Now Matthew would not be returning. Would Danny ever know who his natural father was?

Quietly she said, 'Thank you, Danny,' then more briskly she added, 'I've some scones in the oven. Would you like one with some fresh butter?' She was rewarded by a replica of Matthew's cheeky grin, and as she rose and went to take her baking from the range oven, she spared a moment's thought for Beth.

How the sight of her son must twist at Beth's heart every day of her life!

'Tom – they've taken me 'osses.'

'Eh, Esther, lass, I'm sorry to hear that.' He shook his head. 'You did well to hang on to them the last time they came. I didn't,' he added with feeling.

They were standing in Tom's stack yard. 'I'd help you if I could, lass, but I've none mesen, now. I have to borrow the squire's. You'll have to do the same.'

'Aye, but I'll be at the end of the line, won't I?' she added bitterly.

Tom faced her squarely. 'No beating about the bush, lass. I dun't reckon the squire holds anything against you, personal like.'

'Not like the rest of you, ya mean?'

Tom's huge shoulders lifted fractionally as he said truthfully, 'You're not perfect, Esther Hilton. You've made mistakes and takin' up with that young feller whilst your husband was at war hasn't gone down too well with the folks round here . . .' He held up his hand as she opened her mouth to protest, speaking for her the words she had been about to utter. 'Aye, I know, it's no one else's business. But folks around here, I'm afraid, will always make other people's business their own. It's the penalty you pay for living in a little community like this. Matthew was one of us, an' you were a stranger here.'

Stiffly, she said, 'I'm sorry if you think badly of me, Tom, but there's – things you don't know . . .'

Tom nodded. 'Eeh lass, I've been around a long time. I don't think badly of you at all. And maybe I understand a lot more than you think, but there's some as don't.'

'Tom—' she said, suddenly needing to know. 'You never thought I fired your stack, did you?'

Tom pushed his cap back and scratched his head, but did not answer.

'How can you believe that of me, Tom? How can anyone believe I'd do a thing like that? Me, who loves the land more than I—' She stopped. She had been about to say 'more than I love people'. Once, not so long ago, that would have been a valid statement. Since she had known Jonathan, it was no longer true.

'Besides, I wouldn't hurt you for the world, Tom – even,' she added with embittered truthfulness, 'if I ain't much time for yar wife and that sister of hers.'

'I know, lass, I know. But she reckons you swore vengeance on her and Flo for reporting your – er – friend to the authorities. Then after that ran-tan-tanning they give ya . . .' Once more Tom's huge shoulders lifted in a non-committal shrug.

'Aye, I did threaten her.' Esther faced him squarely, courageously admitting her faults but stoutly defending herself against false accusation. 'And in that moment when her and Flo were in their trap in the lane, gloating over the policeman payin' us a visit, I would have done her a mischief an' no mistake. But – ' her voice softened, not at the memory of Martha and Flo but at the mention of Jonathan's name – '*he* stopped me. Jonathan held me from tippling the trap over.' She met the older man's gaze steadfastly. 'Tom, I'm not vindictive. Yes, I bear her a grudge. I'll never forgive her for what she's done to me. First goading Matthew into volunteering, then reporting Jonathan . . .' She shook her head again in disbelief. 'But I would never, ever do a thing like firing yar stack! Please believe me, Tom?'

As Tom pulled his cap back on his head and opened his mouth, there was a loud squawk of rage from behind him and Martha came striding across the yard waving her fat arms and shouting at her husband, closely followed by Flo Jenkins.

'Thomas – how can you let this creature on to our farm after what she did?'

'What's she doing here?' Flo demanded and her voice rose shrilly with a touch of hysteria. 'Martha, she's come to kill us – kill us all. It wasn't enough to try to set fire to our farm. She's a whore and a trollop. Set the dog on her, Martha!'

Tom turned to look at them both. 'Now look here, Flo Jenkins,' his deep voice boomed as he stepped forward. Esther saw Flo's face turn a funny grey colour and her thin hand fluttered to cover her mouth. 'I've let you live in this house nigh on ten year and in that time you've done nowt but cause trouble between me and me wife with your tittle-tattle. You've a poisonous tongue on you, woman.'

'Thomas . . .' Martha began to plead.

'And you can hold yourn, else I'll leave the pair of you and join up.'

Martha gave a cry. 'No, Thomas. You wouldn't. You couldn't – you're too old.'

'Too old be damned!'

'Thomas!' Martha still had enough spirit to admonish him for his language, but the farmer took no notice. 'There was a piece in the paper last week saying that they'll take anyone – anyone, mark you – who'll volunteer to dig trenches.' He leaned towards her and said slowly and deliberately, 'Now that I could do, Martha, as you well know, for I've dug a few in me time.'

'Thomas . . .' Martha wailed. 'How can you side with – with her against your own wife?'

'Now come, Martha my dear. You know me better than that. I'll not take your part if I think you're wrong – and this time, you are. I never did believe that Esther fired that stack and I still don't.' He laughed suddenly, throwing back his head, his great belly wobbling. 'She's more likely to come an' give you a good hiding, but set fire to a stack? Never!'

Martha all but stamped her foot. Her face grew puce. She turned and, grabbing Flo's bony arm with her fat hand, she hustled her sister away and back into the house slamming the back door behind them.

Unperturbed, Tom merely rubbed his huge hands together and smiled again. 'She dun't like to be beat,

Esther lass, and that's put her in her place this time – and that sister of hers – and no mistake.'

'Oh, Tom, I'm sorry. I didn't come to cause you trouble, but I'm glad you believe in me.'

It was a comfort to Esther to know that she had Tom's support, for apart from the ever faithful Will, she saw no one now. Even Enid came less and less to the farm to help out and Luke, one of the younger Harris boys who had for a time tried to take Ernie's place, had stopped coming. But Kate was still welcomed at the Point cottages to play with the Harris children – and with Danny Eland.

The only person in whom Esther could confide was Will Benson. She looked forward to the days when he visited Fleethaven Point and had his dinner with her. Sometimes she never spoke to another soul – apart from Kate – from one of his visits to the next.

'Y'know,' he said between mouthfuls, 'I miss my little lass on me visits, now she's at school. How is she? Does she like it?'

Esther frowned. 'Oh, yes, she loves it. Getting quite the saucy minx now. All the children from the Point walk to the school in town together.'

She felt Will's perceptive eyes upon her. Quietly, he said, 'An' you don't like that because she's with Danny Eland.'

She glanced at him and pulled her mouth into a grimace which implied agreement.

'I shouldn't let it worry you none, lass. They're only bairns. No harm can come of it.'

'Mebbe, mebbe not. I still don't like it, though. They

361

– they seem drawn to each other, Will. She thinks he's wonderful. It's all "Danny says", and "Danny did this" with her.'

Will shrugged. 'Well, they are brother and sister . . .'

'*Half* brother and sister,' she corrected.

'Half brother and sister, then. Perhaps there's a kind of closeness – kinship, if ya like – that won't be denied.'

'Yes – and it worries me,' Esther said, heaving herself up from the table. She gathered up the empty plates and took them out to the scullery. 'Though there's not a lot I can do about it, I suppose.'

'You'll find the more you try to stop 'em playing together, the more they'll want to. Even at this age, they'll rebel against you, given half the chance. I'd let them be, lass. Really I would.'

'I expect you're right, Will.' She grinned at him with affection. 'You usually are. I should listen to your wisdom sometimes.'

He stood up and laughed wheezily. 'Mebbe you should, me lass, mebbe you should.'

They exchanged a knowing glance, but still the words she would have liked to hear him say were not forthcoming.

The months dragged on and it was only the needs of the animals and the land that kept Esther going. She was saddened to think that Matthew was dead, for, three months after the telegram, another official form arrived. The words were just as informal and impersonal:

It is my painful duty to inform you that no further news

362

having been received relative to Sgt Matthew Hilton, the Army Council have been regretfully constrained to conclude that he is dead.

This letter was not such a shock as the telegram had been for despite what the squire had said, she had not thought that the War Office would send such a telegram unless they really believed that there was little hope of Matthew still being alive.

Poor Matthew. He hadn't wanted to die. He hadn't even expected to die, like many of them had done when they volunteered for the glory of it all.

She realized now that although she had never felt for her husband the overwhelming passion she felt for Jonathan, still in a way she had loved Matthew. She owed him a debt of gratitude and the loyalty that any man ought to be able to expect from his wife. But now, having known the intensity of falling in love with a man, of being loved and desired and almost worshipped by that man in return, there was a tinge of sadness in her memories of Matthew. She had no doubt that Beth had loved Matthew like that, and, too late, Matthew had come to realize that he loved Beth. Then he had felt cheated and trapped by his marriage and had vented his unhappiness upon Esther.

Carefully, she placed the letter in the sideboard drawer and closed it. Matthew was gone and she could not alter what had happened in the past. Even so, it had not been all bad, she comforted herself. They'd had the farm and they had created a daughter.

Now the farm and Kate were all she had left.

*

One blustery afternoon, Esther went into her meadow which adjoined Tom Willoughby's land to check the bloom on the grass. She sighed. This field was ready for cutting now – in fact it had been ready for two weeks. Somehow she was going to have to cope completely alone with the harvests this year, for no one would come to help her. She looked about her at the long grass rippling like waves on the ocean in the stiff breeze that blew in from the sea. Clouds scudded across the sun and their shadows travelled across the fields. Suddenly she was filled with a desire to go to the end of the Spit – just to get away from the never-ending workload, if only for an hour.

She left the fields and walked back down the lane away from the borders of Rookery Farm and towards the sand dunes and the marsh beyond them. She had climbed the bank and was about to run down the other side to cross the marsh towards the Spit, when she heard the rattle of wheels in the lane behind her. She turned to see Martha and Flo in their trap, their smart bonnets suggesting they were heading for Lynthorpe. Not wishing to become embroiled in yet further argument with Martha and her sister, Esther ran quickly down the bank and out of their view.

The tide was high and the wind drove waves against the Spit as she walked along it, but she was determined to get to the end where she could find solace and peace surrounded by the sea and the sky with only the birds to share her loneliness.

Seawards, she could see a small boat making towards the haven. Perhaps it was Robert Eland returning from a day's fishing. No doubt, as he drew closer, he would see her standing there, but he would be too intent upon threading his way between the markers he himself had placed in the marsh at low tide to bother himself with Esther Hilton. The poles, sticking up out of the water when the tide was high and the sea covered the marsh, were to guide him up the deep channel of the river bed.

How long she stood there, she didn't know, nor did she know what made her turn suddenly to see Martha and Flo only a few feet away from her, for no sound of their approach had come to her ears above the sound of the sea and the wind.

Suddenly, Esther was filled with an unaccustomed dread. She was standing on the end of the narrow strip of land with her back to the swirling, rushing water and before her, advancing with menace in every step, were the two women who hated her most in the world. Perhaps even more than did Beth Eland.

Esther was trapped. There was no place to run. Young and strong though she was, she would be no match for the two of them.

They had stopped and were standing side by side on the narrow strip of land, effectively barring any chance of escape towards the marsh. Exultation showed on both their faces. The sea, splashing against the bank, showered their best skirts with salty spray yet they didn't seem to care, didn't even seem to notice.

They had Esther Everatt Hilton at their mercy.

Thirty-three

MARTHA was speaking. Her mouth, twisted into an ugly sneer, was moving, but her words were snatched away by the wind before they could reach Esther.

Together they moved forward and Esther felt the fear rise in her throat. Even out here in the cold wind she found she was sweating with terror. Behind her the sea, once her solace, had become a malevolent monster waiting to devour her. The water was not deep but Esther could not swim, and there were hidden channels and pools that were always water-filled even at low tide. If she should fall into one of those . . .

The two women moved forwards again, coming closer, ever closer . . .

There was no escape for Esther.

Suddenly, with one accord, they lunged towards her hitting her in the chest and sending her falling, arms flailing helplessly, backwards into the sea.

The waters closed over her face and there was a gurgling in her ears. She struggled, thrashing with her arms, trying to find the bottom with her feet, striving to bring her head above the water. She broke the surface and drew great gasps of air into her bursting lungs. She could not open her eyes for the stinging salt water. A wave hit her in the back and sent her tippling forward again, face down in the water. She lost her footing and now she could not feel the bottom, could not feel firm earth beneath her feet. She twisted and writhed and tried to push herself upwards. Her sodden clothes were now dragging her down and she felt as if her lungs would rupture. She tried to open her eyes but all she could see was murky, swirling sand. There was a glimmer of light above, but so far away, too far away . . . Water filled her nose and mouth. Her heart was pounding, there was a drumming in her ears. She had never felt so frightened in her life. She knew herself to be drowning and she so desperately wanted to live. She must live – for Kate – for Jonathan. In that moment she saw his beloved face in her mind – the smile crinkling his eyes, the flop of fair hair falling across his forehead – and then there was darkness . . .

Suddenly strong arms were lifting her and she was hauled upwards until her head was above water. She was being shaken and her face was being slapped and suddenly she was coughing and spluttering and clinging on to someone. She coughed and dragged in gulps of air and coughed again until she was sick. Hanging over her rescuer's strong arm, she retched until she had brought up all the sea water that had entered her lungs. Esther was clinging to a man's arm and being pulled along. She felt herself bump the side of a boat.

'Come on, Esther,' said the man's voice. 'I can't lift you in, you'll have to help me.' She brushed her hand across her face and blinked. Her eyes were sore and swollen so that she could scarcely open them. But she knew his voice. Her rescuer was Robert Eland.

She tried to speak but could make no sound. Her breathing was still painful and there was a dreadful ache in her chest.

'Come on,' he was urging her again. 'Put your arms over the side of the boat. Try and grasp hold and I'll heave you in.'

They struggled for a few moments until a helpful wave gave an extra buoyancy to her tired limbs and she found herself sprawling in the bottom of the fishing boat. She was scarcely aware of Robert somehow getting himself back into the boat and rowing away from the Spit towards the mouth of the river and the Point. She neither knew nor cared what had happened to Martha Willoughby and her sister.

It seemed a long time before the boat bumped gently against the river bank, by which time Esther was shivering uncontrollably. Her head ached and her chest still hurt. She kept blinking her eyes to clear her vision. It felt as if she had a barrow-load of sand in each eye.

But she was safe.

Robert was bending over her. 'Can you get up, Esther?'

Valiantly, she made the effort to pull herself up and he supported her, taking her arm and helping her to step out of the boat and on to the wooden landing stage.

'Oh, dear Lord,' she heard a woman's voice exclaim. 'Whatever has happened?'

Still with Robert's arm to support her, Esther staggered on to the land and fell to her knees. She had never been so thankful in her life to feel the firm earth beneath her.

'What happened?' came the voice again.

Slowly Esther raised her head to see Beth standing over her, bending down towards her and even holding out her hands to help her rise.

After only a moment's hesitation, Esther grasped the outstretched hands and hauled herself to her feet. She stood swaying and then she felt Beth's arm about her waist, supporting her, urging her forward. 'Come on to the boat, Esther. I'll get you some dry clothing. Whatever has happened?' she demanded yet again.

Now, relinquishing the care of Esther to his wife, Robert said, ''Twas them two old biddies from Tom Willoughby's farm. They pushed her into the sea off the Spit. God knows what would have happened if I hadn't been near enough to get to her in time.'

Though she could not yet speak, Esther echoed his sentiments. God alone knew!

Esther did not go to the Elands' boat home. She wanted to get to the farm as quickly as possible and Beth took her. Only when she had seen Esther stripped of her wet clothing and sitting before the range with a cup of hot tea, did Beth leave Esther in Kate's care.

Esther recovered quickly and all she told the child was that she had been foolish enough to walk along the Spit on a blustery day and at high tide, and had fallen into the sea.

'And Mr Eland rescued you?'

'Yes, yes – he did,' Esther croaked, for her voice was still ragged. 'I – I think he saved my life.'

Kate, full of importance, said, 'I must go and find Danny and tell him.' In the next moment the child had rushed from the house and Esther had not the strength to stop her.

The following day, Esther opened her back door in answer to a knock and was surprised to find Tom standing there.

'Tom – come in,' Esther invited, her voice still croaky.

Tom hesitated a moment and then eased his bulk through her scullery and into the kitchen.

He pulled his cap from his head and stood twisting it in his huge hands. 'Esther, lass,' he began, 'Eland told me what happened yesterday. I want you to know – I'm sorry.'

'Tom . . .'

'No, lass. Hear me out – please. They'll not bother you again, I've seen to that. But I'd just ask ya to keep away from me farm for a while – an' mebbe church an' all. Just for a time, like.' The cap was still revolving through his restless fingers. 'I've never in me life raised me hand to me wife an' I dun't intend to, but, by God, when Eland told me – I came close to it, lass.'

Esther shook her head sadly. 'Tom – I've told you before, I never wanted to cause trouble between you and your wife . . .'

'I know, I know.' He shook his head, wonderingly. 'I just dun't understand her mesen. You're like a red rag to her, Esther, an' that's a fact.'

'Tom,' Esther asked, suddenly remembering, 'were you related to Sam Brumby? Is that what started it all?'

'Oh, aye, but years back. Now let's see – my grandfather's sister was Sam's mother.'

Esther nodded. 'There's an entry in Sam's old family Bible. I did wonder.' She sighed. 'Martha thinks all this – ' she waved her arm to encompass all Sam's belongings in the house – 'should have come to you.'

Tom shrugged. 'Mebbe, Esther. To tell you the truth, I never give it a thought.'

Esther believed him. It was only Martha and her grasping sister who resented her.

She also believed Tom when he said that their persecution of her was at an end. For that, she was thankful, yet his advice to stay away, not only from his farm but from the church too, would isolate her from the community more than ever.

Like Ma Harris, but not as bluntly, Tom was saying they wanted no more to do with Esther Hilton.

A few days later, when she had fully recovered, Esther went to the point in search of Robert Eland..

'I came to thank you, Robert. You saved my life.'

The man looked up at her from where he was sitting on the river bank, mending his fishing net. He nodded briefly in swift acknowledgement of her thanks. Then, looking back down at his nets, he said, 'I reckon we're equal now, then. For yar man saved my life that night.'

She knew she was referring to the time Matthew had gone out in the lifeboat and had rescued Robert.

'Please – thank Beth for me, will ya?'

There was a pause, then Robert nodded and muttered, 'Aye, I will.'

There was no more to be said. To say any more would have been an embarrassment to them both. Robert Eland might have saved her life but it had changed nothing in the attitude of the people of Fleethaven Point towards Esther Hilton. Not one thing.

It was the farm that devoured Esther's time and strength through the rest of the summer, autumn and even the winter of 1917. Thankfully, her growing daughter, happy at school and always welcomed by her friends at the Point even if her mother was not, was little trouble. Kate never seemed to suffer from childish illnesses, she was sturdy, strong for her age, and healthy. If anyone's health was in question during those months, it was Esther's.

Apart from Will Benson, she saw no one but to say that she was utterly alone was not quite true for she had two very willing helpers, and for their age and strength they were remarkable.

Kate – and Danny Eland. Without their help she would have lost more of her crops than she did, for when winter set in with a vengeance there were still two fields uncut. As for the rest, Esther cut the corn with a hand sickle. She had tried Sam's scythe but found it too heavy and unwieldy. Day after day she moved slowly down the field locked into a stooping position, grasping a bunch of corn in her left hand and cutting it with the sickle in her right. Day after day until she thought she would never walk upright again, until every limb in her body ached and cried out for rest. Still she drove herself on. On and on until the pain in her body drove out the ache in her heart and left her mind dulled and unable to think of

Jonathan. At night she fell into bed exhausted and slept at once.

The children took on the job of raking, tying the sheaves and stooking. Esther cut down the handles of two rakes to make them more manageable for them and their merry laughter as they worked was the only sound in the fields, normally alive with noisy chatter from the numerous harvest workers. The fields at Brumbys' Farm were silent, waiting their turn under Esther's lone sickle – and some would wait in vain.

'Ya'll kill ya'sen, lass,' Will told her bluntly.

'What else can I do, Will? I can't lose it all. I won't lose it all.'

'Ask the squire for help, Esther. After all, it's his land.'

'I dun't want him to think I can't cope. I don't know what he intends – now Matthew's not coming back. He might only need the slightest excuse to take the tenancy off me.'

Will was silent, scratching his head in defeat.

'And,' she added bitterly, 'I dun't want him to know why none of the others are helping me this year.'

'I 'spect he knows,' Will muttered under his breath, but Esther's hearing was sharp.

'I suppose you're right. I can't understand them,' she said angrily. 'They all came last year, when Jonathan was actually here. They liked him – everyone did. So why are they punishing me now?'

'They didn't blame him, Esther lass,' Will told her gently, unknowingly echoing Ma Harris's words. 'At first he was a hero in their eyes. A soldier wounded in the war and going to go back. But then *you* kept him here. To their way of thinking it was *you* turned him into a deserter. They blame you for everything.'

Esther closed her eyes and swayed slightly as her loss swept over her again. Tiredness made her vulnerable. Whilst for the most part the hard work blotted out her memories, when those same memories did intrude, she had no resistance to the hurt. She groaned and sank down into a kitchen chair and leant her head on her arms on the table.

'Why was it so very wrong of me to fall in love with him?'

'Because you were married — are still, for all we really know — and to one of their own. More than anything else, they can't forgive you for that, Esther.'

'It's different for men, isn't it?' Her voice was muffled, but there was no mistaking her resentment. 'They get away with it. They can have affairs, even bring — bring bastards into the world and are just thought "a bit of a lad". Even envied by other fellers. But a woman! Oh, no, she's a trollop and a whore . . .' She stopped, appalled that she was talking to Will in this way, that she was thrusting the knife of her years of resentment into him of all people.

Will Benson sighed but said nothing. What was there that he could say to her accusation?

'Me husband's dead,' Esther went on. 'Am I supposed to live the rest of me life alone, just because . . . ?'

'No, of course not, Esther. You jumped the gun, that's what's caused the resentment. You hadn't even had word that he was missing before you took up with Jonathan Godfrey.'

It was a fact that she could not deny and it was that fact the people of Fleethaven Point could not forgive.

Through the long winter, Esther threshed the corn in her barn by hand with Sam's old flail, spending long hours in the cold, with the wind whipping between the two sets of open doors, blowing away the chaff and leaving her the precious harvest of grain.

There was no news of Jonathan. Was he dead too, like Matthew? Or was he still out there in the muddy trenches? Did he ever think of her? she wondered. Did he remember Fleethaven Point and the warm sand and the soft, lapping sea, music to their love-making?

By the spring of 1918 the news from the war front seemed no better – worse if anything. The newspapers which Will still brought each week were gloomy. The Germans had launched massive attacks on the Western Front and British-held trenches were overrun and captured. The British faced defeat and fresh fears swept through those left at home. Had they lost so many young men in vain?

Then, like the turn of the tide, the British and their allies were marching forward, breaking through the Hindenburg Line and marching on and on and people began to speak as if victory could be a reality.

One morning she heard Will's whistle; not one blast as usual to herald his arrival, but three shrill notes piercing the air. Esther set down the egg basket she was carrying and ran to the gate. Will was standing up on the front of his cart, excitedly waving a newspaper and climbing down before his horses had stopped. 'Esther – Esther lass. It's over. It's really over.'

Esther stood at the gate staring at him as he came towards her.

'The war, Esther. It's over.' Wordlessly, she put her arms up and he hugged her to him. 'It'll be all right now, lass. Things'll get better – you see.'

At the eleventh hour on the eleventh day of the eleventh month, it was indeed all over. Of course there was rejoicing and in some towns and cities there were joyous celebrations, but amongst the community at Fleethaven Point there seemed only relief, their happiness tempered by the losses their small number had sustained. The squire's son, who would never step into his father's place; Ernie Harris, Ma's firstborn – and Matthew. In the months since Esther had received the final letter from the Army authorities there had been no further word, no hint that there was any hope that he could still be alive.

Now that it was finally all over, Esther clung to the hope that Jonathan had come through, that perhaps he would come home, that he would come to the Point to see her and, maybe, finding her a widow, just maybe . . .

During the weeks which followed the Armistice, Esther grew increasingly restless. There was little she could do on the land in December, nor could she seem to generate any enthusiasm for Christmas preparations. Once again she had struggled virtually alone with her harvest, though this year she had use of the squire's horses for a week and the loan of one of his men. Yet again, no one from the Point had offered help, nor even Tom Willoughby. And Ma Harris, whose coldness hurt more than anyone's, kept stubbornly away from Brumbys' Farm – and Esther.

Wandering around the farm watching the pigs, the hens, checking on the cows, Esther felt as if she were waiting for something to happen, only it didn't seem to be happening.

She sighed and walked towards the farm gate, leaning on it and looking up the road towards the town. If only he would come walking back round the bend. But the lane was empty. There was no sign of a tall, fair-haired soldier marching towards her.

Her gaze travelled round and came to rest on the rise in the road – the Hump – beyond which were the cottages at the Point. Before she fully realized what she was doing, or had even stopped to think, she was moving out of her gate and down the lane towards the Point. She knocked on the door of Ma Harris's cottage and stood waiting, her heart thumping. It was strange that she should feel afraid. She had missed Ma's warmth, her chatter, her friendship so much. As she stood there she could hear the sound of children laughing and shrieking as they played on the scrubland beyond the cottage.

The door opened and Ma stood there, wiping her floury hands on her apron.

'Oh – it's you,' she said, turned away abruptly and went back to her kitchen table to her pastry-making. But she left the door open. At least she had not slammed it in Esther's face.

'Ma – can I come in?' This was a new Esther, a tentative, penitent Esther.

'If ya must.'

'Ma – can't we be friends again?'

The older woman glanced at her and then back to her pastry, thumping it over and over, rolling it out with the wooden rolling pin. For a long time she didn't answer.

'Ya know what the Good Book says, "As ye sow, so shall ye reap." There'll come a day of reckoning, lass. Somewhere, some time you'll be made to pay.'

An angry retort rose to Esther's lips, but for once she literally bit back the words, pressing her teeth into her bottom lip to suppress them.

Ma Harris let out a long sigh and now there was more sadness than censure in her tone. 'Oh, Esther lass, part of me does understand why you were drawn to that young feller, but it's hard for me to forgive you. Young Matthew has always been part of our lives. I helped bring him into the world in that cottage next door,' she nodded her head beyond her own cottage wall indicating the adjoining house. 'He were like one of me own and after he'd lost both his parents, well, he more or less did become one of me family. But more than that even, it was you leaving your bairn in the house on her own that really riled me. Ya know how I am about bairns?'

'I – I know you think badly of me and I'm sorry, real sorry. As for Kate, yes, I felt guilty about that and it never happened again.'

Ma cast her a sideways glance but said no more. To Esther her look said, 'So, you took him into the house then – into Matthew's house.'

Esther's chin came a little higher, but she kept her tone submissive. 'There's a lot I'm sorry for now – a lot that's to do with Matthew — and Beth. But I'll never, ever, say I'm sorry I met Jonathan.'

Ma gasped and stared at her. Esther met her gaze levelly. 'Eeh, lass, you're honest, I'll say that for ya. An' though I dun't hold with what ya've done, ya didn't skulk about it. Ya didn't try to hide what was going on between you and Jonathan from us all, even knowing we wouldn't like it. You're a strange one, Esther Hilton, an' no mistake.'

Then slowly, like the sun appearing as a cloud passed away, a smile began to spread across Ma's shrunken mouth. She shook her head, almost as if in disbelief at herself for what she was about to say. 'I can't go on being mad at ya — an' the Lord knows I've tried. Truth is, I've missed ya, lass. Missed talking and laughing with ya, I really have.'

Now she was smiling broadly and Esther was smiling back.

'So, you'll both be here for Christmas this year, will you?'

'Try and keep us away!'

So it was a merry Christmas that year of 1918 which Esther and Kate shared with the Harris family once more, for Mr Harris and all their brood took their lead from Ma. Her word was law. If she wanted nothing to do with Esther Hilton, then they obeyed, but if Ma forgave and welcomed her back, then they were ready to do that too.

And their country was no longer at war — it was time to forgive and to make new beginnings. They all went to

Midnight Mass together, walking the long lane in the frosty, moonlit night, the children, far from sleepy, skipping and dancing and chasing each other; the grown-ups, walking arm in arm, smiling and content and thankful. Yes, thankful, Esther thought, that despite what they had all lost, there would be no more killing and maiming. Their soldiers were coming home.

Oh, dear Lord, she prayed silently, let one of them be Jonathan.

It was in the New Year that Esther's restlessness grew and became unbearable. She could find no solace in the farm. Even her favourite place on the Spit and the peaceful scenery brought no comfort and serenity. Her anxiety over Jonathan festered until she was sleeping badly and could not eat.

There should have been some word. Surely the soldiers were coming home from France now? He would have got in touch somehow. Perhaps he was still in France. Perhaps he was wounded and in hospital, or – heaven forbid – perhaps he was dead and lying in a grave in foreign soil, alone and forgotten by everyone but her.

It was Will Benson who gave her the idea that there was something she could do.

'Have you heard the latest?'

She was listening with only half an ear to his chatter, but his next words commanded her immediate attention. 'Squire's going over to France to see if he can find his boy's grave. Course Mrs Marshall ain't going. Poor lady – she's never got over the lad's death, y'know. Just the squire and his younger son are going.'

Esther stared at him. Her heart began to beat a little faster and she felt herself go breathless with excitement. 'How's he managed that? Can anybody go? When's he going?'

'Eh, steady on, lass. 'Ow should I know? All I know is, he's got in touch with that there Major Langley. You know, 'im as gave that speech in the town just after the war started.'

'Oh, I remember him all right!' Esther said grimly.

'Now, lass, the man was only doing his duty—'

'Never mind that now, Will,' she cut him off sharply. 'Do you know when Squire's going?'

'Next week some time I think. He found out from the major where young Rodney's company was when he was killed.'

'Oh, next week, eh?' Esther muttered, her mind busy. Jonathan must have been in the same company as the squire's son. She remembered the squire asking Jonathan if he had known his son and Jonathan had said that he knew him by sight. They'd all been in the same regiment, Rodney Marshall, Ernie Harris, Matthew – and Jonathan! Perhaps . . .

'Esther Hilton – what are you up to?' Will was eyeing her shrewdly.

She grinned at him, feeling alive and hopeful for the first time in many months. 'Never you mind, Will Benson, just never you mind.'

'Mr Marshall – please, I want to come to France with you.' Once more – as if time had taken a tilt – Esther was standing facing the squire across his huge desk.

'Eh? What?' The squire's mouth all but dropped open. 'Come to France? My dear Mrs Hilton . . .'

He was patronizing her. Her green eyes flashed and her jaw tightened. She saw that he had noticed, for his protestations died. He ran his hand through his thin, greying hair. He sighed deeply and said, more kindly, 'I can well understand your desire to go out there. Indeed, it must match my own.' He glanced at her shrewdly. 'More so, if you still hold on to the belief that perhaps your husband may be alive.'

Esther opened her mouth and then shut it firmly against what she had been about to say. She made herself swallow hard before she said, 'Exactly!'

Silently she begged forgiveness for the lie.

The squire spread his hands in a helpless gesture. 'My dear, I really don't think it's a place for ladies . . .'

'But the war is over now. Why don't they come home? Why have we heard nothing?' Deliberately, she allowed him to think she was referring all the time to Matthew, when in her heart she was silently crying the name, 'Jonathan, Jonathan! JONATHAN!'

With quiet determination, she said, 'Squire, please help me. I *have* to go.'

He sighed and looked at her steadily. Esther was sure he could no longer find it in his heart to argue with her. He was determined to go, but knew he would discover only a grave. She could read his thoughts, transparent upon his face. How can I refuse her, when perhaps she seeks the living?

All he did not know was the true identity of the person she sought.

Thirty-four

'*G*O where?' Ma Harris's tone was scandalized. Esther might as well have said she intended to fly to the moon. 'But – but what about yar bairn? And the farm?'

Esther smiled her most winning smile, but before she could utter a word, Ma nodded. 'Oh, I get it. The Harrises'll no doubt help out. Tek care of young Kate and all the livestock! Is that it?'

'Well –' Esther eyed the older woman with a coy look, the smile still twitching at her mouth – 'I was hoping . . .'

Ma's laugh cackled. 'Eeh, but you're a bold one, lass. Is that why you came to get round me again?'

'No, it isn't, Ma. You know me better than that.'

'Aye, I suppose I do at that. We'll help ya.' Then her eyes narrowed as she added perceptively, 'What exactly are ya going for?'

Ma Harris was not as easily deceived as the squire.

For a long moment the two women stared at each other. Esther sighed. 'Ma – please try to understand. I – I have to go.'

'You're going to try and find him – Jonathan – aren't you?'

Esther sat down suddenly at Ma's kitchen table and laid her arms on its scrubbed surface. All her strength, all

383

her resolve ebbed away. She felt her mouth quiver and tears spring to her eyes.

'Oh, Ma, don't be angry with me. Not again, please.'

Ma sat down opposite and patted her hands as they lay, trembling a little, on the table. 'Eh, lass, dun't tek on so. I meant no harm. I didn't mean to upset yar, but I dun't want to see ya hurt . . .' She paused a moment, before adding wisely, 'Or bring more trouble on ya'sen. Ya'd do better to forget all about him and get on with yar life.'

'Oh, Ma, I'm hurting now. I've never stopped hurting since the day he went. I don't know what's happened to him. I've never heard a word of him since he walked down that road away from me.' She flung her arm wide in a vague gesture towards the road leading to the town. 'I've got to know, Ma. I've just got to find out. At least, I must try.'

Ma shook her head sadly, but still held Esther's hands. 'Eh, lass, lass,' was all she could say, but Esther knew by the older woman's tone that whilst she might not condone Esther's intentions, at least she had now forgiven her enough to help her.

'Go where?' Will thundered. 'Are ya daft, girl? What about ya bairn? What about little Katie? Not thinking of draggin' her along with ya, were ya?' It was the first time Will had ever been angry with her.

'No, of course not, Will.' She had never seen him so incensed. He was almost shaking, and his hands, straight down by his sides, were clenching and unclenching.

'Oh, I see, going off an' leaving her, are ya?'

'Ma Harris is going to look after her . . .'

'A fine thing, running off after a feller and leaving your child. Don't try to deny it, girl. I've held me tongue these past months, but I knew what were going on. I didn't like it, but I could feel for ya, aye, I could. But to go off and leave yar child,' he repeated as if he could scarcely believe it possible. 'I thought better of you, Esther.'

'I have to go, Will.'

He flung his hand towards her in a gesture of dismissal almost. 'Aye well, perhaps ya'd better go and get it out yar system.' Then as another thought struck him, his frown deepened. 'You're not going with just the two of them, are ya?'

'Well – yes.' Esther was puzzled. 'You told me yourself, poor Mrs Marshall ain't well . . .'

''Tain't right. 'Tain't fitting for you – a young woman to go off with two men.'

Esther laughed. 'Oh, Will, really! Do you think that bothers me? Besides, from what I've read in all them papers you've kept bringing, in the war women have been doing things they never dreamed of; nursing, working in factories – all sorts of things. I reckon the days of chaperoning have gone – and good riddance, I say!'

'You would,' Will muttered, unable to argue with her. However, he was not going to let her have the last word. He faced her then, his eyes boring deeply into hers. 'Ya'll come back? Ya will come back?'

'I'll come back, Will,' she promised him quietly, but that was the only thing she would concede.

'Huh,' he was muttering almost to himself, 'and to

think it were me that was daft enough to tell you about the squire going out there. I could kick mesen.'

The journey, even in the company of the squire and his younger son, Arthur, was for Esther a nightmare. She had never been anywhere other than the village in the Wolds where she had grown up and Fleethaven Point. Now she found herself being pushed on to a huge steam train that hissed and chugged and puthered smoke. She sat on the seat in the carriage at the side of the squire, her hands clenched around the holdall carrying her few belongings, her eyes tightly shut against the scene flashing past the window.

'Do look at the countryside, my dear. It's very different from our Lincolnshire, but every bit as beautiful.'

Esther took a peep, forcing her eyes beyond the rushing hedgerows to the fields further off, rolling by at a more sedate pace. 'Oh, you're right, Squire. It's lovely. Where are we?'

'We're travelling south towards London. We're in Cambridgeshire now, my dear.'

Esther smiled briefly, but said nothing. She was trying desperately to remember the picture of England divided into its counties in her school atlas, but she could not recall where any other county was except her own. She leaned back against the plush seat. Never mind, she told herself, it's all beautiful, no matter where it is.

When they alighted at the huge, bustling station in London, fear washed over her again. It was a world such as she had never seen before – all metal and brick and stone. Not a blade of grass nor a tree to be seen. The engine gave a roar and belched out a jet of steam. Esther squealed in fright and clung to the squire's arm.

Mr Marshall laughed. 'There, there, my dear. Don't be afraid. We'll take good care of you. Just mind you don't get separated from us, that's all.'

There's no fear of that, Esther thought grimly. I'm hanging on tight to you, mester.

They stayed the night at an inn in Dover, although Esther could not accustom herself to someone else waiting on her. As soon as the maid appeared in her bedroom with a jug of hot water for her to wash, Esther made to take it from her. In the dining room, when the waiter brought her food, she stood up to help him. At the end of the meal she began to clear away the crockery. Blushing, she realized her mistake and sat down again. The squire, noticing her confusion, kindly made no comment, but merely patted her hand and exchanged a word with the waiter, thoughtfully taking the attention away from Esther.

The following morning as they took their leave, she was carefully counting out her coins to pay the landlord, when the squire whispered, 'Put your money away, my dear, the bill is all settled.'

She looked up at him, 'Oh, Squire, you are kind.'

Esther was quite relieved to leave the inn, having felt very out of place.

There was worse to come. The ship crossing the Channel rolled and tossed and Esther was sea-sick. The squire was solicitous, but, she noticed, even he looked a little pale by the time they landed in France. Then, what they saw in this strange land obliterated any memory of the fearsome journey. Their own minor discomforts paled into insignificance compared with the destruction and desolation they now beheld.

How the squire found a means of transport, Esther did not know. It was a dilapidated trap pulled by a scrawny pony, yet better than anything owned by the inhabitants of the towns and villages through which they passed.

The people she saw were hunch-backed with misery. Little groups, whole families with children in tow, seemed to be on the move, pushing all their worldly belongings in carts, going somewhere, but not seeming to know where, or to care. As they passed through villages, Esther realized why. Houses and cottages lay in ruins, some reduced to a mere pile of rubble, whilst others had every window broken, the glass hanging jaggedly from the woodwork. Doors hung drunkenly off their hinges, open to the street and huge holes gaped in the sides of houses. People sat about dejectedly, the spirit pounded out of them by the four years of relentless war being fought all around them. Small children wandered alone, dirty and unkempt, their feet bootless even in the cold of winter. These people had watched their homes being shot to pieces, their land ravaged.

Esther glanced at Squire Marshall and saw there were tears in his eyes. Forgetting, amidst all this horror, their relative positions in life – he the squire and she his tenant – she put her arm through his and squeezed it tightly. Seeking some kind of comfort himself, she felt him grip her hand and hold on to it, whilst they looked around them. They didn't speak, their throats constricted by the sights they saw. Beside them young Arthur sat white-faced and silent.

The pony plodded on slowly, making for the area where the squire had been told some of the biggest battles of the war had been fought, the place where he believed his son had died. The sky was grey with heavy cloud and a fine drizzle clung to their clothes and seeped through making them feel chilled. At last they crested a rise in the ground and there it lay before them, stretching as far as they could see through the mist and the gloom, the land ravaged by years of war.

Wordlessly, the three of them climbed down from the trap and leaving the pony standing, they walked forward, drawn by the awful sight before them, mesmerized by the destruction they were witnessing.

No birds flew overhead, no cattle grazed the land. As far as Esther could see there was not a speck of green. No blade of grass, no living leaf, only thick, greasy mud. Shell-torn trees, blasted limb from limb, struck out grotesquely like burnt sticks. Esther looked down into the trench below where she was standing. In the bottom was at least six inches of murky, stagnant water and the slimy, sloping sides were littered with empty cans, discarded weapons, even items of muddy, torn clothing. A single boot stuck up out of the mud. Everywhere ran the rats. A huge brown one came running down the trench, stopping every now and then to sniff and search. It paused just below Esther and sat up on its haunches, staring up at her boldly. The rats back at home in her barn would have scuttled away at her approach but this monster was tame – frighteningly tame. It dropped down on to all fours and sniffed at the boot then pushed its head into the top and with sharp teeth began tearing at the grey, slimy pulp oozing from the boot.

Esther gave a gasp and clamped her hand over her mouth as the bile rose in her throat. The rat was pulling at rotting human flesh.

She turned away, closing her eyes and her mind against an appalling thought.

Supposing that had been Jonathan's boot. Reason told her not to be foolish. But it had belonged to some young soldier just like Jonathan – some young man whose foot had been blasted away by a shell and left to rot in the trenches.

The trenches ran everywhere, twisting and turning, deep ravines gouged out of the ground, like a gigantic warren where men had lived for months and years. Here they had eaten, slept, laughed and cried with only each other – and the rats – as companions. Here they had died.

A low mist hung a few feet above the ground like a shroud. The smell of death was all around them.

It was as if the reaper of death had laid waste the fields of young corn, destroying not only that harvest, but ravaging the land so completely that there could be no future growth. A generation of young men had been wiped out and with them generations of unborn sons.

She turned and with eyes that were suddenly opened to the world that lay beyond the safety of Fleethaven Point, she looked towards the two men. 'Oh, Squire, oh, Squire!' She shook her head. 'I never thought – never in a million years – did I imagine anything like this.'

The squire blinked his eyes rapidly and pulled a large kerchief from his pocket. He blew his nose noisily. 'Nor I, my dear. Foolish old man that I am . . .' He glanced at his son, standing speechless with shock beside him, and then back to Esther. 'I should have known better than to bring you two young people . . .'

Esther ran to him and grasped his arm. 'Don't say that, Squire. It's – dreadful – awful, but I'm glad I've seen it. Now I understand.'

He looked at her questioningly. 'What do you mean?'

'I was so naïve, so innocent,' she said. 'I thought when that Major Langley was whipping up the young men to follow the call of arms, it was just a game to him, to all of them. I was angry, irritated, that they were going off in a blaze of glory, leaving us to cope as best we might. All that talk of honour and duty and – oh, you know what I mean. But this – this is real. This is what they came for – to stop this happening in our land – in England. All this destruction . . .' she waved her hand to encompass the ravaged land as far as they could see. 'It's just sheer wickedness. And they – our men – came to try and stop it. This land won't be fit to grow anything for years, will it? I mean, what are these poor folk who live here going to do?'

The squire shook his head and gazed about him almost in a trance as if he were overwhelmed by the enormity of the devastation. 'I don't know, my dear, I just don't know.' He paused and then went on more to himself than to the other two with him. 'I had this stupid notion that I should find Rodney's grave on a grassy hillside, a pristine white cross above it, and that I'd be able to lay flowers on it and . . .' His voice broke and Esther, still holding his arm, gave it a comforting squeeze. 'How very foolish I've been,' his voice dropped to a husky whisper.

Esther looked across at Arthur. He had said nothing for a long time. His face was pinched, his lips blue with cold and he was shivering visibly.

'Come, Squire,' Esther said gently, the first of them to recover their senses. 'We'd best find some shelter for the night. Your boy looks about done in.'

'Eh?' Roused from his ghastly reverie, the squire looked at his son. 'Oh, dear me, yes. Come along, let's leave this dreadful place.'

Together they walked back to the tired-looking pony and climbed into the trap. The squire turned the conveyance round and they made back towards the nearest village.

Along the road they passed a family – a man, wife and three children. The man was pushing a handcart loaded with all their possessions.

'Excuse me.' The squire halted the trap. The man paid no attention but trundled the cart along the side of the road.

'I say – excuse me. Do you know if there are any British soldiers still here?'

The woman glanced up and the children stared at them, wide-eyed with fear.

Nervously, Arthur cleared his throat and asked the same question in his halting, schoolboy French. One of the children – a girl, barefooted and ragged – ran forward and plucked at the man's coat, but the man trudged on. Arthur jumped down from the trap and followed the man a short distance along the road, and though they could no longer hear what was said, it appeared Arthur was still asking questions.

Esther saw the man let go of one of the handles of the cart and gesture briefly to the road behind him, but he neither stopped nor slowed his pace.

Arthur came back to the trap. He climbed in and sat down. 'I think – though I'm not sure,' he added apologetically, 'he said "at the hospital back there".'

'Never mind, my boy. You tried. We'll just keep going.'

As the trap moved on, Esther took a last look at the forlorn little family, homeless in their own country.

It was growing dusk by the time they came to the village. A huge building loomed up before them; impressive, but bleak and dismal. Miraculously, it was still standing, comparatively unscathed. 'That must be the hospital they told us about,' the squire said. 'I'm sure this must be the one where – where Rodney died. That's why I've come here. I thought he might be buried close by.'

'I never knew where Matthew was,' she murmured and added in the secrecy of her own thoughts, or Jonathan. 'They –' she began and then corrected herself swiftly. 'He – Matthew – was in the same regiment as your son, Squire.' And so, she thought, was Jonathan. 'Do – do you think they might have records of any sort about what happened to people or . . . ?'

The squire was looking at her. 'Do you really think there's a chance that Matthew's still alive?'

Esther drew breath — it was the closest she had come to having to tell the squire a deliberate lie. Fixing her mind, for the moment, on her husband and not on Jonathan, she answered, 'It — it was only — presumed.'

'Well,' the squire said slowly, 'I understand there are still some of our men here.'

'Still here?' Esther repeated, sudden hope flaring in her breast. 'In this hospital, you mean? Why? Why haven't they been sent home?'

The squire shrugged. 'Several reasons, I suppose. Some may be too ill to travel yet. Maybe — maybe they don't know who some of them are, if their identification papers were lost. I've heard of that happening.'

'Really?' Esther gazed up at the square, grey building. It looked more like a prison than a hospital. It was a gruesome place. There was such a mixture of feelings within her, a sudden dread of what she might find.

They were made welcome by a nursing sister at the hospital. She displayed surprise, though not displeasure, at their coming and bustled about making ready a narrow bed for Esther in her own quarters. Embarrassed, she said, 'I'm afraid all I can offer you gentlemen will be a bed in a ward.'

'Don't mention it, dear lady. Are you sure you can spare us that? I mean, are you sure we won't be taking up a bed you need for patients? I wouldn't want to do that.'

'Oh we've the room now, sir.' Her eyes were weary and sad and there were shadows beneath them that told of long months of soul-destroying nursing of the wounded, sick and dying. 'We've a few patients left, of course.

Those still too ill to make the journey home,' she said, confirming what the squire had already thought. She sighed heavily, 'Of course there are several who are so shell-shocked, they don't know who they are or where they come from. Naturally, we shall repatriate them as soon as we can but . . .' She shook her head. 'Oh, dear me, it's so sad, so very sad.'

Esther's heart leapt and plummeted all in the space of a second. Hope soared and then died. Jonathan might be alive, he might be here. Yet if he were it meant he was so ill that he was scarcely alive.

'Could we – could I see the patients?' She knew there was longing in her voice and desperation in her green eyes as she looked at the sister.

'Well,' the woman said doubtfully, looking Esther up and down. 'Most of them are very ill, you know. Not – not pleasant sights . . .' Then she must have caught some of the pleading in Esther's tone, for she added more gently, 'Are you looking for someone? Is that why you've come?'

Esther swallowed the lump that had risen in her throat, and, not trusting herself to speak, she nodded.

'Ah, well, of course, that makes a difference. Perhaps in the morning . . .'

Esther grasped the woman's wrist. 'Now, please. I beg you . . .' There was no mistaking the urgency in her plea.

The sister nodded. 'Very well,' she said, relenting. 'This way. Please be as quiet as you can.'

Holding a lamp high for them to see their way, she led them along cold, dank passages. Stone walls on either side ran away into the darkness, further than the light showed. Their footsteps echoed eerily on the flags as they passed from room to room, and between the rows of beds on either side. Many were in use, their occupants, lying swathed in bandages, motionless and silent, or tossing restlessly, muttering in delirium. Some sat up in their beds staring fixedly ahead of them, taking no notice of the people who came and went, still trapped in their own world of horror, reliving the nightmare played out in their mind again and again and again.

Esther peered into each face, almost holding her breath each time, then letting it go with a mingled feeling of disappointment and yet relief.

Jonathan, oh, Jonathan. I want to find you, but not here, not like this, not maimed and crippled, or deranged. I want you alive and whole and . . .

She stopped at the foot of one of the beds and the sister, glancing back to see if she were following, came back and held the lantern higher.

The man in the bed was sitting up, rocking backwards and forwards, his head nodding continuously as if he had no control over it. His arms were clasped around his own body, and his eyes stared unseeingly into the darkness. From low in his throat came a whimpering sound, like an animal in pain and suffering.

Esther drew in a breath and held it as she stared at the man in the unsteady light from the flickering lamp. His hair was cropped short to his head and there was a growth of stubble masking the gaunt jawline and yet there was something about him that made her pause instead of moving on.

She saw him become aware of the light, conscious that

there were people standing at the foot of his bed. She saw him blink and run his tongue over swollen lips, saw his gaze flicker and come to rest on her. For a long moment they stared at each other. She saw the frown on his forehead as he struggled to remember.

Then he held out his arms to her, arms that trembled. His voice was a hoarse, pleading whisper, 'I knew you'd come. I've been waiting for you. Take me home. Take me home!'

'Goodness me!' the sister said in a stunned voice. 'That's the first time I've ever heard him speak. We don't know who he is – he had no identification on him and he couldn't tell us – couldn't seem to speak.' She looked at Esther. 'Who is he?'

Esther looked down at him. She was overwhelmed with compassion. In that moment as she stood in this makeshift hospital ward, a dark, cold, damp place, she remembered him as he had been. Once so strong and vibrant, his life had now been destroyed. He was no more than a trembling wreck. In that moment, Esther Hilton passed from girlhood to womanhood. Gone in an instant were all her naïve, immature dreams of happiness, all her hopes for the future. Before her, grim reality stretched down the years and became her future. Loyalty and duty and yes, love, but a very different kind of love, must, of necessity, come before the desires of her own heart.

After a moment's hesitation she put out her own hands and grasped his outstretched, shaking fingers.

With infinite gentleness, she said, 'Yes, my dear. I came to find you. I'll take you home.'

The man's thin shoulders were shaking with racking

sobs and he pulled her hands up to his cracked lips and kissed her fingers.

As she leant towards him, only she heard the name he whispered.

'I've been dreaming about you. Oh, Beth, Beth – thank God you've found me.'

'Is he the man you're looking for?' the sister asked.

'I—' Esther hesitated fractionally, trying to evade answering the woman's question directly, then added, 'I – know him.'

'What's his name, then? Who is he?'

'His – his name is Matthew Hilton. He's my husband.'

Thirty-five

*I*T was a difficult journey home, and without the help of Squire Marshall and his son Arthur, Esther acknowledged she would not have managed. Though the hospital had been thankful to release Matthew into his wife's care, being one less burden on their dwindling resources and supplies, he was by no means fit to travel or to be in the hands of someone without proper medical experience. He seemed constantly to be running a fever. Every limb in his body seemed plagued by shaking fits, whilst his head nodded continuously in a nervous tic.

'Whatever's causing that?' Esther whispered to Squire Marshall.

'I think,' he answered soberly, 'it's what they call shell-shock. The continual sound of gunfire and shells exploding all around them for months, years even, finally shatters their nerves.'

He shook his head with infinite sadness. 'To think I sent my boy into all that. With such pride – with such damned, stupid, ignorant pride.'

As the squire blew his nose noisily and cleared his throat, Esther patted his arm. Out here amongst all this carnage, she felt the squire's equal in a way she never would back at Fleethaven Point. 'Don't blame ya'sen, Squire. They all wanted to go. He'd still have gone, your lad, whatever you'd said.'

He sighed heavily. 'I suppose you're right, my dear, but it doesn't help me to think that I actively encouraged him to go.' He was silent for a moment, still watching Matthew. With an almost fatherly concern for her, he covered her hand which was still resting upon his arm. 'I'll tell you something else, my dear, that I never thought I'd hear myself say. Looking at poor Matthew here, I'm almost glad my son didn't survive, not if he were to live a life like – like that.'

They watched Matthew's hands fluttering in the air, uncontrolled and without purpose, watched his nodding head and the saliva dribbling from the corner of his mouth.

'Oh, my dear, I don't envy you your task ahead.' He shook his head. 'You may have your husband back, but at what cost?'

What cost indeed – more than the squire could ever know! Esther thought, though she said nothing.

Those thoughts must remain her own.

Once they were home and when Matthew was settled in bed and asleep exhausted by the journey, Esther slipped away to the Spit. Despite her frightening experience at the hands of Martha Willoughby and her sister, Esther still loved the place, still found comfort and solace there. She didn't blame the sea for having almost taken her life – she blamed the people concerned. The Spit was her special place and she wrapped the serenity of it around her like a cloak.

She walked the full length and at the very tip where the water lapped at the edge, she sank down and dug her hands into the shingle and sand, the sharp stones cutting her palms. She didn't notice the pain. She was so thankful to be home, so grateful that her land and this place were still whole and untarnished. She looked about her, drinking in the tranquillity. The sea lapped softly at her feet. Behind her the land stretched smooth and flat towards the pale gold of the wintry sunset.

Young men had died to keep this land – her land – whole. Perhaps one of them had been Jonathan. Tears blurred her vision and spilled over but she let them run down her cheeks unchecked. They were tears of sorrow for what might have been, and now would never be. For a few moments she allowed herself the luxury of self-pity. Never again would she see Jonathan, yet she still prayed that somewhere he was alive and whole, that he had somehow, by some miracle, survived that slaughter.

The memory of that ravaged land would never leave her. If she closed her eyes she could still see all the horror. She had only been there for minutes; how then had it been for the men who had spent four years there, trapped by circumstance and awaiting inevitable death?

No wonder her husband had come home a broken man.

She knew now what she had to do. She knew where her duty lay. Gone were all her romantic hopes and dreams. Before her lay a lifetime of caring for her sick husband, of running the farm single-handed and bringing up her daughter without the love and support of a robust, healthy man in her life.

She prayed as she had never done before. 'Dear Lord, give me the strength. And – please – please – let *him* be alive somewhere. Somewhere in this same world as me, just let Jonathan be alive and well and – and happy.'

If only I could know, she thought, one way or the other, then I could go on. But her reason told her that it was best she did not know, for if she knew that he was somewhere, maybe back home in Lincoln, not all that far away, wouldn't she want to see him, to meet him secretly? The voice of reason told her that cruel though it was, it was best that she did not know what had happened to Jonathan Godfrey.

Now her duty, her loyalty and her compassion lay with the man who was her husband, for all that he did not truly love her any more than she was in love with him. It was Beth he had been dreaming of, Beth's name he had whispered in his befuddled state, confusing his dream world of longing with reality.

Esther had a kind of love for Matthew. He was the father of her child and the maternal spirit that was within her would always hold a place in her heart for the man who had sired her child. And it was she, Esther, he now needed. A broken wreck of a man, it was her from whom he could draw strength. She could not desert him, whatever the desires of her own heart might be.

She could almost hear within her head Ma Harris's words, 'As ye sow, so shall ye reap.' And down the years Beth's shrill cry still echoed, 'Ya'll reap a bitter harvest . . .'

Oh, what a bitter harvest she must now reap.

Esther waited for the solace of tears, but now they would not come. Not any more. Her time for weeping was over. The future stretched before her, bleak and lonely.

With heavy limbs she dragged herself upright and taking one more look at the calm sea and the gentle sky streaked by the setting sun, she turned away and walked back along the Spit towards home.

As she did so, she knew she was turning her back for the last time on all her dreams of love.

They all came to see him. One by one and from all around, those who knew Matthew, hearing the news, came knocking at the door, a joyous smile of welcome upon their lips. But they went away sick at heart, no longer smiling, no longer rejoicing at such a homecoming.

Yet out of every sadness, usually there's some good comes. Esther smiled, thinking of Ma and her sayings. 'It's an ill wind that blows nobody any good.'

All the gossip about Esther and the soldier stopped just as if it had never happened. The community drew in around itself to protect its own. Not one of them would ever tell Matthew how his wife had taken up with a soldier even before she had been told that he, Matthew, was presumed killed. For how could you tell the poor gibbering idiot such a thing? Besides, wasn't she the angel of mercy herself the way she was looking after him now? And the young soldier – what was his name? They couldn't rightly remember – he'd never come back nor by all accounts had he even written to her. For didn't they all know exactly who had cards and letters at the Point? No word had ever come to Mrs Hilton except the telegram and the official letter about Matthew. Esther guessed — and guessed correctly — at what the talk would be over the pints in the Seagull.

Without a word being spoken directly, Esther felt the change towards her, and, most gratifyingly, the last vestige of any lingering animosity between herself and Ma Harris was swept away.

'Eh, lass, Ah said ya'd have to pay, but Ah wouldn't have wished this upon ya. Not in a million years!'

'I know, Ma, I know,' Esther said sadly.

But it was a comfort to have Ma Harris's robust friendship once more.

Three days after they had arrived home, Esther, washing up in the back scullery, heard the shrill sound of Will Benson's whistle in the lane. Three times he blew on it, just as he had on the day the war had ended. Had he heard already that Matthew was home, she wondered, and it was his joyous greeting to someone they had all believed lost?

Will pulled his carrier's cart into the yard and climbed down from his seat, a broad grin on his face. 'Esther, lass, I've got news for you. Wonderful news!'

'Have you, Will? That's nice,' she said, drying her hands on her white apron. Outwardly she appeared calm, but inside her heart was thudding in her chest.

Will was coming towards her, his arms outstretched as if to embrace her, though normally he was an undemonstrative man. 'Wait till you hear what I've . . .' His glance went beyond her, towards the back door of the house. His gaze became fixed, the smile faded from his face and his arms dropped limply to his side. Esther knew why, for behind her she heard the shuffling, unsteady gait of Matthew's footsteps on the cinders of the yard.

Esther stretched a smile upon her mouth. 'We've got news for you, Will,' she said quietly. 'Look who I brought home from France.'

She turned and went towards her husband, taking his arm and gently leading him forwards. 'See, Matthew, here's Will come on one of his visits. He's come all the time, right through the war.'

She leant forwards putting her mouth close to Matthew's nodding head. 'He spoils our Kate summat rotten, given 'alf a chance. Now, come and sit on this seat against the barn wall. Ya can sit a few moments, but not long. It's not warm enough yet to sit out. Come the spring, we'll all feel better.'

Will was still standing in the middle of the yard, just staring at Matthew.

'You taken root there, Will Benson?' Esther forced herself to laugh. 'An' close yar mouth, ya'll be catching flies.' The older man still continued to stand and watch as Esther lowered Matthew tenderly on to the bench seat against the barn wall.

'Mr Marshall sent this across yesterday, from his own walled garden, so his man said. Weren't that kind? He said he thought Matthew would be able to sit in the garden when the weather gets warmer. I've put it here for the time being, as it's more sheltered near the barn. Later on we'll move it near the pond.'

She kept up the bright, inconsequential chatter, but behind her she heard Will murmur hoarsely, 'Lass, eh me lass!' She did not turn round, did not respond to the sympathy in his tone. She dare not, for the lump that rose in her throat threatened tears. She refused to let anyone except Jonathan see her weep.

Her mind latched on to other thoughts. 'What was your news you were so anxious to tell me, Will?'

'Oh, er, yes, that.' He shuffled his feet on the cinders. 'Oh, 'twas nothing really. Just – er – just that I got a better price for your eggs than usual at the market last week.' His voice faded away. 'It – it was nothing – really . . .'

She glanced at him, but his eyes flickered away and would not meet hers. 'Ya'll stay for your dinner, Will, as usual?' she asked quietly, knowing full well that the price of eggs had not been his news. She had never before seen Will Benson so excited about having secured another couple of pence on her eggs. But it was obvious that he was not going to tell her now – not once he had set eyes upon Matthew.

All through dinner, whilst Esther patiently fed Matthew, Will could only look on helplessly. He picked at the food on his own plate, his anguished gaze going from Matthew to Esther's face and back again. Will seemed, time and again, to try to speak, to try to think of something to say. Easy, natural conversation would not come. Esther could sense that he did not know how to handle this new and uncomfortable situation.

'Where's Kate?' Will asked suddenly.

'At school, of course.'

'Oh – oh, yes. I forgot.'

There was silence, then Will whispered, 'Is she – I

mean – how has she . . . ?' His glance flickered towards Matthew.

'All right.'

When Will's expression showed scepticism, Esther added, 'No, really. She's very good. Fetches and carries for him. Almost mothers him.'

'She's – she's not afraid, then?'

'Not a bit. First time she saw him, she just stared at him for a while and then went and fetched a picture she'd drawn at school to show him. Not that he takes a lot of notice, but she chatters away to him. Sometimes he seems to listen – sometimes not.'

Will was silent again.

At last, almost with a sense of relief, he stood up and pushed back his chair. 'I – er – I must be going, Esther lass. Me wife – she's – not well. I dun't want to be late home.'

Esther, a spoonful half-way to Matthew's mouth, said, 'I'm sorry to hear that, Will. Nothing serious, I hope.'

He shuffled his feet. ''Tis this influenza that started last year, Esther. It's the very devil. Two in our village have died of it already.'

'Really. I hadn't heard of it. It dun't seem to have come round here.'

'Well, you'm lucky then.'

'I hope she'll soon be well again, Will.'

'Aye – well – yes, thanks, Esther.'

He still seemed ill-at-ease, more so than could be explained by his awkwardness with Matthew. She glanced up at him, an unspoken question in her eyes. Again Will avoided meeting her gaze.

'Your – your Aunt Hannah's been very good. Came and nursed the wife.'

Esther smiled. 'Then I'm sure she'll soon be well. The 'flu wouldn't dare defy Aunt Hannah!'

Will laughed but shook his head. 'She's been good. Very good. I've not had much time for her in the past, but she's been a godsend to us these last few weeks.'

Esther nodded. 'I know, Will, I know. She's a good woman, I'll not deny that.'

Satisfied with her acknowledgement of her aunt's virtues, Will backed away from the table, taking a last, almost despairing look at Matthew.

'I'll see you next week, lass. 'Bye, Matthew.'

Matthew did not respond.

Esther laid down the spoon she had been using to feed Matthew and stood up. 'I'll come out and see you off.'

'No, lass,' Will said quickly. 'I mean – you stay with Matthew.'

'He'll be fine for a moment or two,' Esther said firmly and followed Will out into the yard.

Standing by the cart as he climbed up on to his seat she said quietly, 'Will – what was your news?'

He sat down on his seat high at the front of his cart and took up the reins. 'I've told you, lass. I got another tuppence on yar eggs.'

'Will – that wouldn't warrant *three* blasts on yar whistle coming down the lane.'

'I'd 'ave thought you'd 'ave been pleased of a bit extra in these hard times,' he snapped and clamped his jaw shut.

'Will, please – tell me . . . ?'

'Esther lass – there's nothing more I can tell you. Now, will ya let me get on me way to the Point or I shan't be home to the wife before dark.'

Reluctantly, she stood back whilst he turned the cart round and left her farmyard. She followed him as far as the gate, leaning on it to watch him go towards the Point.

Will neither looked back nor waved.

There was something – she knew – that he wasn't telling her. And by the stubborn look on his face, he wasn't ever going to tell her either.

Will did not come the next week, or the week after. In all the time she had lived at Fleethaven Point, Esther had not known Will Benson to miss his regular visits, except during the snowy weather. Now he had missed two weeks running. Esther felt concerned for him. Perhaps he had caught this dreadful 'flu from his wife and was too ill to work. Another week went past but no one at the Point knew anything about Will. She was also distressed by his absence because they had parted on heated words. Surely he wouldn't stay away deliberately just because of that? Or was it because he didn't want to face her further questions?

Then Tom Willoughby came home from market with the news.

'His wife's died, Esther. Never recovered from the 'flu, so they say. And Will, he was took bad, though I hear as how he's better now. But with the funeral an' all, he just ain't got back on his rounds yet.'

'Oh, poor Will.' Esther bit her lip, holding back

further comment. Her feelings for Will Benson were her own secret. Gently, Esther told Kate the reason for Will's prolonged absence and the child listened solemnly to the news. With equal gentleness Esther tried to get the news across to Matthew though she wasn't too sure whether he understood. She was unsure too whether word of another death, when he had lived for so long with so much killing and death around him, would make him even worse. There was no outward sign, however, that Matthew even understood. He sat in his chair by the fire, his eyes staring, unseeingly she thought, into the glowing coals. His mind, if it functioned at all, seemed miles away from Fleethaven Point.

Another week had passed when at last she heard the trundling of cart wheels coming down the lane and the carrier's whistle as he rounded the last bend. Esther ran to the gate to meet him. Slowly Will climbed down and she held out her hands to him. 'Oh, Will, I'm so sorry.'

He seemed to have aged several years in the few weeks since she had seen him. He stooped a little more and his hair showed fewer red glints amongst the white.

'Aye, lass, thank'ee. But – but it's not all that's happened.'

'I know you've been ill, too, Will. Are you feeling better now?'

He shrugged and sighed heavily. 'I'm better, aye, but I get tired, very tired.' His eyes met hers. 'It's yar aunt, Esther. She caught the 'flu nursing the wife and me.'

'Aunt Hannah?' Esther's voice was incredulous. She had never known her aunt to have a day's illness. Even giving birth to each one of her large brood had been over and done with in a matter of days.

'It's a natural thing, childbirth, not an illness.' Esther could almost hear her aunt's clipped tones.

'Aye, she's bad – real bad,' Will was saying now.

'And – Uncle George?'

'He had the 'flu a while back. He's fine again and looking after yar aunt. The girls help, of course. The eldest two are away in service now, but Rachael's taken charge.'

'Rachael! But she's only a child, she . . .'

Will was shaking his head. 'She's seventeen, lass. You forget,' he added as Esther gasped in surprise, 'you've been gone nearly nine years.'

Esther nodded slowly. 'So I have, Will, so I have. you're right, I had forgotten just how long it's been. I've been picturing them to be just the same as when I left.

'Well, you've changed, so – why shouldn't they?'

'Yes – of course.'

It was difficult for Esther to imagine how things must be now. How the children she had known were grown up and working and – most difficult of all – that her aunt was now laid low by illness.

'But,' she asked at last, 'they're – managing all right?'

'Aye.' Will was silent for a moment. Then he put his head on one side and said quietly, 'But if you were thinking of paying them a visit, I reckon they'd be pleased.'

Esther shook her head vehemently. 'No, no, Will, I can't. I can't ever go back.'

'Surely you don't still bear a grudge against Hannah?'

Esther turned away and did not answer him.

The following week the news Will brought was even worse. 'She's over the 'flu itself, Esther, but it's brought on some sort of seizure. She just sits in a chair now, lolling to one side. She dun't speak or do anything now.' He shook his head sadly. 'She's a pitiful sight . . .'

He glanced towards Matthew sitting by the range, his hands shaking, his head nodding continuously. Will looked away, but Esther could read his thoughts. The condition of her aunt was much the same as Matthew's, though brought about by a different cause.

'I feel very guilty, Esther,' Will was saying. 'She caught that 'flu coming to help me and the missus. If she hadn't . . .'

'Now, Will, don't be foolish,' Esther told him briskly. 'She'd have caught it some time if not from you.'

'But she nursed George through it and a couple of her own young 'uns. I don't understand it.'

'There's no telling with illness, you know that.'

Will's face was still distressed. 'I've brought trouble on them two sisters an' no mistake,' he murmured.

'What did you say, Will?' Esther prompted, but Will shook himself and said, 'Nothing, lass, nothing at all.'

She took his arm. 'Sit down and 'ave yar dinner, Will.'

He lowered himself into the chair and looked down at the piled plate she put in front of him. 'I dun't know if I can manage all that, lass. I ain't quite mesen for eating yet.'

'Dun't worry,' Esther assured him cheerily. 'What you leave, the pigs won't!'

Over the following weeks Will brought news of her aunt. 'She's better from the 'flu, but she ain't making any more progress. She just sits all day long and George has to dress and undress her. I dun't reckon she'll ever be right again.'

If the news of her aunt was hopeless, at least day by day there were tentative signs that Matthew was improving. Esther's tender and devoted care seemed to be soothing away his shakes. He made no husbandly demands upon her and she was grateful for that, for her thoughts were still with Jonathan. At night when they lay together in bed, she would put her arms around Matthew and pillow his head against her breast, stroking his hair until the shaking stilled and he fell asleep. She would be left staring into the blackness dreaming of bright, sunlit days in a sandy hollow on the beach.

The breakthrough that seemed to set Matthew on the way to recovery came from a most unexpected quarter, and one about which Esther was not altogether happy.

For one day in the early spring, Kate brought Danny Eland home to see her father.

Thirty-six

*T*HE two children stood in front of Matthew sitting on the garden seat against the barn wall and regarded him solemnly.

Esther, coming out of the back door, stopped in surprise and caught her breath as she saw them. Quietly she moved forward to stand a little way to one side of them so that she could observe them, but, unless they turned, they would not see her. She could see all their faces in profile and she saw Matthew staring up at Danny. His head nodded and his hands fluttered helplessly. Slowly a smile spread across the young boy's face, though there was no answering smile on Matthew's.

Esther saw Kate give Danny a sharp nudge in the ribs with her elbow. 'Don't you laugh at him, Danny Eland. Just don't you dare . . .'

The boy turned to look at Kate, their eyes on a level, staring into each other's.

'I weren't. I wouldn't do that, Katie. I was only being friendly-like.' He turned his gaze back towards the pathetic man sitting before them. 'I wouldn't hurt him for the world. He's been hurt enough. He went to war an' I reckon he ought to have a row of medals. You ought to be proud of him, Kate. *I'd* be proud of him if he were *my* father!'

Esther drew in a sharp breath through her teeth and

held it. Then slowly, as she continued to watch, she released her breath. It had been a statement made in childish innocence, but for a moment it had startled her. What was it Ma Harris was always saying? 'Out of the mouths of babes and sucklings!'

At that instant, Kate turned and saw her mother watching them. Esther saw a look of fear flit across her daughter's face, as if she expected to be in trouble for having brought Danny to see her father in this pitiable state.

Esther smiled quickly to show that she was not angry. 'Hello, Danny. You're just the chap I need to give me a hand.'

Kate was not to know of the connection between Danny and Matthew. If Esther had her way, Kate would never know.

The young boy turned to grin up at Esther, puffing out his thin chest importantly.

'I need to carry this garden seat around and put it near the pond,' she explained. 'Now the weather's better, it's a nicer place for Mr Hilton to sit.'

'I'll 'elp you carry it, missus,' Danny said, taking charge. Turning back he leant towards Matthew with a gesture of solicitude that was strangely touching in one so young. Watching, Esther marvelled that the boy, instead of ignoring the sick man and directing his questions to Esther to answer for her husband as so many of the adults had done, actually addressed Matthew.

'Can you stand up, mester? Lean on my shoulder . . .' and as Matthew struggled to his feet, 'that's it, lean on me. Kate, fetch us a chair out of the house for yar dad to sit on whilst we move the bench.'

Kate, ever Danny's willing slave, scuttled off to do his bidding.

Esther stood by as Matthew shuffled across the yard, his hand on the boy's shoulder. She wondered if Matthew had realized who Danny was. It was difficult to guess just how aware he was, for although he made sounds sometimes, since those first words of greeting in the hospital when he had imagined her to be Beth he had not uttered a word. She had no idea if he understood what was being said to him or if he recognized the people around him, even those he had known all his life.

Danny settled Matthew into the chair which Kate had brought out and then, with Esther lifting one end and Danny the other, they carried the bench seat to a place beside the pond.

'There, that's better. Now there's something for you to look at, Matthew. The willow tree and look, there's still a few snowdrops round the pond and soon there'll be the crocuses and daffs.'

'And the ducks,' Danny added, grinning as two ducks waddled towards the pond and splashed into the water. Now the two children stood back looking at Matthew. Slowly, Matthew turned his head and looked directly at them. His gaze, now obviously intent upon them as if he were really seeing them, went from one to the other. His head still moved in that awful nodding tic, yet at the moment it didn't seem quite so bad. A tentative smile flickered on his mouth and his fluttering hands reached towards them.

'I think he wants you to go and sit beside him,' Esther said quietly. The two children glanced up at her, as if for permission, and when she nodded, they went and sat on the bench, one either side of him.

Esther watched as Matthew looked down at them, first to one side and then the other. Then she heard a deep sigh escape his lips, as he leant back against the seat. She could almost see his tortured limbs relax and the shaking lessened visibly. Before her eyes she was witnessing the beginning of Matthew's recovery.

She was truthful enough to admit that it was down to Danny Eland.

Once the healing had begun, each day saw an improvement, so much so that on Will's very next visit, he remarked upon the change. 'He looks better, lass. That awful nodding's not so bad and I reckon his hands aren't shaking so much.'

Esther told him what had happened the day Danny had come. 'The lad's come every day since, Will.'

Will eyed her sharply. 'Dun't you mind, Esther?'

She shrugged her shoulders. 'How can I if it's helping Matthew to get better? I'm not *that* spiteful or petty-minded!'

'Does Matthew – er – ever see . . . ?' Will made a gesture with his head towards the Point, towards the Elands' boat home.

'Beth, you mean?' Esther said quietly.

'Aye.'

'To be honest – I don't know. Danny and Kate have started taking him for little walks now. You know, a little further each day. They've got him as far as the pub . . .' she paused and gave a grimace, 'though I'm not sure that's such a good idea,' she added with a tartness in her tone. Then she shrugged, smiled and said, 'Ah well, if it helps, why not?'

'I dun't expect landlord'll let harm come to him — y'know, let him tek too much.'

'No, you're right, of course. Matthew sits outside when it's warm enough and watches the children play on the grassland near the pub and the cottages . . .' She stopped and did not add 'and the Elands' boat'.

There was a triangular piece of grassland which lay between the Seagull and the cottages and on the third side ran the river bank where the boat was moored. From the deck of their boat home the Elands had a clear view of the cottages and the pub and beyond them across the marshes towards the sea.

'Of course, all the fellers come and talk to him,' Esther made herself chatter on. 'They're getting a little less embarrassed now.' She smiled musingly, 'Funny, isn't it, Will, how those two bairns weren't afraid or awkward around him, and yet some of the grown-ups — they couldn't get away fast enough when they first saw him.'

'It was a shock for us to see him in such a state, Esther, remembering how he used to be afore he went to war. A fine strapping lad, brought down like that.' He shook his head in disbelief. 'It's wicked, that's what it is. I must admit,' he added, a little shamefacedly, 'I didn't quite know what to do or say that first time.'

There was silence between them and then Esther, struggling with an inner conflict that she could still not

418

quell, said haltingly, 'How's — how's me aunt, then?'

'No change, lass, no change. George — poor chap — he's wearing himself out.'

Again there was a long pause, then Will said softly, 'Won't you go and see them, lass? Even if only for George's sake. He's always asking after you — has done ever since you left. Won't you go?'

Esther, wrestling with her conscience, pressed her lips together, and shook her head. 'I can't, Will, I just can't.'

Matthew made rapid progress. Soon he could walk unaided. Then, hesitantly at first, he began to speak again. Just one word and then two or three, like a child learning to talk for the first time.

Esther would shake her head, a small smile on her mouth as she watched the three of them together. The two children, one on either side of him, skipping and dancing, chattering, glancing up at him, Kate slipping her hand into his, and Matthew placing his hand on Danny's shoulder, not so much now for support as just in affection. Esther watched and smiled and in her heart she was glad. Glad for Matthew, compassionate enough to rejoice that he had perhaps, after all, some sort of life ahead of him. She was still a little fearful of the closeness between Kate and Danny. Yet what harm could it do while they were so young?

So some of her burden eased, at least some of the physical hardship, now that Matthew did not need quite so much help. Yet the farm work still lay fully on her shoulders. Matthew made no effort to do even the simplest tasks. He just wanted to spend his days with the children, and when they were at school, he would sit by the range or near the pond and gaze into nothingness.

Although Esther gave thanks for Matthew's steady recovery, in her innermost heart Jonathan was never far from her thoughts.

She still slipped away to stand on the end of the Spit, to put her face up to the sky and the wind, to close her eyes and let the peace of the place surround her. This time of solitude she allowed herself was her only way of renewing her strength of purpose. Her iron resolve would not let her do any other than what she had vowed to herself to do; to turn her back on dreams and face reality. She would care for her sick husband and she would not let her longing for Jonathan eat away at her and destroy her. Her pledge renewed, she would turn away from the place where the sea and the sky and the land seemed to meet and once more take up the burden of caring for Matthew and Kate and running the farm single-handed.

With the coming of spring came a surprise for Esther. Suddenly, there were willing hands to help with the late ploughing and the spring sowing. Labourers from neighbouring farms appeared unasked and unheralded, sheepish grins on their faces. 'Thought you could use a hand, missus, just till yar man's well again, like.'

Esther held back the bitter retort that she had desperately needed their help during Matthew's absence, but she knew that the reason they had stayed away towards the end of the war was solely because of her association with Jonathan. Now they had come back and she was far too sensible to turn away their help, however much her prickly pride might have liked to do so. Maybe they had talked it over amongst themselves, or maybe they'd just drifted back automatically now that her husband was home and the soldier gone. She had no way of knowing and she was certainly not going to ask.

Matthew made no effort to help, not even with light jobs that in Esther's opinion he could have managed now. He sat in the spring sunshine or outside the pub on a bench and watched the rest of his little world at work or at play, apparently apathetic, locked in his own private existence.

Then something happened which gave him a new interest. At first Esther was gratified to see a spark of enthusiasm for anything, but as time went on she was to rue the day that the squire brought his brand new motor car down the lane to Brumbys' Farm.

This strange chugging noise came nearer and nearer. Esther, in the process of stabling the horses she had on loan from the squire, had a job to calm the younger one. His eyes dilated with fear and he stamped and whinnied and backed away from his stable as if he thought the sound was coming from in there, and then just as suddenly, as if realizing his stable offered refuge from the noise, he shot forward almost knocking Esther over.

The chugging grew louder and Esther stared up the lane towards the town. Coming round the bend she saw a motor car bowling along the narrow lane and to her surprise turning in at her gate. She stood back against the wall of the cowshed, her hands spread against the brickwork behind her, staring wide-eyed as the vehicle, puthering smoke, came to a juddering halt in front of her. She saw the squire lean forward and then the engine died.

He climbed out of the vehicle. 'Good morning, my dear. I hope you don't mind, I thought I'd take Matthew for a little drive in my new acquisition. I thought it might – well, you know – perk him up a bit.'

Esther glanced towards the seat near the pond and saw that Matthew had already risen and was moving, with that peculiar, shambling gait, towards the motor car.

'That was kind of you, Squire,' Esther said.

Matthew was now standing near the motor car, his gaze roaming over it, his hands reaching out to touch the shiny metal.

'If you'll excuse me, Squire,' Esther murmured.

'Surely, my dear, surely. You have no objections to Matthew taking a spin with me?'

'Of course not, Squire, it's very kind of you to think of him,' she repeated. And it was. It was kind of him and unusual for a man in the squire's position to concern himself so with Matthew's welfare. Perhaps, Esther thought intuitively, looking after another victim of the war is helping to ease the loss of his own son.

From the pantry she heard the car start up again and winced as the loud throbbing once more shattered the peace. Gradually the sound died away as the squire drove down the lane towards the town.

There he goes, she thought of Matthew not without a little bitterness, her lips pursing in disapproval. Gallivanting off with the squire, riding in a grand motor car and not even trying to lift a finger to do a few simple jobs. She sat down suddenly on the cold slab of the gantry.

'Esther Hilton,' she said aloud to the empty house. 'You'll become bitter and sharp-tongued just like your Aunt Hannah if you dun't watch yourself!'

She remained sitting where she was for some time, finding herself in a strangely pensive mood. Maybe, she thought reflectively, it had been the responsibility of her family and the sheer drudgery of her life in caring for them that had made her aunt as she had been. For, despite the fact that her uncle had been a gentle, good-natured lump of a man, Esther could see now that he had never taken responsibility upon himself. He had worked hard but it had been her aunt who had made decisions, she who had carried the burden of bringing up the family.

Maybe I'm more like her than I care to admit, Esther thought ruefully, and tried to imagine what her aunt must be like now, struck down by a paralysing seizure. And her uncle, how would he cope? Hannah had ruled her family and organized their daily routine. Without her hand on the plough, the furrows of their lives would be crooked and uneven.

Again Esther wrestled with her conscience, but still the festering resentment clouded her vision and her emotions. She could not forget – nor yet forgive – the sharp tongue and the feel of the rough hand. Never a word of affection or encouragement had come her way.

The cold of the stone gantry struck through her clothing and reminded her that she had been sitting idling away her time. What would Aunt Hannah have said to that? she thought wryly. As she pulled herself upright and went about her work her feeling of guilt could not so easily be dismissed.

Not yet, I can't go yet, she answered her nagging conscience. Maybe one day . . .

When the squire left Matthew at the farm gate and drove away, Esther came out of the back door to see her husband standing staring after the receding vehicle. Drying her hands on her apron she moved towards him across the yard. 'Well, did you enjoy that?'

When he turned to look at her, she could see that his eyes were shining. He pointed with fingers that no longer shook, after the car. 'It's a Ford, the latest model,' he told her and there was no denying the excitement in his voice. And, Esther realized with a shock, he had put together a proper sentence for the first time since he had come home.

'Very nice,' Esther agreed, forcing herself to be thankful for the obvious pleasure the ride had given Matthew, and for its undoubted beneficial effect. She pushed away uncharitable thoughts of how she carried the burden of the farm work alone. How strange it was, she thought, that such a simple thing could lift him out of his despondency and bring about such an immediate improvement.

The squire came every Friday to take Matthew into the town to the market. The first week, Matthew just got up from the bench seat by the pond and climbed into the vehicle and off they went, but the second week, Esther found him in the bedroom pulling on his Sunday best suit. She opened her mouth to say sharply, 'And where do you think you're off to in that, m'lad?' then pursed her mouth against the sharp rebuke. Aunt Hannah was surfacing again, she reminded herself. Her fleeting resentment against his 'gallivanting', as she termed it within her own mind, died when she saw how unshapely his best suit was now. It hung on his emaciated, stooping frame, a pathetic reminder of his suffering and a reprimand to her uncharitableness.

'Why, you 'aven't fastened your collar stud, Matthew. Here, let me.'

'It's — stiff,' Matthew murmured, but Esther knew his fingers, still without strength, could not cope with fastening the collar on to his shirt.

'It's me starching,' she laughed. 'I always get yar collars too stiff. Now put yar jacket on.'

She held it for him whilst he struggled to put his arms into the sleeves. Then she stood back to look at him. 'Let me brush it down for you. It's a long time since you've worn this. I hope the moths haven't got at it.'

Matthew stood meekly whilst she flicked the clothes brush over his shoulders and down his back. 'There now, that's better.'

She stood watching them go until the car disappeared around the bend in the lane, listening while the chugging grew fainter.

Esther was preparing supper in the scullery by the time she heard the chugging sound of the motor car coming nearer and nearer. Outside it was almost dusk and Kate had been in bed over two hours.

Esther glanced at the clock on the mantelshelf above

the range. Almost nine o'clock. Where on earth had they been until this time? She heard the car stop at the gate, and watching from the small scullery window, she saw Matthew climb out and lurch unsteadily towards the gatepost and lean against it. The car reversed into the gateway and then, with a grating of gears, it swung out again and up the lane towards the road leading off to the Grange.

Esther opened the back door. Matthew was still standing clutching the gatepost as if he needed its support to keep him upright.

Esther clicked her tongue in exasperation and walked towards him across the yard. He was lolling against the post, his arms wrapped around it and as she drew near, she realized just why. Even from a few feet away she could smell the ale on him!

She pursed her mouth. Now she knew why the squire had driven off so quickly. He had not wanted to face her anger.

She sighed heavily. What's the use, she thought. He's in no fit state to understand anything I say. Aloud she said, unable to keep the sharpness from her tone, 'Come on with you. Let's get you to bed.'

In his drunken state, the nodding and the shaking had returned. The squire might be trying to help, Esther thought grimly, but he was doing Matthew no favours at all by getting him like this. No favours at all.

Nor her either.

Thirty-seven

*T*HE Friday jaunts into town with the squire continued and there was nothing Esther could do to prevent them – though she tried.

'You're doing yourself no good, Matthew,' she railed at him. 'The drink makes you bad again.'

'Shut up,' Matthew growled, struggling to fasten his collar, too angry and proud to ask for her assistance. 'Ain't I – a right – after what I've been through?'

'You're getting so much better – when you don't drink.'

He raised his hand and swung round as if to strike her. It was a long time since anyone had hit her, yet Esther stood her ground. Quietly, she said, 'Aye, go on then. Hit me if it makes you feel better. If it makes ya feel a man again.'

She knew the words were cruel, after all he had been through, yet she had to try to make him see sense.

Before her, Matthew swayed, his arm dropping uselessly to his side. There was no strength in him now to deal her any kind of a blow.

The gesture had been a futile one and they both knew it.

A bright spring turned into a warm summer and with each day Matthew improved – at least in some ways. He still refused to do anything remotely connected with work and spent his days between the two children, the Seagull and the squire and his contraption, as Esther called it.

He would sit outside the pub in the early evening and watch the children playing on the stretch of grass. Esther found this out because almost every evening she was obliged to go and stand on the Hump and shout her daughter home for bed.

'Why dun't you come when you know it's your bedtime? I won't let you go playing up at the Point again if you're not going to come home on time,' Esther said, almost dragging the reluctant child home.

'Aw, Mam, but I'm looking after me dad.'

'Danny Eland, more like,' Esther muttered to herself. Her daughter's sharp hearing had caught the name.

'Yes, he looks after me dad an' all. He likes me dad, does Danny.'

Esther's mouth became a thin line as she compressed her lips together to prevent the words tumbling from them. Of course he likes your dad, she wanted to shout. He's his dad an' all!

But the words remained unspoken; they were words that must never be spoken – at least not to Kate.

Aloud she said, 'Yar dad can look after himself now.' Her tone was laced with a bitterness she could not prevent.

'He still dun't walk properly sometimes, Mam.'

'Huh,' Esther gave a disapproving grunt, opened her mouth to explain and then closed it again. Inwardly she sighed. How could she tell Kate that Matthew's unsteadiness was caused not by his illness now, but by drink?

The child must have felt her mother's controlled anger for she said no more and walked meekly beside Esther.

Each evening Kate slipped away to play with the Harris children and Danny Eland and however much Esther upbraided her, she could not stop her daughter, short of locking her up somewhere.

So time after time Esther had to leave her work and climb the Hump and shout to Kate. Then one evening as she crested the rise in the lane and stood on top of it, she saw the children playing on the grass near the cottages and her husband sitting on a bench seat outside the pub. Standing motionless on the deck of her boat home, looking down on the scene below her, was Beth Eland. Esther swivelled her glance to look at Matthew and saw that his face was upturned and his gaze was fixed upon Beth. Below, on the grass, quite oblivious of the grown-ups, Danny bowled a ball to Kate who hit it high in the air, shrieking with laughter.

'Catch it, Enid, oh, catch it!'

Esther turned away and, unobserved, returned to the farm. For once she would let Kate come home of her own accord.

Back in her kitchen, Esther set the kettle on the hob and sat down at the table. For a long time she just sat there, staring out of the window that faced out over the front garden and across the flat land she now farmed. Her gaze was unseeing, for before her mind's eye was the poignant picture of Matthew and Beth.

There was a dull ache of loneliness inside her, but the

release of tears would not come. It was a pain — like Matthew's and Beth's — too deep for tears.

When at last Kate came home, Matthew was with her, leaning heavily on the child's shoulder. Esther, busying herself in the pantry, stayed out of the kitchen until she had heard Kate scuttle quickly upstairs to her bed. When she stepped into the kitchen it was to find her husband sitting in the wooden chair at the side of the range, his head lolling back. His mouth wide open, he was snoring noisily.

The summer was well advanced. The hay was gathered and the corn ripening. Soon they would have to think about the next harvest, Esther thought, and her mind fluttered back to the harvest when Jonathan had been here. Working all day side by side in the fields and then lying together in the soft hay . . .

Esther wandered through her fields of corn, splitting open an ear of wheat here and there. Almost ready, but not quite. She heard the rattle of cart wheels in the lane and glanced up in surprise. Today was not one of Will's days for a call. As she shaded her eyes against the glare she could see that it was Will's carrier cart right enough, but he had not blown his whistle to announce his arrival.

He saw her in the field and waved. She returned his greeting and went towards the gate where he pulled the cart to a halt. He climbed down stiffly and leant over the gate waiting for her to reach him.

She smiled a greeting. 'This is a nice surprise, Will. What brings you out here today?'

There was no answering smile on his face. 'Esther lass,'

he said at once. 'It's yar aunt. She passed away last night.'

Esther laid her hands upon the gate, feeling the rough wood beneath her palms. She could think of nothing to say.

'Yar uncle wanted me to come and tell you. He asked me specially to ask you to come to the funeral . . .'

Esther drew in a sharp breath.

'He asked me special-like,' Will insisted, and Esther found her eyes held by his intense gaze. Softly, he said, 'Ya'll not refuse yar uncle, lass, will ya?'

Slowly, almost against her will, Esther found herself shaking her head. For a moment a look of anger flitted across Will's face, but as she said, haltingly, 'No, no, Will, I'll not refuse him, this time,' his anger died and he covered her hand with his own as it lay on the gate.

'I knew you'd not let me down, lass. I knew it.'

They stood a few moments like that until Will seemed to rouse himself and opened the gate for her to pass out into the lane. Briskly now he made the arrangements, and Esther found herself with no chance to withdraw her promise.

'I'll come for you early on Friday morning and bring you back again when it's all over.'

'But Will, it's one of your busiest days, a Friday . . .'

'I'll work the Sunday, then. The Lord'll not mind for once.'

Esther felt the corner of her mouth twitch. There was no arguing with Will when he was in a determined mood.

*

431

Dawn on the Friday morning found Esther climbing up on to the seat of the carrier's cart beside Will. She was dressed in a new black costume, with a neat black hat to complete the outfit.

'Eh, lass, if it weren't the wrong thing to say on such a sad occasion, I'd tell you that you look right bonny!'

Esther had bought the outfit the previous day on a rare visit to the town. She had pondered long and hard, biting her lip in indecision, counting her savings coin by coin, trying to justify the expense. She still kept her money in the box Sam had left under the bed. Over the years, little by little, she had added to the hoard. Every penny had been hard earned, every coin represented a tiny achievement on her part. She had scrimped on new clothes for herself, making do and mending, as Ma Harris put it. As for Kate's dresses, Esther made most of them herself, sitting up far into the night stitching tiny neat seams by hand as her aunt had taught her until her eyes ached in the flickering lamplight.

There was quite a sum now and it gave Esther a feeling of security.

Now, as if in honour of the woman who, Esther was obliged to acknowledge, had taught her all the practical capabilities she possessed, she had spent a small part of her savings on a mourning outfit to attend her aunt's funeral.

'I ain't never spent any of this money – not even when we bought the 'osses,' she told Matthew as she pushed the box back under the bed. 'I've been saving it all these years. Even when it were tough in the war, I managed not to dip into it. I want to hang on to it just in case we gets a bad harvest, or – or . . .'

Matthew was sitting on the edge of the bed to pull his boots on. 'For that rainy day, eh, Esther? Dun't feel you have to – explain it to me,' he added and then hesitated, as if feeling suddenly awkward. 'If anyone deserves a new dress – I reckon it's you.' He paused again as he still did when striving to put sentences together. 'Pity it's got to be black though.'

Esther rose from crouching down to shove the box back into its hiding place, and stood looking down at him. He was a strange mixture of moods and temper, this husband of hers, and it wasn't all down to the shell-shock either.

One moment he was laughing and jovial, swinging Kate up into his arms now that daily he was growing stronger, or kicking a ball about with Danny and the next he would be growling in anger, raging against the unfairness of his life as he saw it. His mood swings were like the see-saw that Kate and Danny had made in the meadow across the fallen trunk of a tree.

Still Matthew made no effort to work. Today though, Esther had deliberately asked him to try to do the milking for her. 'Enid'll be over later, but try, Matthew, won't you?'

He had held out his hands to her, spreading his fingers wide, frowning down at them. 'How can I – with this shaking?' he had asked her morosely.

She had sighed and bitten back the retort that sprang to her lips. She had the sneaking feeling that Matthew often played upon his disabilities now; that he wasn't really as bad as he still liked to make out when it suited him. His hands didn't shake when he climbed into the squire's car and bowled away to the town to get drunk, she thought resentfully.

'You'm quiet, lass.' Will's voice broke into her thoughts now and she turned to give him a quick smile.

'You've no need to feel – well – awk'ard, Esther,' Will went on. 'Yar Uncle George is looking forward to seeing you again.' She felt Will take a sly look sideways at her and knew he could not resist adding, 'Pity it's taken this to mek you go back to visit.'

Esther said nothing.

Thirty-eight

AS Esther climbed down from Will's cart in the yard of the low cottage that had been her home for the first sixteen years of her life, time seemed to spin around her. It was all so familiar and yet at the same time so strange.

Little about the place had altered, except the people. When the door opened and Esther found herself staring into the eyes of her uncle, she scarcely recognized him. The huge bulk of the man she remembered seemed to have shrunk away. His clothes hung loosely on his thin frame, and he stooped now, his shoulders hunched. His face, the skin yellow and wrinkled, was drawn and care-worn. It seemed he did not recognize her either for it was not until she said tentatively, 'Uncle? Uncle George?' that his expression lightened and tears welled in his faded eyes.

'Esther, oh, Esther. How – how you've changed. Come in, come in. The children are all in the parlour.'

Esther followed him through the kitchen she remembered so well. Here she had stood on a stool at the sink to wash the dishes. Here she had blackleaded the range and polished the brass fender. These rugs were the ones she had shaken each week and the red stone flags were the same she had scrubbed. And all the time her aunt had scolded her. She could almost hear her Aunt Hannah's shrill voice now in this room.

Esther shuddered. She glanced at the empty wooden chair by the range. Her aunt's crocheted shawl lay across the back, and in front of it was the hassock where she had rested her feet. Esther looked away and followed her uncle into the best parlour.

He held open the door for her and as she stepped into the room, her resolve faltered and she put her hand on the door jamb for support.

The furniture which Hannah had polished lovingly herself every week, allowing no other hand to touch her best possessions, had been pushed back against the wall. In the centre of the room on two trestles lay the coffin with a posy of wild flowers upon it.

Esther drew breath sharply. She had not expected that her aunt would still be lying in the house.

She blinked and dragged her gaze away from the wooden box with its brass handles and glanced towards the family who stood in a semi-circle around the coffin.

Esther experienced another shock. Instead of the seven little faces of her cousins as she remembered them, there were five grown-ups to greet her. Well, almost, for only Ellen at thirteen seemed still a child. Two were missing, but now was not the moment to ask. Surely Will would have told her if . . . Then she remembered. Will had said the eldest were away in service. Surely, she thought, they would have been allowed to come home for their mother's funeral?

Her uncle's voice interrupted her thoughts. 'Here's your cousin Esther. You remember Esther, dun't you?'

George was saying. Four heads nodded but the youngest girl merely stared at Esther, her eyes large in a pale, pinched face.

There was an embarrassed silence. No one seemed to know what they were expected to say. They stared at her and suddenly Esther felt shy in her finery. She felt out of place as she noticed Hannah's own family were dressed in their Sunday best clothes, a black armband the only sign of their mourning.

She felt the flush of embarrassment creep up her neck. She was overdressed, as if she had put on a lavish display of prosperity, when in truth all her wealth – her very little wealth – had come from Sam Brumby or her own hard work. As if to add to her chagrin – though unwittingly trying to compliment her – George said, 'Doesn't your cousin look fine? You look real handsome, Esther. Your aunt – ' he made an almost reverent gesture towards the coffin – 'would be proud of you, wouldn't she?'

The poor man, trying to do his best to ease a difficult situation, was turning to his family for support, for their approval of their cousin.

It was not forthcoming.

Rachael, the eldest present, pursed her lips and tossed her head. It was the gesture of disapproval that Esther had so often seen her aunt give. In an instant the years fell away and for a moment she was again the young girl at her aunt's bidding, the bastard niece in Hannah's household under sufferance.

She was no longer that child, Esther reminded herself. She was a young woman, a married woman, with a farm of her own, a husband — such as he was — and a child. Esther's head came higher and her chin jutted forward. She had no need now to cower before their disapproval. She opened her mouth but at that moment, out of the corner of her eye, she caught sight of the pain and sadness on her uncle's ageing face. She closed her mouth, bit back the sharp rejoinder and smiled tenderly at him.

'Thank you, Uncle,' she found herself saying instead, and nodded to her cousins, before sitting down on the chair her uncle held out for her.

Will Benson, following her into the room, came and stood behind her chair. They waited in silence, the awkwardness in the room growing with every minute. No one had anything to say. There was so much they could have said, and yet so little. Hannah, even from her coffin, seemed to dominate the gathering.

It seemed an age that they remained in that small, stuffy room, everyone nervously on edge, awaiting the arrival of the undertakers. A sigh of relief wafted through the parlour when there was a knock at the door and the village carpenter, dressed in his funereal garb, entered the room, and he and George carried the coffin out and on to the cart waiting in the yard.

The family, with Esther and Will bringing up the rear, fell into procession behind the cart. Last as always, Esther thought wryly, and most definitely least in Hannah's estimation, even at her funeral.

After the service in the village church and the committal in the churchyard, Esther found herself alone for a few moments whilst George shook hands with all the villagers who had attended the funeral. His children stood dutifully in line beside him to receive the condolences of their neighbours, but Esther felt she had no place there now.

She wandered amongst the gravestones, reading the inscriptions, recognizing some of the names of the elderly of the village she remembered from her childhood. Some of the not so elderly too, for death was no respecter of age. Not all were allowed their three score years and ten. Even her mother . . .

Esther's footsteps had brought her to that part of the churchyard where she knew her mother lay in an unmarked grave.

'I've no money to spare for fancy gravestones, not for the likes of your mother, girl . . .' Aunt Hannah's voice echoed from the past.

Esther stopped in surprise. In the place she knew to be her mother's grave, there was now a small, white marble headstone, simple yet quite beautiful in its simplicity.

She bent closer and read: 'In loving memory of Constance Everatt who fell asleep 9th June 1893, aged nineteen years. The Lord giveth and the Lord taketh away.'

So, Esther wondered, had her aunt relented? If so, it was only in recent years since she herself had left.

She stood up and looked about her. Next to her mother's grave there was an empty space, the ground flat, the turf unturned. But beyond that there was a mound of recently dug earth, on which lay a fresh bunch of flowers. At the head of the grave was a headstone which matched the one on her mother's grave. A simple, white marble stone.

'In loving memory of Rebecca Benson, beloved wife of William Benson, departed this life 30th March 1919, aged 62 years. Her reward is in Heaven.'

Esther stood back and looked at the two identical headstones. First at one and then at the other. A small gasp escaped her lips. Had Will really had the nerve to . . . ?

A voice spoke behind her. 'So you've found them then?'

Esther swung round to see him standing there.

They stared at each other. Silently Esther pointed, first at the stone on her mother's grave then at his wife's. 'Will, you didn't?'

Will Benson grinned, a wicked glint in his eye. 'Oh, but I did, Esther lass, I did. No one would have put up a stone to yar mam, if I hadn't. I bought these two plots at the side of yar mother after she was buried.' His voice dropped. 'God rest her.' He paused and then nodded at the empty space between the two graves. 'That's my spot when I go, Esther lass.'

He looked at her keenly then. 'Can I rely on you to see to it, lass? To see I'm put where I want to be . . . ?'

'Will, dun't talk so, I . . .'

'Promise me, Esther. I mean it.' His tone was insistent – and serious.

For a long moment, Esther gazed into his eyes. She knew, beyond doubt now, just what her relationship to this man was, and yet even now he would not say the words she longed to hear.

She sighed. Even so, he was asking her to undertake

something which was important to him. It was better than nothing, she supposed.

She nodded. 'I promise . . .' she said, biting back the name she so longed to call him but did not dare. It was strange, she thought, here he was almost proclaiming to the world his affection for her mother, and yet still he would not acknowledge his relationship to Connie's daughter.

What if she, Esther, had been wrong all this time? What if, as her aunt had always implied, her mother had really been that cruel name they had called her and had not known which one of several men had fathered her daughter?

No, no, Esther's heart cried within her. She wouldn't believe it – not of her own mother. She glanced down for one last time at the spot where her mother lay. Poor Connie Everatt, whose only sin had been to love too much. And wasn't she, her daughter Esther, now guilty of that same sin for loving Jonathan Godfrey so passionately? Her mother had paid for her sins with her life, a life cut short. Esther, too, was paying, trapped by duty to her husband.

She turned away and saw that her uncle was beckoning to them to rejoin the family as the villagers drifted away. 'You'll come back to the house, Esther – Will, for a bite afore you go?'

'It's very kind of you, Uncle,' Esther began, 'but we should be getting along . . .'

'Oh, you must come back, even if only for a moment,' said her uncle, catching hold of her hand. 'I have something for you.'

441

'Something for – for me?'

He was nodding eagerly. 'Yes, you must have it. Hannah was always most insistent that she wanted you to have it.'

'Aunt Hannah? Me?' Now she could not keep the surprise from her tone. She felt Will's warning grip on her elbow from behind and said no more, merely nodding agreement.

They walked down the village street back to the cottage, George and Will one either side of Esther, the others a little way behind, whispering together.

'Come in, come in,' George fussed. 'Rachael, make the tea, girl. We can't let Esther travel all that way back without a cup o' tea.'

Esther smiled inwardly. When she had left this house the last time, there had been no one to bid her goodbye, to make her a farewell cup of tea. No one had seen her go, or seemed to care about her going.

Her uncle was delving into the far corner of the kitchen, picking up a heavy oblong shape and bringing it to the table.

With a gasp, Esther recognized it. Her gaze met her uncle's eyes. He nodded, smiling in answer to the unspoken question. 'Yes, it's yar aunt's sewing machine. Her pride and joy. She wanted you to have it.'

'Oh, Uncle – no! You must be mistaken. Aunt Hannah wouldn't have wanted *me* to have her sewing machine.' The words were out of her mouth before she stopped to think. Her uncle did not seem to take offence, instead he merely said, 'She did, Esther lass, really she did. Ask our Rachael, if you dun't believe me.'

442

Esther glanced briefly over his shoulder to look at her cousin. The glowering expression on the girl's face and the pursed lips were enough to tell Esther that her uncle was indeed speaking the truth.

He was smiling fondly and shaking his head, running his hand over the smooth wood of the lid of the machine. 'She used to say – after you'd gone, Esther – "She's to have my sewing machine, George, you hear me?" And I'd nod and say, "I hear you, love, I hear you." But I never – ' his voice broke a little but he carried on – 'never thought she'd go afore me, Esther.'

Now Esther, feeling embarrassed by the generous gift, leaned forward and spoke softly. 'What about her own daughters, Uncle? Surely . . . ?'

Now he was laughing openly. 'She always said they were all thumbs when it came to sewing. "Esther's the only one with my gift for needlework and dressmaking," she used to say. Oh, she meant for you to have it, Esther, and no mistake.'

Esther sighed and stood back, looking down at the machine. With tentative fingers, she too reached out and touched the wooden lid. She looked up again at her uncle. 'Then, if you're sure, thank you, Uncle George. I'm real glad to have it.'

As Will's cart rattled its way back to Fleethaven Point, she heard him chuckling softly to himself.

'She's heaping coals on yar head still from the grave, Esther lass,' Will said.

Even Esther had to smile.

Thirty-nine

WHEN Will Benson pulled his carrier's cart into the yard and Esther climbed down, she thought at once that the farm seemed unnaturally quiet. No sound of children's laughter, even though by now Kate should have been home from school. There was no sign of Matthew, nor sounds of the cows being milked in the byre.

Esther clicked her tongue against her teeth in exasperation. She went to the cowshed and swung back the door. The building was empty. Esther frowned. Had Matthew done the milking early and gone down to the Seagull already?

She went to the end of the barn. There in the meadow the cows were clustered near the gate dolefully watching for someone to come and open it and bring them to the farmyard. Even from this distance, Esther could see their unmilked udders bursting for relief. A pitiful lowing reached her ears.

'Where on earth is he?' Esther muttered crossly to herself.

'What is it, lass?' Will was shouting, lifting down the sewing machine and carrying it into the kitchen. 'Is owt amiss?'

Esther marched back across the yard and followed him

into the house, pulling off her gloves and struggling to unpin her hat as she went.

'Matthew's not done the milking. I'll 'ave to get them cows in, Will, but make ya'sen a cup of tea afore you set off back. And Will . . .'

'Aye, lass?'

'Thanks – thanks for everything, for – for taking me and bringing me back – and that . . .'

Will grinned. 'I could have wished to have taken you on a happier jaunt, lass, but I'm glad you went. For George's sake and, if it comes to that, for your own. Though you might not think it now, I reckon in years to come, you'll be glad you went.'

'Aye well, mebbe . . . I – I must get on, Will.' With that she hurried upstairs to change into her working clothes.

Opening the door and stepping into her bedroom, Esther stopped, her hand still on the latch, her mouth wide in a shocked gasp, but eyes staring in disbelief. Then a sudden spurt of intense anger flooded through her.

On the patchwork counterpane of the double bed lay the wooden box – Sam's wooden box – which held the money she had found after his death. His hoard of savings which had then become hers and to which she had added, coin by coin, by scrimping and saving over the years through her own hard work. All the money she had in the world had been in that box.

Now the box lay open on the bed – empty.

She leant forward and grasped the box, flinging it to

one side, then she dropped to her knees and scrabbled under the bed.

The money was gone.

'Will,' she screeched, 'WILL!'

She stood up again just staring down at the empty box lying open on the bed.

She heard Will come to the bottom of the stairs. 'Esther lass, what is it? What's the matter?'

'Here, Will, come up here!'

'Aw, lass, it's not Matthew, is it?' she heard him say, as he pulled himself up the narrow, steep stairs. As he came through the doorway of the bedroom, she glanced up at him to see his face lined with worry and anxiety at what he was to find.

'My money, Will, all my money's gone. Stolen!' She made a futile gesture towards the box. 'It was in that box – the one Sam left under the bed. Someone's been here and – and found it.'

'Good Lord!' Will muttered.

'Who'd so such a thing, Will? Who round here would—?' Her eyes widened as she whispered, 'I bet it's Martha Willoughby and that sister of hers. They're the only ones who—'

'Now steady on, lass, steady on. You can't go accusing people like that. You'll get ya'sen into trouble. They'd not steal, Esther lass, not them. I know they ain't no time for you, but nay, they wouldn't do that.'

She bit back the retort, 'Aye but they tried to drown me once,' for Will knew nothing of that.

The fight went out of her and she sank down on the bed. 'Then who . . . ?'

Will shuffled his feet awkwardly and murmured, 'Esther, lass, where's Matthew?'

Slowly, Esther lifted her eyes to meet Will's unhappy gaze.

'Oh, Will, no . . .' she began, then she remembered. Only three days ago Matthew had eyed the money in the box as she took out a few precious coins to buy herself a mourning dress for her Aunt Hannah.

Surely, surely he would not . . . ?

'Oh, Will, no!' she moaned again, and let her head fall forward.

By the time she had done the milking and Will was long gone, there was still no sign of Matthew or of Kate, though Esther had a shrewd idea her daughter would be at the Harrises.

She went to the gate of the farmyard and stood looking up the lane towards the town, watching through the gathering dusk, her mouth set in a grim hard line. The lane was silent and empty.

She sighed and set off towards the Point to fetch Kate home to bed.

'There you are then, lass,' Ma Harris's kindly round face greeted her. 'Kate's with the bairns. They've gone shrimping in the pools on the beach. Our Enid's with 'em, they'll come to no harm. I know it's past the young un's bedtime, but I thought you wouldn't mind this once.'

Esther nodded and, suddenly weary, sat herself down at Ma's scrubbed kitchen table and dropped her head into her hands.

'Not been an easy day for you, I 'spect,' Ma said gently, and the sympathetic tone threatened to overwhelm Esther.

She felt the tears prickle and a lump come into her throat. 'Oh Ma. It's just – everything.'

'I know, lass, I know.' Ma's fat hand patted Esther's shoulder. 'Funerals aren't easy at the best of times, and, well, if you ain't seen yar family – for whatever reason – for a long time, then there's bound to be – well, awkwardness.'

Esther raised her head and looked up at Ma. How strangely perceptive and wise this simple country woman was, Esther thought. 'She left me her sewing machine, Ma. Me aunt left me her precious sewing machine.' Esther shook her head, still uncomprehending.

'She must have thought summat about ya, then, lass.'

'To be honest, I can't take it in yet.' Esther sighed heavily and added, 'Then when I get back home, Matthew's gone . . .'

'Oh, he'll be all right, Esther lass. He went off this afternoon as usual with the squire.'

'Of course,' Esther murmured, 'I'd forgotten,' and added cynically, 'It's Friday and nothing – not even doing the milking while I go to me aunt's funeral – must stand in the way of his Friday jaunts into town with the squire!'

'Eh, lass, ain't the milkin' been done?'

'It has now, Ma,' Esther replied grimly.

'I'm sorry, if we'd known, we could have . . .'

'No, Ma, it's not right. Matthew's quite capable now of doing a bit of milking. He does little enough . . .'

'Aw but, Esther, he's a sick man.'

'Not too sick to go jaunting into town – spending money!' she finished bitterly.

Ma shook her head. 'Dun't be too hard on him. He's had such a dreadful time,' Ma pleaded his cause.

Esther opened her mouth to tell Ma Harris about her missing savings and then decided against it. She probably wouldn't believe it of Matthew.

But Esther did.

It was almost midnight and Esther was still sitting before the dying embers in the range, a shawl huddled about her shoulders, her anger keeping her weary body wide awake and rigidly upright, when she heard the familiar chugging noise of the motor car echoing across the flat fields long before it reached the farmyard gate. Esther pulled herself up, her face set in hard lines of resentment as she opened the back door and went out into the yard. She stood waiting whilst the car swung in at the gate. Instead of stopping to let Matthew alight and then reversing out again, the motor car came right into the middle of the yard before it stopped. The engine died and the headlamps were turned out.

Esther blinked in the sudden blackness, unable to see anything for a few moments after being blinded by the light. Then she saw only one person climbing out of the car – out of the driver's seat: Matthew.

'Hello, Esther. Look what I've got! Go and get yar bonnet, and I'll take you for a drive. It's a car, Esther, I've bought a car.'

Matthew must have thought he was back in France

449

under bombardment from the Hun by the time Esther had finished with him.

'How could you do it? How could you spend all that money on a useless object like a car? Who do you think you are, the next squire? We ain't in that class, Matthew Hilton. Just because he's been kind to you since you came back from the war, just because he lost his son and is trying to make up to you because of it, it dun't put you in his class . . .'

On and on she railed and shouted, stormed and raged.

'Oh, I know you've had it tough in the war – none knows it better than me. But you're alive – you're back home with your family. But do you care?' She flung out her hand to encompass the whole of the land around them. 'Do you lift a finger to help me? I've struggled all that time to keep things going, and looking after you when you came back. You're getting better now, Matthew. You could help, but you dun't want to, do ya? You think you've done your bit for evermore. Life ain't stopped, Matthew, it goes on, day after day after day.'

'Maybe,' he said quietly, 'maybe it would have been better if me life had stopped – out there. Ya'd be better off if I had died out there.'

Though she heard the words, she didn't listen to their meaning – their real meaning – and she retaliated impulsively, 'Aye, mebbe it would . . .' Her mouth fell open and she stared at him, stricken with swift remorse for allowing the cruel words to spurt, unchecked, from her lips.

Even to her own ears, her words, shrill and venomous, had the ominous ring of her Aunt Hannah venting her frustration on the young girl for whom she had grudgingly taken responsibility. In the same way that, deep down, Esther resented the burden of a helpless husband which the war had thrust upon her.

She saw his hands start to shake and his head twitch and her shrill tongue was silenced.

He was struggling to speak, to explain. 'I just thought the kids – we live a long way from – school – and town. I just thought . . .'

Aye, she might have known, she thought bitterly, his life revolved around Kate and Danny now – and his jaunts into the town with the squire. Jaunts that had resulted in this last act of madness.

Why? She railed, turning her anger inwardly on herself now, rather than on Matthew. Why hadn't she had the sense to hide her money? Even before the war, he'd hardly shown signs of thrift. He had cajoled her into agreeing to buy the horses. Then he'd come home with a new suit without so much as a by your leave or can we afford it! And that because he had wanted to attend his son's christening. Now, it was even worse, he was scarcely stable in his mind. What a fool she had been! She should have realized something like this might happen. Esther blamed herself. She was responsible for him. It was like looking after another child. The man she now called her husband bore scarcely any resemblance to the old Matthew. Except, she thought ruefully, when it came to spending money.

His whole body was now convulsed with the shaking and Esther had to put her arm about him and lead him into the house. He dropped into the chair by the range and she knelt down in front of him and took his hands in her strong work-worn grasp. 'Don't fret any more. I'm – I'm sorry for the things I said, but – well – you made me mad . . .'

Matthew grinned lopsidedly, but she was relieved to feel the shaking ease a little. Even in the midst of her anger, she had no wish to make him ill again.

'It's not a new one, Esther,' he was saying hesitantly. 'A chap had it afore the war and – well – he didn't come back . . .' He struggled to continue. 'His widow was – glad of the money.'

Esther said nothing, but wryly she thought, well, I suppose it's an ill wind that blows nobody any good.

She had the grace to smile at herself. Why did Ma Harris's sayings always pop into her mind at such times?

She got to her feet and sighed as she did so. 'Ah, well, Matthew, 'tis done now.'

Forty

*E*STHER stood in the middle of the yard, her hands on her hips, watching as the squire drew his motor car to a halt at the gate and climbed down. She kept her face expressionless. When he stood before her, she saw that he had the grace to look shamefaced.

'Mrs Hilton – Esther – I am sorry. I feel it's all my fault . . .'

Tight-lipped, Esther nodded. 'Not *all* your fault, Squire, but a part – yes.'

He twirled his hat nervously through his fingers. 'What can I do to make amends, I . . . ?'

'There's nothing that can be done now, Squire. Matthew's bought the car – and what's done's done.'

The squire spread his hands. 'He went off on his own, you see, in the market. I lost him completely and when I found him again, he was tipping all this money into this chap's hands and the deal was done. I couldn't do anything about it without making Matthew look – well – very foolish in front of a lot of fellows stood around.' He paused and looked at her keenly. 'I didn't want to do that, Esther.'

'No,' she said slowly. 'No, Squire, you couldn't have done that.'

'Won't you let me make amends in some way? Let me pay for part of the motor car. After all . . .'

'No, certainly not!' Esther snapped and then remembering just who it was she was talking to, she made a great effort to control her seething anger. 'I'm sorry, Squire. I know you mean it kindly, but we'll manage.'

'Well . . .'

With a supreme effort she forced a smile on to her mouth. 'Please come in, Squire,' she now invited, 'and take a glass of home-made wine with me. I have a nice elderflower just right for the tasting.'

'Why, thank you, Esther, thank you.' Mr Marshall actually looked relieved and accepted her offer at once. 'I'm partial to home-made wine.' As they went towards the farmhouse he added, 'Have you ever tasted Mrs Willoughby's home-made wine?'

Now Esther threw back her head in genuine laughter. 'Oh, Squire! Does she make it from deadly nightshade, because that's the only one she'd give me?'

'Eh? Oh – er – yes, I was forgetting . . .' He grinned. 'You're not exactly bosom friends.'

Again Esther chuckled, though to herself now, to think of the times she had caused Martha Willoughby's ample bosom to heave in anger, not affection.

'To be fair,' she said as she set two glasses on the living-room table and poured out a glass of the clear liquid, 'we haven't clashed much of late. She was almost civil to me the last time I went to church.'

Tom had kept his promise, she thought to herself. His wife and Flo were obeying his command.

'She's not a bad woman, Esther,' the squire was saying. 'Just a bit of a gossip and full of – what shall we say?' He

454

looked up at her somewhat coyly. 'Righteous indignation?'

It was in her power to disillusion him, but instead Esther sat down opposite him and, taking a sip from her own glass, said, 'Aye, well, Squire, I s'pose I did cause a bit of a stir when I came here.'

The squire chuckled. 'You were a trifle – headstrong, shall we say? And I'll tell you something else, Esther Hilton.'

'What's that, Squire?'

'This wine's damned good!'

Across the table they smiled at each other.

Of course Matthew's new and expensive toy created a lot of interest amongst those at Fleethaven Point. From the adults there was incredulity.

'Have you gone quite mad, Esther?' Ma Harris demanded. 'Did you ought to let him be driving around – in his state? He'll kill himself – or someone else in that – that – thing!'

'I've told you what I think about it, Ma,' was Esther's reply. 'But there's not a lot I can do – not without making Matthew look a fool. I dun't want to do that even though I'm mad as heck at him.'

'But to spend all yar money on a car, Esther lass.' Ma Harris shook her head. 'Eh, what will become of him? Ya've got yar work cut out with him, an' no mistake. Ya'll 'ave to keep yar eye on 'im, lass. There's no telling what he'll do next!'

Amongst the young people of the small community, however, there was wholehearted approval for 'Mester

Hilton's motor'. It caused great excitement, and most days would find Matthew at the wheel and the motor car overflowing with children begging a ride. Always in the front seat rode Kate and Danny Eland with beaming faces and lording it over their friends.

Esther could not be persuaded to ride in the motor car, not even to be driven to church.

'You're just being plain awkward, Esther,' Matthew growled. 'You're still trying to make me feel bad for taking yar money and buying it.'

Esther pursed her mouth. 'You know I'm not one for dragging up the past. We had our quarrel about it at the time, so there's no more to be said. But I can't bring mesen to perch up there on that great noisy thing. Now if it could pull the plough or drive the threshing drum, then it'd be some use. As it is . . .' She flung out her hand towards the car standing in the yard, a constant reminder as to where all her hard-earned money had gone and why she was now terrified that the coming harvest would not be a good one.

None of these fears did she ever voice to Matthew. He neither helped with the work nor seemed to care what happened to the farm. She carried the burden alone and knew she would have to go on doing so and reproach him no more, but that didn't mean she had to succumb to his foolishness.

She leant towards him. 'I ain't riding in the thing, Matthew, an' that's that!'

'Please ya'sen,' he shouted. 'There's others that'll ride with me. Aye, an' they mean more to me than you ever could.'

As he went from the house and slammed the door behind him, she leant against the table. Suddenly an intense longing for Jonathan swept over her and the loneliness of her life engulfed her. Even though she had husband, child and friends close by she always felt herself to be alone.

It seemed to Esther this year that no sooner had the harvest been gathered in than Christmas was upon them. To her immense relief the harvest had been a good one – not abundant, but good enough. They would not go short through the winter, despite the disappearance of her savings.

The bad weather seemed to close in earlier than normal. Heavy rain made the late ploughing difficult, and blustery winds whipped bitingly across the flat land. The animals huddled in the farmyard and even Esther found excuses to stay in her warm kitchen and cook and bake ready for Christmas rather than face the dreadful weather.

Come the spring, she told herself, it'll be better.

It turned out to be the happiest Christmas she could remember. Matthew seemed more even-tempered and much better in health. He even made an effort to help with the preparations. He stirred the puddings, urging Kate to make a wish. 'Dun't tell what you wish, not to anyone, Katie, for then it won't come true.' He was smiling down at her as the child shut her eyes and screwed up her face.

Matthew was chuckling. 'My word, that looks as if it's a wish and a half.'

He plucked, drew and dressed the goose ready for the oven – a job Esther hated.

'We must put up the trimmings, Katie, and tomorrow we'll drive into town and get a Christmas tree.'

'Oh, yes, Dad, yes. Like the one in the square in the town.'

'Well, perhaps not quite as big as that, but . . .'

'They're expensive to buy, Matthew. There's some fir trees on the old marsh. You get one of them,' Esther began and then she saw the disappointment written plainly on both their faces.

'They're not the same as a real Christmas tree off the market, Mam,' Kate said.

'It's me first Christmas back home, Esther. Let's have a proper tree, just this year,' Matthew added.

She sighed inwardly. Really, she thought, half-amused, half-exasperated, it was like having two children instead of one. Aloud she said, 'You pair! Ya reckon ya can twist me round ya little fingers!' But she was smiling as she added, 'Oh, very well, then, but dun't you go mad, Matthew. Promise?'

'I promise, Esther.'

When they arrived home the following day, Esther could see at once that his promise, so lightly made, was also easily broken. Kate was dancing around him in excitement and the tree was so large that Danny, who had been invited to go with them into town in the motor car, was having to hold one end whilst Matthew struggled to drag the tree through the door, the full extent of the branches being wider than the doorway. But seeing the children's joy and Matthew's pride in his purchase, Esther hadn't the heart to spoil their fun by scolding.

They set it up in a tub in the corner of the living room and Kate hung paper decorations and painted fir cones on its branches.

'Teacher showed us how to make these at school, Mam. There, doesn't it look pretty?'

'Yes,' Esther nodded. 'I must admit it looks splendid.'

She felt Matthew's arm around her waist and involuntarily she stiffened. He did not seem to notice as he said close to her ear, 'You're not such a bad old girl, Esther Hilton, in spite of your shrewish tongue.' He planted a swift kiss on her cheek, turned away, took his cap down from behind the door and winding a muffler round his neck, he left the house and headed in the direction of the Seagull.

Esther watched him go. Shrewish tongue, eh? Was she sounding to Matthew like her Aunt Hannah had seemed to her? Only concerned with work and duty, and devoid of any capacity to enjoy herself?

Kate interrupted her thoughts. 'Mam, when can I hang me stocking up on the mantel?'

It was late when Matthew staggered in – too late to help Esther fill Kate's stocking with an orange, some nuts and sweets. And lastly, just one main present – a doll with a china face and a cloth body for which Esther had painstakingly made the tiny clothes on her Aunt Hannah's sewing machine.

They had Christmas dinner at the farm – just the three

of them with Matthew sitting at the head of the table carving the goose.

They were invited to join the Harrises' noisy Christmas in the cottage at the Point for the evening, so during the afternoon she had made an over-excited Kate rest on her bed. Matthew, too, was stretched out in the front parlour, snoring in front of a blazing fire which Esther had lit in honour of Christmas. So whilst the others dozed, Esther snatched a few quiet moments to walk alone to the end of the Spit. The tide was high and lapped at the ridge of land along which she walked, but she had no fear of the water now.

As always her thoughts turned to warm, sunlit days. The memory of Jonathan's blue eyes and gentle mouth was so vivid she almost felt that if she turned quickly he would be there, walking towards her. Sometimes, he seemed so close . . .

Pushing away such foolishness, she bent and picked up some flat oyster shells. Leaning sideways she held the shell between her thumb and forefinger and flipped it across the water. It scudded over the surface bouncing three or four times before it sank beneath the waves. She sent three more skimming after it and smiled to herself as she remembered Matthew teaching her the game.

Ducks and drakes, he'd called it.

Her mind was filled with both the men in her life: Jonathan, her lost love, no more now than a sweet memory, and Matthew – poor Matthew – still suffering from his dreadful ordeal in the war. He needed her and deserved her compassion at least.

But would there ever be real happiness for any of them?

She sighed. Pulling her shawl closely around her she took one last look at the bleak, lonely sea and bending her head against the wind, she went back home.

At the beginning of January north-easterly winds blew in from the sea, combining with the highest tides of the year which pounded the coastline and flooded over the Spit and on to the marsh, swelling the haven and the mouth of the River Lynn.

On the first Saturday after New Year it seemed to reach a climax. The gale howled around the farmhouse, battering the windows and rattling the tiles, and the rain lashed against the glass.

Esther, who had never liked storms, blocked the back door with a chair against it. 'It's like that day you went out on the lifeboat. Remember, Matthew,' she said as she came into the kitchen where he was sitting by the range. 'When Robert Eland was out in his fishing boat and—' She broke off as Matthew got up from his chair and stared at her with wide, stricken eyes.

'Why, whatever's the matter, Matthew?'

He stumbled across the room towards the door.

'Matthew!' she cried again. 'Matthew, what is it?'

'The boat,' he mumbled. 'The boat – I must . . .'

'Don't be silly, Matthew.' She pushed against his chest, trying to calm him, to make him sit down again. 'There's no boat out there on a night like this. Sit down . . .'

Suddenly there was surprising strength in his hands as he gripped her arms, his eyes wild. 'No, no – their boat,

461

Elands' boat. It's not safe – not in this storm. Beth – Danny – they're on that boat.'

'Matthew, listen to me – Robert'll have brought them off. He wouldn't . . .'

'He'll not take care of them.' Matthew was ranting now, panic and terror in his frenzied eyes. 'He'll not care for my son. Or for Beth . . . my Beth. He's let that boat go to ruin. The wood's rotten now – I've seen it.'

Esther opened her mouth to argue, but suddenly a memory flashed before her – a memory as clear as if she were seeing it before her eyes right now. It hadn't really registered at the time, yet now amidst Matthew's wild babbling, she knew he was speaking the truth.

It had been when she had received the telegram about Matthew and she had gone to see Beth. It was the only time she had been really close to the Elands' boat home – and now in her mind's eye she was seeing once more the rotting, unpainted wood of the boat and the poles and stays that supported it on the river bank. All had been allowed to fall into a state of decay.

She gasped as realization hit her. In such a storm those poles, rotten with neglect, would give way.

'They won't have stayed on the boat, Matthew,' she insisted. 'Not in this lot . . .'

He wasn't listening to her rational statement. All he was thinking of was Beth – and his son.

With sudden, inexplicable strength – the strength that fear gives for those few vital minutes – he pushed her aside, not caring that she lost her balance and fell to the floor. Reaching the back door, he flung aside the chair and the door blew open, the storm raging into the house.

'Matthew, Matthew—'

But he had gone out into the storm.

Esther dragged herself to her feet and staggered after him. The wind blew her shawl from her shoulders and tossed it into the air. The rain soaked her blouse within seconds and plastered her hair to her head. Leaning against the wind she struggled towards the Point. She saw Matthew crest the Hump and disappear from her view.

As she reached the top of the steep rise and came down the other side, she saw he was striving to reach the boat. Already the swollen river was flooding on to the bank, the water swirling around his ankles. The boat seemed to have been lifted up off its supporting poles and looked to be floating, heaving from side to side, and yet it had not yet broken adrift from its mooring.

Matthew arrived at the wooden jetty and reached out to grasp the rope.

'Matthew! No!' Esther shrieked, but the sound was snatched and tossed away by the gale. She could not even hear her own voice let alone be heard by Matthew.

He was pulling himself up the gangway as she reached the water. Lifting her skirts, she waded through it to reach him. She must stop him. This was sheer madness.

She had reached the bottom of the gangway and had even put her hand on the rope. Looking upwards, she saw him jump from the end of the gangway on to the boat, saw him stagger for a moment and then right himself, though the boat rocked beneath his feet.

Then he disappeared from her view.

As she tightened her grip on the rope and steadied

herself to step on to the swaying planking, she felt herself pushed to one side. Above the roaring wind she had heard no one behind her and so the push, catching her off guard, sent her sprawling into the shallow flood-water on the bank. Gasping and gulping she staggered up again, thinking, irrationally at such a moment, that she seemed to be spending more time on all fours than on her feet this night.

When she looked around it was to see that Beth had taken her place. Now it was Beth's fingers which grasped the rope, Beth's face which was upturned to the boat, her eyes wide with anguish and terror. Her mouth was moving and although Esther could hear no sound above the noise of the storm, even this close, she could see that it was his name Beth was shouting.

'Matthew! MATTHEW!'

Esther too glanced up again, but he had vanished, gone below in search of his other family.

Beth made to heave herself up the gangway, and Esther, too, grasped the rope and made to follow her.

Strong arms seized them, pulling them backwards. Robert Eland's arms were around Beth's waist, but still she clung tenaciously to the rope. Esther felt herself held by Mr Harris.

Close against her ear he shouted, 'Nay, lass, ya'll all be killed. Have some sense, Esther.' Suddenly the fight went out of her and she leant against the huge comforting bulk of Ben Harris. She closed her eyes and dropped her head momentarily against his shoulder as a shudder convulsed her whole body. The man must have felt her fear, for his arms tightened about her. Esther took a deep breath, raised her head and opened her eyes again to see Robert Eland trying to drag Beth off the landing stage. Her hands gripping the rope were grazed and bleeding, but still she clung on, her mouth wide open, her eyes frantic, her face the colour of death itself.

Then from the mouth of the river, a huge tidal wave, blown in from the sea, came rolling up towards them, sluicing on to the banks on either side, sweeping aside all that lay in its path. Esther felt herself lifted from her feet and carried by Mr Harris away from the bank, and only when they were against the shelter of the cottage and Ma Harris too had taken hold of her, did they turn to look back.

They stood in a petrified trio, Esther in the centre with Ma Harris and her husband on either side. They clung together watching the bizarre and awful scene played out before their eyes. The wave came nearer and nearer, yet Beth would not relinquish her hold upon the rope of the gangway, and Robert Eland would not leave her.

The horrified watchers saw Matthew appear at the side of the boat above the gangway. Seeing them below, he seemed about to step over the side to come down. But in that split second he must have become aware of the surge of water bearing down upon him for he half-turned, looked down river and was stilled. His hands resting on the side of the boat, he was motionless. He looked down – just once – at Beth. He had time only to raise his hand as if in final farewell, before the wave crashed against the boat, lifting it like a cork, tearing it from its mooring and wrenching away half the landing stage with it. For a timeless moment, the boat seemed suspended above them, and then with slow finality it rolled over on its side into the river.

They saw Matthew flung backwards, saw his arms flail wildly and then he and the boat plunged beneath the torrent, sending huge waves washing on to the shore, bowling Beth and Robert Eland over and over on the river bank.

The waters subsided and drained back into the river as the wave, lessening with each yard it travelled, rolled on up the river. Then Esther saw the two of them — Robert with his arms still locked around Beth — lying on the ground.

The Harrises and Esther struggled towards them. As they did so, with a cruel irony the wind dropped suddenly. Now they could hear another dreadful sound.

The sound of Beth's shrill screaming that went on and on and on . . .

466

Forty-one

MATTHEW'S body was washed up three days later, ironically on the place which Esther had called her own; the place where so often she had found comfort in her solitude and yet the place where she too had almost lost her life – the end of the Spit.

The storm had blown itself out. It had calmed almost at once after the tragedy, as if it had exhausted its cruelty and was appeased.

Beth and Robert Eland were safe, yet Beth, they told Esther, had retreated into a world of her own, neither speaking nor eating. She sat in Ma Harris's kitchen just staring out of the window at the river, at the place where her home had been. At the place where Matthew had died.

Esther was tormented by feelings of guilt. I should have stopped him, she told herself over and over, and even voiced her feelings to Will. 'I should have gone up after him . . .'

'Aye, then there'd have been two deaths, lass. Where would me pretty little Katie have been then, without father or mother?'

'But . . .'

'But nothing, lass. I've heard it all from Ben Harris. He says you'd have gone up if he hadn't held on to ya.'

'I should have stopped him here, before he went out.

He – he wouldn't listen, Will. I tried to tell him they'd have come off the boat, but – but he didn't even seem to hear me, let alone believe me. He was gone so quick, before I really realized what he meant – what he was going to do.'

Will, not often given to displays of open affection, put his arms about her, and likewise Esther, not used to giving way to emotion, laid her head against his chest and her voice was muffled as she said, 'Oh, Will, I feel so – so guilty.'

Will stroked her hair and she heard his words deep from within his chest as he said, 'Dun't blame yourself, lass. We all feel guilt when someone dies. It's not his death you feel the guilt about, it's the life, all that went before. All the things you've done or haven't done. Now you're denied the time to put it right.'

Esther listened to his wise words of comfort. 'You shouldn't need to feel the guilt, lass, because since you brought him home from the war, no one on this earth could have been a more devoted wife than you.'

His voice dropped to a whisper as he added, 'An' I know, more than anyone else, just how much it's cost you to do it, lass.'

She heard the catch in his voice and she lifted her head a little and, her own eyes brimming with tears, she looked up into his face.

'Thank you . . .' the name she longed to call him hovered on her lips but she ended, 'Will.'

*

They all came to his funeral. Everyone from the Point, and from the surrounding farms: the Harrises, the Willoughbys, the Souters and the Squire.

And Beth came.

Supported by her husband, she stood at the end of one of the pews half way down the aisle, her eyes fixed upon the coffin. By her side stood Danny, solemn and white-faced.

The young boy had lost his friend, a man he had helped towards recovery. The man he knew as Kate's father.

Would he ever know, Esther thought, just how much more he had lost?

Following the coffin out of the church as chief mourner, with Kate on one side and Will Benson on the other, Esther paused in the aisle as she came level with Beth. She felt a soft sigh run through the congregation and knew they were watching herself and Beth in this moment.

Esther glanced at Robert Eland – this compassionate man who had borne so much in the face of his wife's love for another man. Yet even now she read the silent consent in his eyes to her unspoken question. She put out her hand towards Beth and Danny and gestured that the Eland family should take the place in the funeral procession directly behind herself, Kate and Will.

It was a gesture she knew might find censure amongst some and would certainly cause gossip amongst many. But as always Esther Hilton flouted convention, cared nothing for how things looked or what others might say or think. She owed this to Beth and to Danny.

Most of all, she owed it to Matthew.

The two women in his life, who had loved him each in their own, but very different, way, stood side by side as the coffin was lowered into the ground.

Esther heard a sob and she reached out and took Beth's hand in hers. It was like ice. She held it between her own, trying to warm it, trying to comfort the woman at her side. There was nothing she could say that would lessen Beth's pain, nothing that could turn back time and make everything different.

The vicar intoned the words over the grave and then Matthew's family and friends threw handfuls of earth on to the top of the coffin.

Danny and Kate stepped forward, their faces solemn, feeling the importance of the moment. They stood close together and Esther saw Danny take hold of Kate's hand. Together they bent and picked up a handful of earth and together they threw it on to the top of Matthew's coffin. They stood in silence for a moment and then Danny turned to look at Kate, concern for her on his young face.

They were only children, Esther told herself fiercely, and yet in that look there was something she had feared to see. There was a closeness between them that had grown innocently, unaware as they were of their blood relationship.

It was a closeness that put dread into Esther's heart.

The house was strangely quiet without Matthew, and Kate was doleful and lethargic. Esther too felt listless and tired. All the spirit and energy that was her nature had been drained out of her. The hard work and the

470

worry she had known since she had brought Matthew home were now reaping their own toll upon her vitality and strength of will. To say nothing of the sadness locked within her own heart. There was no doubt that she had drawn on her reserves of strength this last year – and long before that too, if she were honest.

She walked along the shore deep in thought. Part of her longed to go to the place she had loved. The end of the Spit. But she could not yet face the spot where they had found Matthew's body. She feared her special place despoiled by the tragedy in a way that it had not been by her own traumatic experience there. That, she could rise above, but with this last disaster she was not so sure – not yet.

She had not seen her husband's body in death – the men had told her she should not. In her imagination she had visualized it bloated and battered, and shuddered at the thought. To think that he had survived the horrors of the trenches only to die in the place that was his home.

Matthew had died trying, so he had thought, to save the woman he loved and his own son. But in that last split second, he had seen Beth on the bank and had known she and Danny were safe. Esther believed that was all he had wanted. He could have saved himself then, he could have jumped towards the willing arms stretched out to help him. Instead he had just stood there, gazing down at Beth. He had indeed gone back to her just as Beth had always predicted. At the moment when death was inevitable – and he must have known that it was – hers was the last face Matthew saw.

Esther sank down on to the sand and gazed out across

the calm water. How deceptively tranquil and innocent the sea looked now, as if it could never have been the foaming fury that had taken Matthew.

She stayed there a long time, until the winter afternoon grew cold and dusk came creeping across the water. Then forcing her cramped legs to stand, she turned her back on the sea and lifting her head she turned homeward – back to Kate and the farm.

Always, there was Brumbys' Farm.

Forty-two

THREE weeks after the funeral when the demands of the farm had forced Esther to return to her routine, she steeled herself to open the big doors of the barn that housed the contraption, as she still called it, which Matthew had bought in his moment of madness.

She stood, hands on hips, looking at the motor car, her mouth pursed with indecision. A shadow fell across the doorway and she looked up to see the squire standing there. It was the first time she had seen him since the day of Matthew's funeral.

He cleared his throat – nervously, it seemed to her. 'Good morning, my dear. I – er – I've been meaning to come and see you, but well, I thought it only respectful to leave – ahem – matters of business, for a little while after . . .'

His voice trailed away. Esther stared at him. At his words, cold fingers of apprehension touched her and her heart began to beat a little faster.

Matters of business! That could mean only one thing. The farm! Now that her husband was dead – and known to be dead – was he going to force her to leave the farm, just because she was a woman?

Where could she go? What could she do? What about Kate . . . ?

The squire was speaking again. 'I realize I was partly

to blame for Matthew squandering your hard-earned money on – ' he gestured towards the motor car – 'this. I wondered – if it is of no use to you – if you'd like me to try and sell it for you, my dear? I know someone who deals in motor cars and I'm sure I could get a good price for it. If not quite all your money back, I could certainly recoup most of it.'

Esther felt herself smiling as relief flooded through her. Was this the 'business' he had meant? He had not come to throw her out of Brumbys' Farm after all, but to put right a folly in which he had played no little part.

She felt sorry for the squire in that moment. He looked so anxious, so genuinely concerned. All he had tried to do all along was appease his own conscience and loss by taking Matthew out with him. Yet his kindly actions had backfired when Matthew had become obsessed by the motor car.

'I'd be very grateful, Squire, for anything you could do. This – thing – is no use to me. I couldn't drive it, and even if I could, well, it's not quite what people of my class ride about in, is it now?'

The squire had the grace to smile. 'I tell you what,' he said, as an idea came to him. 'What you could well do with is a smart little pony and trap. You could drive that, Esther. You could drive into the market, and take your little girl to school. What about it? Will you let me sell your car and sort out a nice little pony and trap? Needn't cost very much,' he added hastily, as her face showed doubt.

She smiled again. 'Very well, Squire, and thank you.'

'My pleasure, my dear, my pleasure.' He bowed a little

towards her, put on his hat and marched away across the yard, more purpose in his step than she had seen for some time.

Esther stood in the doorway of the barn, her hand on the rough wood of the jamb, and watched him go.

He had said nothing about the tenancy of Brumbys' Farm. The way he had talked – about her driving to market and taking Kate to school – it sounded as if he took it for granted she would be going on living here at the Point.

But would she be the legal tenant of the farm?

Now that the thought was in her mind, it would not let her rest and so it was that, three days later, she put on her best black costume and walked up the lane towards the Grange.

When she was shown into his study, the squire rose from a deep leather armchair by the long window overlooking the lawns and held out his hand to greet her. 'My dear, come and sit down. I haven't forgotten about the car, but I have not yet had the opportunity to strike a deal . . .'

Esther shook her head and remained standing in the centre of the room. 'It isn't about that, Squire.'

'Then what is it, my dear? There's nothing wrong, I hope? Please, do come and sit down here.' He indicated a similar chair to his own set on the opposite side of the window.

Esther hesitated and then did as he bade.

How very different was her reception now, she was thinking as she settled herself in the chair, to the first time she had come into this room with wild, flying hair

475

and muddy boots. She smiled inwardly at the memory, remembering her belligerence, her youthful indignation. Now she was older, and more than a little wiser, yet the sense of injustice was as strong as ever.

'Squire,' she began, picking her words carefully, surprising even herself at her deliberate tactfulness. 'Like you I thought a lapse of time was appropriate, but I'm sure you will understand that I must know what my position is now.'

'Your position, my dear? I don't quite understand.' He seemed genuinely puzzled.

She leant forward a little, towards him. 'As regards the tenancy of Brumbys' Farm, Squire. The agreement was in Matthew's name.'

The squire's expression cleared. 'Oh, that. Oh yes – well – of course. Yes, I see what you mean. I really hadn't given it a thought. In fact, I'd forgotten all about it. You see,' he sighed heavily, 'with Matthew going to the war, and you carrying on so admirably on your own, I accepted the fact that you were running the farm.'

He lifted his shoulders in an apologetic shrug. 'With Matthew being posted missing, then coming home and yet not being well enough to run things, well, I'd completely forgotten we hadn't legalized things from your point of view.'

Esther bit her lip, stopping the words from bursting out. But what's going to happen? she wanted to cry. What's to happen now I'm really alone?

At his next words, all her questions were answered and all her fears allayed.

'The war changed a lot of things for us all, Esther my

dear. The biggest change it has brought about has been for women. They've proved they can do men's work when the men are no longer there. And you, more than most, have proved you can run that farm, single-handed if need be.' His keen, knowing eyes met hers and then he glanced away and cleared his throat.

So, Esther thought, the squire had known all along how her neighbours had ostracized her over her affair with Jonathan. He had known how she had struggled to cope alone. Yet he had never censured her, never used his power to oust her as he could well have done.

Now the jovial man in front of her was slapping his knees and beaming at her. 'Well, my dear, I intend to put all this right. You shall have the tenancy of Brumbys' Farm in your own name. Just as you wanted it all that time ago.'

Esther smiled at him in return and expressed her gratitude. She could not let him know that if only he had agreed to this almost ten years earlier, a great deal of unhappiness might have been prevented.

There was a cruel irony in the fact that after all this time she had what she had then wanted most in life. Now, it was not what she wanted the most. Not now, not since she had known real love.

She sighed softly to herself. Once the squire's change of heart would have filled her with ecstasy. Although she did still feel a deep satisfaction at the knowledge that her future, and that of her daughter, was secure, the thrill, the pinnacle of all her dreams as she had once supposed securing the tenancy of Brumbys' Farm would be, was no more.

She was standing shaking the squire's hand and he was saying, 'I'll not forget the business of the motor car, my dear. Just give me a few days . . .'

True to his word, the following week the squire fetched the motor car.

Esther dusted her hands together. 'I'm glad to see the back of that,' she muttered, as the vehicle, coughing and spluttering, disappeared up the lane. But in her own mind she was doubtful she would see her money back.

Esther was wrong.

Two days later a smart pony and trap driven by a beaming Squire Marshall turned in at the gate of Brumbys' Farm. Esther, rolling pastry at her kitchen table, dusted the flour from her hands with her apron and went out to meet him. She walked around the trap and patted the sprightly pony on its neck.

The squire climbed down and stood beside the trap, confident of her approval.

Esther looked up at him. 'Oh, Squire, 'tis lovely, but I don't know whether I really ought to spend the sort of money this must have cost.'

'Now, now, my dear, before you decide . . .' As he spoke he was reaching into an inside pocket of his jacket and pulling out what seemed to Esther to be a sheaf of papers. Holding them out, he added, still smiling broadly, 'Just count that first, and if you're still not happy then I'll take this back and recoup all the money for you.'

Esther held the thin, white pieces of paper in her fingers. Puzzled she glanced up at the Squire. 'Is – is this money?'

'Oh I'm sorry, my dear. Of course, I hadn't realized. Yes, each of those white pieces of paper is worth five pounds.'

'Five pounds!' Esther exclaimed. 'Each?'

The squire nodded. 'Yes, my dear.'

Swiftly Esther counted them, and then looked up once more. 'There's more money here than ever Matthew took from my box, Squire.'

The older man shrugged and avoided meeting her direct, questioning gaze. 'Ah well, I don't know about that, my dear. All I know is, I managed to get a good price for the motor and that is what is left.'

'Is the pony and trap paid for?' she asked sharply.

'Yes, yes . . .' He fished in another pocket. 'Here's the bill of sale. Now, Mrs Hilton, are you happy – or not?'

'Well . . .' Esther frowned over the money and the receipt she held in her hand. She could not be anything but happy, although she had a shrewd suspicion that the squire was not being entirely truthful with her. Had he really got such a good price for the motor car, so much that he had paid for this magnificent pony and trap and still left her with more than Matthew had taken in the first place? Or had he put in some money of his own? There was no way she could know without risking offending him. For once, if her suspicions were founded, she would have to swallow her prickly pride and accept the squire's good intentions with equally good grace.

She looked up again at him, a smile spreading across her face. 'I'm overwhelmed, Squire. Really. I don't know how you've managed it – ' there was a veiled hint in her

tone that perhaps she guessed what he might have done —
'but I'm truly grateful. Thank you.'

Relief spread across Mr Marshall's face and he patted her shoulder benevolently. 'Don't mention it, my dear, don't mention it. About that other little matter — if you care to come up to the Grange tomorrow afternoon, Mr Thompson will bring all the papers to be signed.'

'That other little matter', he called it. If only he knew what havoc that 'little matter' had caused in her life.

Forty-three

*E*STHER Hilton was mistress of Brumbys' Farm — the legal tenant in her own right.

She had the land she loved, she had a healthy, growing daughter and a smart new pony and trap to take Kate to school and herself to the market and to church.

She had good friends; Will still came twice a week, and treated her and Kate as if they belonged to him even if the words of acknowledgement were not forthcoming. She had the Harris family; wonderful, motherly, laughing Ma Harris in whose eyes Esther had exonerated herself for her past indiscretions by her tender care of Matthew, and Mr Harris, quieter than his voluble wife, but always there to lend a hand when needed. And the Harris children — what would she do without Enid and the younger boys helping on her farm whenever they knew she needed extra hands, without her ever having to ask?

And then there was Danny Eland.

Oh, Danny, Esther would say countless times to herself watching him about the farm with Kate, or doing little jobs for her, you're the growing image of Matthew. What am I to do about you?

Despite all this if there was still an aching loneliness in her heart, a secret sadness which she could share with no one, then she would tell herself sternly that she had much to be grateful for and that she couldn't expect to have everything she wanted in life.

Nevertheless, there was a restlessness about her, a longing that even the work-filled days and exhausted nights could not subdue.

'Our Enid's getting wed, Esther,' Ma greeted Esther one morning.

'Oh, Ma, how wonderful. I didn't even know she was courting. Who is it?'

Ma's round cheeks wobbled with pleasure. 'It's a young feller who's come back from the war – Walter Maine. Lost a leg, he has. He's got a wooden one but you should see him get about, Esther. I couldn't believe it. Before I met him,' Ma clasped her hands in front of her ample bosom, 'I have to admit I was a bit doubtful. I thought he'd be a cripple, like. Not a bit of it! One crutch he uses but can he move!' Her laughter cackled so loudly that the hens, pecking in a leisurely way in the yard, squawked in alarm and scuttled for cover. 'He's not idle either.' There was pride already in her tone for her future son-in-law. 'Learning to be a blacksmith, he is, so's he'll have a trade.' Her tone dropped. 'You know our smithy's lad never came back from the war . . . ?'

Esther nodded and Ma went on, 'So I reckon he's glad to have a young 'un to take on.'

So many lives altered by the war, Esther thought, but aloud she asked, 'When's the big day?'

Ma shrugged and stretched her mouth into the familiar toothless grin. 'We thought Midsummer Day – they've no reason to wait any longer. There's attic rooms above the smithy they can have and the smith's wife says she'll be glad to have Enid's help, and,' Ma added, 'our Enid'll even help out in the smithy itself if need be. She ain't afraid of work.'

Esther smiled. 'No, I can vouch for that.'

Ma's round face took on a dreamy expression. 'Eh, but what wouldn't Ah give to see me girl in a fine white dress on her wedding day?' She sighed and then added in a more matter-of-fact manner, 'Ah, well, there it is – frippery's not for the likes of us. She'll have to have a new costume that'll serve her after her wedding day.'

As Ma waddled away down the lane towards the Point, Esther watched her go, a plan forming in her mind.

The sewing machine she had brought back from her Aunt Hannah's was now in constant use. She made smocks and dresses for Kate and simple skirts and blouses for herself. Could she, Esther asked herself, make a wedding gown for Enid?

It would be the most complicated thing she had ever tackled, but she could afford to buy a length of material out of the extra money the squire had got for the car – or that he said he had got.

Esther smiled. The squire had been good to her, so why should she not pass on a little of that kindness to someone else? She owed the Harris family so much. First young Ernie, and now Enid and the younger boys. And Ma herself. Even though there had been a time of estrangement between them over Jonathan, now it was as if their differences had never happened.

The very next day found Esther bowling along the lane towards the town in her smart pony and trap. It gave her a sudden thrill to be driving her own trap, to be dressed in a smart costume — even though it was the one she had bought for her aunt's funeral and therefore black. But she was still in mourning for her husband and only the ruffle of her white blouse showed at her throat in the open neck of the close-fitting jacket.

On her arrival in the busy main street, however, some of her newfound confidence ebbed away. She was not used to coming shopping, frequenting what were to her the smart shops in the town.

As she entered the largest drapery store in the main street, the bell clanged loudly, heralding her arrival. She felt that everyone in the shop turned to look her up and down and suddenly Esther felt very much the country mouse come to town.

For a moment her nerve almost failed her completely when a woman customer at the counter turned to leave and saw Esther standing uncertainly just inside the door. As she came towards her, Esther recognized her as a member of the church congregation and a woman of whom Martha Willoughby always made a great fuss.

Esther drew a sharp breath and waited for the woman's scathing look and sarcastic remark. In readiness to do battle, Esther's chin came a little higher and her green eyes sparkled with defiance.

The woman was on her way out, but as she drew near to Esther she said, 'Good morning. Mrs Hilton, isn't it? How nice to see you in town.' The woman did look her up and down, but there was no disdain in the glance. To Esther's astonishment, it was more a look of admiration.

'G-good morning,' Esther managed to stammer in

reply and then she gazed about her almost in awe of the large shop with its shelves of bolts of cloth, its prim woman assistant behind the counter.

The customer, her hand resting lightly on the door handle, made no move to leave the shop but stood, her head slightly on one side, watching Esther. There was a friendly smile on her mouth.

Esther felt she could confide in her. 'I – er – I'm looking for some material suitable for a wedding gown.' As she saw the woman's eyebrows rise Esther added hastily, 'Oh, not for me! It's for a friend of mine who's getting married and I thought – well – I'd like to try and make her a wedding dress.'

The woman's smile broadened. 'Then I know just the person to help you.' She turned and led the way back towards the counter and Esther followed.

'Miss Davenport, would you be kind enough to assist Mrs Hilton with the choosing of a fabric suitable for a wedding gown?'

'Certainly, madam.'

The woman turned back to Esther and made her farewells. 'Miss Davenport will look after you. She is a fine dressmaker herself – ' she leaned towards Esther with a conspiratorial air – 'she'll give you a few tips, my dear.'

Esther smiled. 'Thank you. You've been very kind.'

'A pleasure, my dear. A pleasure. I'm so glad we met.'

Esther watched her go as the doorbell clanged behind her. How friendly she had been, and yet Esther was sure that the woman – whose name she still did not know – must have witnessed several of Martha Willoughby's sarcastic remarks towards Esther in the past.

'If you'd like to come this way, madam, perhaps I can be of assistance.'

'Of assistance' Miss Davenport certainly was and when Esther finally left the shop, she couldn't think when she had last enjoyed herself so much.

Her arms were full of material and lace trimmings, and her head was bursting with advice and suggestions.

'Do come back and see me again, Mrs Hilton, if you have any problems,' Miss Davenport insisted as she held open the door for Esther.

When her work was finished that evening and Kate safely in bed, Esther spread out the creamy silk material on her parlour table. She wrinkled her brow thoughtfully. Now, she thought, Enid's slightly shorter than me, but her size and shape are much the same as mine. So I reckon if I make it to fit myself, I shan't go far wrong.

The most anxious moment was actually putting the scissors into the lovely fabric, but once she had cut out the pieces and begun to pin and tack them together, Esther's confidence grew.

Two weeks before the wedding, the dress was almost finished. Esther chewed her thumb thoughtfully as she stood looking down at the gown which she had spread out on the narrow bed in the little room beyond the nursery that so long ago had been her bedroom when Sam Brumby had been ill.

She heard voices from downstairs and carefully shutting the door, Esther went down to find Ma Harris and Enid sitting in the kitchen talking to Kate. Esther jumped visibly at seeing them there, thinking for a moment they had found out about her making the dress.

They were both smiling up at her as she looked from one to the other.

'We've come to ask you summat, Esther lass,' Ma began. 'Go on, Enid, you ask her.'

Enid giggled nervously. 'I – we – was wondering if you'd let Katie be me bridesmaid . . .'

At this Kate jumped up and down clapping her hands. 'Oh, Enid, Enid! Oh do say I can, Mam.'

'Now wait a minute, Kate,' Esther said. 'Be still, child. Let me talk to Enid.' She turned back. 'I don't understand, Enid. What about your own sisters?'

Ma Harris and Enid exchanged a knowing look and shrugged their shoulders.

'That's the very reason we're asking your Kate,' Ma said. 'And we're asking Danny Eland to be a page boy. Just the two of them, that's all we want. Enid dun't want a lot of fuss and you should hear the squabbling that's been goin' on in our house over who's to be her bridesmaid. She can't have 'em all and so we thought this was the best way to settle it. That way none of 'em's noses is out o' joint!'

Ma and her sayings, Esther thought irrationally, and then she murmured, 'Danny, you say?'

It was strange how circumstances seemed always to contrive to bring those two – Kate and Danny – together, however much she might wish it otherwise.

Kate was tugging at her mother's skirt. 'Mam, do say I can be bridesmaid and wear a pretty dress, can't I?'

The smile on Enid's mouth faltered. She glanced at her mother before saying quietly, 'Yes, lovey, you shall have a pretty dress.' There was a slight emphasis on the 'you' which did not pass unnoticed by either Esther or Kate.

With a child's directness, Kate said, 'Why, you'll be having a lovely wedding dress, won't you? Like in the picture books?'

Enid shook her head a little sadly. 'It ain't practical for the likes of us. You can't wear a wedding dress for anything else afterwards, Katie.' She forced herself to laugh. 'Can't see me helping Walter at the anvil in a wedding dress, can you?'

The wistful tone in the girl's voice was not lost on Esther.

'Wait here a minute, Ma – Enid. There's something I think I ought to show you.'

She turned and ran upstairs to fetch the wedding gown that was all but finished apart from the final seams. It's only sensible she knows, Esther told herself, and besides, I can fit it on her properly now.

The look on Enid's face as Esther held up the gown before her was thanks enough. Tears of joy ran down her face and all she could say was, 'Oh, missus, missus!'

'I was trying to keep it as a surprise until a night or two before your big day, but I think you should know now.' Esther laughed, 'Especially as it looks as if I'll have to tackle a smaller dress for Kate.'

Enid reached out with fingers that shook. 'It's beautiful, missus. How kind you are – I dun't know how to thank you.'

Even Ma sniffed noisily and, not trusting herself to speak, just nodded at Esther and beamed.

*

Enid's wedding was a joyful affair. There seemed to have been little fun and merrymaking for so long. The long years of war, the loss of Ernie and then the homecoming of an invalid Matthew and the deprivations the war had caused even in this small, close-knit community, had weighed heavily upon them all. And finally Matthew's death.

Now they had something to celebrate. Enid looked beautiful in the wedding gown and Kate was quite the little show-off in her flounced pink dress. Even Danny puffed out his chest and strutted down the aisle behind the bride and her father.

He was growing so like Matthew it was uncanny, Esther thought, and glanced across the aisle towards Beth. He was a living, daily reminder of the love between Beth and Matthew.

Esther's glance rested upon Robert Eland. What an unusual man he was to care and go on caring for his wife's child by another man. Esther sighed. Robert Eland must love Beth very much, and it must hurt him to see how she still pined for Matthew.

Always there was an air of quiet sadness about Beth. Though she looked after her husband and son – they were now living in one of the cottages at the Point – and though she smiled and talked, the sadness never quite left Beth's eyes. Yet Robert still went on loving her and her boy. He was a remarkable man, Esther thought.

Will stood at Esther's side in the church, beaming with pride as he watched Kate in her pretty dress, her red curls glinting in the shaft of sunlight slanting through the stained glass window.

Will – a favourite with all the folk at Fleethaven Point, not just with Esther – had been invited to the wedding. He had arrived that morning leaving his carrier's cart in Esther's yard and setting his horses loose in her meadow for the day.

'Kate's just like you were at that age, Esther lass. A bonny bairn, you were, an' so is she.'

Esther put her hand through Will's arm as they walked behind the merry wedding group. 'Known me all me life, haven't you, Will?'

'Yes, lass, I have. Watched you grow – and watched over you, though you might not always have known it.'

Esther wrinkled her forehead. 'I remember climbing up on to yar cart when you came around the village and me aunt never shouted at me for it. I could never understand that. She shouted at me for everything else.'

Will laughed. 'Aye, well, she knew better than to cross me.'

Esther glanced at him and bit her lip. Will stared straight ahead as they walked together down the lane towards the Point. The bride and groom rode in Esther's pony and trap whilst all the other guests walked behind them.

'I remember you always used to listen to me and talk to me as though I *was* somebody. No one else ever did that, Will. Not when I was little, anyway.'

Briefly his hand covered hers where it rested on his arm. 'You were always special to me, Esther lass, always.'

They had reached the Hump and once over it were enveloped in the wedding celebrations and her moment of intimacy with Will was lost.

From her little cottage, Ma Harris produced the biggest spread that the people of Fleethaven Point had ever seen. Luckily it was a fine, warm afternoon and so the guests played and danced on the grass outside the row of cottages. Trestle tables had been borrowed and the wedding feast was held out of doors.

Enid's new husband was a tall, thin young man, with a slight stoop caused by the loss of his leg. In some ways he reminded Esther poignantly of Jonathan. When the light glinted on his hair or he stooped down to speak to Enid, his head slightly on one side, his eyes smiling into hers, he was so like Jonathan in his actions.

Watching the young couple in the church and now here sitting side by side at the wedding reception, shy and not a little embarrassed, but so happy, Esther felt again the aching loneliness. She ought to be content, she told herself fiercely, she had so much and today she was surrounded by so many happy people. All the Harris family were there, the young ones capering and chasing one another in a noisy game of tag after the wedding feast was finished whilst the adults chatted amongst themselves.

There were new faces too amongst the small community: the bridegroom's family. Ma introduced them to her friends and neighbours. 'This is Walter's mam and dad, Mr and Mrs Maine, Esther, and this is his grandad.'

Esther found herself shaking hands with an old man with a long white beard, who leant heavily on a walking-stick, his legs as bowed as she remembered Sam Brumby's being. At her side, Kate gazed up at the old man with trance-like fascination.

The old man laughed wheezily and grasping his long beard, he tickled Kate under her chin with its wispy ends. 'Now, little girl, ain't you ever seen a beard like this 'un afore?'

Kate shook her red curls. 'No, Grandad,' her little voice piped and she put out her hand and gently stroked the silky waves of his beard. 'It's lovely.'

'Kate,' Esther admonished her daughter swiftly, 'you call this gentleman "Mr Maine". He's Walter's grandad, not yours.'

'She can call me grandad if she wants,' the old man laughed. 'Lots of folks do – even though I ain't their grandad – just 'cos I'm as old as Methuselah.'

'Who's Methoosy?'

At that moment, Danny interrupted Kate's question and, grabbing her hand, pulled her away into the game of tag.

'You've a lovely bairn there, missus.' Old Mr Maine's bright eyes followed the child skipping and hopping amongst the rest.

'She is that,' murmured Will who, standing next to Esther, had heard the exchange of conversation. His eyes were thoughtful as he watched Kate.

Mid afternoon the bride and groom took their leave, riding into town in Esther's pony and trap to their new home above the smithy.

''Tis kind of you, Mrs Hilton, to lend us the trap,' Walter said in his low, soft voice. 'I'll see you get it back in the morning.'

Esther put out her hand to shake the young man's.

'Don't worry. So long as the pony is fed, I dun't mind if you keep it a day or two. Perhaps you could take Enid out tomorrow.'

The young man nodded. 'Aye, well, if you're sure. It'd be nice, being Sunday, but I'm back at me work on Monday.'

He smiled and his blue eyes crinkled, reminding her so keenly of Jonathan that her heart turned over. She squeezed his hand in hers and there was a catch in her voice as she said, 'Good luck to you, Walter. To you both.'

The bride and groom were waved off and the other guests began to drift away. Esther looked around for Will and saw he was in earnest conversation with Ma, who was nodding and smiling. To Esther's astonishment, she saw Will plant a kiss on Ma's cheek and then Ma laughed aloud and smacked him playfully on his arm. 'Get away with you, Will Benson, and do what you have to do.'

They turned and saw Esther coming towards them and for a moment she thought they looked a little sheepish, for they glanced at each other and then quickly away again. Coming to meet Esther, Will said, 'I'd best be on me way, lass.'

'Oh, Will, you dun't have to go yet, d'ya? It's only early and I've a bite of tea ready for you at home afore you set off back.'

Will shifted uneasily from one foot to the other and twisted his hat round and round in fidgeting fingers. 'I'll get off, lass, if ya dun't mind. There's something I've – er

493

– to see to, like.' He glanced at Ma Harris, who grinned and nodded.

'You get off, Will. He'll be back again afore you know it, lass.'

Esther felt a stab of disappointment. This had been such a lovely day and she didn't want it to end. She didn't want to let Will – of all people – go. Oh well, she supposed, his next call on Tuesday wasn't so long away.

'Goodbye, Mrs Harris,' Will was saying, 'and thank 'ee for asking me. It's been a grand wedding.'

Ma beamed broadly, nodding her head towards him as if sharing a secret. 'Mebbe it won't be the last, eh? Goodbye, Will. We'll be seeing ya again very soon, eh?'

Esther was sure she saw Ma Harris wink at Will.

When Will had gone, Esther, seeing Kate still intent in her game with Danny, slipped away to the shore.

Mechanically her footsteps brought her to the Spit and she was drawn, unwillingly at first, to walk along its length, the water lapping on either side, to its very end, to the point where they had found Matthew's body. She had not visited this place since, but she knew she must face it again.

It had been her favourite spot and she expected it to be haunted by the tragedy and robbed of its tranquillity. As she neared the very tip she found she was holding her breath. She stared down at the shingle where his body must have lain. Slowly she released the breath and lifted her head. Her gaze scanned the gently rolling water. She closed her eyes and lifted her face to the sky, feeling the warmth of the sun.

Everything was just the same as it had always been.

Nothing was spoilt. The peace of this place was almost tangible. She felt she could reach out and embrace it.

She sank down on to the shingle and felt the balm of tears which blurred her vision, so that the water danced before her eyes.

'Oh, Matthew, I'm so sorry, sorry for you and for Beth,' she whispered. 'Sorry I – couldn't make things right.'

She allowed herself the luxury of a few moments of self-pity. After seeing the happiness of Enid and her new husband, after being part of a large and loving family even if only for a few hours, the loneliness of her life ahead overwhelmed her.

'Oh, Jonathan, Jonathan, where are you?' Tears ran down her cheeks and, as she bent her head forward, dropped and were lost in the vastness of the ocean.

Forty-four

WHEN she returned to the wedding party, most of the guests, other than those who lived at the Point, had departed. Only Mr and Mrs Maine and Grandad Maine were still there. Old Mr Maine was sitting outside Ma Harris's cottage watching the sun sinking into the flat horizon, streaking the sky gold and pink. On his knee, her cheek against his silky beard, was Kate.

Esther stood before them and the old man looked up at her with twinkling eyes. 'We've become good friends, yar little lass an' me. Ya'll have to bring her to see my cottage. 'Tis only a few miles inland – nowt for that smart pony and trap of yourn.'

Esther smiled. 'We'd love to come. Thank you.' Gently, she added, ''Tis time you came home now, Kate.'

The child's eyelids were already heavy with tiredness, but like Esther she didn't want this lovely day to end.

'A bit longer, Mam, then I'll come.'

'All right, then. Only a few minutes, mind, just whilst I get yar tea ready.'

'I'll send her home, missus, in a little while.'

Esther nodded and said, 'Goodbye, Mr Maine. It's been lovely to meet you.'

As Esther walked up the lane towards home, she passed the meadow, the rippling grass just ripe for harvest.

'We'll be able to start this week,' she murmured and smiled to herself. 'My first haymaking as the tenant of Brumbys' Farm in my own name.' Shading her eyes, she stood in the lane and looked towards the farmhouse silhouetted against the setting sun, her gaze travelling over the house, the orchard, the barn and other buildings and then beyond to the fields of ripening corn. She sighed. How beautiful it all was and yet that very beauty brought a lump to her throat.

In the distance she heard three shrill, excited blasts on a whistle and the rattle of cart wheels.

Will? But he had only just left an hour or so ago. Was something wrong? Why was he coming back?

Her heart leapt. Three whistles – why three?

As the cart rounded the bend in the road, she could see that there were two figures on the front of it. As it slowed, one jumped down and began to run towards her. A tall man with an unruly lock of fair hair that glinted in the sunlight and fell forward over his forehead . . .

'*Jonathan!*' She couldn't even take so much as a step towards him, her legs refused to move. 'Oh Jonathan!'

But he was coming towards her, that dear, familiar smile crinkling his eyes. Then he was taking her face gently between his hands and kissing her forehead, her eyes and at last her mouth.

'Oh, my love, my dearest love,' he was murmuring.

And all the time, Esther had not moved. Breathlessly, she whispered, 'Is it really – really you?'

He put his arms about her and drew her close against his chest and she felt the solid reality of him.

She was vaguely aware of the cart wheels rattling on towards the Point, and then they were alone.

'But where've you come from? How . . . ?'

'Later.' He stilled her questions with his lips and she clung to him, knowing he would never leave her again.

They drew apart for a moment, their eyes shining with joyful devilment. They both spoke at once. 'The hollow!'

Hand in hand, they were running, across the lane, over the dunes and across the marsh to their special place . . .

Much later they came back to the farm and were standing in the middle of the yard, their arms around each other, when they heard the wheels of the cart returning from the Point. Perched beside Will sat Kate.

'Mam, Walter's grandad's gone home now . . .' Kate began, as the cart drew to a halt in the yard. Then she stopped, her eyes widening, at the sight of the stranger standing there with his arm about her mother's waist.

Will climbed down from his seat and held up his arms to Kate. The child allowed herself to be lifted down, but all the time her gaze was on the tall stranger.

'Will Benson,' Esther began with mock severity, though she could not hide the happiness from showing on her face. 'You have some explaining to do!'

Will was grinning happily as he set Kate down on the ground. She made no attempt to leave him and go to Esther, but stood close to Will, leaning against him and slipping her hand into his. But all the time her eyes were intent upon Jonathan.

'Do you remember,' Will was saying, his expression more sober now, 'the day I came all excited with some news to tell ya, and then I found you'd brought Matthew home?'

Esther nodded. 'Yes, I remember,' she said quietly. 'When you saw Matthew, you said your news was another tuppence on me eggs.'

'That weren't true, lass.'

'No, I knew it wasn't.'

'You did?'

'But you wouldn't tell me. You – you got almost angry when I tried to press you.'

Will shook his head at the memory. 'I didn't dare to tell you – not after I'd seen Matthew.'

There was sadness in Will's eyes now and a look too that begged for her understanding and her forgiveness.

Jonathan took up the story. 'When I got back from France, I went to see Will. I knew he'd know how things were with you. He said he'd come and break the news that I was alive and – coming back to you.'

'Oh, Jonathan,' she breathed.

'Then,' Jonathan added gently, 'he came back and told me that you'd found your husband in France. Of course, I couldn't – wouldn't – come then. But I've kept in touch with Will ever since.'

It didn't surprise her that this man of principle, who despite all her desperate pleading had put duty and honour before everything else, had kept away when he'd heard Matthew had returned.

'I couldn't tell you, lass. You do understand?' Will was saying, anxiety in his tone.

Her voice broke as she reached out and patted Will's arm. 'Of course I understand.'

'I brought Jonathan as far as Lynthorpe this morning . . .'

'We didn't think it right that I should arrive at the wedding. After all it was their day, and besides, I wasn't really sure what my welcome from the folk at the Point would be!' Jonathan added with a rueful smile.

'But everything's going to be all right.' Will grinned broadly. 'I had a chat with Ma Harris at the wedding. Asked her if she thought enough time had gone by since – well – you know . . .' He broke off, cleared his throat, and continued. 'She was that pleased, said you'd earned a bit of happiness and that I'd better get off and fetch the young man as quick as I could.'

'Oh, so that was what all the whispering was about?' Esther smiled.

Esther became aware that all the time they had been talking, Kate had been standing quietly, holding Will's hand and still staring solemnly up at Jonathan.

Jonathan's blue eyes twinkled down at her. 'And just who is this very grown-up young lady?'

Suddenly, Kate beamed.

'Kate, I don't suppose you'll remember Mr Godfrey. You were only little when he was here before . . .' Esther said.

'Yes, I do,' Kate said promptly. 'You made me a fishing net, didn't you?'

The three grown-ups gaped at her.

'Fancy you remembering that, Katie,' Esther said.

The girl wrinkled her smooth forehead and added, with candid honesty, 'It's all I do remember.'

They all laughed.

Kate was still eyeing Jonathan, her head on one side as if surveying him. 'I dun't suppose you're me grandad, are ya? You're not old enough.'

Jonathan looked startled and glanced towards Esther for explanation.

Esther laughed. 'No, lovey, he's not yar grandad.'

The child looked disappointed. 'I did so like Walter's grandad. Mam . . . ?'

Esther held her breath, knowing what was coming next.

'Have I got a grandad?'

Kate's clear gaze was directed at Esther, who, for once, did not know how to answer her daughter.

It was Will who answered the child, saying in a strong vibrant voice, 'Yes, Katie, you have. I'm your grandad.'

Kate gave a little squeal of delight and threw her chubby arms around him. 'Are you really? I *am* glad!'

Above the child's head, Will's eyes met Esther's. 'Yes,' he said at long last, speaking more to Esther than to Kate. 'I'm your mother's father.'

Tears filled Esther's eyes and ran unashamedly down her cheeks but she was smiling as she reached out and clasped Will's hand. 'Oh, Dad, oh, me Dad . . .' was all she could say.

A happiness such as she had never before known flooded through her.

Now, at last, she had everything she had ever wanted.

www.panmacmillan.com